ALL I NEED

THE KNIGHTS SERIES
BOOK 1

E. SALVADOR

Cover design by Books & Mood

Editing by Emily A. Lawerence

This book is intended for an 18+ audience.

Content Warning: explicit language, sexual content, brief mention of cheating(not by MMC or FMC), mention of postpartum depression, mention of anxiety.

For the over thinkers who just need a little reassurance.

PLAYLIST

Electric - Alina Baraz, Khalid
Pink + White - Frank Ocean
Beautiful Boy - John Lennon
Groupie Love - Lana Del Rey, A$AP Rocky
Freakin' Out on the Interstate - Briston Maroney
Partition - Beyoncé
Melting - Kali Chis
Golden Hour - Kacey Musgraves
Cloud 9 - Paravi
See You Again - Tyler, The Creator, Kali Uchis
Pretty Little Fears - 6LACK, J. Cole
Sex on Fire - Kings of Leon
Floating - Alina Baraz, Khalid
Beige - Yoke Lore
My Favorite Part - Mac Miller, Ariana Grande
Did you know that there's a runner under Ocean Blvd - Lana Del Rey
Taking Pictures Of You - Camille Jansen (cover)
Sunsetz - Cigarettes After Sex
Coffee - Miguel
Sure Thing - Miguel

1

LOLA

RATIONAL THOUGHTS AND ALCOHOL DON'T MIX.

Actually, any rational thought doesn't exist when I'm with my two best friends, Daisy and Cara. Alcohol just happens to always be around when we're together.

In my drunken stupor, it seemed like a good idea, a great idea even, but the more I think about where I am and where I'm heading, I think I fucked up.

The plan was to go to Myrtle Beach, South Carolina, with my best friends for senior week and to celebrate my birthday. We've just graduated from high school, so we were going to spend a few days at the beach with our friends and my boyfriend, Matt.

But everything changed. I'm not at Myrtle with my boyfriend. I mean, ex-boyfriend now. Instead, I'm in an Uber in Miami, Florida.

The snap of a finger interrupts my thoughts. I blink a few times until my blurred vision is clear and I'm staring at the bracelet wrapped around Cara's deep bronze wrist.

"Stop thinking about him. He's not worth it."

"I'm not."

I plaster a smile, but her arched brow and tilted head tells me she doesn't believe me.

"I'm not thinking—"

I pause mid-sentence when Daisy cuts me with a pointed look.

"This is your special day, babe. Don't let him ruin it. If you want help to forget him, think about his tragic haircut and atrocious laugh. Nothing worth remembering." She grimaces, shuddering.

I chuckle because she's right. Matt had a hyena-like laugh and a shaggy-like haircut, but I looked past it because we were together.

"Okay, I am thinking of him, but mostly my parents."

They have no idea I'm here, and I hope to God it stays that way.

I wish I were more concerned about my breakup with the guy I dated for two years, but all I can think about is what my parents will do if they find out I'm miles away from home.

It took a full year of begging to get them to agree, and after they did, I could tell they regretted it. A few weeks before graduation, it felt as if I were walking around eggshells, worried they'd change their minds.

I wish I were like my best friends, without a care in the world, but my mind likes to screw me over, thinking of the worst-case scenarios.

Especially because in a few hours, they're going to call me like they promised they would to make sure *I'm safe*. Though it's their way of making sure I'm in my hotel room and not out doing something I shouldn't.

Cara's face softens, her expression sympathetic. "We promised they wouldn't find out and I swear they won't."

It's easier said than done, but I don't know how I'm going to tell them that I broke up with the guy who they thought I was going to marry, used half of my savings, and some random guys invited me to their beach house to celebrate their friend's birthday.

"And that's a promise we intend to keep. I know that's not

enough reassurance for your overworking mind, so if by tomorrow morning you don't feel comfortable, we can leave," Daisy adds, a genuine smile curving her lips. I know that has nothing to do with the pregame she did before we left the hotel room.

Despite what my mind tells me, I can't do that to my friends. They've done so much for me, and after this week, we're all going our separate ways. We'll be in different states, and because of that, who knows when we'll be together again.

I drum my fingers against my thigh, hating that it's a nervous habit I've picked up over the past few years. I should have pregamed, but I was too busy thinking about my parents.

"No, it's okay. I'm sure they won't find out, but either way, fuck it." I don't feel that way, but I'm hoping if I say it enough, I'll eventually not give a damn. "We're in Miami and it's my birthday."

"That's right, it's your fucking birthday! Your special day!" Daisy excitedly says.

Cara drapes her arm over my shoulder, tugging me close to her. "I swear after tonight, you won't want to leave Miami."

I don't know what I was worried about, but Cara was right. I don't want to leave Miami. Regardless of not knowing anyone but the two guys who invited us, we're having the best time. Not to mention the house is right next to the beach, and they have an unlimited supply of alcohol.

We have yet to meet the birthday boy, but I truly couldn't care less and I'm sure the girls feel the same way.

While Cara and Daisy are in the restroom, I stand in the kitchen in front of the counter, staring at all the alcohol, energy drinks, and juices. From the entire assortment, there are only two things I want.

Crown Royal and peach juice.

Picking up the glass bottle, I pour the amber liquid into my cup. But I can't do the same for the peach juice because as I'm about to pick it up, a hand beats me to it.

"Hey!"

"Hey!" A deep, amused voice draws my attention away from the large hand grabbing the bottle to a pair of mischievous eyes.

I blink once, then twice, my words getting lodged in the back of my throat. My lips part to say something, but embarrassingly, nothing comes out. All I'm able to do is stare like I'm stuck in a daze.

I've seen a lot of good-looking people, but this guy is on a different scale of attractive. Rich, whiskey-colored eyes, a sharp jawline, dark brown curls that tempt me to reach out and touch them, and a smile that feels like a warning. Despite it, I can't help but be drawn to it.

And he's immensely tall, causing me to tilt my head back due to how close he is. Though now that I'm looking at him closely, I realize the right corner of his lip tugs upward, morphing into a cocky smirk.

I force myself to snap out of it, but embarrassment crawls up the side of my neck because he knows I was checking him out.

Ignoring the awkwardness that grips me, I wrap my hand around the neck of the bottle and pull it toward me.

"I had it first."

"Technically, I grabbed it first." He tugs it in his direction and the infuriating smirk lifts higher.

I scoff, glaring at him. "I would've grabbed it first if you had waited your turn." I pull it back with more force, but he's just as stubborn as me because he doesn't let go.

"My birthday, I do what I want." He shrugs unapologetically and tugs it back.

It takes a moment for my brain to register that he's the reason we're invited.

Begrudgingly, I let go. His smile falters, his brows pinch

together, and he tilts his head to the side, intently staring at me until that same infuriating smile curls on his lips again.

"Here, you have it." He holds it out for me to take.

"No, it's fine." I push it back to him. "You use it first. It's your birthday."

A deep chuckle falls from his lips as he pushes it back. "No, I want you to have it."

"You're frustrating, you know that? Use it first." I place my hand back on the bottle but freeze momentarily. My palm is on top of his, but it hardly covers it. Our size difference isn't the only thing that catches my attention but the number six tattooed on his right wrist.

"Do you flirt like this with everyone?" The smugness in his voice drags my attention away from his wrist.

His statement catches me off guard, but I smile nonetheless. Wait, no, what am I doing?

"I'm not flirting with you," I deadpan, shaking my head just as Caleb, the guy who invited us, stands next to the infuriating man still smirking at me.

"I've been looking for you." Caleb lazily smiles at his friend, then looks at me. "Oh good, you're here too."

"You two know each other?" Whiskey eyes bounce between me and Caleb.

"No," we answer at the same time.

"Met her at the beach. She's the birthday girl I was telling you about." He slyly smirks, eyes briefly flickering in my direction before shifting back to his friend.

Something between them goes unspoken as they look at each other. I don't have time to analyze what it could mean because I feel a soft vibration against my skin. I'm close to ignoring it, but realization quickly hits me like a bucket of cold water. It's my phone tucked inside the waistband of my skirt.

Pulling it out and without sparing the two guys in front of me a glance, I walk out of the house and hope to God I sound sober enough.

2

TJ

I'M LOSING MY MIND.

I've spent the last thirty minutes searching for a girl who could quite possibly have been a figment of my imagination. There's no other explanation because despite how much I drank tonight, I know I'm not drunk.

Or at least I thought I wasn't.

A sassy redhead won't leave my mind. Her hair was a golden copper color, and her striking eyes an earthy, forest green infused with specks of brown.

But I think my favorite color on her was the rosy hue on her cheeks when I caught her checking me out. I felt smug as fuck and did the same. I blatantly let my eyes roam over her body, but when I locked eyes with her again, she stared at me apathetically. Like she couldn't give a shit that I was checking her out and purposely flirting with her.

And that alone made me want to do it again.

Taking one last look at the crowded living room, I run my fingers through my hair before I turn on my heel and walk back into the kitchen.

Caleb and the rest of my friends are congregated near the keg stand, except for the one person I want to see again.

Standing next to him, but keeping my eyes on the crowd, I raise my voice. "Hey! You seen birthday girl?"

My friends said they had a gift for me, an extremely hot birthday gift. I genuinely thought they meant a stripper. Only because they've always made jokes about getting me one for my nineteenth birthday. But I was in for a surprise when they invited three random girls they met at the beach.

His lips rise slowly and lazily, glossy eyes dropping down to the bottle in my hand. "You still carrying that around?"

I ignore his question. "Have you seen her?"

His eyes lift to the camera strapped around my neck. "Can you take some pictures?"

"Caleb." I slap his hand away before he touches it. "Have you seen her?"

He chuckles, taking a pull of his beer, knowing he's annoying the fuck out of me. "She's outside." He points his thumb over his shoulder toward the glass sliding door that leads to the beach.

I turn on my heel, walking away as he yells out if I'm going to take pictures.

Stepping outside, I search for birthday girl, but she's nowhere in sight. Every spot is taken up by drunken bodies. I almost go back inside, but when I spot a silhouette standing by the shore, hair flowing on a soft gust of wind, my feet immediately move in that direction. I have no idea if it's actually her, but it has piqued my curiosity.

There's a one hundred percent chance I'll never see her after tonight, so I'm not going to miss the opportunity to talk to her one more time.

Weaving through the drunk bodies, I jump off the ledge that divides the beach and the house and slip my shoes off before trudging in her direction.

She paces back and forth, occasionally stopping to overlook the water, and then continues. I don't realize until I'm a few feet away that she's on the phone talking to someone. She holds it away from her face and then she presses it back to her ear.

I don't approach her. Standing where I am, I run my fingers through my hair again to make sure it doesn't look like shit. Having curly hair fucking sucks sometimes. Most of the time, it works in my favor, but occasionally it doesn't.

"Yeah...Myr-Myrtle Beach is really great. W-we're having a great time," she slurs and I'm sure she realizes that because she forces a laugh that sounds awkward.

Myrtle Beach? Myrtle Beach, South Carolina?

She stills, nodding and listening to whoever she's talking to.

I faintly hear the muted music that plays in the distance, but the waves that lap over one another almost drown out the noise. They roll to the shore and fizzle out before they're pulled back and the process repeats all over again.

Shifting my gaze away from the waves, I admire the way the full, bright moon illuminates her body.

The burnt orange dress she's wearing is tight at the top, accentuating her curves, and goes past her waist, flowing freely, the hem reaching right above her mid-thigh.

"Yes...Mom, I know." She clears her throat, pulling my thoughts and gaze away from her waist to her head. "I...I promise I'm behaving." She clears her throat again and I realize now that she's trying to hold back a laugh. "See you guys Saturday night. I love you."

As she pulls her phone away from her ear, the laugh she was fighting back finally manages to break through.

I approach her, shaking my head and smiling. "Last time I remembered, this isn't Myrtle Beach."

She shrieks, jumping back, her phone falling on the cool sand with a soft thump. I'm not sure how she managed to do it, but the flashlight on her phone comes on, illuminating the space between us.

"Shit, sorry, Peaches." I press my lips together, doing my best not to laugh as I bend down to pick up her phone. "I didn't mean to scare you."

"What's wrong with you?" She places her hand on her heaving chest, glowering at me. "You scared me!"

I cover my mouth, but it's not enough to mask my snicker. "I'm sorry, Peaches, I didn't mean to scare you."

"It's not funny." She huffs, snatching her phone from my hand. "It's creepy that you—" Her brows knit together. "Did you just call me...Peaches?"

"I never got your name." I tighten my hold on the neck of the bottle of peach juice I've been carrying around to give her.

Though the name is really fitting.

"So you thought of Peaches?" she asks, keeping a straight face, but I can see through her facade because the corner of her cheek keeps twitching.

I stretch my arm, holding the bottle out. "You never got to use this. After all, it's your birthday."

"I'm good," she hesitantly replies, taking a step backward.

Guilt rises, understanding what she's doing.

"It's brand-new." I twist the cap off, showing her the plastic liner that's sealed tight on the rim. I also flip it over to show her it won't leak. "But that should be the least of your worries," I say, capping the bottle back. "You shouldn't be out here by yourself. I was standing behind you for a solid ten minutes and you never noticed."

This is private property. No one should be roaming around here, but she doesn't know that.

"Right, I should get going." She's already walking away, not giving me a chance to say anything.

"Wait, Peaches," I call, following her until I'm walking next to her.

She quickens her pace. "Stop calling me Peaches."

I smile because, in my peripheral, I see her legs move faster. Either she's oblivious or doesn't care that I'm walking nowhere near as fast as she is. She could be doing a light jog and I'd still be walking at her same pace. "You walked away before giving me your name, again. What else am I supposed to call you?"

"Nothing." She abruptly stops, spinning to look at me. "After tonight, we won't see each other again, so does it really matter?"

She's right, but she also isn't.

Jesus fuck, I sound desperate as hell but fuck it.

"TJ," I extend my hand out to her. "My name is TJ."

She considers my hand for a second, those warm hazel eyes flickering to the number six tattooed on my wrist and then back at my hand.

"It *was* nice to meet you. Happy birthday, TJ." She grins, placing her hand in mine. The size difference between our hands is comical. Mine completely swallows hers, but I don't focus on that for long because I get distracted by how soft it feels.

Wait, did she say *was*? My foggy brain is too preoccupied with how her hand feels, and I don't realize she's already retracted her palm and is walking away, again.

I fall into step next to her. "Oh, come on. Don't be like that."

"I'm not," she simply replies, turning off the flashlight from her phone. "I don't have to tell you anything."

"All right, so Peaches it is." I grin, hearing her grumble as she picks up her pace. I could point out that she's only overexerting herself, but I don't. I'm enjoying this way too much. "So, *Peaches*...last time I remembered, this isn't Myrtle Beach."

Silence.

"So your parents don't know you're in Miami?"

Silence again.

"You made the right choice." I scoff. "I promise Miami is so much better than Myrtle."

She's stubborn. I like it.

"I would've lied to my parents too. I don't know who the hell would go to South Carolina for senior week of all places."

I expect silence, but instead, she throws her head back, letting out a loud, exasperated groan.

"What?"

"Coming to Miami was a last-minute decision." She stops walking when we reach the ledge and considers how she's going to get back up there. I'm about to tell her there are steps to our right, but then she looks at me. "Look, I'm not going to sleep with you, so if you think that's what's going to happen, you're wasting your time."

I chuckle, rubbing the back of my neck. "That's not what I—"

She folds her arms against her chest, pinning me with a stare.

"So it crossed my mind," I reply honestly, shrugging. "But I'm here to give you this." I shake the bottle in my hand. "Happy birthday."

I anticipate her to push it back, to tell me to fuck off, but to my surprise, she takes it.

"Thanks." Removing the lid, she rips off the plastic liner and sets them both on top of the ledge. "Glad to know some people still are." She humorlessly chuckles, staring off into the distance.

I lean against the ledge as she does, her shoulders sagging in defeat.

"You're glad some people are what?"

"Honest. Thanks for the gift." She sighs, dropping to the sand. She holds the bottle close to her chest, stretching her legs out and crossing one ankle over the other. "Have a good night."

I could go back and do what I originally planned, get drunk as shit and possibly get laid. That's the entire point of senior week. After high school graduation, everyone comes to the beach to drink, fuck, and party.

But I can't do that. I can't leave her out here alone. It'd be a shit thing to do.

"And to leave you alone with all this juice? I don't think so." I flash her a smile.

Her eyes follow my movements as I sit down next to her, still leaving an inch or two of space between us. "Didn't you say this was for me?"

I shrug. "Semantics. It's my birthday too. Don't be stingy."

"Stingy? I am not stingy." She aggressively shoves the bottle into my chest.

I smirk, taking the bottle from her hand. "Thanks, Peaches."

"Lola, my name is Lola."

I sit up straight, staring at her incredulously.

Lola. Cute. "I think I like Peaches better."

"You're frustrating, you know that?" Despite the annoyance in her voice, there's also a subtle amusement behind it.

I may be buzzed, but I'm sure that's her way of saying she likes me.

"So, want to tell me what you're doing in Florida and not in South Carolina?" I ask, ignoring what she said before taking a drink. "Though I don't blame you. Who wants to go to dirty Myrtle?" I've seen the water there; nothing worth going to.

A stretch of silence settles between us and then she bitterly laughs.

"My boyfriend cheated on me. He accidentally sent me a video of a girl blowing him off. A girl he told me to *never* worry about."

My eyes bug out and I choke on a breath. Now I wish I had something more than peach juice because what the fuck am I supposed to say to that? I've never been in a relationship. They're too messy and complicated for my liking.

I wait for the tears, for her to lose it, but it doesn't happen. She inhales and exhales and holds her palm out. I place the bottle in her hand and wait until she's ready to talk.

"Because my parents are strict, they didn't let me leave until a few days after Matt, my boyfriend, had already left. The morning my friends and I were supposed to leave, he accidentally sent me the video." She digs her toes in the sand, taking a pull of the juice. "Long story short, I got drunk, my best friends booked a hotel here for the rest of the week, and now I'm here telling you this..." she trails off. "God, this sounds pathetic."

"It's not pathetic." I shake my head. "If anything, he's pathetic and a fucking piece of shit, but you know, it's a good thing it happened."

"A good thing?" She blinks, stunned, and takes another drink, then hands it to me. "Finding out that your boyfriend is cheating on you with the girl he told you never to worry about is not a *good* thing."

I take a drink before I elaborate. "We would've never met, and you would have never known what it's like to have a *real* boyfriend."

Lola takes the bottle from my hand, staring at me, utterly confused.

It could be the alcohol clouding my mind. Or maybe it's because I'm extremely attracted to her. Or it could be knowing that I'll never see her again, but I open my mouth, not thinking through my thoughts.

Grabbing the bottle from her hand, I take a quick sip. Fuck, I wish I had something stronger. Here goes nothing.

"How would you like to have a boyfriend for the last few days you're here?" I sweetly smile at her, although the confusion deepens on her face and she stares at me like I've lost my goddamn mind. Yeah, I probably have, but maybe this could be a great thing...or maybe not. "Show you what an actual boyfriend is supposed to be like."

"A boyfriend?" The word sounds foreign coming from her lips. Hell, it sounds foreign to me and it came out of my mouth. "You want to be my *boyfriend*?" This time she laughs like she can't fathom the word.

I don't think I've ever liked the sound of a laugh more than I do now.

"I do. Granted, I've never been a boyfriend, but I swear I'll make a damn good one, and I promise I'll show you a good time." I grin but press my lips together as I realize how that sounds.

She doesn't respond, nor does she make a comment about the innuendo that I didn't mean to make. She only stares at me dumbfounded, lips slightly parted.

I wave my hand in front of her face. "Lola?"

She bursts out laughing. "I'm sorry, but that sounds crazy.

You want to be my boyfriend? I leave in three days. Why would you do that for me?"

I raise my hand to her face and tuck the few strands that got caught in her eyelashes behind her ear. She tenses but doesn't pull away. "Consider it a birthday present."

Truthfully, I don't know why I'm doing this. I just met her a few hours ago, but for some reason unbeknownst to me, she intrigues me.

"Come on." I cup her cheek, feeling her smooth, warm skin, and inhale her coconut-scented breath. "What do you say? Just two days, you and me. I swear I'll make it worth it."

"You don't know anything about me, and I don't know anything about you. I don't see how this could work out."

"I don't need to know much to know that you're it for me." I have no idea where any of this is coming from, but I'm going to blame it all on the alcohol.

"But—"

"What's your favorite Shrek movie?"

She snorts. "You're not really determining whether we're meant to be over my preference of a Shrek movie?"

"Just answer the question. It's important."

Lola beams. "Two, of course."

"I knew it, Peaches, we're meant to be." I smile, reveling in the sound of her laugh and the way her knee grazes mine. I'm not sure she notices it, but if she does, she's not doing anything to move it.

"Over Shrek 2?"

"No." Licking my lips, my gaze flickers to hers. "Over this moment."

We stare at each other, silence enveloping us for a beat before those earthy eyes fill with resolve, and her lips curve upward into a small smile.

"Okay, but if you suck, I'm taking all your money and the kids," she teases.

"The kids?" My jaw drops, my voice laced with feigned hurt. "Let's not bring the kids into this. We want to do what's best for them." I try to keep a serious face, but this conversation sounds fucking ridiculous and yet, I don't mind it.

"Fine." She chuckles. "So what now?"

I didn't think about it this far out, but an idea goes off in my head. "What's a place you've always wanted to go on a date but never did?"

"A museum." She doesn't hesitate to answer. "Matt always thought it was lame, so we never went."

I may have never wanted to be in a relationship, but I don't understand why anyone would get into one if they aren't going to put in the effort or cheat. It seems pointless and a waste of time.

"A museum?" I absentmindedly hum, dropping my eyes down to her jaw.

"Forget it."

"No, it's not that. You have dry paint here." I graze the pad of my finger underneath her jawline, where the dry orange patch is, feeling her steady pulse.

Her eyes widen. "I thought I had cleaned it all off. My friends took me to a painting class this morning for my birthday." She smiles, and it's not the kind that seems forced, but a genuine one that looks brighter than the fucking moon.

"Don't worry, I'm pretty sure I'm the only one who noticed." I swallow, feeling her pulse spike up when her eyes shift down to my lips. The temptation to pull her in and kiss her is suddenly strong, but she's been drinking tonight and so have I. "Museum, got it." I drop my hand.

"And what about Friday?"

"I get to pick our date." I wink at her, watching her eyes fill with curiosity. "I promise you'll love it."

"Okay." Lola smiles and looks down at where her phone vibrates at her side. Her eyes double in size and she jumps to her feet. "I have to go." I'm about to tell her about the stairs, but she easily pulls herself up on the ledge and stares down at me. "Where—"

"I'll see you tomorrow at the beach where my friends met you."

"Okay."

"Lola, wait." I turn my camera on, almost forgetting that I have it on me. "Can I take your picture? How am I supposed to obsess over you if I don't have anything to look at?"

I think she blushes, but I'm not sure. "Use your imagination."

"Come on, Peaches. Don't make me beg."

She cocks a brow, letting me know she wants me to do just that.

"Beg."

There are many things I don't do, and begging is one of them, but for her, I'm going to do just that.

"Please Lola, please let me take your picture."

"Make me look good." She beams, cradling the bottle like a baby.

I quietly laugh as I get the camera ready. "You already do." I snap the picture.

"Happy birthday." Lola hands me the bottle. She jogs off, but before she completely disappears, she peers over her shoulder and shouts, "Good night, boyfriend!"

"Happy birthday and good night, girlfriend!" I laugh, shaking my head.

Even after she's gone, I stare like a dumbass with a wide grin on my face. Until I raise the bottle to my lips and realize it's empty.

3

LOLA

"I SWEAR I'M NEVER DRINKING LIKE THAT AGAIN." Daisy groans, scrunching her nose in disgust. "If I ever pick up another bottle of tequila, I give you both permission to slap the shit out of me."

Cara snickers, shaking her head. "I tried to stop you, but you didn't want to listen. Here." She digs in our cooler and pulls out a container of coconut juice. "Stop whining and drink."

She slides her sunglasses down the bridge of her nose, glaring at me when I laugh. "I wouldn't have gotten so drunk if you hadn't disappeared with the birthday boy."

"What does me disappearing with him have anything to do with you getting drunk?" I quip, drifting my gaze to the light blue water that stretches for miles.

"I had to take all your shots." She twists the cap off and chugs half of it down.

"Oh, poor you."

She flips me off, pushing her sunglasses back up to cover her tired brown eyes. "Anyway, are you going to tell us what you and the birthday boy were talking about? Since you say you guys did absolutely *nothing*."

They stare expectantly, waiting and hoping to hear that I hid behind a bush or went to the pool house with him and did something wild. Nothing *wild* crossed my mind, but the thought of kissing him a time or two did.

"I swear nothing happened." I repeat the same thing I said last night about twenty times. "We just talked."

"About?" they both ask, leaning closer to me as if that's going to pry the information out of me.

"It's nothing exciting..." I trail off, digging my hand in the sand and scooping a handful. I let it slip between my fingers, my mind screaming that it was more than nothing. I can't stop replaying the memory in my head. Some bits are fuzzy, but I remember mostly everything.

TJ's cocky smile, the bottle of peach juice, his hand on my cheek, and him asking me to be his girlfriend.

Nothing earth-shattering happened. We talked, we laughed, and shared juice. It was just that and nothing more. I just wish my brain would accept that and not overanalyze how he looked at me and how he said it. And I wish more than anything that I could stop replaying the part where he proposed to show me what an actual boyfriend is supposed to be like.

"Nothing my ass." Daisy's voice interrupts my thoughts and when I lift my head, she knowingly smiles, as does Cara's. "That smile says otherwise. Come on, tell us."

"He overheard me talking..." I sigh and tell them everything. They listen, their smiles growing and the hangover long forgotten. "He said he would meet me here," I say at last, my smile fading.

We've been at the beach for three hours now, and I still haven't seen him. It's embarrassing that I keep looking around in the hopes he'll appear. There's no way I'd miss him. Someone like TJ is hard to miss and it doesn't have anything to do with how insanely attractive he is. He's over six feet. Someone that tall can't go unnoticed.

"Wow." Cara is the first to break through the silence, but she looks as speechless as Daisy.

I shrug, hoping to look indifferent. "It doesn't matter, though. We'll never see each other again."

It would have helped if we had agreed on the time, but everything happened too fast. I didn't think. I was buzzed and stuck on the feel of his fingers on my cheek.

"Peaches."

The familiar voice catches me off guard, causing the rest of the sand to quickly slip through my fingers.

"I finally found you." Relief is evident in his voice.

The girls' mouths part open, their stunned eyes peering over my head.

"Thank fucking God," one of his friends says. "We've been looking every—" He stops mid-sentence, grunting and mumbling a low *fuck*.

"Peaches?" the girls ask, their gazes lowering to my waist. "Peaches." They smile knowingly.

"That's not why—" I stop myself, shaking my head. Though pretending to be annoyed is not working out for me because a traitorous smile rises, and my heart speeds up excitedly. "I told you not to call me that."

I tilt my head up, forcing my lips to remain flat, but the attempt is futile. He crouches down so that we're at eye level, and the smile I was trying so hard to hold back breaks free until it mirrors his. It's hard to pretend to be annoyed when he's wearing nothing but swimming shorts and a camera strapped around his neck. The same one he had yesterday.

My eyes trail down his smooth, tanned skin, from his shoulders to his taut chest, following every dip and ridge in his stomach.

"Ready for our date, *girlfriend*?" His smug tone snaps me out of my stupor. When I meet his whiskey-colored eyes, he cocks a brow and a breathtaking smile stretches across his face.

Pull yourself together!

"Date?"

"Have you already forgotten about our date? About me?" TJ

places a hand on his chest, feigning disappointment. "Does she do this often?" he asks the girls, though his attention is solely on me, and I'm sure they're not paying attention to me as they're too busy talking to his friends.

"Do what?" I ask him.

"Break hearts."

I don't have any words, but I laugh at how corny that was.

"Lola." Daisy's voice pulls my attention to her. "We'll be back."

She and Cara are up on their feet, walking away with TJ's friends toward the shore before I say anything. I watch, jaw dropped as they both get farther away from us.

"So, Peaches, about our date?"

"You know you can call me by my name."

TJ shakes his head, eyes trailing down my body before he takes a seat next to me. "Nah, I like Peaches better." I stare at him, unimpressed, but he doesn't take me seriously and laughs. "Don't look at me like that. You're my girlfriend. I'm supposed to have a cute nickname for you."

"Cute?"

"You are."

"Wow." I bite the inside of my cheek, doing my best to keep a straight face.

"What? I thought that was good." He softly elbows my side, tapping his knee next to my leg. My entire body burns and I wish it were because of the scorching Miami heat. "Or was it not?"

"I would say it was really corny," I reply, staring down at the sand and scooping up another handful to hide the smile on my face.

He scoffs. "As *my* girlfriend, you're supposed to love all my corny words. It's part of the package deal."

I laugh at that, letting the sand slip between my fingers. "Package deal?"

"Lola, how are we supposed to make this relationship work if we don't do what first base couples do?"

Looking at him, I indulge him with a smile. "And what exactly do first base couples do?"

"Clingy, obsessed, happy, and all over each other." TJ's gaze drops to my hands, and it lingers there. He doesn't have to ask for me to hear the unspoken question, "*can I hold your hand?*"

I want to do just that, but I hesitate because this all seems too good to be true. I can't help but think there's a catch.

"You were being serious last night?"

"I wouldn't be here if I hadn't been," he responds, resting his hand next to my lap, his palm facing up. "Come on, take my hand."

My heart speeds up, beating erratically against my chest as I decide to not overthink for once, and lay my hand on top of his, interlocking our fingers together.

It's two days. What's the worst that could happen?

"We're really doing this?" I ask, swallowing as he rubs his thumb in soft circles on my hand.

"There's no going back. You're stuck with me for life and by life I mean until Saturday."

"For life."

"For life, Peaches." He squeezes my hand and lets it go as we hear our friends' voices in the distance. "Meet me at The Miami Gallery and Garden at seven."

"The Miami Gallery and Garden at seven. I'll be there," I repeat back to him as he stands, and Cara and Daisy sit on their towels, while TJ's friends stand a few feet away from us, waiting.

"I'll be waiting for you." He winks, turning on his heel to head back to his friends, but before they walk away, he jogs back to me and kneels down until he hovers slightly above me. "What kind of boyfriend would I be if I didn't kiss my girlfriend goodbye?"

TJ tucks two fingers underneath my chin, tipping my head back. His lips briefly brush against mine.

"Bye, *girlfriend*."

"Bye, *boyfriend*." My cheeks flare uncontrollably.

He smiles, content before standing to his full height. Giving me one more glance, he jogs to his friends and leaves.

Releasing a shaky breath, I wipe my sweaty palms on my dress.

My eyes wander aimlessly over the massive, white Mediterranean-style building. It's beautiful with vibrant colors peaking from the corners, and in front of the museum stands a huge three-tiered fountain. I wish I could focus more on the details, but I'm too nervous to do so.

Looking away from the building, I stare at the mini sage linen dress I chose to wear for my *date*. The neckline droops in between my chest, the dress tight at my waist, and flows freely to my mid-thigh.

I love this dress, the color, the way it fits my body perfectly, and how it makes me feel. It's not too much for my date, but still, I wonder if I should have worn something else.

But I know my mind is rioting because I willingly agreed to go on a date with someone I don't know. A guy whose last name I never asked.

I bite the inside of my cheek, inhaling and exhaling slowly as I try to get my thoughts together. Even if I hadn't dated Matt for two years, I wouldn't have stepped out of my comfort zone for a guy I don't know, or at least I thought I wouldn't have. Because with TJ, it doesn't feel like I did. With him, everything feels so... comfortable...so normal.

In spite of my frenzied heart and how fevered my body feels when I talk to him, I can't help but feel at ease with him.

And I hate myself for feeling like this because despite neither one of us saying it out loud, we haven't gone out of our way to truly get to know one another. We know after I leave on Saturday, we'll never see each other again.

Why start something that's bound to come to an end?

"Peaches." TJ's voice brings my thoughts to a stop. Our eyes connect as soon as I lift my head. He stands at the top of the stairs, the corners of his mouth curved upward into a grin. "I thought you had stood me up." His eyes trail down my body appreciatively as he comes down the steps.

My lips part, but they close as I decide against reminding him that my name is Lola. Something tells me no matter how many times I remind him, he'll still call me Peaches.

"I thought about it, but then I would've never been able to give you your birthday present."

"You got me a gift?"

It's not something I planned to do, but earlier when the girls and I were shopping, we passed by a shop that made custom souvenirs. Cara jokingly said I should get TJ something to remember me by. It was a joke at first, but then I saw the faux brown leather bracelets hanging on display, and the salesperson said she could add an engraving free of charge.

"Just something small, so you never forget me," I tease, taking out the bracelet wrapped in white tissue paper from my purse, and hand it to him.

"I don't think I could *ever* forget you." He shakes his head, taking the gift, and slowly and carefully pulls the tissue paper back. "A bracelet?" His lips quirk up, but when he grabs the faux leather and holds it up to the sky, a megawatt smile takes over his face. "Peaches." He quietly chuckles, reading the name engraved, then wraps it around his wrist and snaps it closed.

"Obsessed. Check." I lift my wrist and twirl it slowly so he can see I have the same one.

He wraps his hand around mine, lifting it up to inspect the letters engraved on my bracelet. "TJ." His voice is low as he reads his name.

As corny as this is, I'd be lying if I said I didn't like it. Even if it's all fake, I'm going to pretend that he genuinely loves that I got us matching bracelets.

Matt would have never pretended to like this kind of stuff. He would have made a joke and refused to wear it. I was afraid TJ would too, but he smiles and stares at them like they're matching Rolexes.

I can't believe how all of this is making me realize how bad of a boyfriend Matt was and how I overlooked everything.

"It's not matching T-shirts, but I figured these would do."

He runs the pad of his thumb across his name. "First base couple shit."

"First base couple shit," I repeat, the smile on my face growing as tiny flutters erupt inside my stomach.

"That's the spirit." He slowly drags his fingers down my palm until they're in between my own fingers and interlocks them. "Now we just need to be clingy and all over each other."

"You forgot happy."

"Lola." Standing in front of me, he cups my neck with his free hand, gently grazing his finger along my cheek as his eyes bore into mine. "I'm so damn happy, and if you're not, I've already failed as a boyfriend."

My heart races and the flutters manically spread everywhere, but I have to remind myself that this is all *fake*.

"I am happy," I admit, squeezing his hand.

Something flares in his eyes as they descend to my lips, but whatever lies in them disappears as a drop of water lands on his cheek.

"Welcome to Florida." He drops his hand, wiping the stray drop away. "Where the weather is unpredictable as fuck."

I nod at that. There was a storm last night, but this morning the sun was out, shining brightly as if nothing had happened.

Though the weather in Florida isn't the only unpredictable thing.

"We should head inside. You don't want to get wet on the first date," TJ says, guiding us up the stairs. He peers over his shoulder, his eyes sweeping over my body. "You look beautiful."

The three words sound sincere, but I still narrow my eyes at him, unsure if there's going to be another innuendo next to those three words.

"I mean it." He keeps his gaze glued on me as we head up the steps. "You look beautiful. Even with the paint in your hair, you still—"

"Are you serious?" I cut him off, my hand instantly going to my hair.

We liked the painting class we went to yesterday, so we went to another this morning.

"Don't worry about it. It makes you ten times more alluring. I don't think I'll ever be able to look at paint the same." He smiles, wrapping his hand around my wrist and pulling it away from my hair. "I promise no one will notice."

"But you did," I point out, raising my hand to my hair, but he stops me again before I can touch it.

"It's my job to notice the little things."

Any second now, my heart is going to combust into nothing if I hear something like that leave his lips again.

I eye him keenly. He's a little corny, but I guess that's how every relationship always starts. "Are you sure I'm your first girlfriend?"

"You're the first. How am I doing so far?"

I silently muse, considering how he's treated me from the moment I met him to now.

"Better than I expected. I sort of expected you to stand me up."

"I thought you were going to stand *me* up."

We look at each other and laugh.

"So what would you rate me?"

"What would I rate you?"

"Yeah." He eagerly nods. "One out of ten."

I hum, pretending I'm deep in thought. "I don't know...the date hasn't ended yet. So I can't make a decision."

"Okay, fair enough, but I'm confident that by the end of the night, it's going to be eleven." And he means it, the expression on his face filled with nothing but confidence.

"Wow, an eleven?"

"An eleven." He not only says it with so much self-assurance, but there's also a bit of cockiness laced in his voice.

"We'll see. So what's up with the camera?" I ask as he holds the door open for me to step inside.

He had that same camera hanging from his neck last night and this morning.

"Can I really be considered a boyfriend if I don't have pictures of my girlfriend?" TJ doesn't wait for me to respond as he continues. "Thought I could take pictures of art next to art."

I stupidly smile at his words and it has nothing to do with how cheesy they sound, but with the fireworks going off inside of me.

4

LOLA

"You Decide." TJ reads the name off the didactic plaque that's placed next to the painting. "I don't get it. What's this supposed to be?" His arms are folded against his chest, brows drawn together, and lips pinched and twisted to the side as he thoroughly examines the large canvas.

I'm not entirely sure how long we've been here, but unfortunately, we're at the end of the exhibit.

I should be looking at the painting, but I'm stuck staring at the single dark-brown curl that rests on his forehead and the way his eyes attentively follow every brush stroke with admiration and confusion.

"This doesn't make sense to me." He peers down at me. "What do you think it means?"

My breath hitches as he takes a step back and stands behind me. I stand still, veering my focus on the letters engraved on the plaque. Though it's hard to center my attention on it because my body is acutely aware of him.

"Hmm?" The hum is mildly faint, but it triggers a shiver to run down my spine.

"I think..." I trail off, feeling the pads of his fingers gently glide up my arms and then back down. *Focus.* "You Decide," I quietly read, then look at the painting. It's the only one on this wall and probably half the size of TJ.

On one side of the canvas, the brush strokes are rash, fast, and done aggressively sloppy with different shades of reds, oranges, whites, and yellows. The other side has the same colors except they're soft, careful, and detailed, making what looks like a sunset. And in the middle, the abrasive and soft strokes mesh together beautifully.

It makes sense why it's alone. It makes everything in comparison look dull.

Unlike the other plaques giving a brief summary of who the painter is or what the painting means, this plaque gives nothing away.

"I think it's supposed to be about life."

"Life," he muses.

"I could be wrong, but I think that side is meant to be chaos." I tip my head to one side. "And that side is calm." I pause, taking my time to slowly study the painting. "I think the purpose is to let us decide. Calm, chaos, or a little bit of both. One side is aimlessly erratic and the other purposely neat, but when they come together, they balance each other out and create something beautiful."

"Just like us," he murmurs, lacing his arms around my shoulders, but leaves a small gap of space between us. The strap of his camera dangles from his hand.

My heart drastically slows. "You think we balance each other out?"

"No, I *know* we do," he whispers, his minty breath ghosting over the shell of my ear. "You're calm, I'm chaos, and together we can create something beautiful...don't you think?"

"Yeah...I think we could." I take a step back until I'm firmly against his chest.

I could be overanalyzing it, but it feels as if he was letting me decide whether I closed the gap or not.

A comforting silence falls over us, but it hardly lasts a second as someone clears their throat. It takes everything within me not to groan and tell the person to go away.

"I'm sorry to interrupt, but we're closing in twenty minutes," one of the museum employees says.

When TJ and I pull away and turn around, a friendly smile lifts on the employee's face and her eyes fall to the camera.

"Would you like me to take a picture?"

"Yes, please," he replies, handing her the camera. "Thank you."

TJ stands next to me, slipping his arm around my waist to pull me close to his side. I stare up at him as he stares down at me. "Clingy. Check." He smiles down at me.

Something *intense* stirs inside my chest. I trace over the seam of his lips, wandering to the wild curls on his head before they meet his eyes again and a glint of mischief shines in them.

The bright flash of the camera pulls our focus away from each other and to the employee who holds the camera to her face.

"Oh, to be young and in love." She happily sighs, snaps another photo, and hands it back to him. "You two make such a beautiful couple."

We're not in love. We're just really good at pretending.

He smiles at her in appreciation. "Thank you."

"My pleasure." She glances down at the watch on her wrist. "Don't forget we close in twenty minutes," she reminds us, and with a smile, walks away.

TJ threads our fingers and ushers us to the front door. We walk in silence, his focus on the camera and mine on the way his thumb rubs soft circles on my hand.

Now that we're outside, he stands in front of me. "So how did I do? Did I meet your expectations?"

"Well...I would give this a solid six out of ten. If you had bought me that painting, maybe I would've given you a nine." I shrug as if unimpressed, but I struggle not to smile at the offended look on his face.

"A nine? You realize that painting is like twenty thousand dollars?"

"So? Am I not worth it?"

As soon as he laughs, my serious expression wavers and I laugh with him.

"You were right, this is an eleven."

This is more than an eleven. I don't think I could even rate this date because it exceeded every single expectation. Not that I had many to begin with.

"Tomorrow is going to top this." His voice holds promise.

My brows rise, folding my arms against my chest. "Is it now?"

"Yeah." He grabs my waist, tugging me to him. "Meet me at the Miami Davenport Marina, pier B at five."

"Miami Davenport Marina, pier B at five," I repeat, my voice breathless as he leans down until his lips hover over mine.

"I'll be waiting for you," he says before brushing his lips against mine.

"I'll be there." I smile against them.

"Peaches?" He grins when I roll my eyes at the nickname. Although it's kind of grown on me.

"Yeah?"

"You're worth it."

I stand in front of a white gate, awkwardly smiling at the guard who sits inside the booth, eyeing me warily.

I got here exactly at five, but TJ isn't here yet. I keep telling myself that he wouldn't stand me up, but I've been waiting for twenty minutes now.

The guard clears his throat. "Ma'am, you can't stand here. You're going to have to—"

"I'm so sorry I'm late." TJ comes out of nowhere, sounding winded. He stands next to me and takes my hand in his, lacing our fingers. "Hey, Greg, she's with me."

The cautious expression on Greg's face morphs into a welcoming smile. "Hey, TJ, it's good to see you. Are your parents—"

"No, just us." He quickly cuts him off.

Greg's brows pinch together and he looks like he wants to say something but shakes his head. "It should be ready. Be safe out there." He presses a button that unlocks the door.

"Always." TJ leads me through the gate and onto the dock. "Sorry I'm late. I had to do a few things that took longer than I thought they would."

I tighten my hold on the canvas in my hand. "It's okay. I'm just glad you didn't stand me up."

"I wouldn't do that to you. I'm in too deep and I can't go back now, figuratively and literally speaking."

"What do—" The rest of my words get caught in the back of my throat when we stop in front of a large boat.

He squeezes my hand, pulling me with him. "Come on."

My body feels as if it's stuck on autopilot as he guides me.

Just like the beach house, the boat is just as pretty and extravagant.

"I couldn't let you leave Miami without seeing dolphins and the sunset."

I gasp, not able to control the excitement in my voice. "Really?"

"Yeah." He chuckles and stands in front of me, gripping my waist and pulling me closer to him. "Anything for *my* girlfriend."

I suck in a breath when his fingers slide underneath my top and softly graze my skin, evoking goose bumps.

"This is too much." The words leave my mouth before I can stop them. I want to take them back and enjoy this moment, but we're merely strangers. I've spent a total of thirty dollars on him. I don't want to imagine how much he paid to rent this boat. "I mean, this is the best and sweetest thing anyone has ever done for me, but I can't let you do this. I can only imagine renting this boat—"

He laughs, amusement dancing in his eyes. "It's my dad's *yacht*." He removes a hand from my waist and tucks a lock of my hair behind my ear.

My jaw falls slack.

"Don't worry about anything."

I close my mouth when he cups my neck.

"It's your last day here, so let's just have a good time." A mesmerizing smile curves his lips, making it hard for me to say anything. So all I do is nod. "What's that?"

"Oh." I take a step back and hand him the canvas wrapped in brown paper. "A thank you isn't enough, nor is this, but thank you for making this one of the best summers."

"You didn't have to—" He stops mid-sentence as the brown paper falls to the ground. His eyes grow wide, gaze bouncing between the canvas and me a few times until they finally stop on the canvas. "Lola, holy sh—whoa—you painted this?" He drags his fingers along the sunset I painted.

"It's not my best, but—"

"Are you kidding me?" He stares at me like I've just said the most absurd thing. "This is insane. It almost looks realistic. You really painted this." It isn't a question but a statement of disbelief. "You're fucking incredible."

He hugs me tightly, melting everything inside of me. My heart moves erratically, but I swear his feels just the same. Beating simultaneously, evoking a tiny hole in my heart that's going to be hard to fill when we part ways.

I stare at the ocean, unblinking, the steady ripples that flow back and forth rhythmically captivating me. They're endless, vast, and completely mesmerizing with two different shades of blue, royal and indigo. And then the burnt sienna, deep champagne, and tangerine colors are beautifully painted across the sky.

They pour onto the sea and together coalesce, creating a breathtaking view that stretches as far as I can see.

I sigh at the reminder that this is all pretend. I want to continue pretending this is all real, but the sense of reality is slowly creeping in.

TJ's done an amazing job of making me forget about everything. I was solely focused on his eyes, his heart-shattering smile, and everything we did.

Even if I had wanted to think of anything else, I couldn't. Not when I sat on his lap at the helm of the yacht and he steered, when his fingers grazed and dug into my skin, or when he placed tender kisses on my bare shoulder. And it got harder to focus on anything else when we saw the dolphins. I wish I could say that topped the entire day, but then he took us swimming to an area where there were hardly any people.

The water was so clear, the sand was so white, and the heat from the sun was perfect.

I'm not sure how I'll ever get over this, but one thing is for certain: I'll *never* forget him.

"What are you thinking about?" he asks, his voice dissolving the cloud of my dreadful thoughts.

We're sitting on the bow lounge side by side, staring as the sun slowly descends below the horizon.

Bringing my legs to my chest, I wrap my arms around them and lay the side of my face on my knees. My hair cascades down my face and before I can move it away, TJ beats me to it, tucking the damp frizzy stands behind my ear. As our eyes meet, a soft smile lifts on his lips.

I return the smile. "Nothing...I don't want to ruin the moment."

"Tell me. What's on your mind?" He stares at me with intrigue and patience as he waits for me to reply.

"How I'm going to hate stepping back into reality...going back into the real world." I don't elaborate, but he nods as if he understands.

It's depressing to think this is almost over, and I'll be starting school and I'll have to take courses I'm not ready for. My parents insisted that I become an accountant like them, and even though that's not what I want to do at all, I don't have much of a choice. After all, they'll be paying for my college tuition.

He stares straight ahead, seemingly deep in thought as if he's contemplating what he wants to say. "Can I tell you something?"

"Whatever happens and is said here, stays here."

His smile grows just as the sun casts a perfect golden hue across his face, making the whiskey color in his eyes look like an incandescent amber.

"I'm a little anxious about the real world..." he trails off as if he's doubting what he just said or is unsure if he should have said that. "I mean, I'm ready, but sometimes I think about how *one* thing could fuck everything up."

I'm not sure what he's referring to, but I've never related to something so much. My parents have high expectations, and sometimes I worry about letting them down.

"It's nerve-racking, isn't it? One domino falls, and the rest fall and there's nothing you can do but watch it go to shit."

"Yeah, that's exactly how I feel," he sounds relieved that I understand.

I glance at him as he looks at me. "We should make a promise to each other."

"What kind of promise?"

"Finding our happy and reminding ourselves that *everything* will be okay."

"I promise." He slips his middle finger around mine.

I cock a brow. "You don't want to pinky promise?"

"Nah, those are overrated."

I quietly chuckle, gripping his finger, and stare off into the sunset, letting it seal our vow.

"Thank you for this. For everything."

He threads the rest of our fingers together. "Don't thank me. Just doing what any boyfriend would do."

"You don't have to pretend to be my boyfriend anymore. You've surpassed all the boyfriend qualifications. Congratulations, my standards have now been set extremely high, and it's going to be hard finding someone who will be worthy."

He grins. "Good. Never settle for less."

"I won't. *I promise...*"

I can't stop my eyes from dropping to his lips. It was only supposed to be a quick and subtle glance, but when he drags his tongue along his bottom lip, I can't look away.

"Lola?"

"Hmm?" I absentmindedly hum, forcing myself to look up at him.

"Are you ready to go back?"

The answer is yes. Even though we don't have to check out of the hotel until ten in the morning tomorrow, we still need to pack and make sure we have everything we need before we leave. On top of the packing, we have a twelve-hour drive ahead of us.

I should say yes, but...

"Lola?" My name leaves his lips in a low, desperate tone.

He only said my name, but I understood the question in his voice. Though it doesn't matter as sound becomes nonexistent. The seagulls flying in the distance, the waves rocking back and forth, the hammering of my heart, and the warning in my head become nothing.

My focus is solely on the shade of his irises, pools of dark amber that set every nerve in my body on fire.

I don't let myself dwell on the what-ifs because, after tonight, I'll never see him again. Without giving it much thought, I close the space between us and connect our lips.

5

LOLA

Two Years Later...

Eight dollars for iced coffee should be a crime. And as a semi-broke college student, I have no business substituting my milk for oat milk, adding three shots of espresso, and swiping my card.

It's not a necessity and I know my bank account is currently in shambles, crying over the fact that I spent eight dollars on something I don't need. Considering I'm on a tight budget, have student loans, bills, and a baby, I shouldn't have swiped my debit card.

But as I thought about it long and hard, I deserve it.

It's what I keep telling myself as I walk out of the café inside the Student Union.

I could say it's my *congratulations on almost making it through your first day of classes as a junior*. I'm also running low on energy, and I'm not confident I'll be able to keep my eyes open through my last class of the day, Healthy Lifestyles.

The class didn't sound too bad when I signed up for it. The issue is that it starts at four and lasts an hour and a half long. And the worst part is that I live an hour away; by the time I get home, it'll be almost seven in the evening.

It wasn't my choice, but my advisor said I needed this elective in order to graduate. She did give me three different options; Statistics, Geology, and Healthy Lifestyles. I would've preferred anything but these choices. Unfortunately, it was all I could pick from. So the latter option was the best and easiest. Luckily for me, it's only twice a week and I sort of know someone.

Well, I don't really know this girl. She's best friends with Gabby, a girl I met in my Studio Art class this morning. We sat next to each other and immediately clicked. After class, we compared schedules and though Studio Art is the only class we share together, she told me her best friend, Polly, is also taking Healthy Lifestyles.

So now I'm waiting outside the Student Union for Polly, and while I do, I sip my coffee and text my babysitter.

Me: Hey, how's he doing?

Elena: He's good, enjoying his snack :)

Elena: Attached: 1 Image.

I smile at the screen, staring at my baby, Phoenix, as he smiles at the camera with a cheeky grin on his chunky face.

It was never a part of my plan to bring my one-and-a-half-year-old kid with me to college, but it was also never in my plans to have a baby at nineteen to begin with.

A lot of things happened that weren't part of my plans. Finding out I was pregnant a month after I left Miami, my parents disowning me, and everything else that transpired after.

Chaotic is an understatement of what my life has been since Miami, and it all started the moment I met TJ.

"Lola?"

A pretty girl with strawberry-blond hair and deep green eyes stands in front of me, a friendly smile spread across her face.

"Hey," I greet, returning the smile. "Polly?"

"The one and only."

"I hope you didn't have to go out of your way to meet me," I say, pushing my bangs away from my eyes. "If you did, I'm sorry. I'm sure I would've—"

"Nonsense," she cuts me off, waving her hand dismissively. "I was heading in this direction, and even if I wasn't, don't worry about it. This campus is huge and the last thing we need is for you to get lost. Trust me, I know from experience. First day of freshman year, I walked into the wrong room."

I sheepishly smile at the reminder of me walking into the wrong class this morning. "Well..."

She snuffed a laugh. "It was bound to happen, but hey, at least you didn't walk into a lecture hall of three hundred students." A wry smile graced her lips.

I shake my head because I definitely couldn't relate. The class I walked into hardly had thirty students.

"Anyway"—she tipped her head to the side, motioning for us to get going—"how are you liking NCU so far?"

"I'm loving it," I giddily reply, finding it hard to contain the excitement I feel at being at my dream school.

If I hadn't gotten pregnant, I would've been here my freshman year. I received my acceptance letter in my senior year of high school and was ready to move into my dorm in August. But then I found out why I'd been feeling sick for a month and had to withdraw.

We walk side by side down the brick lane, talking about our majors and mostly her college experience. She talks about the parties, the hangovers, and the boys. I just listen and absorb her words and expressions. I would vicariously live through what she was saying if I didn't already do that through Daisy and Cara.

Now that I'm a mom, my life is different and I can't just do whatever I want when I want. If I'm not at home with Phoenix, I'm at school, and if I'm not at school, I'm at work. I do go out with the girls, but it only happens once a month. I also don't have the luxury of spending money because my only source of income comes from me.

We step into the lecture hall and take a seat in the last row as we spot four seats available. We sit down and save the seats right next to us for Polly's friends, who are running late.

"—and don't let those pretty faces fool you, especially the athletes. Most of them are arrogant and cocky as fuck. There are a few good ones, but the rest"—she pauses, lips pursing as she considers what she wants to say—"are entitled assholes, to say the least."

"Thanks for the heads-up." Setting my backpack on the chair next to me, I take my laptop out and set it on the joke of a table attached to my seat. "But I'm not looking for anything right now. I have a lot going on and relationships are complicated."

I don't mention that I have a kid. As soon as a guy finds out I'm a mom, they turn in the other direction. I could tell Polly and Gabby, but the last thing I need is a judgmental comment or look about me being a young mom. I shouldn't assume they would do that, but I've gone through it enough these past two years.

I'll tell them eventually.

"I aspire to have your level of self-control." She cocks a brow and inhales deeply. "Don't judge me. I know I said they're entitled assholes, but they're extremely *hot* entitled assholes."

I hold back a laugh. "I like sports, but I don't have enough time to keep up with them."

"You don't have to keep up with the sport. You just need to look at the guy. It's like window-shopping or you can buy and return it back later. Do you have a favorite sport?" Her eyes brighten and a teasing smile curls her lips as she unlocks her phone and goes to Instagram.

"I like basketball and—"

"Oh my God, if you love basketball, then I need to show you T—"

"Move over, Pols." A deep voice stops her finger from tapping the screen.

When I lift my head, I stare dumbfoundedly at the two immensely tall guys staring down at Polly. She smiles at them and moves her stuff from the seat she was saving. "You better be glad we got here in time, and you're welcome, by the way."

"We?" the one who spoke first asks, his dark brown eyes falling on me. "Hey." He flashes me a crooked grin as he takes a seat next to Polly.

"Don't even think about it," she warns him.

The guy makes a comment, but I don't pay attention as his other friend stands next to my seat and eyes my stuff.

"Sorry." I grab my bag and set it on the floor.

"Thanks, Lola." He smiles, taking a seat.

His friend is good-looking, but this guy...he's beautiful. I can't believe I just called a guy *beautiful*, but it's unreal how attractive he is. Immaculate jet-black hair that's swept back with a few strands resting on his forehead, thick and impeccably styled black brows, insanely clear blue eyes, flawless ivory skin, a killer smile, and a perfectly symmetrical face.

"How did you—"

"It's on the cup." His smile widens. "I'm Saint." He stretches his hand out.

"Right." I mentally roll my eyes at myself and place my hand in his. I note how large it is and the ring on his forefinger. A scar that looks like a burn mark covers half the top of his hand. "Lola, but you already know that."

Amusement glints in his eyes, but it morphs into something else as his gaze drops to my laptop. I cringe, looking down at the black Sharpie scribbled all over the top silver panel.

Somehow, Phoenix got into my stuff and got a little too excited.

"I don't blame you. I get bored too." He pulls out a thick paperback out of his bag that looks like it's seen better days.

"It must be one hell of a book."

The cover looks completely worn and faded. Creases upon creases mar the front, making the picture and letters on the front look hardly legible. Some pages are folded at the corner, and multiple tabs peek out from the side.

"It's decent."

I smile at his casual shrug and the nonchalance in his voice.

"I'm Jagger," the guy sitting next to Polly says, a playful smile on his lips. "Louise, right?"

My legal name is Louise Larson, but I typically just go by Lola. I took the first two letters of my first and last name and combined them. I do have two other nicknames, but only my two best friends use them—Lo, or Daisy's personal favorite, milf.

"You can just call me Lola."

"Lo—" His smile falters, eyes slightly narrowing. "Do I know you?"

Polly softly slaps her forehead, shaking her head disapprovingly. "Oh my God, Jagger, are you seriously trying to flirt right now? It hasn't even been two minutes. You couldn't have waited at least until class was over?"

"Jesus fuck, Jag." Saint stifles a laugh.

"I'm not flirting. She—" He pauses, tilting his head, studying me. "You look familiar. Have we met before?"

"Uh, no?" I reply unsurely, knowing I would remember meeting someone like Jagger. There is no way I'd ever be able to forget someone who looks like him. Warm brown skin, dark brown eyes, thick curly eyelashes that are truly unfair, and a small indent on his chin. He's good-looking and he knows it. "I just transferred here."

"Hmmm..." he hums absentmindedly, swiping his hand over his short black curls. "You just look familiar and I would know. I don't see a lot of redheads. You are a true redhead, right?"

Polly thumps him on the cheek. "Ignore him. He's an idiot."

I chuckle, pushing my bangs away from my face. "Yeah, I'm a *true* redhead."

It's not the first time someone asked if this is my real hair color. Though it's more on the spectrum of a golden copper with undertones of red. "And I'm sorry to disappoint, but I don't know you."

"Well, now you can." He pushes Polly out of the way and leans closer to me, wiggling his brows suggestively.

"Like I said, an idiot." She shoves him back in his seat and rolls her eyes. "Just pretend he doesn't exist. I do most of the time."

I nod, holding back a laugh, but fail at the offended expression on his face.

"I think we're going to be great friends, Lola," Saint whispers as the professor stands at the front of the class next to the podium and introduces herself.

"I'm home!" I shut the door behind me. I kick my shoes off, drop my backpack and purse on the floor, and stand in my spot.

I wait until I hear the soft padding against the floor and get on my knees, spreading my arms wide open.

"Ma!" Phoenix comes from around the corner and runs toward me, his wild brown curls bouncing with every movement along with his chubby cheeks.

He doesn't resemble me in the slightest. No red in his hair, no green in his eyes, absolutely nothing that screams he's my son. He looks every bit like TJ, from the brown curls, the whiskey in his iris, the nose, his long fingers, breathtaking smile, and height.

He may only be one-and-a-half, but the doctors said that from the looks of his growth chart, he's going to be tall. I don't doubt it. He weighed almost ten pounds when he was born.

"Hi, honey." I laugh as he jumps on me and wraps his little arms around my neck. I wind my arms around his small body and inhale the sweet scent of maple syrup.

I hold him against me until he decides that he's had enough and pushes away from me.

"All right, all right, I'm sorry." I pinch his cheek and set him down, letting him run back to whatever he was doing. "Sorry I'm late!" I yell out as I pick up my stuff and head into the living room.

Our professor said we're going to be working in groups for the rest of the semester and allowed us to pick who we wanted to work with. So after class, I exchanged phone numbers with the guys and Polly. It took longer than necessary because Jagger kept insisting he knew me even though I told him I'd never met him in my life.

Daisy stands in the kitchen, holding a spatula in one hand and a shaker cup in the other. Her black hair is in a low ponytail. A few of the black strands stick out and her golden tan skin is flushed from her workout.

"You're right on time. Food's almost ready." She peers over her shoulder, giving me a quick smile before she looks at the pan on the stove.

I round the couch, drop my stuff next to it, and grin down at Cara, who's sitting on the ground with Phoenix. His Winnie the Pooh and a few other toys are scattered along the floor, along with a few cereal puffs.

"Thanks for picking him up."

Even though my best friends have insisted on helping me, I still feel guilty because I know it's not their responsibility.

"Don't." She gives me a pointed stare, knowing exactly what I'm thinking about. "I wanted to pick him up and I got out of class early. I don't have homework or have to work, so it's all right. Isn't that right, Phoenix?" She twirls his curl around her finger.

"Mmhm." He hardly acknowledges what she said as he's too busy playing with the ball in his hand.

Cara and Daisy don't want me to thank them, but I do it anyway. "Thank you."

From the moment I found out I was pregnant, they've been there every step of the way. Even when they were in different states, they were always supportive. Daisy even convinced her parents to let me move in when my parents kicked me out, and when I gave birth, the girls were there.

It hadn't been in our plans to go to college together. Daisy said she was homesick and hated being on the other side of the country, so she left California and came back to North Carolina. It was a little odd considering how much she loved California, but I didn't question it. And Cara said she was tired of paying out-of-state tuition and felt left out.

When they moved back to North Carolina, Daisy had the idea that we get an apartment together. After going through our finances, we managed to make it all work out. Unfortunately, I'm still not making enough from my small painting business, so I can't afford any of the apartments near campus. We did manage to find a decent one, and Daisy's parents know Elena, my babysitter, so it worked out. The only downside is that it's an hour away, but it could be worse.

But it doesn't matter because things are finally starting to look up for me.

6

TJ

I GROAN, PULLING MY DUVET OVER MY HEAD, SHIELDING the bright streams of light that filter through my curtains. I groan again, wishing that the duvet had the same effect on my thrashing headache.

My intention had been to stay in last night and catch up on homework. Even though school started two weeks ago, I'm already behind. Despite having mandatory study hall since I'm an athlete, I still managed to procrastinate. It's not the smartest thing to do, but I can't help it. Though I feel like I work best under pressure.

My roommate and teammate, Saint Arlo, convinced me to go out, but it didn't take much effort from him. All he said was that one of the guys on the football team was hosting the party and there'd be an unlimited supply of alcohol. It helps that the athletes who live off campus live on Ashford Drive, so we're only a five-minute walk from our place to theirs.

I didn't get black-out drunk, but I drank enough to make my headache last. And that isn't the only thing I did last night.

An arm thrown over my bare chest reminds me that Alexia is lying next to me, completely naked.

My headache slowly diminishes as her hand trails down my chest to my stomach.

Pulling the duvet away, I sit up on the side of my bed and peer over my shoulder, looking down at her.

"Morning," her sleep-laced voice greets me. She sits up and leans against the headboard, stretching her arms above her head, showing off her tight, toned, hot as fuck body.

Alexia and I met freshman year at a party during a game of drunk Jenga. She was a horrible partner but amazing to look at. And she knew that, with the way she was rubbing her ass all over me and the way she carried herself with all the confidence in the world.

After that night, we mutually agreed to keep things simple. No feelings and we could fuck whenever and whoever we wanted. It's the best of both worlds because we aren't looking for a relationship, just for a good time.

My only focus is basketball and preparing to declare for the NBA draft in April next year.

The last thing I need or want is a relationship. They're anything but easy. They require too much time and attention, which is something I can't afford to give up.

"Wanna join me in the shower?"

She gets off the bed in all of her naked glory and saunters to my bathroom.

"You want to hang out?" Alexia asks.

She stares at herself in my mirror, combing her fingers through her damp black hair.

"I have homework I need to finish," I answer, strapping the brown leather bracelet around my wrist and then twisting, dragging the pad of my thumb over the faded name.

"That's fine. We could—"

"I have a lot of homework."

It wasn't a complete lie. Thanks to mandatory study hall, I was able to do most of my homework, but I still needed to work on my portfolio. I'm a Studio Art major, concentrating on photography. Two weeks ago, they asked us to pick something that empowers us, and at the end of the year, we're supposed to present it. I haven't decided what I want to do yet. I thought of basketball, but that's too predictable. I want to do something different. I'm just not sure what.

Homework set aside, I'm not in the mood.

She's not horrible to hang out with. I like that she's not attached to me and isn't using me for attention. I sound conceited, but people are always trying to get close to me because of who I am and who my dad and sister-in-law are.

With Alexia, I don't have to worry about that. She gets enough attention as it is on social media.

We fuck, occasionally hang out, and then we go about our day. It's pretty great if you ask me. She doesn't have expectations and neither do I.

But all that aside, I just like my space.

"Do you at least want to grab lunch?"

I'm not a morning person, never have been and never will be. The only exception to waking up early is if it deals with basketball. Other than that, I never wake up before 11:00 a.m. Especially on days after I've partied.

I'm surprised it's already two in the afternoon.

"I'm going to eat here. I really need to start on my homework."

She steps out of my room and I trail right behind her. "Well, if you change your mind, text me."

"All right," I absentmindedly answer, not focusing on whatever she's saying but on the music that slips from underneath the door of one of my roommates, Landon Taylor.

There are five of us who live in this house, and out of the five, he's the most reserved. He's always in his room unless Jagger Spears, my other roommate, forces him to come hang with us, or unless it involves school or basketball. He hates it and I'm pretty sure hates anyone who's near him. Somehow, he still puts up with Spears despite their different personalities.

"Have you made up your mind?" she asks as we stand at the front door.

"Huh?"

"Have you decided if you want to come out to Liquid next weekend?"

Liquid is a club that opened about a month ago and since its opening, it's become extremely popular. Alexia has asked me a few times to go with her, but when I want to, something comes up, and I have to change plans. Though it works out better this way. Sometimes when we're out together, people assume we're dating, and that's the last thing I want any girl to assume.

"I don't know yet. I'll let you know."

"Text me if you change your mind about hanging out later." She twists the doorknob and walks about, thankfully not giving me a chance to reply.

I shut the door behind her and step into the living room. Jayden Thompson, my other roommate, sits on the couch with a PlayStation controller in his hand.

He side-eyes me briefly before shifting his focus to the game. "You want to play?"

"I'll play but not on your team."

He flips me off, aggressively moving the cursor with his thumb. "I'm getting better, but this shit is hard."

"Getting better?" I mock, looking at the score.

1-5

And those five points aren't his.

"As if you're any better than me. Damn it." He grunts, throwing the controller to the other side of the couch as the other team scores a goal.

"Yes, you're *definitely* doing better."

He rubs his eyes, breathing harshly. "Fuck you. This shit is hard. I still don't understand why Taylor calls this football."

"That's what they call it where he comes from." I remind him, though it's not necessary. Taylor's British accent is a dead giveaway. "But it makes sense. They kick the ball so—"

"Let's test this theory right now," Jagger says from the kitchen, followed by the sound of a bottle being slammed on the table.

"Jag, it's two in the afternoon. Put that shit away," Polly says.

My brows pull together at her voice. She's best friends with Jagger and Landon and occasionally visits them with Gabby, their other best friend.

"You forgot about the project, didn't you?"

Saint mentioned something about a project he's working on with Jagger and Polly and some other girl in their class. They said they were going to use the kitchen, but I forgot they were working on it today.

"Well, if you're going in there, don't be loud. Polly chewed my ass out because I didn't know they were in the middle of recording something." He scoffs, folding his arms against his chest, annoyance etched on his umber face. "How was I supposed to know? It doesn't even sound like they're busy. Jag's been mad flirting with the girl in there since she got here."

"Don't tell me you're scared, Little Red," Jagger taunts.

"I told you not to call me Little Red," the girl says with agitation in her voice.

"Little Red?" I ask.

"She's hot." Jay picks up the controller again, eyes bouncing toward the kitchen and then back to me. "But not your type."

"Not my type?"

"She's a redhead." He grins, knowing it's all I need to hear.

It's not that redheads aren't my type, but the last redhead I was with, I accidentally called her by someone else's name. It was a shit thing to do and I apologized. It hadn't been my intention, but *her* name just slipped out of my mouth before I could stop it. I wish I could say it was the only time it happened, but it wasn't. I met another redhead at an away game and did it again. I couldn't help it. The lights were off and I saw *her* face.

I hardly think about her anymore, so if I wanted to, I could mess around with a redhead and *she* wouldn't even cross my mind.

"I like redheads," I state matter-of-factly.

He laughs condescendingly. "Good for you, but it doesn't matter anyway. Jagger has been flirting with her for the past hour, and either she's oblivious or doesn't give a shit. She's not even flirting with Saint—"

"Saint is a freshman," I cut him off. Not that it matters. Even though he's a freshman and only nineteen, girls are always flirting with him whether they're nineteen or twenty-four.

"You know that's never stopped anyone."

"Well, I'm not Jagger or Saint." I challenge.

He resumes his game. "Yeah, okay. Good luck, Kingston."

Rolling my eyes, I saunter into the kitchen but falter in my footsteps. The redhead stands next to Polly, her back to me, and although I can't see her face, I get an amazing view of her ass.

Damn.

I'm stuck in a daze until Saint clears his throat. When our eyes meet, he smiles knowingly. No one else says anything to me, and that lets me know they're probably recording, so I don't say anything.

Shoving the stupor away, I stand in front of the refrigerator and pull the door open. I look at the variety of drinks we have, but all I can focus on is the redhead's voice and the laugh that follows after Saint says something.

Inhaling sharply, my hand tightens around the handle, willing my thoughts not to stray to the *girl* from two years ago. I'm really fucking insane because the girl standing just a few feet away from me sounds familiar.

I shake my head, annoyed that she's the first person I think of when I see a redhead. Fuck, I am insane and I need to go back to sleep. Homework and food can wait.

Grabbing a water bottle, I shut the door and right as I'm about to walk out, Saint stops me.

"Wait, don't leave. We need to get your opinion on something."

I turn around and lean against the fridge, doing my best not to let my eyes drop to her ass again.

Uncapping my bottle, I then chug half of it down. That's until the redhead turns around, and when our eyes lock, the water gets lodged in the back of my throat and I choke.

"Jesus, are you okay?"

I hear someone say, but I'm coughing too hard to respond. I would be embarrassed about the water dripping down my chin if it wasn't for my loud cough taking over the kitchen.

Once I get myself under control, Jagger throws a wad of paper towels in my direction, and just like Saint and Polly, he stares at me, amused.

"You good?"

I ignore the question and stare dumbfounded at the girl in front of me. "Lo—" I cringe at the sound of my hoarse voice. Wiping the water away, I clear my throat. "Lola."

"TJ." Her voice is a mere whisper of disbelief, eyes wide with something I can't read.

"You two know each other?"

7

TJ

"WELL, I'LL BE DAMNED." JAGGER'S VOICE PULLS ME OUT of my stupor and forces my gaze back to hers. "What a small world."

"Yeah, small world indeed." I smile at her, although she doesn't return it. She doesn't even look remotely happy to see me. "It's been what? Two years?"

She weakly nods. "Yeah...two years..."

Saint coughs, slicing the invisible string of awkward tension. "So, how do you two know each other?"

When she doesn't answer, I do. "Senior week in Miami. We met on our birthday."

The memory flashes through my head as if it were yesterday.

May 26. Peach juice. Our talk on the beach. The bracelets. The museum. The pictures. The painting. The dolphins. The sunset. Her.

I hover over her naked body, hands on either side of her shoulders.

She looks beautiful, her hair splayed on the white pillowcase, cheeks stained pink, a sheen of sweat on her face, and swollen lips.

"Why are you looking at me like that?" She sheepishly smiles.

Ask for her number, dumbass.

"I'm thankful for peach juice."

"Me too." She cups my sweat-covered cheek.

"Thanks for making this night memorable."

"You two share a birthday?" Polly's eyes drift between Lola and me, eyebrows raised in disbelief.

"May 26," I reply just as a thought comes to mind. I probably shouldn't, but I really can't help myself. "Isn't that right, *Peaches*?"

The nickname I gave her does the opposite of what I hoped it would do. Instead of her telling me not to call her that, she turns around and packs up all of her stuff in her backpack.

"Yeah...May 26." Her response is low, almost inaudible, but we all hear it.

Saint's brows knit together and Jagger's arch; both of them stare at me with a *what the fuck did you do* look. I'm just as confused as they are because she's the one who left without saying goodbye.

I shrug, rubbing the back of my neck, trying to figure out where I could have fucked up two years ago, but nothing comes to mind.

Lola almost knocks her iced coffee on the floor, but Polly catches it before it happens. "Wait, where are you going? We still haven't finished."

"I, uh, I—" she stammers for a second before she huffs a breath. "I just remembered I need to stop by the store before work."

"Oh, that's right."

Lola hesitates when Polly picks up her pencil pouch and hands it to her.

"I forgot you had told me about that. You need to buy more paintbrushes, right?"

"Yeah." This time, her smile is genuine. Nothing ever bothers me, but I'm extremely offended right now. "More paint brushes." Lola zips up her bag and throws it over her shoulders. "I'll finish the rest of the assignment and submit it tonight."

I keep my gaze glued to the back of her head and don't allow it to trail down to her ass like it's begging me to. She's wearing dark green leggings, and holy fuck, it looks like they've been painted onto her body. They mold to her, the material showing off just how big her ass is.

"Don't forget about our bet, Little Red."

"Jagger, stop calling me Little Red." She pushes her bangs away from her eyes. Did she have bangs two years ago? "And I never agreed to the bet."

"Then how am I supposed to know you're not lying, Little Red?" He flashes her a crooked grin.

She rolls her eyes, but still, she smiles. "I don't care if you believe me or not."

"Then you're lying—"

Saint elbows his side. "Jag, leave her alone. Come on, Lola, I'll walk you out." He jerks his head toward the living room.

She nods, smiling as she picks up her iced coffee.

Not that I care, but why the hell is she smiling at everyone but me?

"No." The word leaves my mouth before I can process it and all eyes fall on me, except for Lola's. The shocked expressions on their faces dissolve in a matter of seconds, and they all grin at me. "I mean, I can walk her out."

"No," she replies not even a second after. "It's fine. I can walk myself out. Bye, everyone."

She hurriedly walks out of the kitchen, leaving a scent of something sweet I can't pinpoint.

Once we hear the front door shut, everyone looks at me with questioning eyes.

"Well, well, well, Teddy, what the fuck did you do now?" Jagger chuckles, leaning his hip against the counter and crossing his arms against his chest.

I raise my middle finger at him, hating the stupid nickname he's been calling me since freshman year. My name is short for Theodore Jackson, but everyone calls me TJ. Mom couldn't decide which grandfather she wanted to name me after, so what did she do? She named me after both of them, and if that isn't enough, she insists on calling me Teddy.

Ever since Jagger heard the stupid nickname, it's all he calls me. Granted he has a nickname for everyone, but I still hate it.

"Nothing," I reply defensively, raising my hands. "What makes you think I did anything?"

We fucked all night, though I'm not sure *fucked* is the appropriate term for what we did. It was slow and *so* damn good.

The only mistake I made was never getting her number or last name. At that moment, it seemed pointless, but I regretted it when I woke up and she was nowhere to be found.

"The fact that this is *the* first girl who has left a room you're in. Matter of fact, the first girl to not look remotely interested in you," Polly points out.

Saint snorts a laugh. "That was funny as shit. I like her."

"Please don't tell me that you and her—"

The tight smile on my face gives everything away.

"Nice." Jagger nods in approval. "Louise is..." he muses, rubbing his chin, deep in thought.

"Louise?"

"Her full name is Louise Larson," Saint answers as he taps away on his phone. "But she uses the first two letters of her names and together they make Lola."

"Hmmm." She hadn't told me that. Not that we shared much to begin with. We didn't voice it out loud, but we both knew it was pointless because we assumed we'd never see each other again.

But little did we know.

Now she's here, I'm here, but it doesn't matter. We don't know each other, and really, we're *just* strangers. If it wasn't obvious by the way she walked out and hardly acknowledged me.

Not that I care. I don't care what she does or doesn't do.

I really don't care...

I don't.

"Jagger, don't finish that sentence." Polly narrows her eyes at him in warning, and I find myself doing the same thing. Jagger isn't shy to state how he feels about a girl. I can definitely see the interested spark in his eyes and the thoughts that are probably circling his mind about her. "And you." She looks at me. "I don't know what you did to her, but don't make things weird. I really like Lola. She's the first girl I've met to not thirst or obsess over any of you."

I don't bother to argue that I don't really know Lola and that I didn't do anything. I don't mention that I made sure I gave her the best two days of her senior week. Or that I had been the best goddamn boyfriend despite me hating the thought of being in a relationship.

They can believe what they want to believe. I don't need to explain myself to them. It was two years ago. For all I know, we're *just strangers.*

8

LOLA

All this time, TJ's been in the same state, just three hours away.

"Lola?"

From my peripheral, I catch sight of something fuzzy, but it isn't until I blink that I realize Julianna is waving her manicured hand to get my attention.

"Sorry, what?"

"Is everything all right?" she worriedly asks. "Were the kids not good today? Because if they weren't, I can—"

"No, no, they were great," I quickly supply. "Sorry, I just—I just couldn't sleep last night."

She nods understandingly. "Phoenix kept you up?"

I met Julianna a few months ago when I came for two job interviews. Luck hadn't been on my side that day because I had to bring Phoenix with me after my sitter canceled, and all my backups couldn't help me. The two managers I had met with didn't appreciate that I brought my son with me, and after two brief five-minute interviews, they said they would call me back.

It didn't take a genius to figure out that meant there was no chance in hell they would call me back. I know they thought I might be unreliable due to having my son, so they weren't going to waste their time on me.

After the disappointing realization, I went to the Hall of Arts Museum to clear my head, when I met Julianna. Well, Phoenix met her first. I had let him walk around to tire him out before we drove back home. As he was walking, he got distracted by the sweet melody coming from the piano, and that's when we met her.

It was never my intention, but I ended up ranting to her about my day. She listened and held Phoenix while we walked around the museum. After I was done talking, she said she could help.

I left the museum that day as the new museum guide and the new art teacher for the kids at the community center. I wasn't getting paid to work at the center, but it was for a good cause and I only had to go every other Sunday.

Not only do I get to work with Julianna, go to school with her, but I get to do something I love, which is to talk about art. The best part about working at the museum is helping out when they have exhibitions and meeting new artists.

"No, but he did wake up early." I wrinkle my nose at the thought, but I couldn't be annoyed even if I wanted to. "But with his bear on my face and a kiss on my nose."

Phoenix is part of the reason I'm exhausted, but it's also a multitude of other things. On top of TJ being on my mind, I kept thinking of all the homework I had to do, the bookings I had coming up, and everything else that my chaotic life entailed.

Besides working at the museum, I have my own business, doing live paintings for any event. The idea came to mind when I was at my lowest, struggling with postpartum depression and unsure of what I wanted to do with my life after I gave birth.

Business has been slow, but I'm staying hopeful it'll eventually pick up.

"Stop," she cooed, her face in awe. "That's so cute. I swear I love your kid."

I smile at the sincerity in her voice. Juls is one of the most genuine people I've ever met and also one of the most stunning. It's no exaggeration that she's the literal definition of perfection. With golden blond hair, long lean legs to die for, and flawless skin I envy. She's the kind of girl you see in fashion magazines.

"Yeah, he's pretty cute..." I trail off, my thoughts straying to TJ.

He smiles. "It's been what? Two years?"

"I'm sorry I made you come out with me." Her voice drags me back to where we're at. After we left the community center, Juls invited me out for coffee, and who was I to turn down free coffee? "We can leave so you can get some rest. I can't begin to imagine how tired you must be."

"No, you're fine. I was just thinking of the conversation I had with one of the guys in my group." I internally cringe at the memory of how I panicked and walked out. "We were on the subject of depressants, and I accidentally let it slip that I have a slightly high alcohol tolerance, and Jagger—"

"Jagger? As in Jagger Spears?" she cuts me off, her perfect dark brown brow arching high. "That's the guy whose house you went to earlier for the project?"

I nod. "Yeah, his house. His roommate Saint is also part of our group. Why?"

She deeply glowers.

"Why are you looking at me like that?" I chuckle, pulling off a piece of my blueberry muffin and plopping it in my mouth. "Do you know them?"

She grabs her mug, drumming her fingers along the white porcelain. "Of course," she answers less than enthusiastically. "*Everyone* knows them, but it's not them I can't stand. It's the tallest one. If you haven't already met him, stay the fuck away from him. He's the biggest asshole you'll ever meet. Trust me."

I don't process her last statement because my mind is circling back to the first one, *everyone knows them*.

"What do you mean everyone knows them?"

She stares at me incredulously. "You're kidding, right?"

I shake my head.

"Do you follow any of the athletes or sports here?"

I shake my head again. "I don't have the time to."

"You're lucky." She pulls her phone out of her purse and unlocks it, going straight to Instagram. She goes to the search bar and types *ncu.basketball*, and it immediately pulls up the men's basketball team account. She clicks on a picture of the team and staff that was taken inside the arena and lays the phone in front of me. "I present to you NCU's basketball team, also known as the cockiest assholes. Besides the football team, that is."

I should've known considering how tall they are. I never cared to question or pay attention to their conversations about the NBA draft, stats, or anything else that didn't have to do with our homework.

"So if Saint and Jagger are on the basketball team, then TJ..." I suck in a breath as my eyes stop on his face. He's in the third row, standing with his arms behind his back, a beaming smile on his face. He's wearing a light blue jersey with a white number six that's outlined in black in the middle.

"I don't know how well you know them, and I'm not trying to talk shit about them because I can't stand athletes, but just be careful with Jagger and TJ."

"Why?" I find myself asking, although I'm afraid to find out the answer.

"They like to get around *a lot*. Not that it's a bad thing, but they're not looking for anything serious. So if you aren't, just stay away from them. Trust me, for the sake of your mental health, don't do it. Especially with TJ of all people."

"Oh." I feel an odd dip in my stomach and my appetite is completely gone.

She retracts her phone and turns it off. "Yeah, TJ is the one person you definitely want to stay away from. He's great to look at but not worth the trouble. Everyone has this weird obsession with him and they all adore him. Especially the girls. They go feral for him."

"Oh..."

"This is..."

"Insane." Cara finishes off for Daisy.

As soon as I got home, I told the girls everything. From the moment I saw TJ to everything Juls told me. Now I'm sitting in between them, holding my phone, staring at his Instagram account.

It's not only verified but close to seven hundred thousand followers.

"I can't believe all this time he's been here. All this time, he's been three hours away from us." The shock in Daisy's voice matches exactly how Cara and I feel. "I can't fucking believe it."

I can't bring myself to tell Daisy to put a dollar in the jar. All I can do is stare at the stupid username that taunts me.

When I found out I was pregnant, I tried to find TJ on social media, but trying to find a guy whose last name I didn't know was futile. I'm annoyed that I never found him because the username is simple *tj.kingston*. In hindsight, I would've never found him because I don't follow any athletes or keep up with any sports, especially college basketball of all things. All of my social media consists of art, babies, and coffee.

A heavy silence falls over us as we all muse over the news, staring at his Instagram page but never scrolling down.

My thoughts spiral out of control, going in all different directions, still in disbelief that he's been here all this time.

"I can't believe how much they look alike." Cara breaks the silence. "TJ has some strong genes."

In my peripheral, I see her phone in her hand and notice she has his account pulled up. On her screen, there's a picture of TJ sitting on a chair in his uniform, arms resting on his thighs as he holds a basketball in his hands, a smug and all too confident smile on his face.

Daisy plucks my phone out of my hands and clicks on one of his posts. In the picture, there's an immense crowd behind him and he's smiling, wearing the light blue uniform.

Even though it's been two years, I can tell he's changed. The last time I saw him, he didn't have stubble and his arms weren't as defined and muscular. He didn't have a full tattoo sleeve covering his right arm, and he didn't have a fade with his curls in place.

I wish I could say that he didn't look as good as he did two years ago, but he looks even better than I remember.

"God really said duplicate," Daisy adds.

I shove away my thoughts, realizing that I was gawking at him and not thinking about what truly matters.

"Phoenix looks like me." The moment those words leave my lips, they look at each other and snicker.

Daisy eyes me up and down. "Lo, I'm sorry to break it to you, but Phoenix looks nothing like you."

"Yes, he does. H-he—" I stammer and fail to point out one thing where he and I resemble.

We simultaneously stare at him playing with the toys Daisy's parents gave him for his birthday.

I could deny it all I want, but even my subconscious won't let it slide because I know the truth. My son looks nothing like me.

"Whatever," I grumble.

"So when are you going to tell him?" Cara tosses her phone to the side, twisting her body to look at me.

I drum my fingers, unsure of how to answer that, feeling a tightness in my chest.

"Lo, you're going to tell him, right?" Daisy warily asks, and even though I'm not looking at either one of them, I feel their scrutinizing gazes.

"It's not that I don't want to tell him, but..." I trail off, finding it hard to swallow. It feels as if a boulder grew and got stuck in the middle of my throat. "Life is finally getting better.

Imagine if I tell him and he doesn't take the news well? Or he meets Phoenix and doesn't want any part of his life? Or he's actually a jerk? What if—"

"Whoa, whoa, whoa." Cara abruptly stops my rambling. "Breathe." She instructs, rubbing my back in soft, small circles.

I inhale and exhale slowly, wiping my clammy palms on my leggings. "I'm just afraid. I don't want a repeat of my parents." I attempt to block out the memory, but it manages to sneak its way into my head and play in a loop.

The reminder causes my temples to throb, and the air around me becomes thicker. Releasing a harsh breath, I rest my head on the back of the couch and stare at the ceiling.

"You know we love you, and we'll support whatever decision you make." Daisy's voice softens, surprising me because she's far from soft or gentle. She's more of an in your face, tells you how it is kind of person.

"But?"

"But one day, Phoenix will have questions about who his dad is," she replies.

"I know you're afraid because you don't want a repeat of two years ago, but we all know TJ's the dad. No one can deny how much they look alike, and if they do, that's what DNA tests are for," Cara adds. "If you tell TJ and he denies it or doesn't care, at least you did your part and it won't be on your conscious because Daisy is right. One day, Phoenix will grow up and ask questions."

I glance at Phoenix. He's still busy playing with his toys, with no worries in the world.

The girls are right. I should tell him. I *need* to tell him, but there's this lingering feeling of anxiety that once I do tell him, everything's going to blow up in flames and the only one who'll be struggling to put them out will be me.

9

TJ

"MOTHERFUCKERS, *STRONZIS*, *VAFFAN*..." SAINT GOES on a rampage, saying words in Italian that I have no idea what they mean. "Why did you all let me sleep in?"

"We thought you knew," Jayden replies, doing his best to suppress his smile. Giving Jagger and me knowing looks. "He sent out a text to everyone."

"Yeah, I know that, but you all told me it wasn't mandatory. You all promised we didn't have to go." He seethes, glaring at all of us as we take a seat at one of the tables inside Cameron Hall.

We just finished training and are now going to have lunch inside one of the dining halls. Well, *most* of us finished with training. The freshmen and transfers had not only trained but also had a lengthy *chat*—in other words, a punishment—with our coach, Frank Warren, about the importance of following directions and being on time.

"*I* didn't promise anything," Landon says, his voice filled with boredom. "It's your fault you're daft. The only person to blame is yourself for listening to them."

Yesterday, we all got a text stating that we had *optional* 6:00 a.m. morning conditioning. Anyone who knows Coach Warren knows that *optional* doesn't mean shit. He expects everyone to be at the arena at 5:45 a.m. and not a minute later.

We made Saint believe he didn't have to go to morning conditioning, as did the other guys on the team with the other freshmen and transfers. This and a few other things are just part of us welcoming them into the family. It's light hazing at best. It could've been worse.

"I thought we were all friends." Feigned hurt laces Saint's voice, but I see through it as a small smile rises. "What the hell, guys? I'm so hurt."

"Good." Landon stabs his lo mein with his fork and twirls it until he gets enough. Before he lifts it, he looks at Saint with a disdainful expression. "We're not friends. I don't even like you."

His apathetic expression and voice are nothing new to me. Not only is this my third year playing basketball with him, but this is also my third year being his roommate.

With that being said, there are a few things I know about Landon Taylor. And by a few, I really mean *a* few.

One and foremost, he's antisocial. If Jagger can't convince him to come out with us, he won't. Two, he's not the person you want to ask for advice unless you want nothing but brutal truth. And three, he's smart as fuck.

"I know you don't mean it." Saint waved off his statement with a dumbass grin. "I know behind those dead, cold, soulless eyes, there's a guy who loves with his whole heart, and you can't tell me otherwise."

Landon chews, staring at Saint apathetically, then ignores him and the rest of us.

Saint shrugs, not fazed by his cold shoulder. He only smiles like always. I'm not against smiling, but he smiled like it was his fucking job.

"Back to pressing matters, I'm still hurt that you all would do me so dirty." He picks up his sandwich, shaking his head disappointedly.

"Stop being a little bitch. You're lucky you weren't the only one who decided to sleep in." Jayden stares off into the distance, remembering the time he was the only one to sleep in when he was a freshman.

"I know but—"

"Oh look, it's Little Red," Jagger cuts him off, tipping his head toward the sea of students looking through the multitude of menus from the various restaurants inside Cameron Hall.

I have no idea why my head instantly turns. For some reason unbeknownst to me, I feel like I'm stuck on autopilot. My body, my brain, and my eyes work of their own accord. As if hearing *Little Red* and spotting the girl with golden copper hair was an everyday occurrence.

Because somehow, amongst the sea of students, I instantly spot her. The worst part about staring at her is not being able to look away. There's this voice in my head that tells me to stop looking, to think of anyone else, but the voice is low at best. It's hardly audible compared to the blaring one that's telling me *not* to look away.

My traitorous eyes oblige and stay glued on Lola. She stands to the side, brushing her fingers against her bangs to push them out of her eyes as she stares down at her phone.

She didn't have bangs before. I only remember because I *might* have gone back through my pictures to see if she had them and she didn't. She also didn't look like...*that*.

I need to stop myself from openly gawking at her, but I can't. She looks different than she did a few years ago. The white top she's wearing outlines her breasts, which are bigger now, and the pastel orange leggings cling to her thick thighs like a second skin.

"Damn, Teddy, close your mouth."

I don't know when it happened, but my lips are in fact slightly parted. I clear my throat and look away, not saying anything to Jagger as he smirks. I know he's waiting for me to say something, but I don't.

Especially now that I meet Landon's eyes. It's minuscule—anyone who doesn't know him wouldn't notice it, but I do. I see the interest pique in his gray eyes and the slight twitch on his cheek.

Of course the one time it's about me, he cares.

"That's Louise?" Landon asks, his gaze drifting in her direction. "*The* one TJ was choking over?"

I roll my eyes at the reminder. It's something the guys can't seem to let go of. It's been two days since it happened, and since then they've been giving me shit about it. They'll even mimic me, pretending they're choking on their water like fucking assholes.

"*The* very one," Jayden cheekily replies.

"Hmmm..." he hums thoughtfully as his eyes sweep over her body. "Okay."

There's another faint twitch on his cheek, but he doesn't say anything else as he looks away from her. I want to ask what that was about, but I don't want to give him the benefit of knowing he's getting under my skin.

The guys on the team think I don't know, but everyone is in on a bet to see who can get under my skin first. I don't know who started it, but I know it's there. Little do they know that I'm a master at this shit. I have no other choice, being a D1 college athlete who's projected to be the number one pick in the draft this coming year. And possibly being ranked the number one team in the country for the second time in a row is already enough pressure as it is.

I'm constantly under a microscope, being compared to my dad and brother when they played college ball, players before me who were the number one draft picks the previous years, and players now. If it isn't the sports analysts, it's the people on social media. They never fail to state their unsolicited opinions and advice.

I know everyone deals with it, but my gosh, it's draining.

If anyone sees anything that resembles a crack in my life, they'll tear me apart. They did my freshman year after my injury. I don't need that again.

"I'm going to tell her to join us."

"No," I immediately say but regret it as they look at me with questioning stares. "I mean why? She's probably busy."

"No, she's waiting for her friend," Saint supplies.

"How do you know that?"

"I texted her." He holds his phone up as if that's enough explanation.

"You text her?" Jayden steals the words right out of my mouth.

"Yeah," he replies as if it's an everyday occurrence. "Anyway, she's just waiting for her friend."

He places his phone in the middle of the table, letting us all stare at the selfie she sent him. She's staring at the ceiling, almost as if she's rolling her eyes and her nose is scrunched. The text says, *Waiting for my friend at Cameron Hall. I'm starving. What do you recommend?*

She sent him a picture?

"Are you fucking kidding me?" Jagger plucks the phone and raises it to his face. "Why the fuck did she reply to you but not to me?"

He texts her too?

"Because she knows I'm not trying to fuck her," he retorts, snatching his phone back.

Jagger scoffs dramatically. "I'm not trying to fuck her. I'm just trying to get to *know* her."

"Jag, that's the equivalence of you trying to fuck someone," Jayden says through a mouthful.

His jaw drops and his brows pinch together, feigning offense.

"I—"

"Stop bullshitting, mate," Landon says simply. "You want to fuck her."

"Can you all shut the fuck up?" I snap, clenching my jaw. "Jagger, there are tons of hot girls around campus. Stop obsessing over *some* girl."

"But she's not just *some* girl." Landon cocks his head, the corner of his lip rising just a tad, gray eyes glinting with mischief. "Is she, TJ?"

"Don't look at me like that. You look creepy as fuck." I ignore the patronizing way he's staring at me and stab my grilled chicken with my fork.

"Don't deflect," he counters.

I hold back the urge to roll my eyes at his idiotic comment. Landon thinks he's so damn smart with his analytical bullshit, but he's far from it.

"She said she's coming, and she's bringing her friend."

I stare at them indifferently. "Okay."

I don't mean to, but I find myself searching for her through the sea of students, but she's nowhere to be found. I discreetly let my eyes coast from one direction to the other, but still, there's no sign of wavy golden copper hair.

"Smile." Saint pulls my gaze back to him. He holds his phone in front of my face, his brow arched as if he knows what I'm doing, but he doesn't call me out on it. "You too, Landon. You looked murderous in my last video."

Saint is famous on social media. He's always on his phone, either making videos on a day in his life or going live and cooking while he talks about his day and responds to questions.

Since Saint moved in, he's been trying to get Landon to smile. I told him he'd only be wasting his time. I vaguely saw him do it once and that was when we won the NCAA championship in April, but even then, I'm not sure I saw it right.

But Saint doesn't give up. He loves a challenge.

Landon shoves his phone away. "Piss off."

"Aren't you a ray of sunshine? Matter of fact, I like that, *Sunshine*. It's fitting, don't you think? Instead of The Grim, they should call you Sunshine." He beams and records the food he ordered.

"You know it'd be a pity if you *didn't* wake up tomorrow."

I'm not sure what was more unsettling—the fact that Landon meant every word or the Cheshire grin on Saint's face.

"You know I—" He pauses mid-sentence. I follow his line of sight to see he's staring at Lola's friend.

When my gaze draws back to Lola, our eyes lock and I swear there's a moment of...of I'm not sure exactly what that *moment* is, but I look away. I consider that maybe it's because she's attractive as hell, and with a body like that...maybe we should finish off what we started. Not dating, but physically getting to know one another.

Saint rests his arms on the table, interlocking his fingers, eyes shining with interest. "Hey, Lola and *friend*."

"Hey, guys." Lola smiles, eyes bouncing to each and every one of us. "This is Daisy, my best friend."

"Daisy," Saint repeats as if he's testing out the name on his lips. "Nice to meet you."

"Nice to meet you *all*." She briefly smiles, but it doesn't reach her eyes. She doesn't even look a bit interested in Saint. If anything, she looks annoyed, but her expression changes when her eyes meet mine.

She stares at me, perplexed. It's nothing like the kind of reaction I typically get from fans or random girls. No, it's almost as if she's shocked, but it hardly lasts for a second before her expression becomes blank.

Spears smirks, amusement shining in his eyes. "And this is *my* best friend, Landon."

Lola tucks a tattered planner and what looks like a sketchbook under her arm, and she waves at him. "That's right, we hadn't met yet. You're the other roommate. Nice to meet you." She greets him with the sweetest smile, but me? I get nothing.

"Yeah...it's nice to meet you." Landon's brows pinch together ever so slightly. His eyes shift and narrow on the tattoo wrapped around my forearm.

I quickly hide it behind my other arm but realize now that I gave myself away. Surely, he couldn't have figured it out.

"We're not going to stay long. I just need to talk to TJ in private."

My ears instantly perk up and I almost choke on fucking air. It's pathetic, but there's a sense of gratification I feel that it's me she wants to speak to.

"If that's all right with you?"

She fucking smiles at me. A genuine, warm smile that feels unreal.

"Yeah." Ignoring all the glances directed at me, I get up and stand next to Lola.

"I promise I won't be long," she says to Daisy.

"Take your time." Saint pats the now empty spot next to him. "We'll keep *Daisy* company."

Daisy mumbles something under her breath, shaking her head at the obvious interest in his voice. Despite that, she takes my seat and sets her food on the table. "Don't worry, Lo."

I tip my head in the direction of the double doors that lead outside and gesture for her to follow me.

"So..." I don't know why I'm contemplating what I want to say. The words are right there, but when I take a peek at her, my thoughts fade away. The green streak of paint on her elbow distracts me. "You have paint on your elbow. Some things don't change, huh?"

The memory of paint on her resurfaces in my head as if it were just yesterday.

"Just pretend you don't see it. Don't be surprised when you see me again and there's paint somewhere else on my body."

I know she didn't mean it that way, but I still can't stop my mind from spiraling.

"That's not what I meant." Her response is quick and a faint tinge of red coats her cheeks.

I chuckle and hold the door for her to walk out first. "So does this mean I'll be seeing you more?"

We step out and walk around the side of the building, toward an alcove.

"Yeah... I hope so."

My thoughts go in different directions, but they all lead back to the same place. My bedroom, naked, and so many different positions.

"Sorry that I walked out on Sunday. I—you still have the bracelet?" She stares astounded at the brown leather around my wrist.

I was going to take it off, but I could never bring myself to do it. Unless it's practice or games, I always keep it on, and when I don't have it on, it's weird. It's extremely worn out, and the name Peaches is faded, but I like it too much to take it off.

"How could I not?" I twist my wrist to show it off. "It was a birthday gift from my *ex-girlfriend*."

Her brows shoot up in disbelief. It was all pretend to her, but it was real to me. She was my first and only girlfriend.

We stand in front of each other inside the alcove, so close, I catch the scent of vanilla.

"Oh," she muses, dragging her teeth along her bottom lip. The action pulls my mind to the memory of her tugging my bottom lip in between her lips. She was gentle, soft, and *unforgettable*.

I blink out of the haze and clear my throat.

"So what's so important that you wanted to talk about in private, *Peaches*?"

Her cheek twitches and I know she's desperately trying not to smile, but she fails as it creeps up on her lips. "Again with the nickname? I have a name."

"I know, but Peaches is very fitting." I shamelessly let my eyes wander down her body, taking my time to slowly soak in how her waist curves in and then out to her hips. "We met over peach juice."

I can tell a debate plays in her head, no doubt wanting to argue with my statement. She knows it's not the complete truth, but she lets it go with a resigned sigh.

After a second of silence, she releases a shaky breath. "The reason I wanted to talk to you in private is because—"

"TJ!"

Lola and I both turn in the direction of the voice. Alexia stands a few feet away from us, holding her phone up and her other hand up as if she were saying *where's your phone?* That reminds me that we had planned to meet up for a quick fuck.

I hold my finger out, telling her to give me a second. Her eyes drop to Lola and her brows pull together as if she hadn't realized that she was standing next to me.

"I don't have all day," Alexia says.

I curtly nod at her and look back down at Lola. "Sorry about that. We had agreed to...study."

"Right. Either way, this isn't the best place to tell you."

My brows furrow. "Tell me what?"

"Are you busy this Friday?"

"No, I'll be home, but what do you want to tell me?"

"I'm going over again to work on another project. We can just talk there."

I've never excelled at patience or being careful at thinking before speaking. It's a bad trait, but I'm working on it.

"You can tell me now. I can study with Alexia later."

"It's all right. I promise I'll tell you Friday. You should probably go study."

I'm about to tell her that I'd rather hear what she has to say, but she's already made up her mind as she walks away.

Alexia decides she doesn't want to wait and approaches me. "Are you ready?"

I can't explain what I feel as I watch Lola walk away, but I shove it away and look at Alexia.

"Let me grab my stuff."

10

TJ

I FEEL LIKE A GRADE A STALKER.

I should be working on my class discussion, editing my pictures I need to submit tomorrow, or eating my lunch that I'm one hundred percent sure is cold. I should be doing anything but thinking of Lola and stalking her Instagram account.

It's not even her personal, but her business one because the other one is private. I hadn't meant to find this one, but it appeared on my feed a while ago. Now I'm pathetically scrolling through it, looking at her posts, especially the ones she's in. Which aren't many.

Not that I mind; her paintings are incredible. I've met some extremely talented people, but Lola, her level of talent is something else. I shouldn't be shocked considering she gave me a canvas with the sunset painted on it.

Currently, it's hanging on my bedroom wall here in North Carolina. I'm sure if I had left it back home, my sister, Hazel, would've taken it to her room.

The next post I click on is of a kid with curly brown hair, honey eyes, and the cutest fucking smile. Reading the caption, my eyes do a double take on the kid because she captioned it *My Muse. My Little Bear. My Phoenix.* My mind spirals to weird thoughts, but I quickly bury them away because the kid looks nothing like her.

Instead of looking any further, I exit out of Instagram. Not only because I feel like a stalker, but I'm also pathetically waiting to get the confirmation that Lola accepted my request.

There's no reason to follow her, but my curiosity got the best of me. I can't help but wonder what she's been up to for the past two years.

All I know is that she transferred from a community college, has her live painting business, and is obsessed with iced coffee and blueberry muffins. That's as much as Saint told me because *apparently*, he and Lola are best friends now.

"What are you doing here?" Jayden's voice interrupts my train of thought.

"Waiting for Saint."

I don't realize Landon is standing next to him until I lift my head and meet his stare. His eyes feel like a black hole sucking the life out of everything.

He arches a brow, his gaze drifting down the hall and then back to me. "Just *some* girl?"

"Stop overanalyzing everything."

"Why are you waiting for Saint if you drove to campus?" Jayden asks, folding his arms across his chest.

"Don't you both have somewhere to be?" I grab my stuff and shove it all in my bag, knowing any second they're all about to step out of the classroom.

"We should be asking you the same thing." The idiotic grin on Jayden's face widens. "Correct me if I'm wrong, Landon, but when was the last time TJ was on campus if it didn't involve basketball or fucking a girl?"

"What does it fucking matter if—" My gaze jumps to the wave of students pooling out of the room. Though it's none of them I focus on, but Lola as she steps out with the guys and Polly right next to her. Feeling Landon's and Jayden's eyes burning into me, I look at them again. "What I do or don't do shouldn't concern you."

"Right," Amusement drips from Jayden's voice. "Are you going to eat that?"

I roll my eyes, giving him my leftovers before grabbing the last of my stuff, making sure I'm careful with the bag that has my camera inside. From my peripheral, I see people glancing curiously at me as well as Lola, who is laughing at something Jag says. Not only do I notice that, but his arm is also slung around her shoulder.

Jagger must have sensed that I'm looking because when our eyes connect, a shit-eating smirk stretches across his face. He leans down and whispers something in her ear that makes her look up at him. She smiles but shakes her head, to which he laughs and drops his arm.

I know what he's doing, and I'm not buying it. I know he's trying to fuck with me, but little does he know that I don't care.

"Hey," Polly says, hardly paying attention to us as she looks down at her phone.

"Hey, guys." A small, sheepish smile lifts Lola's lips when her eyes land on mine.

That smile, those lips, her goddamn eyes. They shouldn't be running through my head. They shouldn't be what I've been thinking about lately. Especially thinking of her long, wavy hair wrapped around my fist.

I snap out of my impulsive thoughts, hating myself for thinking that again and for how easily I gave myself away in front of the guys. The only two oblivious to my thoughts are Polly and the girl who's been looming in the back of my head since Sunday.

"Hey," we all say, although by the look on the guys' faces, I can tell they're dying to say something stupid, except for Landon. I can't ever tell when he wants to say something or what he's thinking.

Lola looks down at her phone, her eyes growing wide. "I gotta go, but I'll see you all tomorrow at five?"

"Sounds good." Saint cheekily smiles. "Are you still getting coffee?" He looks at me, although his question is directed at her.

"Yeah, I won't make the drive back if I don't have caffeine." She covers her yawn with the back of her hand, and that's when I notice a red phoenix tattooed on her wrist.

"TJ's also getting coffee. He *owes* me."

"Oh." She looks as shocked as I do.

There's no warning with Saint. He's the *let's do it and ask questions later*, but mostly he's the *let's do it and never ask questions* kind of person.

"I'm going to the Union Center. My car is parked on that side of campus."

"That's all right. I parked nearby." That's a lie. My G-Wagon is parked on the opposite side of campus, but whatever, it's not a big deal.

"Okay, well, I'll see you guys tomorrow." She smiles and waves them goodbye.

"Bye, Lola," they all say in unison and stare at me as she turns around.

Jayden and Saint don't fail to be childish as fuck and make low whipping noises.

As I turn on my heel, I raise my middle finger at them and fall into step next to Lola. The last thing I hear before we walk out of the building are those two idiots I call Thing One and Thing Two making whipping noises. I don't know what it is, but when they're together, they tend to do stupid shit.

Crowd surfing. Dancing on coffee tables, chairs, and roofs. If it has a flat surface, they'll be there dancing. Betting who can make out with the most girls or who can get the most phone numbers. The insane dares. Hosting a back-to-school waterslide and beer pong competition for girls only. The list goes on, but when they're together, the inevitable is bound to happen.

We walk in silence down the brick lane, and the realization hits me that for the first time, I have no idea what I want to say to a girl. I could ask her a variety of things. Questions linger at the tip of my tongue, but I can't bring myself to ask her anything.

Glancing down at her, I notice how the sun casts a golden hue around her, the warm sunrays falling on her face making her eyes more vibrant and her lips a slightly darker shade of red.

"Do I have paint on me again?"

The question drags me out of an odd fog, and I'm thankful for it because I found myself getting a little too comfortable in it.

"Paint?"

"You're looking at me." She lifts one arm and then the other, searching for any signs of said paint. "Don't tell me it's on my face?"

Her question throws me off until I realize that I'm stupidly staring at her.

I look straight ahead. "No, I was looking at the tattoo on your wrist. You didn't have it two years ago, right?"

Lola hesitates but shakes her head. "No, I didn't. It was all on a whim." She chuckles softly as if remembering the moment she got it. "One minute, I'm drinking with Daisy and Cara. The next, we're getting tattoos and piercings. Word of advice, never drink with Daisy because she'll convince you to do things you never thought you'd do."

I laugh. "Sounds like Saint."

She nods in agreement. I contemplate asking her what it is that he convinced her to do because they hardly know each other. I quickly decide against it because what do I care.

She lifts her arm and twists her wrist, showing me the red ink.

"I really like it," I say.

Without thinking it through, I wrap my hand around her wrist. Everything happens in slow motion. My brain tells me to stop, to retract my touch, but my hand isn't getting the memo.

Now it seems like everything is short-circuiting because the moment I feel her smooth skin beneath my palm, I'm taken back to two years ago.

Touching her is nostalgic. I find myself wanting to grasp onto a moment from the past and not let go. But I don't let myself dwell on the past and shove the memories away, focusing on the now, the present.

"Why a phoenix?" I ask, ignoring the way my hand heats up against her skin and how I can feel her erratic pulse before I let go of her wrist.

"The meaning. It symbolizes the renewal of life." Her voice is low, almost a whisper. "Overcoming the odds in life."

I swear I see a flicker of sadness cross her eyes.

"Damn, mine are nowhere near as significant as a phoenix." I look down at my right arm and tuck my hand in my pocket. Most of them are random things that I like, but there's one in particular that's my favorite.

"That's the *only* significant one I have."

I arch a brow. "You have more?"

I scan every inch of her, but she's wearing sage green cargo pants and a beige top. She looks so damn good, and I'm getting off track.

"Yeah." Her cheeks coat in a soft shade of pink as she tucks a strand of hair behind her ear. "In other places."

My brows rise. "Other places?"

"Yeah...other places."

I stare unblinking, trying to figure out where the rest of her tattoos could possibly be. That's a mistake because the harder I think about it, the more inappropriate my thoughts become.

I should stop and consider what I'm about to say, but I really can't help myself. "What other places? You can't just tell me you have other tattoos and not tell me where."

She playfully smiles. "It's five tiny ones, but they're nowhere crazy."

Her tone is casual, but that smile and those eyes tell me otherwise. Something tells me I should find out where they're located, preferably in a place where it's just her and me and absolutely no clothes on.

"You're really going to leave me in suspense?"

She laughs and I can't help but get absorbed in it. It's great to know it isn't directed at one of my friends for once.

"They're just tattoos. The location isn't important."

There's this desperate voice in the back of my head begging me to ask her, but I refrain from doing so because I don't want to look desperate. There is one thing I refuse to do and that is to beg.

"All right." I shrug, not pushing the subject any further. "So Saint tells me you transferred. What made you come to NCU?"

What I really want to ask is what Jagger whispered in her ear, but I decide against it.

"NCU has always been my dream school. They have an amazing art program and I like the atmosphere. I'd already gotten my acceptance letter and had planned to come here my freshman year"—she pauses for a brief moment before she continues—"but stuff happened and I had to go to community college. What about you? What made you come to NCU?"

I laugh. I've been interviewed countless times, but that's a question I never get asked. Even people who are *trying* to get to know me never ask that.

"You're serious?"

Her brows knit together. "Why wouldn't I be?"

Everyone knows that my dad, my brother Ben, and my sister-in-law Mariah played basketball here. My dad was also in the NBA and Mariah is currently in the WNBA. Though Lola isn't everyone because she stares at me like she has no idea about that piece of information. Or maybe she does, but she doesn't care. I can't tell.

"A lot of people assume it's because of my family, but the truth is I'd met countless coaches and no one made an impact on me like Coach Warren has. There are many great things about him, especially his passion for the game and how he treats us players like people and not trophies. Playing for him makes me fall for the game all over again."

She nods like she understands exactly what I mean. "That's

how I feel about the art professors here. They make me fall in love with art all over again."

I smile as I hold the door open for her, letting her walk in front of me. We head to the café and place our orders.

I learn that Lola likes to try new coffee. I like to stick with my regular only because I'd hate to pay for something that might not be good, but she persuaded me.

Now we're both walking to her car holding Irish cream cold brews with oat milk because she said she'd never tried it before. Who was I to refuse? Especially when she looked so damn excited. Luckily for both of us, we end up liking it.

"You didn't have to walk me to the garage," she says for the tenth time as if that's going to make me change my mind. Not that I think the parking garage isn't safe, but it's six in the evening and she's a girl walking alone. "And please let me pay you back."

"You really think I'd let you walk alone? And I don't want your money, so stop."

"Okay. Next time it will be on me."

That's not going to happen. "Okay."

"Well, this is me." We stand in front of her car, the only one in the parking garage. "Thanks for walking with me. It does get creepy walking alone at this time."

"If you want, I can walk with you the other days." There are days I won't be able to because of games or practice, but I'm sure I could make it work.

"No, it's fine. It's not a big deal. I have a taser and pepper spray." She dangles the keys in her hands. "I'll be all right."

"Don't be stubborn. I really don't mind."

She reluctantly agrees. "Okay, but seriously, don't feel obligated. I promise I'll be fine."

"This isn't an obligation. I want to do this." The thought of her walking alone doesn't sit right with me.

"Well, I should get going. Traffic is going to be brutal." She opens her front door and gets inside. "Thanks for this."

"Yeah, anytime. Are you still going to tell me this big secret that has to wait until tomorrow?"

"Yup, as promised. I'll tell you tomorrow."

"Until tomorrow, Lola."

"Until tomorrow, TJ."

She drives off and I don't realize until her car is completely gone that I'm standing in the middle of an empty garage with the most idiotic smile on my face.

11

LOLA

"'He's insane. Truly and utterly talented. He has it all. He's graceful on the court. He moves fast. He can block any shot. He's got everything that any team would want.'" Daisy dramatically reads from her laptop. "And that was just what Cane Williams said. There's more just like this raving about TJ like he's the second coming to the NBA," she says, less than impressed about what NBA players have to say about TJ.

"Can you blame them? He's that good," Cara says, not looking up from the book laid on the kitchen table in front of her. "Did you see what Karson Riley called him? *The Invincible.*"

They call him that because during his first game in his freshman year, he got injured. He didn't break anything, but it took longer to heal than anticipated. Everyone thought he was done for, but he proved them wrong his sophomore year and now they call him *The Invincible.* Since then, he's all anyone in the basketball world talks about.

So I might've searched him up on Google and ended up spending a few hours reading everything about him. I didn't mean to, but one article led to a tweet, which led to a post on Instagram, which led back to another article on Sports Illustrated and so on.

His stats weren't the only thing I stumbled upon. Julianna wasn't kidding when she said he's adored and the girls go feral for him. Not only did I find fan accounts dedicated to him, but there are videos of girls asking TJ for a *chance*. That's just me putting it lightly because they definitely want more than just a *date* with him.

I can't forget the pretty girl he had to *study* with on Tuesday. I'm not an idiot. I know what that meant.

"Okay, can we stop talking about TJ?" I hate how just saying his name causes my heart to beat a little faster and my palms to get clammy.

I shouldn't be nervous, but I can't stop myself from overthinking about how wrong this could go.

"Ma." Phoenix pats my forearm, letting me know it's time for another maple puff.

He holds a star-shaped puff in his palm. Plucking the little star from his hand, I toss it in the air and catch it in my mouth. He claps and smiles giddily.

I watch as he grabs two, but I raise a brow and shake my head. He knows what he's doing because he giggles and only puts one in his mouth. He may only be a year and a half old, but he's smart enough to know better. Despite the puff easily dissolving, I just worry he might choke.

I peck his forehead. "Thank you."

"Mhm." He smiles and resumes painting.

To get my mind off TJ, I grabbed my art supplies, a white sheet, and some canvases for Phoenix and me to paint on. If there's one thing that can relieve my stress, it's my son and painting.

"Sorry." Daisy closes her laptop, gets up from the couch, and sits on top of the sheet next to Phoenix. "I looked him up once, and ever since then, it's all that pops up. TJ or basketball."

My brow quirks and my lip curls upward. "Is that just it?"

She scoffs, letting herself dramatically fall on her back. "*Cállate*."

"You're so dramatic. He's good-looking. I don't see what the problem is," Cara states exactly what I'm thinking, or pretty much what any person who sees Saint thinks.

"He's two years younger than me." She holds two fingers up in the air for Cara and me to see. "Two."

"*Dos*." Phoenix also holds two chunky fingers covered in paint, giddy that he not only can say the number but can hold his fingers up like she is.

Daisy lies on her side, propping herself on her elbow and laying her head on her shoulder. She smiles at him proudly and ruffles his curls. "*Muy bien, bebé*."

Daisy and her family are adamant that Phoenix learns Spanish and I'm all for it. I know a little bit of Spanish, but I'm definitely not fluent.

"So you agree that he's hot?" Cara rounds the couch and sits on the sheet next to me.

"That's not the point. He's two years younger than me, and I'm sure he wouldn't..." Her eyes flick to Phoenix and then back to us. "*Know* what he's doing."

"That's never stopped you before. You've been with people with *no* experience before."

"Yes, but never with anyone younger than me." She grabs one of the maple puffs, tosses it in the air, and catches it in her mouth. "It's already hard enough finding mature guys our age who know what they're doing. I can't imagine someone like him knowing anything, and his looks won't change my mind."

A taunting grin curves Cara's lips. "So you admit he's hot."

"You're insufferable." She lets out an exasperated scoff. "Anyway, back to you."

I intently focus on my canvas and try my best to ignore their burning stares.

"It's all going to be okay." Cara's soft voice should reassure me, but it does the opposite of that. All I can think about is how everything is *not* going to be okay. "I know it's hard for you to see it that way, but if you say that he's still the same guy from two years ago, then I know it'll be okay."

I inhale a deep breath, letting my mind wander to yesterday. Despite the odd tension, our conversation and interaction felt completely normal. It felt as if we were back to two years ago minus the fake dating.

"And just keep in mind it's been two years since you both saw each other. It's going to be shocking for him, and if he doesn't believe you, he can take a test," Daisy adds. "And you know we'll be around if he wants to see Phoenix."

The girls are going to drop me off at his house but stay near in case he wants to meet Phoenix.

I smile at my son as he glances down at his bear sitting next to him and then at his painting. I think his bear is his muse because the canvas is only covered in light brown strokes of paint.

Despite the nerves lingering, I know telling TJ is the best thing to do. He has the right to know he has a son, and Phoenix has the right to know who his dad is.

"And that's how we would incorporate Maslow's Hierarchy of Needs in our lives," Polly says, ending the presentation.

We would've finished recording a while ago, but it took longer than expected. Saint was late, Jagger accidentally deleted his part of the assignment, and when we first started filming, we didn't realize until halfway through that we never pressed play.

"You should probably put some ice on that," I say to Saint as Polly grabs the camera and turns it off.

Saint not only came in late, but he came in with a gash on the corner of his lip. It's a little swollen, but it doesn't look too bad.

"I'm fine." He waves his hand dismissively and, to prove he's all right, he licks the corner where the cut is. "Nothing a little saliva won't fix."

I roll my eyes at his double meaning.

"I'm still trying to figure out how the fuck you did that to yourself?" Jagger questions, brows furrowed.

"I told you I was trying to fix the fitted sheet on my bed. I didn't hold the corner right, and I accidentally punched myself in the lip," he replies, twirling a small dagger in his hand.

"You're a fucking idiot. Of course you would do something like that. Only you, Freshman."

"I told you to stop calling me Freshman. The girls don't take me seriously when you call me that shit." Saint directs his attention to me, flashing me a lopsided grin. "Speaking of which, have you talked to Daisy?"

"She's not interested. You're too young."

He scoffs, taken aback. "Too young? I'm only two years younger than her. I seriously don't understand what the issue is. You know people tell me I'm very mature for my age all the time."

"She's too hot for you," Polly answers while she puts all her stuff into her bag.

"I agree with Polly." Jagger smiles, amused. "Maybe I should—"

"She's not interested, so don't even think about it." I laugh at the shock on both of their faces.

"I know she'll come around," Saint states, so sure of himself.

"Right, keep dreaming. Anyway, Little Red, you want to come out tonight after you and TJ..." Jagger trails off.

"It's not like that," I quickly say, but I can tell by the look he's giving me that he doesn't believe me. It's the kind of look that says, *I've heard that one before*.

I don't bother explaining myself to him because I don't owe him anything, and I wouldn't even know how to tell him.

Polly throws her bag over her shoulder and punches Jagger in the arm. "Leave her alone, Jag, but if you change your mind, we'll be at The Tap House. They have good drinks, food, and karaoke. Gabby and Jagger's favorites."

"I'd love to, but I have to finish a painting tonight."

I typically do live weddings, but I occasionally do regular paintings on the side.

A man reached out to me and asked if I could paint a picture of him and his fiancée on their first date. I'm pretty much done with the painting, but there are still a few things I need to add before I drop it off tomorrow. I also have no one to babysit Phoenix, so I wouldn't be able to go even if I wanted to.

"You're still going to do my painting, right?" Saint asks.

I'm not entirely sure how it happened, but since the first day of class, Saint and I instantly bonded. Not only have we become really great friends, but we have similar interests. Like our love for blueberry muffins, having no siblings, and art.

When I told him about my business, he didn't hesitate to ask for a painting. He hasn't seen my work, but he says he trusts me.

I figured once I told him the price, he'd back out. Surprisingly, he didn't, and not only did he not back out, but he paid me on the spot and tipped me more than necessary. I didn't want to take his money, considering I hadn't even started on his painting, but he was persistent.

Either he's never heard no in his life, or he refuses to take it for an answer.

Still, to this day, he hasn't seen my work or at least that's what he says. He says he wants to be surprised. He also said that he can easily distinguish between an honest person and a fake person. Something about telltale signs, which I have yet to figure out what that means.

"I am, I promise. I have three more to get to and then I'll do yours."

"Good." He smiles like he always does and pulls me in for a hug.

"You better let her go before T—never mind." Jagger chuckles as TJ steps into the kitchen with two cups of coffee in his hands. "Speaking of the devil."

I try to tell my heart to calm down, but it doesn't. I don't know how to make it stop or how to tell it to slow down, but when our eyes meet, my palms get clammy.

He holds my stare for a few seconds before his eyes flicker to Saint's arm around me. His gaze doesn't linger long before it shifts to Jagger.

"Yeah, he's right behind me." TJ throws his thumb over his shoulder, pointing to where Landon is behind him.

He steps into the kitchen with the most deadpan expression I've ever seen on anyone. There's nothing bright or warm about him, just an empty gaze that somehow manages to scream 'fuck off.'

"I have better things to do." He disregards TJ's words and looks at his friends. "Are we leaving or not?"

"Hi, hello to you too. I swear, Landon, we've been best friends for seven years and you still can't say hello?" Polly says, unbothered by his clipped tone.

I guess I wouldn't be bothered either if my best friend had a deep but smooth English accent.

"Hello, Polly," he replies in a flat tone. "Are we leaving or not?"

"Can we stop to get food? I'm starving!" Jayden shouts from the living room. If he hadn't said anything, I would've never known he was here.

"Me too." Saint pats his stomach as he lets go of me. "Bye, Lola."

"Bye." I smile at him and everyone else as they all walk out of the kitchen until it's just TJ and me.

Once the front door shuts, he inches forward but leaves a small gap of space between us. He hands me one of the cups.

I quickly mask the shock at the gesture and attempt to tame the smile on my face as I take the cup. I inhale, getting the sweetest, earthiest aroma.

"I thought we could try something new today. I typically like to stick to my usual coffee order, but you've encouraged me to step out of my comfort zone." He tentatively smiles as he looks at the label on his cup. "I have no idea what the hell matcha is, and I hope you like coconut milk because this is what the barista suggested. So if you don't like it, we can blame her."

I chuckle. "You didn't have to do this. In fact, it was my turn to get us coffee."

"Next time..." he trails off as he blows into the tiny hole of the lid. "Be careful, it's *hot*."

If I wasn't here to tell him we have a kid, I might have found the courage to be bold and play along. That isn't the case, though. I can't flirt with him knowing everything is going to change for better or worse.

I don't expect TJ to be jumping with joy after he finds out. I do expect confusion and maybe denial, but I hope he's willing to let me explain what happened after I found out I was pregnant. I also hope he'll want to meet Phoenix today, but if not, I'm also good with baby steps. Something is better than nothing.

I bring the cup to my lips just as he does and slowly, we take a sip at the same time. We both stare at each other in shock and in silence as we take another sip.

"This is—"

"Fucking delicious." TJ finishes off for me. "Wow, that barista deserves a raise."

I nod in agreement, taking a longer sip and sighing in contentment as maple, coconut, and something nutty blend together in my mouth.

"So what is it that you wanted to talk about? You know, you've exceeded in keeping me in suspense."

I laugh awkwardly, looking around him, hoping that his friends are really gone.

He peers over his shoulder and then back at me. "You want to talk in my room? Or we can stay here. It should be a little while until they're back. Although Landon might show up. He's not very...social."

"Do you mind if we go to your room?"

"Not at all. Come on."

12

LOLA

"I can't believe you kept it." I stare in disbelief at the sunset I painted two years ago. The canvas hangs on TJ's bedroom wall. It's strategically placed in the middle and all around it are picture frames filled with people he's close with and other random stuff.

I'm not only shocked that he kept it, but that it's here and not in Florida. It's been two years, but it looks like new, as if it was meticulously taken care of.

"Why wouldn't I keep this?" he asks. "This is a masterpiece."

"It's definitely not a—"

"Don't do that. Don't sell yourself short," he interrupts me. "This is really good. It looks almost realistic."

It's true what they say, we're our own worst critics. While TJ sees a masterpiece, I see a painting that still needs a lot of work. I shouldn't be overanalyzing something I did in a span of a few hours, but I can't help my probing thoughts.

"Trust me, I'm not saying it's good for the hell of it. I've never been one to tell people what they want to hear."

It's like he dove deep into my thoughts and knew exactly what I was thinking.

When I look up at him, he's already staring down at me. A

small smile on his lips and rich whiskey eyes, so inviting, I almost forget what was said.

"You can't do that to yourself, Peaches," he chastises.

I hold back the urge to roll my eyes at the nickname because I've realized now that even after two years, it's not something he's going to let go of.

"Do what?"

"Downplay yourself. Be confident in what you do all the time. Even if it doesn't always come out the way you want it to the first time. You don't always have to be humble." The small smile grows into something cockier.

"Let me guess." I pause, arching a brow. "Like you?"

From his interviews and the things I read about him online, I found out that TJ isn't so humble. There are a lot of things being said about him, but the one thing they say the most is that he's extremely cocky. Although many people feel this way about him, they all agree that he's one hell of a player.

"Exactly." He nods, grinning proudly. "Sometimes you just have to say fuck being humble."

"But you know sometimes showing a bit of humility is good."

"Yeah, but it won't always get you very far." He shrugs with indifference, although by the wavering look in his eyes, I can tell he's talking from experience. "Some people don't care about humility, and some only pretend to care to put on a show. I'm not saying being humble is a bad thing, but there are times you should be and other times you shouldn't. Being humble doesn't always put you on top."

I consider his words and think back to my own experiences. I realize he may have a point.

He doesn't say anything, but I'm pretty sure he knows I've come to understand that he's right. I don't know why, but I expect a big I told you so or something equally arrogant, but instead, he surprises me.

The smile on his face softens and he looks ahead, staring at my painting as if it's the most fascinating thing he's ever seen.

A comforting silence falls over us as I get immersed in the pictures hanging on his wall. They don't look like your average pictures. They must have been taken professionally or edited because they look like something you see in a magazine.

"Did you take these?" I ask, taking a sip of my drink.

"Yeah," he replies, sounding almost shocked that I asked that. "I did."

"These are good."

"Thanks. I worked hard on them," pride laces his voice.

We continue looking in silence, but my sight gets stuck on one picture as I feel the warmth of his hand close to my arm. I try my best to focus on what's in front of me, but my body is acutely aware of his hand. I'm pretty sure if I stretched my pinky out, I would be able to touch him.

My fingers twitch at my side, almost like they're tempting me, but I decide against whatever signals my brain is sending them. I return my focus to the picture I've been staring at for the past few seconds, but it's futile when I feel the faintest graze of his knuckle against my arm.

I don't move. I stand still, holding my breath as I feel it again. The grip on my cup tightens. I should be careful considering how hot the cup is even with the sleeve around it. But the warmth emanating from it is nothing compared to the heat coming from his knuckles.

Soft, gentle, and slow is the best way to put it. It's a hardly there touch, almost ghost-like, but my body reacts to it more than it should and I wonder...does he feel it too?

For a second, I find myself wanting to lean into his touch, but the odd warmth encasing us dissolves when his phone vibrates.

We both step away from each other as if we got caught doing something we shouldn't have been doing.

He clears his throat, giving me an apologetic look as he holds up his phone for me to look at. **MOM** with a heart emoji pops up on his screen. "I have to answer this."

I point my finger over my shoulder, letting him know I'll step out to give him privacy, but he shakes his head. “Stay,” he mouths before he answers.

“Hey, Mom...”

Not that I mean to eavesdrop, but since I’m standing right here, I can’t help but smile and hold back a laugh at the conversation between the two. I’m not entirely sure what exactly she said, but when he swears he didn’t mean to use his brother’s fake ID, the laughter I was trying to hold escapes me.

“It was one time.” TJ defends. “I didn’t think they would recognize me.”

Their conversation continues with something else and his voice softens. I can’t help the twinge in my chest. Knowing I’ll never have that with my own parents.

Now I wonder...how will his parents react when they find out they have a grandson?

“Louise.”

I gasp, startled at his hand on my shoulder. “Sorry, what?”

“I called your name like six times.” His hand lingers on my shoulder before he drops it. When I give him a pointed stare, he raises his hand in surrender. “Okay, so maybe not your actual name, but I still called you.”

“You’re never going to let that name go, are you?”

“Fuck no. I really like *Peaches*,” he quips, eyes not so subtly coasting down my body before he quickly raises them back up. “It’s a really great fruit. Sweet...juicy...round.”

“Yeah, they’re great, Theodore, or should I say Teddy?” I tease him. Jagger and Saint might have told me how much he hates when people call him by his actual name or the nickname his mom gave him.

“Fucking assholes,” he mumbles before he takes a sip of his drink. “Please don’t call me Teddy.”

“Then don’t call me Peaches.”

“I guess it’s only fair. Only *you* can call me Teddy.”

“You’re frustrating, you know that?” I attempt to keep a serious expression but fail when he chuckles. “What?”

"This just feels like...déjà vu." His brows furrow, lips flattening into a straight line. He stares off into the distance like he's trying to recall a memory.

"What?"

"Nothing." He smiles, shaking his head. "So what is it that you wanted to talk about in person?"

I had done a pretty good job of keeping my nerves at bay, but now they've come back and all of a sudden, my palms are drenched in sweat. *I shouldn't be nervous*, is what I keep telling myself as he looks at me, waiting for a response.

"Right." I take a sip of my drink, hoping it will help my dry throat, but it does nothing. "I, uh, wanted to talk in private because I need to tell you something really important."

"This is about senior week?"

I nod, but my neck feels strained. Releasing a shaky breath, I brush my bangs from my eyes and lick my lips.

Before I get the chance to open my mouth, a knowing smile lifts his lips and he nods as if he knows what I'm about to say. "Listen, it's okay if you don't want to talk about it. We can pretend it never happened if you'd prefer it that way, and don't worry, I won't tell anyone."

"No, that's not what this is about." I chuckle awkwardly, drumming my fingers against the cup.

He stares at me, shocked. "Oh, okay. So..."

Inhale. Exhale. "A month after I left Miami, I found out I was pregnant. With your baby."

TJ stops the cup midway to his mouth and his furrowed brows flatten. He lowers the cup and stares at me as if he's trying to process my words.

I assumed it would take a lot longer for him to register what I said, but he resumes drinking. "Who put you up to this? Was it Spears? Is that what he whispered in your ear the other day?"

"Whispered?" I shake my head, having no idea what he's talking about. "I'm ser—"

He snaps his fingers and points his index finger like he's

figured something out. "It couldn't have been him. It had to be Arlo. I know he's still upset over the hazing—" His smile becomes tight as if he's realized he said too much. "Don't tell anyone I said that."

"They didn't—"

"No, Arlo isn't that petty. It was Taylor, wasn't it? Son of a bitch. I should've known he'd pull some shit like this." He laughs to himself, running his fingers through his hair. "I have to admit that was pretty good. I almost believed it."

"This has nothing to do with them. This is the truth. I—"

"Lola, come on, I know one of them put you up to this. It's okay, you can tell them they got me."

"TJ!" I raise my voice, feeling exasperated. "I'm serious."

Panic flashes across his eyes, but he shakes his head and chuckles. "And I'm serious too. Are they hiding around here somewhere? Those fuckers—"

"I'm serious," I cut him off. I swallow hard before I repeat myself again. "I'm serious."

The amusement dancing in his eyes and the smile that curves his lips falter for a brief second. When I say the five words again, his expression becomes blank.

"We have a baby together."

A beat of silence passes. One second. Two seconds. Ten seconds. Thirty. The prolonged silence becomes deafening.

I try to gauge his expression, but I see nothing.

"I know it's hard to believe and I know you probably have so many questions, but—"

"Yeah." A muscle in his jaw ticks. "I do have *a* question."

"Of course, ask me anything."

He smiles, but it doesn't reach his eyes. "What did you expect to gain out of all of this?"

His question throws me off, and the voice in my head is screaming that I'm not going to get the outcome I expected. It's also telling me this is going to be much worse than I realized, but I decide not to overthink.

He's in denial. I just told him we have a kid. His reaction is normal. He's just in shock.

"I just wanted you to know that we have a baby. I wanted our—"

TJ scoffs, his lips tightening in a straight line. "Just cut the bullshit and stop pretending. What did you expect to gain out of all this?"

A cold sweat breaks across my back and my heart races faster than it ever has. I keep telling myself to breathe, but the thump of my heart feels like it's in my ears. "I'm not lying. I'm telling you the truth. I promise we have a baby together. I know it's hard to believe, but it's the truth."

He tenses, blinking a few times before looking away. I could have sworn a trickle of fear flashed in his eyes. But it was just my imagination because when he looks at me again, I can tell that he's already made up his mind about whatever he's about to say.

"This all makes sense. You're desperate for attention." He chuckles sardonically and pauses for a moment. "This is what you wanted, huh? Funny how you have classes with my teammates who happen to be my roommates. Isn't that just a coincidence?"

"What?" The word barely comes out in a whisper.

"Lola, for fuck's sake. You really thought I"—he points his thumb at his chest—"was going to believe this? You really expect me to believe that you and I have a *baby*? A fucking baby?" He laughs with no humor. "You thought you were clever, didn't you? This is some next-level stalker shit."

My heart plummets to the ground. "I'm not a stalker. I didn't even know that you were here until—"

"What was it, huh? Money? Popularity? What the fuck did you expect to gain out of me?" His eyes darken, jaw clenching. "Because you really outdid yourself."

The anger coursing through his eyes and his tone that's laced with disgust take me back to June, two years ago. When I was in this same situation with my parents. I told myself I'd never let anyone make me feel small again, but right now he's excelled at doing just that.

My bottom lip trembles and my nose stings. I have to stop myself from blinking as tears prick my eyes.

"If you don't believe me, you can take a test."

"I won't be doing shit, but what you'll be doing is getting out of my house. I swear to God, I never want to see you again," he bitterly spits out, his words icy with rage, sending a chill down my spine.

I bite the inside of my cheek hard until I taste something metallic. Words get clogged in the back of my throat, begging to be heard. Instead, I wipe the lone tear that manages to trickle down my cheek.

"Don't worry, you won't."

I stalk out of his room, calling Daisy as I grab my stuff from the kitchen and leave his house.

"Do you want us to bring—"

"Please just come pick me up," I beg, walking as far away as I can from the house while wiping the tears that won't stop rolling down my cheeks.

13
LOLA

I SHOULDN'T BE DROWNING MY SORROWS IN ICE CREAM, but I could be doing a lot worse things.

"Ma?" Phoenix holds a spoon barely filled with ice cream to my mouth.

I smile and part my mouth, letting him place the spoon between my lips. He removes it and dunks it back into the pint of strawberry and caramel cheesecake. He scoops more of the ice cream, and funnily enough, his spoon has more than mine did.

"Really?"

My son thinks he's clever, but he forgets the more ice cream he puts into his mouth, the bigger his chances are of getting a brain freeze.

I should stop him from making that mistake for the second time since I pulled out the ice cream, but I think he keeps hoping that the outcome will be different. He plops the spoon into his mouth, closes his eyes tight, winces, and his little body shudders.

"Cold." He pouts, pointing at his forehead, staring at me like I'm supposed to fix the issue.

I shouldn't laugh, but I've warned him multiple times not to do it. Suppressing a chuckle, I lean down and kiss the crown of his head. I let my lips linger for a few seconds until I hear a low, content sigh.

"Better?"

"Mmhm." He cheekily grins and continues to scoop more ice cream onto the spoon as if nothing happened.

I may not know what I'm doing half of the time, but one thing I do know is that my kisses are like Winnie the Pooh in Phoenix's eyes. And that says a lot, considering he's obsessed with that bear.

I watch him repeat the process and try to listen to whatever he's saying, but some of his words sound like gibberish. I do my best not to focus on the wild mess of curls on his head and how the color in his eyes is the same shade as *his*. I try to revel in this moment, but so many of his features remind me of him.

It almost feels like someone out there is screwing with me because what the fuck? Am I supposed to learn something from this? And if so, then what? Because this all seems like one big joke and I'm not laughing.

Dropping my head back on the kitchen cabinet, I stare up at the ceiling. My nose stings again and my eyes prick with tears for what seems like the fifth time today. I don't allow them to fall, though, because I told myself I wouldn't cry. Especially not in front of Phoenix.

Yesterday was the one and only exception, but I refuse to do it again. My tears aren't going to fix my situation. I'm still a single parent, and Phoenix is still not going to have a father.

My temples pound incessantly, the pain spiking with every passing second. It doesn't help that my mind replays his hurtful words and the look of disgust on his face.

I hear my best friends' voices in the distance. When the front door opens, their voices become louder. I should get up from the kitchen floor, but I can't bring myself to care.

"Lo, really?" Cara's voice pulls my gaze away from the ceiling and onto her and Daisy, who stand at the entrance of the kitchen. "Two pints of ice cream?"

"In my defense, one of them was almost empty," I lied.

I unashamedly devoured an entire pint of ice cream and yes, I am onto the second. But I didn't do this all by myself. I had an accomplice.

He definitely looks guilty with the ice cream smeared on his hair and face.

"We talked about this," Daisy chastises, bending down to pick up the empty pint and the one sitting on my lap. I tighten my grip on it, but with a threatening glare from Daisy, I let it go.

Phoenix stares in disappointment as she caps the pint and stores it back in the freezer.

"M-more," he begs.

"No, that's enough. Your tummy is going to hurt." I pat his belly just as Cara hands me a damp paper towel to clean him off. "Go play with your toys," I say once I've cleaned him all up.

He picks up his bear and runs to the living room.

"He's a piece of shit, Lola. Fuck him," Daisy says once Phoenix is out of earshot. "You should've let me slash his tires."

"We know where he lives and what car he drives." Cara lowers herself to sit next to me.

"No," I deadpan. "There will not be any tire slashing, window breaking, or paintballing him or his house."

I say this mostly to Daisy because while Cara might consider it, Daisy will one hundred percent do it. Once she has her mind set on something, there's no stopping her. It's a little scary to see the wheels in her head turning. She's not crazy per se, but if she says she's going to do something, then she's going to do it.

She groans in frustration. "Why do you always have to ruin my fun?"

"You're trying to get into law school. The last thing you need is to get arrested over something stupid." I point at Cara and then look up at Daisy. "And you...you don't need to get arrested...again."

Daisy leans against the counter, crossing her arms against her chest. "It was worth it, and it'd be worth it again."

"But I don't want you to get expelled. I need you both here." Not only to keep my sanity intact, but they're my family. I'm not sure what I'd do without them. "Look, I know you're both mad, but I'd rather just move on."

"Move on?" Daisy scoffs, staring at me, bewildered. "It's not fair that you—"

"It's not. Life isn't fair, but what do you want me to do? Beg him to be there for Phoenix like I begged my parents to be there for me? Make him do something he'll probably end up resenting? Make him be a part of Phoenix's life, only for him to be there when it's convenient for him? Or worse, getting my son's hopes up? I know you two don't agree with me, but I'm done. If and when Phoenix has questions, I'll answer them, but as far as I know, I'm his only parent."

Cara and Daisy look at each other. I can tell they're tempted to say something else, but they don't. Daisy drops to the floor and sits across from us.

"Okay." She sighs. "But as far as I know, I'm still Phoenix's favorite aunt."

"Get over yourself." Cara laughs. "It's pretty obvious who's the favorite, and it's definitely not you."

I suppress a laugh, feeling relieved they're not going to push it. I know they mean well, but I can't continue to dwell on something that's pointless and neither can they.

Running into him was something I've been dreaming about since I found out I was pregnant. It's ridiculous now, but at the time, I created scenarios in my head of what life would've been like if I'd found him. Each one was different, but they always ended up happy.

Now it's become a reality and it's harsher than I ever wanted. He's not the same person I met two years ago, and neither am I.

"We should go." Cara nudges my side with her elbow.

I take a deep breath, willing the ache in my chest to go away. "What?"

"Go to Liquid." Daisy beams.

My brows pull together. "Liquid?"

"It's a club that recently opened up. It's not too far from us, probably a thirty-minute drive," Cara explains.

"And one of the girls in my class said their drinks are good *and* affordable," Daisy adds excitedly. "We're going tonight."

"I can't. It's too late to call Elena and ask her to babysit, and I don't have anything to wear."

And I have plans to do nothing but eat ice cream, order some tacos, and watch TV all night.

"Don't worry about that." Daisy jumps to her feet. "We already got it taken care of."

"What did you guys do?"

"Just trust us. Either way, it's the end of September, and we haven't had our girls' night out. We're going out and that's final."

The girls weren't kidding when they said they had it under control.

While I was wallowing in my misery Friday night, they contacted Elena. She wasn't busy tonight, so she agreed to take care of Phoenix. After the girls informed me of our plans this evening, it didn't take long for Elena to pick him up.

They also paid her and refused to accept my money. They said the only thing they'd accept is for me to go out. Not that they gave me much of a choice, but I wasn't going to fight them on it.

I'm not the only one who needs to go out. On top of classes, Cara's working a full-time job and is on a hunt for an internship at a law firm. So far, she's found nothing, and I know she's stressed about it.

Daisy's a student athletic trainer. Part of the program requirement is to do clinicals with two of the athletic teams for the entire year. She got placed with the swim team and the football team.

Daisy needs this because if she doesn't get drunk tonight, she'll murder one of the football players on Monday.

We're currently waiting in line to get inside Liquid. The line is ridiculously long, but the group of girls standing in front of us said the wait is worth it.

"Damn, *mami*," Daisy whistles, her eyes coasting down my body. "You look good." She pinches her fingers together, brings them to her lips, and kisses them before she tosses them in the air.

"I don't want kids, but you're honestly making me reconsider it." Cara's gaze slowly descends down my body, stopping at my chest and hips for a second before they lift back up. "Seriously, your body is insane, Lo."

"All thanks to Daisy," I chime.

If it wasn't for her constantly motivating me to go to the gym and meal prepping, I wouldn't be in the shape I'm in now. After I gave birth, my body changed drastically.

Accepting the change hasn't been easy. I wish I could say I've come to love and accept that my body is different now, but there are days I hate looking in the mirror. Then there are days when I change my clothes because I feel self-conscious.

Tonight is the first time in a while that I really dressed up, and the first time I didn't change after the first outfit.

Courtesy of Daisy, I'm wearing her strapless terracotta corset. It pushes up my breasts and pulls in my waist. And the black leather pants make my ass look great.

And thanks to Cara, my makeup is amazing. I can do the minimum, like putting on mascara, but nothing compared to what she can do.

"You're welcome." She beams proudly, flicking her pin-straight hair over her shoulder.

We talk about other things while we wait and once we're inside, we understand why everyone is obsessed with coming here.

I know it's a special effect, but the walls look like they're made out of water. In the center of the building hangs an immense bottle flipped upside down. Underneath it is a glass catching the liquid that flows out of the bottle. Light mist and strobe lights in vibrant colors cover the dance floor. There's also a second floor for VIPs.

"Oh fuck!" Daisy shouts over the loud music. "Lola, don't look at the VIP section."

But it's too late. I spot TJ with his friends and a few girls gathered around them. I immediately recognize one of the girls. She's the one who needed to *study* with him.

As I go to look away, our eyes lock. It's as if he sensed me looking at him, and now we're gazing at each other from across the club. A beat passes before I avert my eyes.

"We can go to The Tap House, The Lucky Jersey, or there is also—"

"No, it's fine. We're here. Let's just have a good time," I cut Cara off.

"Are you sure?" Daisy questions. "We can go anywhere you want."

"No, we're staying and we're going to have a good time. Now let's go to the bar. Drinks are on me." I grin, not giving them a chance to say anything else as I walk away. I don't have to turn around to know they're behind me.

I also don't want to turn around because I swear I can feel his eyes on me.

14

TJ

"*We have a baby together.*"

That's all I've been able to think about since yesterday. I've attempted to distract myself, but it's been useless because every few seconds, those five words force themselves back into my brain. It's as if they're stuck on repeat, and it's all my mind wants to focus on.

The hurt expression on her face and how *sincere* she sounded.

What if it's true? What if I am really a father? That means I missed out on a year of his life. Is he walking? Does he talk? Who does he look like?

No, fuck, no, it's not possible. There's no way I'm a father.

That's why I'm at Liquid with my friends, surrounded by unlimited alcohol and attractive girls. I wanted to drown my thoughts, but it seems the universe has a fucked-up sense of humor.

Lola is here and she looks...damn it.

Inhaling sharply, I take a long pull of my beer because fuck me.

Just twenty-four hours ago, she told me we have a kid together. I should've already wiped her away from my memory.

Blocked every single detail that my mind is still grasping onto from two years ago, but I can't.

An ugly realization settles deep within me. My friends, the alcohol, and girls aren't enough to permanently erase *her*.

Everything she said yesterday should have been enough, but my brain *suddenly* isn't registering or connecting with the rest of my body. And I know I'm extremely fucked because I can't stop looking at her.

Blowing out a breath, I down the rest of my beer and watch her turn around with her friends in tow as they head to the bar.

Unfortunately—it's wrong that I'm even thinking this—Alexia stands in front of me, slipping her arm around my waist. She curls her finger, motioning for me to lean down. Once I do, she steps closer until I feel her lips at my ear.

"I need to go to the restroom. You want to come?"

I hear the suggestive tone in her voice loud and clear. I know exactly what she wants and normally, I wouldn't hesitate to say yes, but I can't bring myself to feel excited about a quick fuck.

"No, I'm heading to the bar. You want anything?" I hold my empty bottle for her to see. The last thing I want is to be anywhere near Lola, but I really need a drink. I can't get drunk if I don't have alcohol.

She ignores the bottle and frowns. "You don't want to—"

I'm not sure if Saint was listening, considering the music is extremely loud, but he intervenes at the perfect time. "I'll come with you. I think I saw Lola and her *friends*."

And by friends, he's referring to Daisy. I'm pretty sure he wasn't focused on Lola or Cara. Ever since he met Daisy, he's been obsessing over her.

"Oh, I'm definitely coming." Jag grins like a fucking dumbass, chugging the remainder of whatever is in his cup. "Come on, Landon."

"Don't worry about it. I'll get the drinks," I quickly say, pulling away from Alexia's grasp.

"Who's Lola?" Alexia's question drips with irritation.

Saint replies before I get the chance to, "TJ's senior week *lover.*"

They don't know the details of that week, and they know I never plan to tell them what happened. Surprisingly, Lola hasn't said anything. I assumed she would have told someone for attention, but no one knows anything but me, her, and maybe her friends.

Since they don't have any idea what happened, they've created fake scenarios of what they think did.

The corners of Jagger's mouth curve into a devilish grin. "She's a hot redhead."

I can see everything register in her eyes, but I don't wait for her to speak or for my friends to make any other comments. I walk away from them and head toward the bar.

God, I desperately need something stronger.

"What's up with you?" Saint asks, walking alongside me.

"Nothing."

"Doesn't seem like it's nothing. You look tense."

"I'm fine," I grit.

"You sure?"

My jaw ticks and my temple throbs. "Saint, I'm fucking fine."

I'm not looking in that direction because I know she's there, but I follow his line of vision and sure enough, he's gaping, staring wide-eyed at Daisy.

"You don't see—damn..." His voice is almost inaudible due to the loud music.

"Don't even bother. She doesn't want you." It'd be great if he'd stop whatever fixation he has on her. The less we're around them, the better.

I didn't tell the guys about Lola because it's pointless. I trust my roommates more than I trust anyone, but it's better if fewer people know. The last thing I need are rumors going around.

And confessing what she said makes it feel way too real.

"She can't be arsed with you," Landon says. I know he's not physically smiling, but inwardly he's relishing that fact.

Saint stares at us, annoyed. "Why are you both being so negative? It's only been a few weeks, and I'm a very likable person. If she doesn't like me yet, she will soon."

"Damn right." Jayden appears out of nowhere. "You talk to Daisy and I'll talk to her friend."

I cock a brow.

He flashes me an easygoing smile. "Don't worry, not Lola. Cara."

"Do what you want. Talk to Lola for all I care."

"Right," they say in unison.

I roll my eyes and stand at the bar. Thankfully, the bartender notices me and when I lift my bottle, he's quick to grab another one.

I should leave. I don't need to be here anymore, but when I hear her laugh, I can't help but look over at her. And the reason behind her laughter is none other than the little shit Jagger.

She has to be faking it because he's *not* funny. I would know as this is my third year living with him.

As I take a pull of my beer, I'm able to momentarily block out the sound of her laugh, but I'm still aware of her presence.

I'm pretty sure it's only because of what she said. I'm also certain it's all the alcohol I've drunk tonight that's making my body buzz. So it makes sense I'm hyper-aware of her.

That's how I find myself getting lost in her. I try to force myself to look somewhere else, but my hazy gaze is not willing to look away. I blame this on the alcohol because if I were in my right mind, her presence wouldn't enthrall me.

It's not even about the way she's dressed. Stunning isn't enough of a word to describe how she looks. She's wearing a dark orange top and leather pants. Her top is tight. Her tits strain against it, and they're pushed up, almost spilling out.

My eyes linger on her chest until I force them down, but that's a fucking mistake. When they stop on her ass, I feel so many things I shouldn't be feeling.

I wish I could look away. I wish I could focus on anyone but her, but it's not her body or the way she's dressed that completely distract me. It's just her being.

When I lift my gaze back up, the strobe lights shine on her, casting an orange glow around her face like a halo. I tell myself not to go there, but before I can terminate any thoughts, I find myself stuck in a memory from two years ago.

I've never paid attention to the sky. Never paid attention to the colors that blend and spread vastly. Not until right now, in this very moment with Lola. She stares at the sky with awe, like it's the first time she's witnessing a sunset. But I stare at her like it's the first time I'm seeing her.

Though I am. This is the first time I am seeing her, feeling her without even touching her. She feels like a blaze, setting every inch of me on fire. I'm not sure how it's possible to feel a burn when all I'm doing is staring at her.

It could be the sunset reflecting onto her or maybe it was the other way around. Her smile, so soft and warm, her wavy golden copper hair cascading past her shoulders, flowing gently as the wind picks up. She's the embodiment of a sunset: warm, electric, and mesmerizing.

"Mate, close your mouth." Landon stands next to me, his expression blank, but I can feel his judgment. "You're embarrassing yourself and me."

The memory fades into nothing as I come back to the present.

I don't remember opening my mouth, but my lips are slightly parted.

"You?"

"I'm standing right next to you." He grimaces, uncapping his water bottle. Before he takes a drink, his eyes dart to Lola, specifically to her chest. "I see the appeal."

He's taunting me. He wants a reaction out of me. It's what I keep telling myself.

As I'm about to take a drink, I stop myself as Jagger leans down. He doesn't close the space between them, but he's close enough that his lips are hovering over her ear.

I don't understand why they're so close. He's not known her for long, so what could he be telling her?

"You know..." He pauses, eyes dipping to my right forearm. I almost hide it but decide against it. Surely, he doesn't know. "I thought that face was familiar."

"I thought you didn't drink? You sound drunk."

Landon doesn't ever drink. I know that. Everyone knows that, but I need to change the conversation.

"Just *some* girl, yet *her* face is tattooed on your arm," he dryly retorts, his tone patronizing.

Freshman year, I got drunk, and I'm not saying that lightly. I've been drunk before, but that time was different. I was way past the point of no return. I'm positive I was somewhere in oblivion because I willingly allowed a football player—who was also a freshman—to tattoo my arm.

That night, I wasn't in the right headspace. I was upset thinking my career was over before it even started. I went out with the guys and ended up at one of the football players' houses. All I can remember from that night is alcohol being handed to me or poured down my throat, and everything else is a big-ass blur.

Jayden told me I lost a bet and my punishment was to get tattooed by one of the guys. He also said I willingly agreed to let them tattoo whatever they wanted. Chance, the guy who gave me the tattoo, decided on a mermaid. Apparently, he took pity on me and let me choose what I wanted her to look like, and in my drunken stupor, I showed him a picture of Lola.

Why her? I don't know. I wasn't in the right state of mind, but thankfully, Chance is talented and didn't screw me over. Unfortunately, the tattoo is not only big, but it wraps around my forearm, and it's permanently inked on my skin with Lola's face. It's only the side of her face, but it's still her.

"I don't know what you're talking about."

As expected, he doesn't say anything. I know he can see through my bullshit, but he doesn't care enough to call me out on it. Though I don't put it past him to use it against me later.

My head snaps in her direction as I hear her laugh again.

Her head is thrown back as she laughs at whatever Jagger said. I don't understand what the hell is so damn funny. He's *not* funny.

I don't even know what I'm still doing here. I don't give a fuck if she laughs at his lame-ass jokes.

Not contemplating it any longer, I step away from the bar and head back up to the VIP section.

"Are you sure you don't want to dance?" Alexia asks, exasperated.

I shake my head for what seems like the thousandth time tonight. She and a few other girls have asked me to dance. I'm not sure if I'm not making myself clear enough, but they won't stop insisting.

"No. Go dance with someone else."

She has options. I've seen guys approach her, but she keeps turning them down.

"Oh, come on, TJ. Just once." She tugs on my arm.

I inwardly groan. I'm not only annoyed because she keeps asking, but also because Lola is down there dancing. She danced with Jagger and now with her friends.

Not that I'm keeping tabs on her, but the last thing I want is to be around her. I made it clear that I don't want to see her again, but obviously that's impossible considering we attend the same university.

"I already told you—" I clamp my mouth shut, eyes drawn to Lola as she ambles to the restrooms. "I'll be back."

I should think through what I'm about to do, but I'm so fucking frustrated. The last time I felt like this was freshman year after my injury. I never thought I'd be this annoyed again. I wanted to have a good time. Instead, I watched my friends flirt with her.

Even Landon spoke to her tonight. Typically, he doesn't give many girls the time of day, but for *some reason*, he spoke to Lola.

I don't pay attention to the other people who attempt to talk to me. Everything is irrelevant as I keep my gaze straight ahead. I'm not entirely sure what I'm going to say, I'm not even sure why I'm bothering, but I'm blaming this on the alcohol.

Pushing past the throng of people, I finally make it to the hallway that leads to the restroom. The hall is long and narrow and despite the dim lights, I'm able to see her silhouette at the end of the hall.

She stands by herself. I look behind me, wondering if her friends are going to show up. After a few seconds of waiting, I realize they're not coming, and that alone pisses me off more than it should.

"Why are you here by yourself?"

She gasps loudly, jumping back a little.

I suck in a breath as I tell myself to calm down, but as I approach her, I only get angrier.

"You shouldn't be here by yourself. What the hell are you thinking?" I snap.

The shock on her face evaporates and her brows pull together. Her lips part and I wait for her to reply, but it never comes. She looks away, completely ignoring me.

"Do you not realize how dangerous it is to be alone?"

Again she ignores me.

"I'm talking to you. It's not safe to be alone." I inch closer, noting how glossy her eyes are and the flush in her cheeks, but she doesn't look drunk. At least I don't think she is.

And again, nothing but silence.

"Lola, stop ignoring me. You shouldn't be here by yourself."

Her frown deepens, eyes hardening. "Louise. My friends call me Lola. Strangers call me Louise."

"The last thing you should be concerned about is what I call you. You should be concerned that you're here by yourself. With fucking drunk assholes out there." I throw my hand over my shoulder, pointing to the other side of the hall.

She crosses her arms against her chest. I swear to God, I don't mean to, but my gaze drops to her breasts.

"What do you want? You told me to stay away from you, and that's exactly what I'm doing. Actually, let's pretend we don't know each other. So kindly fuck off."

Her attitude should piss me off, but it's doing the opposite of that. Quickly shaking that thought, I release a harsh breath.

"Hard to do that when you're being careless."

She scoffs. "Careless?"

"Yes, on top of being a liar, you're being careless by being here by yourself. Do you not realize how fucking easy it is for any guy to come here and trap you? Drag you to one of those restrooms?" I don't even mention that no one would be able to hear her if she were to cry for help. The music is so loud, I can hardly hear myself.

She humorlessly laughs. "Yeah, I was careless sleeping with you. That's for certain, but I'm not a liar. If you choose not to believe me, that sounds like a personal problem."

I'm speechless for a second, unsure of what to say. This is what I get for drinking so much because now I'm dwelling on her first statement.

"Just admit that you're lying," I demand.

"I don't need you to believe me, and honestly, I don't care anymore. From now on, we're nothing but strangers. Either way, it's not like I ever knew you anyway."

This time, I don't know what to say and before I can gather my thoughts, she sidesteps me and marches away. I'm not sure how long I stand in this damn hallway, but I realize in the moment I can't bring myself to care about her lie. I need to make sure she's with her friends.

I head to the bar, standing next to Saint, who's talking to Jayden. I look around, skimming the crowd, but she's nowhere in sight, nor are her friends.

I elbow his side, getting his attention. "Where's Lola?"

"She left. Said she wasn't feeling good."

"Give me your phone." I pull my phone out and click on a new message.

"For what?"

"Just give me your phone."

He eyes me warily but pulls his phone out of his pocket and hands it to me. This has nothing to do with the alcohol. I don't know what to think anymore, but I feel like shit.

I find her contact and type her number in my phone.

Me: It's TJ.

Me: I just want to make sure you made it home safely.

I don't expect a reply, but for the next few hours, I stay glued to my phone. Patiently waiting for it to say **Read** underneath my message, but that doesn't happen.

15

TJ

"Hey," Saint softly knocks on my door. "We're leaving now. Are you sure you don't want us to wait for you?"

"No, go ahead and leave without me. I'll be there in a few."

"You sure you're okay?" Now it's Jay who asks.

Am I okay? Fuck no, I'm far from okay. There are too many thoughts running through my mind, but only one seems to be coherent and consistent.

"We have a baby together."

It's Tuesday morning, and that's all I've been able to think about since Friday. I wish I could shut it down and think of something else. Hell, I would welcome anything, but that persistent *thought* keeps hammering at my head.

What if she's not lying?

What if she's telling the truth?

What if I really do have a kid?

I tentatively reply, "I'm sure."

After a beat, I hear them head down the stairs. Once the house becomes dead silent, I exhale a long breath, but it does nothing to alleviate the tightness in my chest.

I keep thinking about that night.

We were safe. We used a condom, and we only fucked once.

I've been with many girls, some more than once, but none of those girls have ever told me they were pregnant.

Though they've done other shit that almost tops the baby card.

I've woken up to random girls in my bed, uninvited. After parties, girls have snuck into my room while I'm passed out, to sleep next to me without my permission. I've had girls blatantly cup my dick through my jeans. And then there are some girls who don't know how to take no for an answer.

Needless to say, I keep my door locked at all times now. I keep my distance from certain girls, and I'm very clear about my intentions. I'll never lead a girl on. If I'm interested, they'll know. If I'm not, they'll also know.

It makes me sound like an asshole, but is it a bad thing to want boundaries? I don't mind hanging out and I don't mind inviting them over to my room, but sometimes it becomes too much.

Sometimes they get a little too comfortable and ask questions. Out of the many questions, the one I get asked the most is how much I think I'll make once I get drafted. I'm confident in my abilities to get into the NBA, but nothing is certain. Anything can change in the blink of an eye.

Like Lola's confession to me the other day, if I can call it that.

I don't know why I'm dwelling on that thought. What I should be doing is getting ready and heading to the arena. Coach Warren is going to chew my ass out. No, he won't just chew my ass out, he'll throw one hell of a punishment.

That is if he's not already annoyed that I'm not the first or second one there. It's always either Jag or me who are there first. We're co-captains and because of that, a lot of responsibility falls on us.

I'm certain I won't be the second one there or even the fifth, but this is a one-time thing and it'll never happen again. At least I'm not late. If there's anything Coach hates more than losing, it's tardiness.

I've never been late and I don't plan to start now.

My head is pounding by the time I get to the arena. To make matters worse, the guys have been blowing up the group chats. I have a group chat with just my roommates, and then I have one with all of my teammates. And both chats are getting flooded by messages.

They're probably wondering where I'm at, so that is why I've silenced my phone. I should probably answer, but I can't be bothered.

It's only 5:55 a.m., and my head is already killing me.

I just know it's going to be one of those days, and I'm dreading it. I would skip class, but I know if it's not my advisor assigned to me, then it will be Coach reaching out to my professors to make sure I'm in class. My freshman year, I skipped a few classes and learned the hard way why it's important I don't.

Before I head into the locker room, I go straight to the arena. I typically wouldn't, but I'm sure if Warren doesn't see me, he'll call me and that's the last thing I want.

When I step in, all heads snap in my direction and the entire court becomes silent.

"Is it true?" Saint asks, cutting through the tense, awkward energy radiating around the arena.

"Is what—"

"Frank wants to see you in his office now," Reggie, one of the assistant coaches, says, clapping his hand to get the guys' attention. "All right everyone, focus!"

I stand in the same place, dumbfounded. That is until Jared, another one of the assistant coaches, stands in front of me. "Don't go to the locker room. Head straight to his office."

"What's going on?"

A line of apprehension creases his brows. "You haven't been on your phone, have you?"

I shake my head. "No."

I've made a habit of not looking at my phone first thing in the morning unless it's my parents or Coach who are trying to get in touch with me. It's what my therapist recommended after my injury.

Getting on my phone had always been the first thing I did when I woke up, but after everything went to shit my freshman year, I had to stop. I was letting the comments on social media fuck with my head and I had a panic attack.

No one except my parents and Coach knows it happened. After it happened, they got me a therapist and advised that I cut back on using social media. I still use it but not as much. Especially on game days. I don't get on it at all.

"Just...go talk to Frank and don't look at your phone." He gave me a tight-lipped smile.

"Okay," I reluctantly reply and turn on my heel.

My phone feels heavy in my pocket as I walk to his office. I almost pull it out, but I decide against it.

Once I reach his office, my steps falter as I hear his deep voice echo throughout the empty hall.

"This isn't a fucking joke. Tell your staff to take that shit down. Now!" Is all that he says before I hear the phone being slammed down. "Come in, TJ, and shut the door behind you."

Questions run through my mind as I step into his office and shut the door behind me.

"Take a seat," he says in a clipped tone.

"Is everything all right?" I ask, taking the seat across from him.

My mind wanders to the past few weeks, but nothing goes off in my head. Nothing that screams *I fucked up*. I'm not stupid enough to get myself in trouble. Even though I don't see my therapist anymore, I've been following all of his suggestions. I don't skip classes, nor am I late for them. I don't drink as much as I used to, and I eat pretty healthy. I'm making sure Saint isn't doing any stupid shit, or at least doing as much as I can. Watching over him is like taking care of a fucking child. He does the opposite of what anyone tells him, though recently he hasn't done anything stupid. Coach asked me to keep an eye out for him. It's why he's living with us and why he's my roommate when we're at away games.

He leans back in his chair and takes off his glasses, tossing them on his desk. He closes his eyes, pinching the bridge of his nose before loudly exhaling.

I awkwardly cough. "Coach?"

He drops his hand and opens his eyes. "I assume you haven't gotten on your phone this morning?"

"I haven't, but I can—" I go to pull it out, but he raises his hand, telling me there's no need for me to do that as he turns his monitor around.

The air around me ceases to exist. I stay frozen in the chair as I reread NCU's news article over and over again, staring at the picture of Lola and me at Liquid.

Our junior point guard, Theodore Jackson Kingston, also known as TJ, has a child with Louise Larson.

I stare at the fucking screen until my vision blurs, but still, I don't blink, don't move. I don't do anything until my lungs burn and beg for me to breathe.

My lips part and I attempt to say something, but no words come out. My mouth is too dry and my thoughts are all over the place. I attempt to collect myself, to gather my thoughts, but they're all scattered in a frenzy.

"TJ." Coach Warren's voice drags me away from my drowning, rambunctious mind.

"Hmm?" I'm too focused on the words on the screen to pay attention to anything else. I must have already looked over the words a hundred times because my eyes start to burn, but still, I don't blink.

That is until he shifts the monitor so that the screen is facing him again.

"We have a baby together."

"I spoke with Nancy, the director, and she said she'll take it down." His words pull me out of my stupor, and then he sighs. I already know I'm not going to like what he's going to say next. "But this isn't the *only* article *this* is on. It's...everywhere."

"Everywhere?" It feels as if someone knocked the air out of me.

"Look..."

His words become distant and his presence almost nonexistent as my thoughts shift to the one person who could have done this. Of course, who else would do this? No one knew but her, her friends I'm sure, and me. Unless she told someone else. I mean, why wouldn't she? I can't believe I was stupid enough to believe she wouldn't do this.

"TJ."

"Sorry, what?" I release a shaky breath.

I'm doing my best to remain calm, but the more I think about her words, the stupid article, and the thought of this being everywhere, the more I get pissed off.

I drop my gaze to where my phone is stuffed in my pocket. It feels hot and heavy. All I want to do is open it so I can see what everyone is saying.

"It's not worth it. Don't do it," he says as if he can read my thoughts.

"I had no idea—I didn't think—she—" I stammer, unable to find the right words.

I'm never like this. I'm always calm and collected, except for the one time I had a panic attack.

"Take a deep breath, and talk slowly."

I tilt my head back, staring at the ceiling as I inhale and exhale slowly. My heart rate steadies for a second, but when I look at him again, it spikes back up.

"Lola, the girl from the article, she told me about the baby. I didn't believe her and—"

"Wait a minute," he raises his hand to stop me from talking. "So this isn't entirely false? You knew about this?"

"Yes, I knew about this, but it's not true."

His expression becomes impassive, and I can already tell whatever I'm about to say is going to piss him off. He crosses his arms against his chest and leans back in his chair.

"Okay, well, I'm listening. I'd love to know how my starter is all over fucking social media and the goddamn news."

My jaw physically drops, as does my stomach.

"Don't worry, it was only the local news, but nonetheless *you* made it on the news. Though I'm certain ESPN will pick it up before twelve this afternoon. So please enlighten me."

I stare at him like a fucking idiot, unable to process everything he just said.

The news. Social media. The baby. Fuck.

"She told me this past Friday..." I tell him everything that's necessary, from meeting Lola two years ago to her telling me we have a kid.

It's eerily silent for a few seconds until he stands up, picks up some papers lying on his desk, and rolls them up. He walks around his desk and stands in front of me.

"Damn it, TJ!" He raises his voice and smacks my head with the rolled-up papers. "She told you earth-shattering news, and you didn't think to tell anyone or do anything about it?"

Coach tosses the papers on top of his desk and sits on the edge, crossing one ankle over the other. I can tell he's trying to rein his anger in because his nose flares as he folds his tense arms against his chest.

There aren't many people who scare me but two: Mom and Coach.

If Coach could, I'm sure he'd choke the living shit out of me. Even though he's told me countless times that I need to be careful not to injure myself because I'm his star player. At this moment, I'm sure he wouldn't care. Now that we have Saint, I wouldn't put it past him to end my life.

He may be forty-one years old, but he's built like a fucking machine and won't hesitate to knock your lights out. If he did commit murder, no one would ever question it was him. Everyone's too obsessed with his looks and they wouldn't care. They all think he looks like Jalen Hurts. Some have gone as far as calling him *the* Jalen Hurts of basketball.

"I didn't think she would—"

He laughs sardonically. "Of course you didn't. If you had been thinking, you wouldn't have been so careless."

"I wasn't careless. I *was* thinking that I hadn't seen her in two years, and she shows up two years later and tells me we have a kid together. Two fucking years, Coach."

"We have a baby together."

"After practice, you're going to meet Janet—"

"You want me to meet with the head of public relations?"

"I'm glad you think this is all a game to you, but this doesn't only affect you. It also affects your team. Janet will guide you through what you can and can't say until we can prove whether this is your kid or not."

"You're really not suggesting that I—"

Everything happens way too fast because Coach rolls up the papers on his desk and hits me with them again. "It's your responsibility to make it right. I don't give a damn if you met her five years ago. As the captain and someone a lot of kids look up to, you need to take responsibility."

"Responsibility?" I don't mean to raise my voice, but I can't believe he just said that. "She's the one who started this shit."

"And yet, she's the one who they all might feel sorry for."

I grind my teeth, fisting my hands at my sides.

"You're going to meet with Janet today after practice. You talk to no one and you answer to no one."

That means anyone who could potentially twist my words.

"But—"

"No buts, TJ. I can't believe how irresponsible you were. This is not something you take lightly, and I'm honestly disappointed at how you handled this. You should've known better." He grunts, shaking his head. "This not only affects you, but it also affects the team. If you think they weren't already looking at us, they'll definitely be looking now. They'll dissect every little thing, every minuscule mistake, every fucking little thing you probably hadn't considered they'll look at. That's the last thing you or anyone needs. We don't—"

"Coach—"

"Do not interrupt me." He hits me again with the rolled-up papers. "We don't need the center focus of our new season to be this." He turns his monitor around, smacking the rolled-up paper on the screen. "If she's so adamant that this child is yours, then you will have to take a test because this is the only way we'll be able to clear everything up."

16

TJ

Basketball's the one thing that'll never fail me in life. I could be having the shittiest day, but during practice or game day, everything dissipates. Any kind of possible emotion expels from my body, and I'm left feeling nothing but elated.

Even when it all ends, I still feel like I'm floating on fucking clouds. That's what basketball does to me. The elation, the adrenaline, the surreal feeling unlike no other. There has never been a day where I didn't feel like that...until today.

During practice, I was able to forget until it ended. Once it was over, I was reminded of what was waiting for me.

"We have a baby together."

Those words replay in my head as I walk back to the locker room. Typically, I'm the first in there, but I desperately needed silence to think through all of this. Not to mention the guys are going to ask questions. I was able to ignore the looks and block out their subtle questions when we took breaks, but that won't be possible now.

Letting out a resigned breath, I step into the locker room and immediately regret the decision to shower here. I instantly recognize the obnoxious voice that echoes throughout the room. Mark Simpson. The creator of Behind the Athlete Podcast.

Most of the time, that asshole talks shit about the players he hates and praises the one he loves. Especially NCU, it doesn't matter what the stats say or how well we play, there is not a single good thing he has ever said about any of us. Not even Saint, who everyone loves.

Needless to say, I'm not surprised when I hear, "Is it shocking that TJ Kingston has a kid? Are you all really going to pretend to be shocked? If you are, get your heads out of your asses. I'm just shocked it didn't happen sooner." He wholeheartedly laughs.

"Turn the shit off." I head to my locker and grab my stuff, ignoring their eyes burning through my back.

"So is it true?" Jagger asks.

I clench my jaw hard, stopping myself from going off. I take a long second before I turn around with my stuff in my hands. "What's the point of asking me if you're going to listen to his shit?"

"Mark isn't the only one who's talking about it," Trae, one of my teammates, says. "Everyone's talking about it."

I heave a sigh. "Everyone likes to talk shit. I don't know why you're all surprised."

"So that Lola chick made this all up?" Wyatt, another one of my teammates, asks. The mention of her name makes my head pound and my jaw ache due to how hard I'm clenching it. "Fucking bitch, that's all these—"

"Shut the fuck up," Saint snaps and it's the first time I've ever heard him sound so serious. "You don't know if it came from her. Nowhere has it been stated that it did."

"I'm just saying," Wyatt counters with a shrug. "I'm not the only one who thinks this. You all know how fucking desperate all these girls are, chasing attention and shit. You all know what they're willing to do just to say they've been with us. She's no different. Isn't it funny how she was mentioned and nobody else? You're all stupid to believe that fucking bitch—"

I black out. I push Wyatt against the locker, shoving my forearm against his throat. His eyes widen, my sudden reaction catching him off guard. When he snaps out of the shock, he attempts to push me away, but I don't move. I shove my arm further until he's gasping for air, but still, I don't relent.

"Don't fucking talk about Lola. If I hear you talk shit about her, I don't give a fuck that you're my teammate. I'll beat the shit out of you."

I feel the guys hover behind me, but before they get the chance to pull me away, I shove away from him. Feeling ten times angrier than before. I'm not sure what I'm more pissed about, but I don't bother to think about it as I walk out and head to the shower room.

My meeting with Janet finished thirty minutes ago, and I'm still trying to reel everything in. There is so much she said, but the one thing she's the most adamant about is not getting mad during interviews.

Not sure why she would even suggest I'd get mad. I've done countless interviews and during some of those, I've been asked extremely idiotic questions, but never have I lost my cool. I'm always good under pressure, and I know how to handle myself.

No matter how fucked-up this situation is, the one thing I'm not going to do is lose my shit on national live television. Especially now more than ever. Everyone who cares about basketball will be watching, will have their own thoughts, and give their unsolicited opinions. It never fails to happen.

"You want to talk about it?" Saint asks, setting a cup on the coffee table in front of me.

No one is supposed to be home right now. That's why I came here. Two of my classes got canceled, so I came home because I needed peace and quiet, and I was getting tired of the stares I was getting. The so-called baby news didn't take long to spread.

I guess I won't be getting my peace and quiet after all. Sometimes Saint doesn't know how to take a hint.

"There's nothing to talk about." My eyes flicker down to the cup and when I read what it is, I groan.

"What? I thought you liked matcha?"

After Lola and I tried it together, I started ordering it. Now I can't think of the stupid green drink without thinking of her. Whether it's cold or hot, I smell it, I see it, and all I can think of is the smile on her face as she inhales the drink. How her eyes brighten and how she licks her lips as if she's trying to make sure she doesn't miss a single drop.

"I do...I'm just not *craving* it, but thanks anyway."

He shrugs, a smile spreading across his face. "Not right now, *anyway*."

When I lift my gaze to his, he stares at me with a look I can't decipher. I don't question it, though. I'm not in the mood for his or anyone's shit right now.

I texted her after I was done talking to Janet, but she didn't reply.

"Why are you here? Don't you have class right now?"

"Yeah, but I have a meeting with my father." He stands, walks over to the TV stand, and opens the drawers, pulling out a matte black box. He lets himself fall on the couch next to me and opens the box.

"Oh..." Is all I say. I don't think Saint and his father have the best relationship. Every time they talk, he always rolls a joint. No one is allowed to smoke. We get tested before, after, and in the middle of the season. Yet somehow, he got away with it when we got tested a week ago. "Everything all right?"

"Yeah, everything is great." He beams, setting the box on the table. He pulls out a grinder, filter, paper, and weed. "Is everything all right with you? After all, you just found out you're a father."

Nothing is all right, but I'm not going to admit that to him or anyone.

I hesitate before I answer. "I'm not a...*father*."

"You already knew about this, didn't you?" He stops grinding the weed and looks at me with no judgment. "She told you on Friday. That's what she wanted to talk to you about."

The memory of that day replays in my head. My knuckles grazing her arm, the painting, the awe on her face as she looked at my pictures, the matcha, her *confession*, my words, the lone tear.

I rest my head on the back of the couch, staring up at the ceiling. "Yeah, she did."

"Let me guess, you didn't believe her?"

"No. You know the story of how we met. It's been two years since we last saw each other, two years since we spoke. You can't tell me you would have believed her?"

"I get where you're coming from, but I would have considered everything before deciding whether I would've believed her or not."

I look at him like he's lost his damn mind. "Consider what? Tell me, Saint, what is there to consider?"

He takes a slow drag of his joint before he blows a puff of smoke into the air. "For starters, she chose to tell you in private instead of telling anyone else."

I laugh bitterly. "Private? The news is everywhere. Everyone thinks I have a kid because she didn't get her way."

"I've seen the videos, the posts. Nothing stated that she was the one who said anything. They didn't even insinuate that it was her who said something. If I'm not mistaken, everyone said that someone overheard your conversation when you two were arguing at Liquid."

The only thing I saw and heard was what Coach showed me this morning and the podcast the guys were listening to in the locker room. I knew if I looked and saw what they said, it would mess with me, so I've stayed away from my phone. I've only been checking it every so often to see if Lola replied.

"It's funny you believe someone you hardly know," I reply, feeling agitated. "I thought we were best friends? Aren't you supposed to be on my side?"

He smiles lazily, taking another slow drag. "It's not about

sides but considering the facts. You're always too busy checking her out to notice. And it's not that I'm *not* on your side, but she's my friend too."

"I-I don't check her out," I lamely counter.

Saint snorts, arching a brow. "Whatever you say, TJ."

"Don't you have a meeting with your father?"

He lifts his hand, looking down at the watch strapped around his wrist. "I still have a few more minutes. So are you going to take a test?"

I stare at him. "Are you serious?"

"Yeah. I'd love to know if I'm going to be an uncle. I don't have siblings, so I'll never have blood nieces or nephews. This will be the closest thing to it."

I search for any trace of humor in his expression, but I quickly realize he's being serious.

I frown at the stupidity that comes out of his mouth. Leave it to Saint to say something like this. "You're a fucking idiot."

"Nah, that's you, *stronzo*." He places the joint between his lips and picks up his phone from the coffee table. He types something out before he stands up and grabs his box. "I texted Lola and told her to meet me at Midnight Brew at four."

"Don't you have class with her at that time?"

"I figured she was going to skip. You're not the only one they've been talking shit about." The smile on his face becomes tight before it softens. "I don't know if she'll show. She hasn't replied to my messages I sent two hours ago, but it's worth a try. Just don't fuck it up."

"Why would I fuck anything up?"

"You don't always have the best way with words. I swear you and Landon tie for the biggest *stronzo*. It wouldn't kill either of you to be a little nice once in a while."

"No, but people like to take advantage," I argue. He's starting to piss me off more than he usually does.

"You're right, they do, but trust me when I say that's not the case with her. Anyway, when you meet up with her, don't be an asshole, or I'll beat the fucking shit out of you." A sickeningly sweet smile stretches across his face. He doesn't say anything else as he walks away and up the stairs until he disappears.

"You're not the only one they've been talking shit about."

Resting my elbows on my knees, I close my eyes, hating how tense I feel as anxiety grips my chest painfully. But it gets worse when my phone vibrates in my pocket. I don't have to look at it to know who it is. I've ignored this call all day and I know I can't put it off any longer.

"Hey."

"Why have you been ignoring my calls?" Hazel yells, making me pull the phone away from my ear. "Mom and dad are losing their shit!"

"There's no need for that. Tell them it's all figured out." I let my head hang, dragging my fingers through my hair, pulling on it hard.

"So are you a dad then?" I don't miss the beat of excitement in her voice.

"Hazel, don't be fucking stupid. I'm not a dad."

"Don't be mad at me. I'm not the one who knocked up a girl." Before I get to reply, she continues. "So is it true? Because it's everywhere. Holy fucking shit, you're a dad. A dad!"

"Don't believe what's been said. I don't know where they got that information from, but they're—"

"Is that your brother on the phone? Let me talk to him." I hear mom's voice in the background, and then there's shuffling until she speaks.

"Theodore Jackson Kingston!" Her voice rises with each name.

I rub the back of my neck. "Hey, Mom."

"Please, please, please tell me you didn't get *some* girl pregnant?" Anger seeps from her voice, but I hear a tinge of disappointment. "You're only twenty-one and you're still in college! Should I remind you your cooking is shit!"

"Mom, please stop yelling." I hold the phone away from my

ear. "I didn't get *some* girl pregnant, and just to inform you, my cooking has...progressed."

Truth is, my cooking is shit. I've cooked a total of three times since I've lived here, and all three times were shit. I don't even bother anymore, and the guys don't let Jagger or me anywhere near the kitchen.

"Theodore," Dad says. Great, I'm on speaker. "They're saying you knocked up some girl. Son, there are condoms and—"

"Really, Phil? This is not the time for the condom talk. This is past the condom talk. The baby has already been born!"

"When can we meet the baby?"

"Hazel!" all three of us say.

"What? I'm excited to be an aunt," she replies, amused, clearly enjoying this.

"You're a fucking idiot. There's no kid."

"Theodore, watch your language and, Hazel, this is not the time for this. For all we know, it's a lie. It's all a lie, right? We talked about this." The worry in dad's voice tells me he's unsure whether he believes what he's saying.

"Yes, I know how to use a condom and pull out."

Hazel chimes, "Apparently not."

"Hazel, shut up," Mom scolds. "Theodore, we need to sort this out. Your name is everywhere. If this is a lie, we need to make sure this girl gets some kind of punishment for lying. Who is this Lola girl anyway?"

Hazel gasps loudly and then squeals like a child. "This is *the* Lola?"

"*The* Lola?" Mom and Dad ask.

"Lola is *the* girl from senior week." I hear the giddiness in her voice. "The girl you had asked me to help you find. Oh my gosh, it's *that* Lola. How did I not think of that earlier? No wonder she looks so familiar."

I had forgotten that I had asked Hazel to help me look for her on Instagram. So maybe...I was a little desperate to find her after she left Miami.

"She's not just some girl. Lola is *the* girl TJ got grounded for. The reason why he took the yacht without Dad's permission. And if I remember correctly, we found the condom foil, so the baby has to be TJ's."

I regret ever saying anything to her.

Mom sighs with resignation. "You need to talk to this girl, and if she's adamant it's yours, you need to take a test."

My jaw drops. "Mom, please tell me you're not—"

"I will take the next flight up there and don't test me because I will."

"Dad—"

"Listen to your mom. Talk to Lola and if she's adamant, then take the test. End of discussion."

I say nothing else because I start to feel panic rise. I try to think of every scenario where this could all be some kind of nightmare, but I'm only lying to myself.

This is reality...I could be a dad.

17

LOLA

Why didn't I think of this?

This is what you call a clout chaser, ladies and gentlemen.
If there's a child, where's the proof?
I swear people will do anything for attention.
At least she's hot.
Gotta get that paycheck.
It's funny what people will do for attention.
Of course someone would use TJ.
Someone call Maury.
Don't worry, TJ, we don't believe this.
She's for the streets.
It's obvious this nobody is lying.
Jersey chasers are really on the next level.
Who the hell is this girl even?
She really said child support.

The comments are endless. I don't have to continue reading to know what they're all saying about me. Meanwhile, everyone pities TJ. They all think he's a part of *my scheme* to get attention and money.

I bite the inside of my cheek, staring at the one comment that makes my stomach drop. It's not only because of who said it, but because under that one comment alone, it has almost one thousand likes and sixty replies agreeing with her.

This comment came from the girl TJ had a *study session* with, the girl who was all over him at Liquid.

alexiawatts *Nobodies always doing the most for attention, even if it means hurting someone else in the process. Anyone who knows TJ, knows this isn't true. Anyone who believes this lie shouldn't call themselves a fan or be associated with TJ.*

I shouldn't have clicked any further, but my fingers have a mind of their own and when I tap on her name, I see that she posted not even an hour ago.

The post is a picture of them together. He has his arm around her waist and she's pressed to his side, while they're both smiling. When I look at her caption, I can't help but bite my cheek harder.

alexiawatts *Always rooting for you!*

My nose burns at the bridge and my eyes well with tears. Making my vision blurry until all I can see are indistinguishable colors meshed on the screen as one.

I keep telling myself it's not worth it. That they don't know the truth. That it's all going to be okay, but the comments make me feel like shit and remind me of what happened two years ago. My parents' reactions when I told them, and my ex-boyfriend and his friends finding out and calling me a slut.

I try hard to keep my tears at bay, but it's too late as one tear trickles down my cheek, followed by another.

It's not until I hear the door being pushed open that I wipe them away and grab my stuff.

"I'm sorry. I hadn't realized I'd gone over my time." I sniffle, doing my best not to break down in front of whoever came in.

"Lola," Cara says from behind me, and when she wraps her arms around me, I melt into her embrace.

When I feel another pair of arms wrap around us, I don't have to look to know it's Daisy. I heavily sigh, letting myself relax into them as a few tears trail down my cheeks and cling to my chin.

I bask in the silence for a few seconds until I clear my throat. "I'm sorry."

"You have nothing to be sorry for," Cara softly says.

"We've talked about this before. You don't apologize unless it's necessary," Daisy chastises.

They both pull away from me and take a seat on either side of me. I don't look at them, but I know they're both looking at me. It doesn't dawn on me until a second later that they should both be in class, not here with me while I wallow in self-pity.

I didn't find out the news had leaked until I got to class this morning and saw Gabby. She was the first to tell me because apparently, it's everywhere.

I couldn't believe what I was hearing until I saw an article, followed by a post, followed by something else that led me to fall into a rabbit hole.

That's how I found myself holed up in one of the study rooms of the Atkins library. I needed to decompress before I stepped back out onto campus. To say I felt overwhelmed is an understatement. My hands won't stop shaking and sweating, and I'm overthinking the worst-case scenarios.

"How did you guys find me?" I sniffle, wiping some of the last tears with the back of my hand.

"Remember, we have each other's location," Cara supplies.

I nod, remembering that since school started, we decided to share our locations with each other in case of an emergency.

"They're saying a lot..." I don't have to explain for them to know what I'm talking about. "And nothing they say about me is good."

"Of course it's not, and it never will be good."

Cara scoffs. "She already feels like shit. There's no need to say that."

"Why pretend like we haven't seen what's been said? Those *hijos de puta, pinches pendejos, cabrones*...fuck, they got me cussing in Spanish," Daisy grumbles. "Those idiots feel defensive and they think they have the right to feel that way because they all live in this illusion that they know TJ. I *know* it hurts and I hate that you're hurting. If I could, I'd slap everyone who's talking shit."

A smile cracks on my lips because I wouldn't put it past her to do just that.

"I can't do that, but what I can tell you is that we all know the truth. We all know that TJ's the father, and I know it's not what you want to hear, but they look so much alike."

Daisy never fails to be honest.

"Those people don't know anything about you or TJ, and despite them knowing that, they'll continue to talk shit because they feel entitled to their opinion. Especially when it doesn't deal with them, but if the roles were reversed, it would be a different story."

Cara dryly chuckles. "Ain't that the truth."

"None of those people know and they won't know unless TJ decides to take the test." Daisy's jaw twitches, her nose flaring.

I told the girls that I'm not going to beg him to take the test. After what he said to me on Friday, I'm done. I can't go through what I went through with my parents again. It was exhausting, and the last thing I need is to fall into a hole of depression like I did two years ago.

So it's not going to happen. If Phoenix ever asks, I'll tell him the truth, but until then, I'm not going to bring it up.

"Regardless of a test, you don't need to prove yourself to anyone. Please don't feed into those negative comments," Cara sympathetically adds, rubbing my back.

"You've come too far to let this bring you down. You're a badass milf who gave birth to a child. Not only are you going to school full time, but you're working, and you have your own business."

"I wouldn't be here if it weren't for you guys." I smile at both of them, feeling tears prick in my eyes.

I will forever be grateful to my best friends as well as Daisy's parents for helping me. If it weren't for them, I wouldn't be where I am now.

"We didn't do anything but give you a little push. You did everything yourself, and we couldn't be any more proud." Cara smiles at me.

"But I seriously don't know what I'd do without any of—"

"Okay, okay," Daisy cuts me off, probably feeling awkward. She's affectionate but only to a certain extent. She's not a crier or a hugger. The last time I saw her cry was when Phoenix was born, and even then she tried to play it off. "Now that we've got that out of the way, I just want to know who started this shit."

I sigh, picking at the paint stuck underneath my fingernail. I've been wondering who could have said something, but no one comes to mind. The only people who know are the girls and TJ. At first, my mind went to TJ—I can't believe that I'm saying this —but I don't believe it was him.

I shrug. "Who knows, but I don't think it was TJ. His friends didn't act differently when we saw them on Saturday."

Surely, they would have said something if that were the case. They were all over us at Liquid, but not once did they make a suggestion about a baby. Though they did say a few things that frustrated me. It had been the reason why I went to the restroom to begin with.

The guys insinuated that TJ was jealous.

If only they knew he never wants to see me again. I didn't mention it to them, but I made it clear that I didn't care.

"And he texted me."

"What?"

"When?"

"What did he say?"

"Not too long ago." I unlock my phone and regret that I didn't exit out of Instagram because they see the picture of Alexia and TJ. "I saw her comment on one of the posts that was talking about me..." I tell them what happened and what led me to click on her page.

"You better hope I don't see her."

"She's not worth it, Daisy. She actually knows TJ. They're

close." I swallow hard, but the lump in my throat remains. "Anyway, this is what he said."

I exit Instagram and open his messages.

Nothing: We need to talk.

Nothing: This isn't a joke. We need to talk.

Nothing: Stop ignoring me.

Nothing: I just want to talk.

"What are you going to do?" Cara asks, setting my phone back down in front of me.

"I don't want to talk to him. I'm sure he'll want me to admit that I started this and that I was lying."

A devious grin lifts on Daisy's face. "You should meet him and while you're distracting him, I'll slash his tires," she says, pulling out her pocketknife.

I snort, pushing the tip of the blade down with my finger. "No, you're not going to do that."

Cara looks at me like I'm the one making irrational calls. "He drives a G-Wagon. I'm sure he can afford new tires."

"No," I deadpan.

My eyes drift down to my phone as it lights up. Three messages from Saint appear on my screen.

Saint: Midnight Brew at 4?

Saint: Come on, don't leave me hanging.

Saint: Coffee and anything you want will be on me.

He and a few other people texted me earlier, but I couldn't bring myself to reply. Especially Saint. He's been nothing but nice to me, but he's still friends with TJ.

"I can't believe you're still talking to him." Daisy wrinkles her nose.

"He's really sweet." I reread his messages, debating whether or not I want to meet him. "You would know if you gave him a chance as a friend."

"Fuck no." She stands from the chair, picks up her backpack, and slings it over her shoulder. She places her hand on my shoulder and squeezes it softly. "I'm sorry. I wish I could stay with you longer, but I need to go back."

"It's okay. You shouldn't have left your clinicals. And you"—I look at Cara—"shouldn't have skipped class."

Cara never misses class. Not only because she says she's going to get her money's worth, but because she genuinely enjoys going. If I were as smart as her, I'd definitely enjoy it just as much.

"You're important. End of story," Cara replies as she picks up her bag. "We're here for you, always."

"Always," Daisy says and with one final squeeze to my shoulder, she lets go. "I'll see you home, and whatever you do, don't look at those stupid comments. They're not worth it."

"And whatever you decide to do about TJ, we'll understand."

Once they're gone, I debate whether or not I want to skip class and meet up with Saint. What if he ends up being like TJ or worse?

Saint: Come on. You can't say no to free coffee.

Me: Okay. I'll be there.

18

TJ

Saint: She's here.

Saint: Don't be an ass.

As I step out of my G-wagon and stroll into the café, I know what I'm going to say to her.

Midnight Brew is a thirty-minute drive from campus. I never come here, but Saint does.

I don't see or recognize anyone from campus. There are a few booths and tables taken. The people who are sitting are too busy looking at their laptops or reading to focus on anyone coming in or out. Other than that, there are five baristas behind the counter, and when I lock eyes with one of them, she smiles at me.

I return the smile and head to the counter, placing two orders. I have no idea what I ordered, but the girl said it was their new fall drink and promised I'd love it.

As I wait for the drink at the other end of the counter, I search for Lola, but she's nowhere in sight.

"TJ," the barista calls my name, placing both of the drinks on the counter. "Looking for someone?"

"Yeah, I'm sure she's—"

"She's probably downstairs," she points at the black spiral stairs to our left.

"Oh, okay, thanks," I say and head down the stairs.

Unlike upstairs, there are shelves filled with books and people looking at them, reading, or on their laptops.

Walking a little farther into the room, I search for her until I find her sitting in a booth, tucked in the back. My heart accelerates and I hate that it does. Even when she's not around, it happens and when the guys talk about her to be assholes, it unnecessarily beats a little faster.

The thought of her makes my heart beat rapidly.

Blowing out a breath, I head in her direction but falter in my steps when I realize she's not alone. A guy sits right across from her, holding a notepad and a pen. He draws something on it, while she smiles and says something. She tries to peek at the pad, but he moves it right before she does.

I have no idea who the fuck he is, but I'm not going to stand here while they fucking flirt. I stalk toward them, keeping my eyes on him, and I know he senses me coming because his eyes instantly connect with mine.

"What are you—oh, you've got to be kidding me," Lola says, her voice filled with disdain. "I can't believe he set me up."

I ignore the idiot and look at Lola, who's frowning.

"I need to talk to you. You've been ignoring my messages."

"Hmm..." She smiles condescendingly. "Really now?"

The guy sitting across from her laughs, but when I glare at him, he looks away.

"Lo—"

"*You* made it abundantly clear you never wanted to see me again, and fortunately for you, I never want to see you again either. So you can leave." She dismisses me with her hand, turning her head to look back at the dumbfuck sitting across from her. She continues her conversation with him as if I'm not standing right in front of her.

I'm stunned for a second. No one has ever dismissed me like that.

"Lola, I need to talk to you."

"Louise," she corrects me. "And we have nothing to talk about. Anyway, like I was saying—"

Trepidation fills my chest, but I push through my anxiety. "I'm here to do what I should've done on Friday."

She cranes her head back to look at me. Anger swirls in her eyes, but it wavers when sadness mixes with it. A lump forms in my throat as I notice how puffy her face is and the red rimming her eyes.

It takes me back to Friday and the regret I felt at seeing her cry.

She peels her eyes away from mine and stares at the idiot, giving him an apologetic smile.

"I'm sorry, I—"

He slides out of the booth, and I move away so he can leave. Though it seems like he wants to prolong it because he doesn't immediately leave.

"My break is over anyway. I gotta go back, but I'll see you later."

"Okay, I'll see you later." She smiles at him.

"And you were right. I drew a latte." He shows her the notepad with the picture of a perfectly drawn cup.

She chuckles. "You're a little too predictable."

Okay, I'm over this. "All right, well, bye."

His smile tightens, but he doesn't say anything to me. "Bye, Lola, I'll see you later."

"Bye, Darius." She smiles at him, but when he's finally gone, she glowers at me. "I know what you want to hear, and it's not going to happen. You're wasting both of our time."

My lips part, but I can't bring myself to say what I need to say. I know I need to get it over with, but instead, I stand here like a dumbass, staring at her.

She lifts a brow, unimpressed. "Well?"

I sigh and slide into the booth across from her, and in the process, my legs end up grazing hers. One would think she was set on fire because she jolts in place and quickly moves her legs away. Though she can only move so much because the booth isn't the biggest and my legs are long as fuck.

One of her legs ends up in between mine and the other on the other side of me. She doesn't say anything, but she glares at me like it's my fault.

"Don't look at me like that. I can't help it."

"Whatever."

I hold back the urge to make a smart-ass comment, knowing it's not going to do me any good. She's already pissed, and I know if I'm not careful, she'll end up leaving.

I sigh, setting one of the cups in front of her. "I got this for you."

She stares at it for a moment too long and then slides it back. "I don't want it."

"But I bought it for you." I slide it back.

Lola closes her eyes for a moment as her chest rises on an inhale. She releases a long breath and reopens her eyes. I think she's going to push it back, but then she picks up her purse that was sitting to the side and pulls out her wallet. She pulls out a twenty-dollar bill and places it right in front of me.

"I'm going to take this because I hate wasting, but I don't need nor want *anything* from you. This is for today and the last two times you bought me coffee. Don't do it again."

"Lol—Louise," I correct myself when her scowl deepens. "I don't want your money. I chose to buy this for you." I slide the twenty back in her direction.

"I'm not doing this." She goes to stand and in my panic, I wrap my hand around her wrist.

I realize how wrong this is the second I do it, and I instantly regret it but not for the reasons I should.

Dropping my hand, I swallow and take the twenty. "Don't go."

Hesitation sets in her eyes as they flicker to the stairs. I think at any second, she's going to leave, but she doesn't.

"I never wanted this to happen and I didn't say anything. If you came here to get me to lie to you because it's what you want to hear, it's not going to happen." She wraps her hand around the cup, softly drumming her fingers along it.

"I thought you had said something, and I—"

She scoffs. "Do you not realize why I wanted to tell you in private? You can't tell me you haven't seen what they've been saying about me. You really think that's what I wanted?"

"About you? They're talking shit about me too."

I stare at her, confused, when she pulls her phone out of her purse and unlocks it. She taps the screen a few times until she looks at me then back down at her phone.

I feel so sorry for TJ. He doesn't deserve this. Of course someone would use TJ for attention. No one believes her. It's always the jersey chasers doing shit like this. Everyone knows what she's after. I wouldn't be surprised if she got passed around by the entire team. It's bitches like this who crave attention. TJ is going to enter the draft and she's going to try to take all his money. Desperate, attention-seeking cunt.

If I didn't feel like shit before, I definitely feel it now. My jaw hardens at the way her lip quivers and her voice cracks.

"Okay, that's enough."

"Enough? You think that's enough?" Lola's nose crinkles as sets her phone down. "You think you can just say enough and the comments will somehow disappear? They're not, but don't worry about what they're saying about you. The majority pity you, and if they're not feeling sorry for you, they're just shocked you knocked up *some* random girl. Although the shock didn't last long because they say it happens *all* the time. So don't worry, you'll be another guy who knocked up a girl, but me, I'm the one who ruined everything for *you*. I know you believe I said something, but I didn't. You're *not* worth any of this."

She raises the cup to her lips and looks away, but I still see the gloss that coats her eyes and the way her hand trembles around the cup.

I've never hated myself more. This is the one time I needed to think before I spoke and I didn't.

"I-I just thought—"

"You don't need to explain yourself to me. You told me exactly what you thought on Friday." The harsh expression on her face tells me she's done, and at any second, she's going to get up.

Nerves rise and the trepidation returns. "I want to take the test."

I know I was adamant I didn't want to take one, but as I was driving, I couldn't stop the thoughts that whirled in my head. Nor could I stop the overwhelming need to know if it's true. Although there is this niggling feeling that it is, and I can't shut it off no matter how hard I try.

I tried to make myself believe it was a lie, but no matter how many times I told myself, I couldn't believe it. The longer I sit here and stare at her, the deeper the realization nestles inside of me that she's not lying.

Lola's eyes go round. "You want to take a test?"

I nod and swallow thickly, wiping my sweaty palms on my jeans. "Yeah. I should have agreed to that on Friday, but I was too angry and...I thought you were lying."

I pick up my cup, but I don't get to drink it when I feel Lola's palm on my knee.

"Your leg was bouncing and it was rubbing against mine."

How didn't I realize I was doing that? It took a lot of therapy sessions to control my bouncing knee every time I got nervous, and I thought I got better at controlling it, but I guess not.

"No, I'm sorry," I say and try to shift my legs to the side again, but it's pointless when my legs graze hers again. I sit still and take a sip of my drink to control the urge to move again.

The drink is delicious, but it's hard to enjoy the taste of cinnamon and maple when Lola is staring at me with a look I can't decipher.

"Do you really want to take a test?"

"Yeah, I do."

She muses, pursing her lips. "I'll need to find a clinic and—"

"I've already found one. It's not too far from here. If you want, we can do it tomorrow?"

After I came to terms with the idea of taking a test, I had Mom and Dad help me find a place that would give us the results as soon as possible.

She fiddles with the sleeve of her cup. "I have to work tomorrow and Thursday, but I'm free on Friday."

"Okay, well, I'm going tomorrow because I'm going to be busy Friday, but I'll send you the location."

"Oh...okay."

"Because of basketball." I don't know why I explain myself to her, but I can't bring myself to stop. "With the season coming up, we're practicing more."

"Right, I'll go on Friday," Lola says before she slides out of the booth.

For some reason unbeknownst to me, my fingers jerk and I feel the need to stop her. I don't have a clue why, but I don't do it. I watch her grab her stuff and stand at the end of the table.

Lola hesitates, her lips parting and then closing, but then she shakes her head. "Bye."

There's more I want to say, but I stop myself. I did what I needed to do, and that's all that matters. Right?

"Bye..."

I watch her walk away, and just like Friday and Saturday, it feels wrong.

19

TJ

Ten days.

That's how long I've had to prepare for this moment. I should've known that no amount of time will be enough to prepare for this. As I sit on the side of my bed, holding the white envelope that will determine the rest of my life, nothing has ever felt heavier.

Anxiety has taken over, my palms won't stop sweating, my knee won't stop bouncing, and my heart is beating haphazardly against my rib cage.

"TJ!"

"What?" My head whips to my door.

I didn't realize I zoned out until I see Saint poke his head through the small crack.

"I knocked on the door a few times, but you didn't answer. I'm just making sure you're okay." His clear blue eyes flicker to the still unopened envelope in my hands. "I know it's not any of our business, but we're here if you need anything."

Saint pushes my door wide open. The rest of my roommates stand next to him. Aside from Coach, my parents, and Lola knowing about the test, I told the guys. Despite our arguments and disagreements, I trust them more than I trust anyone else.

I jerk my head, ushering for them to come in.

Saint sits next to me, Jayden takes the chair, Jagger takes the floor, and Landon leans against the wall. They don't say anything, but their silence is louder than words as they all look at the envelope.

It might be because they're here, but some of the tension and pressure subside. With a deep inhale, I rip the side and pull out two pieces of neatly folded papers inside. Releasing a shaky breath, I unfold them and read the first letter.

Paternity Test Certificate
Theodore Jackson Kingston May 26.
Phoenix Larson March 6.

I skim the letter, skipping over the parts I already know. Laying the first paper on the bed, I read the second one, and my eyes instantly land on the results. There is a chart with three rows. One titled DNA-System, the second row DNA-criteria with my name, and last DNA-criteria Phoenix Larson.

I skim over the chart. When I get to the bottom, I hold my breath.

Conclusion:
Based on our analysis, it is practically proven that Mr. Theodore Kingston is the biological father of the child Phoenix Larson.

Ten, twenty, thirty times, I reread the conclusion. Each time, I still find it hard to believe. Although I shouldn't because deep down, I knew this would be the outcome.

I'm a...father.

Oh my God, I am a father.

"What does it say?" Saint asks, breaking through my shock.

My lips part, but no words come out. I try again, but my mouth feels too damn dry.

"TJ..." Jayden cautiously says.

"Hmm." I can't focus on anything he's saying because it's all on the paper. The words blend together until all I see are black dots dancing in my vision.

"What does it say?"

My silence is answer enough, but I know they need to hear me verbally say it. They weren't the only ones; the paper is enough confirmation, but I know I need to hear myself say it out loud.

"I—" I clear my throat at the gruffness and strain in my voice. "It's positive, the test." I swallow, shifting my gaze away from the paper to the guys. "I'm a father. Phoenix, the kid, he's—he's my kid."

All of their expressions are the same except for Landon. His is stoic. Shockingly, he doesn't say anything, doesn't make a smart-ass remark, nor do any of the other guys. Though what could they say? Congratulations?

Saint takes the paper from my hands. When he's done reading it, Jagger takes it and then Jayden. Landon is the only one who doesn't look at it, not that he looks interested.

"Okay, but Phoenix is a bad-ass name." Saint grins, nodding to himself.

"Are you serious?" Jagger stares at him.

"Yeah. I mean, could you imagine if Lola named him Stewart or some shit?"

I can't believe it, but I really like the name, but I can't share Saint's enthusiasm.

"Jesus fucking Christ, TJ," Landon sharply says, pinching the bridge of his nose.

"What—"

"I get it's not what you wanted, but what did you expect? You had sex. Kids come from sex, you dumb fuck." There's a bite in his tone as he looks at me, annoyed. "I get you're shocked, but you're going to have to get your shit together. You have your answer. Now you need to make a choice. Be a father or leave this shit behind and act as if you never knew. And if you decide to walk away, make sure you *never* look back because the last thing that kid will ever need is hope from someone who will never be there."

His words are like a shower of cold water, pulling me out of a haze and bringing me back to reality. Never put it past Landon to be so harsh and blunt, but he's right. I need to get my shit together and make a choice.

"You're right."

"So what are you going to do?" Jagger asks.

20

LOLA

Nothing: I'll be there in 5 minutes.

TJ TEXTED ME TWO HOURS AGO, ASKING IF WE COULD meet up because he finally got the results. He didn't go into specifics, but I know he's going to say one of two things. Either he's going to want to be part of Phoenix's life or he'll tell me he doesn't.

If it were up to me, I wouldn't have agreed to meet him. If it were up to me, I would have ignored the message. I would have pretended as if he didn't exist and moved on with my life, but despite physically wanting to do that, mentally, I can't move on.

Even though I never want to see him again, I know I can't make that decision for Phoenix. If there's a chance TJ actually wants to be in his life, I'm not going to be the one to take that away from him. Even if it means I'll have to interact with TJ in the process.

I don't care that he went out of his way to tell his followers to stop harassing me. Surprisingly, that's all it took for most of it to stop. Occasionally, I'll get stares around campus, and there are a few people on social media still calling me names, but it's not as bad as last week.

None of his friends have said anything to me. I've seen them around campus, and they think I don't notice them looking at me, but I do. As far as Saint and Jagger go, I haven't seen them in class, but Saint occasionally texts me. Polly doesn't treat me differently. She must have sensed I was uncomfortable talking about it because she hasn't brought it up.

If only everyone else were like that.

I heave out a sigh and before I get to close my eyes, I hear a car pulling up. When I turn my head, I see TJ's black G-Wagon parked next to me.

This is for Phoenix. I tell myself as I step out of my car.

"Hey, sorry I'm late."

"It's fine."

His hair is damp and his shirt is wrinkled, but despite that, he looks good. I'll never admit this out loud, but I can't deny how good he looks.

"I had practice. This is embarrassing, but I washed my clothes and never took them out of the hamper," he explains. His gaze drops to the wrinkled part of the long sleeve on his shirt and back up to me.

"You don't need to explain yourself to me." I shrug, hoping I don't look as annoyed as I feel.

I shouldn't be annoyed. I know why he's late and it doesn't look like he did it on purpose. Especially when I notice two cups in his hands. But I don't focus on them as I notice the bracelet. It barely peeks from under the sleeve of his shirt, but I see it.

He holds out one large cup, distracting my thoughts from the bracelet. It takes everything in me not to take it. I barely slept last night.

"I got you this."

"I don't have money with me right now, and I don't want it." I fold my arms against my chest and take a step back. "Can we just talk so I can leave? I have things to do."

He swallows, his Adam's apple rising and falling, but he doesn't retract his hand. "I don't want your money, and I—"

"TJ—"

"Lol—Louise." He sighs. "I'm sorry for everything I said. I know this isn't going to fix anything and I didn't bring this so you could forgive me. I bought this because I...I thought of you. It's something we haven't tried before. Please...just take it."

"But you said—"

"I know what I said and I'm really fucking sorry, and I know no amount of sorrys will ever be enough, but I really am. I'm sorry, Louise."

The sincerity in his voice, along with the warmth and softness of his eyes, *almost* crumble the wall I built. But he's right. No amount of sorrys will ever be enough.

I take the cup, making sure my fingers don't touch his.

His brows lift, probably stunned that I took it without arguing with him, and a faint, relieved smile curls his lips.

"I'm taking this because I really need it. Next time I see you, I'm going to pay you." As his lips part, I shake my head, letting him know I'm not going to argue with him. "And just to make it clear, I don't care about your apologies." The smile on his face fades, and there's a slight tug in my chest, but I ignore it. "I'm not here for you or me. I'm here for Phoenix."

I used to dream of these unrealistic scenarios where TJ, Phoenix, and I could have been a... family. It sounds stupid and immensely far-fetched, but it's not like I have control over what I dream. When I'd wake up in the middle of the night, sometimes those dreams felt so real...I'd continue living in the dream while I was awake.

But in the end, they were all just dreams. Nothing real. Just like this moment right here.

As TJ and I stand in front of each other, we'll always be nothing more than two people who have a baby together.

"Right, that's what I'm here to talk to you about."

He tips his head in the direction of the park, eyeing a wooden table that's next to a pond. I smile to myself, knowing Phoenix would love to come here.

"Have you been here before?" TJ asks.

"No, it's my first time here. Why?"

"You asked me to meet you here. I thought you'd been here before."

"This park falls right in the middle. I thought it'd be fair if we met halfway."

"Halfway?" I hear the confusion in his voice.

"I live an hour away from campus. I'm too exhausted to drive an hour back, so I found this place. It's the same distance for both of us."

"If I had known, I—"

"Don't worry about it. It's not a big deal."

The last thing I need is for him to feel like he has to go out of his way for me. Like getting this stupid coffee that I have yet to try.

He says nothing as we get to the table. When we take a seat, right across from each other, his leg grazes mine like they did at the coffee shop. I try to move my legs, but somehow they still end up touching his legs.

"Sorry, I really can't help it."

"Of course you can't," I sardonically say.

"I can stand if you want?" I offer.

"No, you're fine."

I bring the cup to my lips and slowly take a sip, making sure I don't burn my tongue. I attempt to focus on the sweet taste of caramel and what tastes like brown sugar cinnamon, but his knee rubs on the outside of my thigh.

"So..."

"I, uh." He releases a low breath and rakes his fingers through his hair. "I know it's not what you want to hear, but I'm sorry. I can't change what I or anyone said, but I just want you to know that I'm really sorry. When you told me, I thought—I thought you were trying to use me. You wouldn't believe the people who've tried to use me..."

I dryly chuckle.

"Say it," he says.

I contemplate it, but instead, I shake my head. "It's pointless. I just want to—"

"An asshole. A piece of shit. You can say it, Lola, I know that I'm the biggest fucking asshole for making assumptions. Don't hold back."

I brush my bangs away. "It wouldn't make me feel any better." I shrug as the reminder of what's been said about me online filters through my head. The ache in my chest returns as if it were the first time I was reading those hateful comments. "I just want to move on. Like I said, I'm not here for us. I'm here for Phoenix."

I shift my gaze away from his and stare off into the distance, staring at the sun as it slowly starts to set. Making the sky look like cotton candy with shades of pink, purple, and streaks of yellow.

"I want to be in his life, and I don't want you to hate me."

TJ's words draw me back to him. They replay as if they're stuck on a loop, but still, I have a hard time believing that what he said is true.

It shouldn't be shocking considering this is something I anticipated, but I was leaning more toward him not wanting anything to do with Phoenix.

"You really want to be in his life?"

TJ sits up straighter and rests his hands on the table, interlocking his fingers together, but he releases them and instead wraps a hand around the cup. His knee bounces, rubbing against my leg. His shoulders are tense and apprehension marks his face.

"Yeah, I do. If I'm being honest, this scares the shit out of me. I'm having a hard time wrapping my head around the fact that I'm a...father, but if you let me, I want to be part of Phoenix's life."

"I don't regret having Phoenix, but being pregnant at nineteen wasn't something I wanted. There were many opportunities I missed out on, things I had to turn away, and people I...lost."

"I can't believe that we trusted you. After everything we've done

for you, this is how you repay us? I can't believe our daughter is a whore."

"I'm not sure we can call her our daughter anymore."

"Peaches?"

I blink, pulling myself out of the flashback. I hate myself for going there, for thinking of them.

I glare at him. "Don't call me that."

"Sorry." His cheek twitches, and I can tell by the amusement that flashes in his eyes that he's not sorry at all. But then the expression on his face softens, and from my peripheral, I see his free hand reach out toward me, but he never touches me. "I'm sorry about everything. For what I said, for how I reacted. You didn't deserve that. I'm really sorry."

"I told you it's fine. I just want to—"

"I know what you want, but I just don't want you to hate me." He runs his fingers through his hair, dropping his head for a moment. And when he picks it up and our eyes lock, I see the desperation shining in his eyes, but I must be seeing things. "I really don't."

Despite what my brain may or may not want to believe, I remind myself who I'm here for.

"I don't feel anything for you." I don't understand why the sinking feeling in my stomach returns, but it does, and when I see his shoulders sag and the warmth in his eyes evaporate, it sinks deeper. "I don't hate or like you. I already told you why I'm here, and if you're serious about being there for Phoenix, then I need to say this.

"If you want to be in his life, I need to know that you're *really* going to be there. I need to know that you're not only going to be there when it's convenient for you or because you feel like it. I understand your life is hectic and you have a lot going on, but so do I and I still make time for him. So I'm here to tell you I don't have time for excuses or bullshit. The last thing I want is to disappoint him because you decided this was too much for you." I pause, licking my dry lips. "I understand this is all new to you. I know it's nerve-racking walking into something you were never prepared for, but I'm not going to let you do this alone. I'm going to be here every step of the way until we can figure out a way to co-parent."

Silence envelops us until he stretches his hand out and lays it on top of mine, completely engulfing it. I don't understand why he's touching me until I look at my other hand and see how it trembles.

"I'm sorry. I shouldn't have touched you." He removes his hand but keeps it right across from mine, to where our middle fingers graze. "I don't make many promises, but I promise, no excuses or bullshit. Birthdays, holidays, parent-teacher meetings, I'll be there. I promise. I'll do everything I can to be there for him, and if you—"

I cut him off, pulling my hand away. "You only need to be there for Phoenix. That's all I need you to do."

A resigned exhale falls from his lips and he curtly nods. "Okay. So when can I meet him?"

"I have to work tonight and tomorrow morning, but we could meet tomorrow, here at four?"

"Are you sure you want to meet here? I can drive to your—"

"Phoenix doesn't know you. It would be best if we didn't take this too fast."

"You're right. I'll be here tomorrow at four."

Neither one of us says anything. We revel in the silence as the sun hides beneath the lilac cotton clouds.

For the next few minutes, we say nothing but watch the sunset and drink our coffee until we're finished.

21

TJ

SOMETHING SMACKS MY FOREHEAD, DRAGGING MY thoughts away from Lola and Phoenix down to the crouton on the table in front of me. When I look up, Jag tosses a crouton in the air and catches it in his mouth.

"I called your name. You didn't answer," he says through a chew, giving me a half shrug.

"I told you to stop calling me that shit." I huff.

The corners of his lips twitch. "Oh, come on, don't be like that. It's either going to be Teddy or *baby daddy*. Take your pick because TJ is too boring."

"Neither." I raise both middle fingers at him.

Jagger grins, clearly amused by my annoyance. "I'm not the one who started it." He holds back a laugh as he slides his phone across the table until it's lying in front of me. "Look."

I know I'm going to regret looking, and I do when I drop my gaze to the comments on Saint's live. The guys weren't going out today, so he decided to go live and cook with Landon and Jayden.

I skim over the comments, attempting to ignore the ones that talk about me, but it's hard when most of them are about me.

Are we not going to see our baby daddy cook too?

Where is our baby daddy?

If TJ was my baby daddy I wouldn't know what to do with myself.

Are we going to see the kid?

Honestly TJ being a dad is the hottest thing ever.

DILF!

TJ I'd make a great stepmom!

I'm very good at changing diapers if you need a nanny.

"Damn," I mumble under my breath as I slide the phone back to him.

"You should give the people what they want, *baby daddy.*" He snickers, tossing another crouton in the air.

I pick up the crouton he threw at me and toss it at him. Unfortunately, he moves in time before it hits him.

He laughs and says something else, but I ignore him. I focus on the guys as they cook just a few feet away from us. While Landon hates going live, he loves to cook, and Jayden loves both. He knows how to cook and loves the attention. Although when Landon's on it, the attention is always on him and his accent. I don't understand what the big deal is, but the girls go fucking crazy over it.

"All jokes aside, when are you going to announce that you do have a kid or are you not going to do it?"

I blow out a breath, hating myself as my knee starts to bounce. Thankfully, he can't see it, but still, the thought of him seeing through me makes me feel anxious.

"If Lola's okay with it, I'll announce it today."

There were a lot of things I should have asked her yesterday, so many things I should have said, but I froze. It's pathetic, I know, but today I'll make sure to say everything I need to say.

My phone buzzes on the table.

Alexia: Are you free tonight?

Alexia: You know I'm here for you if you need to talk or need a distraction.

She's been texting me since the news leaked and has offered to let me vent or to use her as a distraction. As tempting as it all sounds, I'm not in the mood. The distraction would be great as hell, but I know it would only be temporary.

And knowing her, she'll try to pry information out of me. She may come off as empathetic, but she's far from it.

Flipping my phone over, I slide it to the side and away from me.

"*Buon appetito stronzis.*" Saint sets two steaming plates of pasta in front of Jagger and me.

I'm not sure when they stopped cooking, but the guys are setting everything up on the table. I don't even ask if they need help because they pull their chairs back and take a seat.

"I can't believe TJ wasn't on the live, and still he got more attention than Landon normally does," Jayden says, picking up the bowl of salad and adding some to his plate. "Maybe I should have a kid."

Jag bursts out laughing. "You with a kid, Thompson?"

"You really want to go there? You don't even know how to cook. I'm sure your child would starve before making it to the second day," Jayden quips.

The guys, Landon included, nod in agreement, murmuring a low yeah as they stuff their mouths with pasta.

"Fuck all of you. TJ doesn't even know how to cook. Did you all forget he almost burned the house down?" he replies defensively, pointing his fork filled with pasta at me.

"*You* and TJ," Landon corrects him. "You and TJ almost burned the house down. TJ panicked because the pasta caught on fire, and you put the dry rag on top of it."

Landon and his ability to remember everything down to the detail is not only freaky but annoying.

A reminiscent smile curves Saint's lips. "That's right. I feel bad for Phoenix. He's fucked."

"Just because I don't know how to cook doesn't mean he's fucked," I argue, but when they become silent, their forks clicking against the plate, I roll my eyes. "You know what, I'm done talking about this."

"Doesn't matter. Your cooking is irrelevant. What I want to know is what that big-ass bear is doing in your car," Jayden asks through a mouthful. "And did I see candy in there? Isn't the kid one? Can he eat that?"

I arch a brow. "You looked inside my car?"

Saint raises a hand. "I looked too, but you can't blame us. The bear is sitting in your passenger seat."

"Phoenix likes Winnie the Pooh."

After Lola and I left the park, I drove around for a while to clear my head. It wasn't until I passed an outlet mall that I got the idea to get Phoenix something. I may not know a single thing about being a parent, but I do know a thing or two about kids.

The past three summers, I've been part of the summer basketball camp that NCU hosts for kids. And over the holidays, we not only buy Christmas gifts for kids, but we also spend time with them. Some of them don't even want presents. They just want to spend time with us. I've not spent a lot of time with kids under the age of five, but I've held a lot of babies and toddlers during meet and greets.

Jagger cackles. "I'm sorry, but isn't it funny your name is Teddy and your son likes bears? Isn't that fitting?"

"No," I deadpan.

"And what about the candy?" Jayden arches a brow. "Isn't he too little for that?"

"Phoenix is a year and six months old. He's not too little, and they're maple puffs that easily dissolve. They're his favorites and Lola said he eats them all the time."

My knee starts to bounce at the thought that he might not like them. I don't know why I'm worried, but when I try to get my knee to stop, the other starts bouncing. I try to focus on the pasta in front of me, but when I feel all eyes on me, the bouncing stops and I look up.

"What?"

"Nothing," they say in unison and continue eating.

"So when are we going to meet him?" Saint questions.

The rest of the guys don't have to voice it out loud for me to know they're also curious when they're going to meet him.

There are only a few people who know about me having a kid. Though most speculate that it's true after I pretty much told everyone on social media to fuck off and leave Lola alone. Coach and Janet didn't approve of how I went about it, but it worked. Although people are still talking shit, it's not as bad as before. It's not what I want, but I only have so much control over what people do on social media.

I also had Gabby, Jagger, Landon's best friend, and our media coordinator for the basketball team make a post on not bullying.

With my fork, I drag my pasta from one side to the other. "I don't know. My parents want to meet him, but I don't know what Lola will say. I still have to talk to her and see how all of this is going to work out before anyone can meet him."

When I shared the results with my parents, I thought they were going to cuss me out or tell me what a disappointment I am. I thought they were going to say that I ruined my life, but they didn't.

They said it's pointless to dwell on something that already happened and to keep moving forward. They gave me a speech on the importance of being a good father, and then they asked when they could meet him.

"You know you're going to do all right." Jagger's tone is serious but reassuring.

"A lot of people have kids at a young age, and they do just fine. By the looks of it, Lola seems to be doing all right and you will too." Landon doesn't look at me, but his words are enough to ease some of the tension.

"And we got your back if you need anything." Saint flashes me a genuine smile, letting me know he's all in and won't hesitate to be there for me.

I've been interviewed countless times. I've played in front of thousands of people. I've given speeches in front of large crowds. But all those things seem so minuscule compared to what I'm about to do.

I've been on national television more times than I can count, but the thought of meeting a kid who happens to be mine makes my nerves skyrocket.

I stare at the bear I got Phoenix and the container of maple-flavored puffs Lola says he loves so much. I don't know if this is too much, but when I told Mom and Dad about it, they said it's one way to win him over.

That thought makes me nervous because what if he doesn't like me? It's ridiculous to think that because he's only one, and I'm never an overthinker, but what if he doesn't?

The sound of a car parking next to me brings me out of my thoughts. When I see Lola step out of her car, I wipe my sweaty palms against my thighs and grab the stuff I bought for Phoenix and the coffee I bought for Lola and me.

I didn't buy her coffee in hopes that she'll forgive me, but if it helps her like me even a little that'll be great. Not that she needs to like me, but it only makes sense that we get along for the sake of Phoenix, right?

Getting out, I shut the door behind me, but my lungs constrict, making it painful to breathe. Lola stands just a few feet away from me with Phoenix propped on her hip.

I'm not entirely sure how to explain every single emotion coursing through me, but as I stare at Phoenix, whatever I was feeling seconds ago withers into nothing.

And then I'm reminded of her post and caption.

My Muse. My Little Bear. My Phoenix.

I remember thinking he looks nothing like her, and of course he doesn't. He looks...just like me. He has everything I have while there's not one part of him that resembles Lola.

From the curls on his head, down to the color of his eyes, he looks every bit like me. And he's only one, but he looks tall.

Phoenix nestles deeper onto Lola's chest, trying to get as physically close to her as he can. He lays his head on her shoulder and eyes me warily, but when he looks at the bear, I see the curiosity in his gaze.

He timidly smiles and I swear if I was looking at a picture of myself at his age, I wouldn't be able to tell the difference.

The words leave my mouth before I can stop myself. "He looks nothing like you."

I know I fucked up gravely when a deep scowl pulls on her face and she rolls her eyes. "Yeah, I know. I don't need the reminder, but at least now you can't deny him."

I feel the bitterness laced in her voice, and her attempt to make me feel like shit for what I said. But despite her jab and the sting I feel, I can't be mad. I deserve it.

"I'm not. I promise." Inhaling deeply, I slowly exhale and when I finally lock eyes with her, I feel okay. And everything feels as if it's going to be okay. I have no idea where that came from, but I ignore it and hold out the cup toward her. "I got you this."

"I told you—"

"I got him the bear and snacks. It's only fair I got you something."

I can't help the way the corners of my lips rise at the excitement that grows in his eyes. He still looks hesitant, but slowly it crumbles away the longer he stares at the bear.

"You didn't have to do that." She breathes out a heavy sigh, but her eyes do a double take at the two cups in my hand. "I only brought you money for one—"

"I don't want your money. I just want you to take the cup, please. It's something new," I plead.

Her lips tighten into a straight line, and I think she's not going to take it, but then she uses her free hand to grab it. I suck in a breath when her soft fingers graze mine. Out of nowhere, I feel a shock that disrupts the way my heart beats against my chest.

"Thanks. You didn't have to, and you didn't have to get Phoenix the bear. He has a lot of them at home." She smiles down at him.

I revel in the smile. I know it's not meant for me and I know it won't last long. Since the day I fucked up, she hasn't smiled at me. I know I deserve it, but fuck, I hadn't realized how nice it would be to see her smile again.

"B-bear."

He stretches a chubby little hand, wiggling his fingers for me to give it to him. The hesitation is gone, replaced with excitement.

She peers down at him, softly chuckling at his giddiness and the way he squirms against her. "You want the bear?"

"Yes!" He eagerly nods, his curls bouncing with every movement.

"Before you get the bear, I have to tell you something, okay?"

He bobs his head, eyes laser focused on the bear.

"This is TJ. He's..." She pauses, contemplating what she wants to say. "He's your...dad."

I freeze, not expecting Lola to flat-out say it. Although I'm not sure there is a perfect way to tell him. Because how does anyone drop news like that?

There's a moment of silence as Phoenix's gaze pulls to mine. He tilts his head to one side, staring at me curiously. I didn't expect that wide, toothy smile that spreads across his face next.

"Bear!"

I chuckle at his enthusiasm and hold out the bear for him to take. "It's all yours, buddy."

When he takes the bear from my hands, I swear his eyes glitter and grow in size. He hugs it tightly as if he's afraid I'm going to take it away.

"I take it he really likes it." I smile.

"More like loves it. Phoenix has an insane obsession with Winnie the Pooh. Isn't that right?" She pokes his belly a few times.

I'm not sure what it is, but as I watch them, I feel the strong urge to hug them and protect them. I have no idea where that comes from, but the thought comes to a pause when he squirms against her and demands to be put down.

"Down," he says again until his wish is finally fulfilled.

I reach out to him when he wobbles, but Lola lays her hand on my arm and stops me.

"He's okay." She sheepishly smiles and removes her hand. "Sometimes he gets a little shaky but don't worry, the worst that can happen is that he'll fall."

My brows knit. "But if he falls, won't he—"

"He might, but he'll learn to be careful." She smiles at the look of confusion on my face. "I promise he'll be okay. If we hover, he'll become too dependent on us."

Us.

"Okay, but we can watch from a distance?"

"Oh yes, we're going to have to because—" It all happens too fast. Phoenix peeks over his shoulder at us, and without a second thought, makes a run for it. "Because that will happen."

It's shocking how fast he is, but I catch up to him in two steps and grab him before he can trip over the bear. "Slow down, buddy, you're going to fall." I lift him with one hand but instantly realize I did exactly what Lola said not to do. "Sorry, I—"

"It's okay. This is good for him, familiarizing himself with you and feeling comfortable around you. By the look of it, it doesn't seem like it will take much. I think you won him over with the bear."

A wave of relief washes over me, but soon it's mixed with different emotions that are hard to process.

"Down," he demands like he did to Lola.

As soon as I do what he says, he makes a run for it, but instead of grabbing him like I'm tempted to do, I let him be. Despite the worry that gnaws at me that he'll get hurt.

"Welcome to parenthood. This is only the beginning."

22

LOLA

"MORE!" PHOENIX LAUGHS, RAISING HIS ARMS IN THE air as I push him on the swing. "Push Win!"

TJ's eyes flicker between the bear and Phoenix, and then he looks at me. Because there's hardly anyone at the park and no one using the swings, I sat his bear in one of them.

I shrug, fighting back a smile. "It's better not to argue with him. Just push the bear."

His lips part as if he wants to say something, but instead, he smiles and does as he's told.

We push the swings without saying anything to each other. The only noise comes from Phoenix, the metal chains that squeak every so often, and a nearby family at the jungle gym.

I know what I need to say, and I know the longer I let this silence linger, the longer we'll be here. The last thing I want is to be with TJ more than I need to. We're here strictly for Phoenix. I should be happy that he came for him, but the hurt still lingers from his words. I should let it go, but I can't.

"Lola?"

I consider whether it's worth telling him not to call me that, but for the sake of not arguing in front of Phoenix, I don't correct him. I should be grateful he's not calling me Peaches.

"Hmm?"

"Do you like your coffee?"

As much as I want to tell him that I don't, I can't deny how good it is. Especially because it has the chocolate cold foam on top and four shots of espresso. If I wasn't mad at him, I'd hug him because this is exactly what I was craving this morning.

"Yeah, it's fine," I replied indifferently.

"If you don't like that one, I can buy you another."

I want to stay mad at him. No, I need to stay mad, but it's hard when he's looking at me like he'll drop what he's doing to buy me another coffee.

"There's no need for that. I really like this."

"You sure?"

"I promise." I force a smile.

"Okay."

I take a sip of my drink. I hate that at this moment, my eyes land on the stupid bracelet I gave him. Memories of that week resurface in my head, and as much as I dread the mere thought of them, the only good thing that came out of it is right in front of me.

Which brings me to the point of why we're here.

"I've been thinking about how we're going to make this work, and I think it'd be a good idea to see him at least once or twice a week. The more you're around him, the more familiar and comfortable he'll be with you."

"That sounds like a good idea." He smiles and it pains me to see it because it reminds me of how much he and Phoenix look alike and how much I liked that smile in the beginning.

"As far as our schedules go—"

"Oh, I almost forgot," he cuts me off, slipping his hand into his front jean pocket. He pulls out a neatly folded piece of paper and hands it to me. "It's the basketball schedule. I know you can look at it online, but I figured I'd go ahead and give it to you," he explains as I take it from him.

I'm not sure if I should be shocked or impressed that he went out of his way to do this.

"The season doesn't technically start until November, but we have Live Action this coming Friday," he says as I skim through the schedule, noting that their first game is right at the beginning of November. "They introduce the staff, the players, there's a scrimmage, and at the end, we do a meet and greet. It's cool and everyone has a lot of fun..."

TJ trails off and when I glance at him, he's staring at Phoenix and then his gaze shifts to mine. The smile on his face becomes small and I swear I see anxiety flash in his eyes, but when I blink, it's gone.

"If you want to come, I can get you tickets. Phoenix won't need one since he can sit on your lap, and if your friends want to come, I can also get them tickets."

My brows lift in surprise. "You want us to come?"

"Yeah, I do. My family is also going to be there, and they'd like to meet you and Phoenix."

If my eyebrows could rise any higher, I'm sure they would.

"They want to meet...us?"

He chuckles at the shock in my voice. "Yeah, they'd really love to meet you both.

Especially Phoenix. They want grandchildren and know my brother Ben and his wife don't have plans to have kids anytime soon, so they're excited."

"Oh..."

I know I need to let it go and move on, but nothing hurts more than knowing my parents wanted nothing to do with me or Phoenix, yet his parents are excited.

My heart clenches in my chest, and my eyes stupidly burn as the emotions I'm trying hard to bury away resurface again.

They didn't want me. They didn't want us. I tell myself over and over again.

"I have to work that night," I manage to say. I wasn't supposed to, but Juls begged me to work with her. My business has slowed down, so right now everything I make is coming from the museum.

The smile on his face falters. "Oh, that's all right. Maybe next time?"

"Yeah, next time." I look away, hoping that my stupid emotions don't expose me.

"Just let me know. I know how much Saint would like that."

I grin at the reminder of Saint texting me and begging me to give him Daisy's number. "She's actually not a fan of basketball. She's never watched a game and said the only way she would do it is if it was obligatory. So that should tell you enough."

"Wait, but do you like basketball?"

I laugh at his apprehension. "Yeah, I like it. I just never have time to watch it."

Relief washes over him. "Okay, good, but if you had time, would you come watch me—I mean come watch the team?"

"Yeah, I'd love to go. It just gets a little hard with work."

"I'm sure we could make something work." He coaxes with hope in his voice.

"Yeah..." I take another sip of my drink and redirect our conversation. "So back to you visiting, we'll just work around our schedules. It shouldn't be too hard to figure it out."

"I—" He clamps his mouth shut but only for a second. "Do you mind if I take a picture of him? My parents would really like to see him."

Once again, the ache returns, but I ignore it and force a smile. "Yeah, that's fine."

I stop pushing the swing and step to the side. "TJ is going to take a picture. Smile big for him, okay?"

"Kay," Phoenix replies giddily.

TJ stands in front of him and holds his phone out, but before he snaps the picture, he looks at me. "Is everything okay?"

Damn it. "Yeah, I'm fine."

He hesitates but doesn't pry. "Say cheese for me, buddy."

"Eese!" Phoenix smiles, bearing a wide, toothy grin as he looks at TJ's phone, but then his eyes dart to a tube filled with puff snacks. They triple their size, shimmering with happiness. "Want!"

"Is it okay if I give him some?" TJ questions.

"Yeah, it's all right." I lift Phoenix and set him to his feet on the mulch. TJ grabs his bear, and in awkward silence, we walk to the same table we sat at yesterday.

As I'm about to pick Phoenix up, TJ does it as if it's something he's always done and sets him in the middle of the table, facing the pond.

"Sorry, I should have—"

"No, it's okay." I round the table and sit right across from him. In the same spot as yesterday. And just like yesterday, I ignore how his leg grazes against mine.

"How many can he have?"

"Just five."

He opens the container and places five on top of the lid, then sets it in front of a very happy Phoenix.

"Can I ask you something?"

"Sure." I grin, watching Phoenix set a puff on the bear's leg. TJ watches him too and sets another puff on the lid.

"You said five," he supplies when I cock a brow.

I shouldn't smile at how cute that is nor do I argue with him because he has a point. Knowing Phoenix, he won't eat it because it's for his bear.

"I wanted to ask if you're okay with me making an announcement about Phoenix being *mine*." He fiddles with the sleeve of his cup, glancing at our son.

"You want to do that?"

His eyes drop back down to me. "Yeah, and I won't post his picture or anything like that. I just want everyone to know."

It's wrong I made the assumption that he would've been too embarrassed to do that. I didn't expect him to do it anytime soon. Maybe in a few weeks but not now. I didn't even think his parents would want to meet him.

Nothing is what I thought it was going to be, and I don't know how to feel about it.

"If that's what you want to do, but I don't care whether people know or not."

The damage is already done. Occasionally, I think about the things said about me. I shouldn't care because I'm not what those people say, but it still hurts.

He deeply sighs. "I don't care either, but it will shut a lot of people up and stop talking shi—crap."

Leaning forward, I rest my elbows on the table. "Just letting you know, for every bad word, that's ten dollars in the swear jar."

"You have a swear jar?" he asks, amused, as he also leans forward, resting his elbows on the table.

"Daisy is short-tempered. Sometimes it slips, and sometimes I let a word or two slip."

He flashes me a lopsided grin, leaning in closer. "I promise to do my best not to let it slip."

I pull back, realizing how close we are. "But anyway, I don't care what people say."

"But I do. I know I'm not any better than they are, but I'm not going to sit here and not do anything about it."

Nothing about his response sounds like a lie or something that he's forcing himself to say because he has to. There's nothing but genuine sincerity, and it's wrong to think this, but I wish there wasn't. It would make it easier to dislike him.

23

LOLA

"I DON'T UNDERSTAND WHO WOULD WANT TO SEE *THAT* on TV."

The pure, utter look of disgust on Julianna's face would make anyone think she's watching something disturbing, but the only thing on the screen is Landon. "I can't believe anyone watches *that* for entertainment."

Juls and I sit in the break room of the museum as we watch the Live Action. I wasn't going to watch it, and I'm definitely *not* doing this for TJ, but I promised Saint I would for him.

One by one, each player is being presented. Currently, Landon is walking across a walkway as an announcer calls his number, height, hometown, and name.

I stifle a laugh. "I mean, he's not bad to look at."

She scoffs dramatically, her dark brown eyebrows pinching together. "Not bad to look at? Just look at him. He has the personality of a rock. I seriously don't understand how anyone finds *that* fascinating."

I attempt to keep my smile at bay. "I never said he's fascinating to look at. And you know you can say his name."

"Absolutely not! It's like saying Beetlejuice three times. The last thing I want to do is summon the devil."

I snicker at the severity of her tone.

"And I didn't mean you. I meant my roommates and every other girl in my sorority. They all find him fascinating."

"Well, you have to understand..." I trail off, amused at the betrayed look on her face. I swear anyone would think I stabbed her in the back. He's immensely tall. The screen doesn't do him justice." TJ and the rest of the guys are tall, but Landon is the tallest among them all. "He has tattoos and an accent. You really can't tell me that's not hot."

She folds her arms against her chest, staring at me, unimpressed. "I've seen better looking sewer rats."

I snort, snatching a slice of cucumber from her Tupperware, and plop it in my mouth. I shift my gaze back to the screen and see that it's now Jagger's turn.

"Are you ever going to tell me why you hate him?"

"It's not worth talking about." She sighs and picks up a baby carrot. "Anyway, thanks for working with me tonight. I know this isn't how you want to spend your Friday night."

"I need the money and there's no one else I'd rather work with."

"I still feel bad that I didn't consider you probably wanted to go to the Live Action."

"It's okay. I didn't. I'd rather be away from anything that has to do with TJ." I wouldn't say this to anyone else, but I trust Juls. Not as much as I trust Cara and Daisy, but I know I can confide in her. "Some people stare, and they think I don't hear them talking about me, but I do."

Juls found out about TJ and me like everyone else did on social media. And like everyone else, she was shocked. She didn't bombard me with questions, only said if I needed anything, I could reach out to her. When he officially announced Phoenix was his son on Monday, she texted me and said she wasn't surprised because they look so much alike. Thankfully, she didn't pry because it seems that everyone is making it their mission to know about Phoenix, and how TJ and I met.

These past five days have been nothing but weird.

There's a podcast called The Unfiltered Three, run by three girls that go to NCU. Athletes, Greek life, parties, and anything that revolves around the university, they'll talk about it. TJ and I have been the center of their attention. On the front page of their website, there's an article about him and me.

Juls snuffs a dry laugh. "I swear I don't understand the obsession everyone has with these athletes. It's ridiculous." She aggressively dips the carrot in avocado-lime ranch and plops it in her mouth. "Most girls are talking about it because they wish it were them. They can't fathom it will *never* be them."

"If only they knew there's nothing great about this situation. Just a week ago, I was a clout-chasing jersey chaser. Now I'm known as *TJ's baby momma*," I grumble. Now that the news is out, no one refers to me by my name. "You know, I miss clout chasing jersey chaser. At least that had character."

Her lips quirk up into a sly smile. "You know, it should be the other way around. *Lola's baby daddy*. Speaking of *your* baby daddy." She glances at the TV.

The arena is semi-dark. Strobe lights produce white-and-blue lights, and there are flashes coming from the audience's phones.

Light fog surrounds the area that the players come from but becomes thicker when they're brought up. Like now, the fog has become denser and all the lights are focused on TJ as he's risen up to the stage wearing his jersey. The crowd becomes louder than before, clapping, whistling, and cheering his name as the announcer introduces him.

"A six-foot-six, from Miami, Florida, he wears number six. Ladies and gentlemen, TJ Kingston!"

People rise to their feet, cheering him on. By the beaming smile on his face, I can tell he's enjoying every second of this. He doesn't immediately start walking. He stands there, looking left and right as he takes in the crowd. He waves and smiles at everyone, and eventually, he walks across the walkway, giving everyone near him a high five.

I must have been staring for too long because when I look at Juls, she's smirking.

"Why are you looking at me like that?" I don't look at the screen again, in case my eyes betray me.

She grins, shaking her head, making her small, golden hoop earrings dangle. "No reason. We should get back to work. Break is over."

I don't push for her to tell me what she's thinking and grab three more cucumbers, stuffing them in my mouth. "Thanks for sharing your snack with me."

"Sorry it wasn't much."

"It's okay. I wasn't that hungry."

That's a lie. I was in a rush earlier. I forgot my lunch bag on the counter. Now I'm starving and counting down the minutes until it's time to go.

Grabbing my phone from my bag, I type out a quick message to Saint and then to Daisy.

Me: You looked good out there!

Me: I'll be out by ten and I know it's late but do you want to grab tacos? It will be on me.

My car is currently at the shop, and I won't be getting it back until tomorrow. I was going to get an Uber, but Daisy refused to let me do that. She said that because it's Friday night, it's going to be more expensive. I didn't argue and let her bring me to work.

I don't expect a reply, knowing she's probably working out. Tucking my phone back in my bag, I peer over my shoulder at the screen. The camera is focused on TJ as he warms up.

Shaking my head, I walk out before I start staring again.

"Don't forget we won't have class tomorrow," Juls reminds me.

Tomorrow the building where we teach class is going to be fumigated.

"I got it down in my planner." I hold it up along with my sketchbook that's cradled in the crook of my arm.

"You should seriously consider getting a new planner."

I smile at the concern on her face. "I know, but then I'd have to move everything over to the new one. And I'm worried that I'll forget to add something to the new one, and knowing me, that'll happen."

"That's fair because that would also be me."

We wave goodbye to Bill, the security guard, as we step out, but I don't make it far before I falter in my steps. The abrupt stop causes Juls to bump against my back and when the stuff in my arms almost falls, I snap out of my stupor.

"Did you forget something? Bill hasn't locked the door yet. I can—"

"No, I didn't forget anything," I quickly say. "Daisy's not here, but TJ is."

Grabbing my phone from my bag, I unlock it, and the second I do, I freeze.

"I don't know how it happened. I accidentally sent this to TJ instead of Daisy."

Juls peers over my shoulder, but hearing her laugh is not the reaction I expected. "You have him as *Nothing*? Oh my gosh, this is great."

"That's not the point."

She cackles. "I know it's not. I'm sorry, but you don't understand the *number* of girls in my sorority who would kill to have his number. It's hilarious that you not only have his number, but it's under *Nothing*. I'm sorry, but this made my night."

"I'm glad you find this amusing."

I go back to all my messages and click on Daisy's. The last thing I said to her was to have a good workout and that was the end of our conversation. When I click on TJ's, I see that I sent him the message I meant to send to Daisy.

"You were subconsciously thinking about him."

"I was not. I don't think about him at all."

That's a lie. It's hard not to think about him when I have a mini carbon copy of him at home. And then he texts me to see how Phoenix is doing, and sometimes I see him around campus.

"Okay." The amusement that drips from her tone tells me she's not buying it. "Do you want me to give you a ride home?"

The idea sounds tempting, but it wouldn't be fair for her. We live an hour away from each other. "No, it's okay. I'm just going to talk to him and call Daisy. Either way, Bill is still here."

"Are you sure?"

"I'm sure."

"If anything changes, just give me a call. I seriously don't mind." She pulls me in for a hug. "Good night, Lola."

"Night, Juls." I let her go and watch her walk to her car.

After she's gone, I stall in my spot, contemplating if I should text him and tell him to leave. But the longer I stand here, the more I realize how stupid it all sounds.

Making my way over to his SUV, I blow out a breath and tap his window. He surprises me when he doesn't lower it but gets out.

TJ's eyes sweep over me before they meet mine. "Hey, is everything all right?"

I look down, making sure I don't have any of the avocado dressing on my black dress or on my oversized burgundy blazer. But I see nothing, not even a wrinkle.

"I'm sorry that you drove all the way over here, but I didn't mean to text you."

He chuckles, nodding to himself. "Well, that explains everything. It makes sense now."

"Wait, how did you know I was here?" I never told him where I worked. When we were at the park, I kept our conversation to a minimum and only about Phoenix. Despite his attempt to make small talk, I didn't want to fool myself into believing he cares about anything I have to say.

"Saint."

Of course. He's the only one of TJ's friends who knows anything about me.

"I'm sorry that you drove all the way over here, but you don't have to wait for me. I'm just going to call Daisy and—"

"I'm already here. I don't mind dropping you off." A small, hopeful smile lifts on his face.

"I live an hour away and—" The rest of my words die at the back of my mouth as an embarrassingly loud grumble comes from my stomach.

"I know a really good taco truck just a few minutes from here and they have homemade drinks."

My mouth salivates and my stomach grumbles harder. If there's one thing I love more than tacos, it's fresh drinks, especially horchata.

"We live an hour away from each other, and—"

"We could live five hours away from each other and it still wouldn't make a difference. Come on, let me take you," he pleads, the smile on his face lifting higher, making it hard for me to say no. "I promise they will be some of the best tacos you've ever had."

Looking over my shoulder at the museum, I debate whether I should or shouldn't. When I glance back at him, there's something like hope that lingers in his eyes.

I know I should call Daisy because the last thing I need is to be around him, but instead, I send her a text.

Me: Don't worry about picking me up. I promise to explain everything when I get home. Love you!

"You know now my expectations are going to be high. If they're not good, you're going to pay," I say as I round his G-Wagon.

"And who said you're paying?" He follows me and opens my door. "Come on, get in. Prepare to be amazed."

24

TJ

"WHY DIDN'T YOU TELL ME THEY MAKE THEIR OWN tortillas?" Lola stares in awe at the plate of tacos in front of her.

"Forget the tortillas for a moment. I didn't know you spoke Spanish."

"I know a few sentences, but I'm not fluent." She picks up a lime wedge and squeezes it onto the meat. "Daisy and her parents taught me a few things. They've also taught Phoenix."

My brows rise, stunned by the new information Lola's giving me. When we met at the park last week, she hardly spoke to me, and I can't say I blame her. Honestly, I'm still surprised she agreed to come with me tonight, but I'm not complaining. I'll take every moment she decides to give me.

After all, we need to get along for the sake of Phoenix.

"You're telling me Phoenix can understand and speak Spanish?" I pick up the plastic bottle of green salsa and squirt the sauce on the tacos.

She laughs. "Ahh, sort of. It's still a work in progress."

I nod, handing the bottle to her. I tense when her fingers momentarily graze mine. She quickly takes the bottle, but I still feel the warmth of her fingers lingering on my skin.

"But back to the important topic. Homemade tortillas." She

holds the taco up, staring at it with admiration. It's amusing seeing her this excited. I don't think I've ever met someone who loves tacos as much as Jayden loves them when he's drunk. Granted, he loves any kind of food, drunk or not.

"So did I pass? Are you impressed?"

"I don't know. I have to try it first."

She chews slowly and then her eyebrows rise, as does the smile on her face. But that's not what sends me into sensory overdrive. It's the soft moan and the way her eyes flutter closed.

She shakes her head, taking another bite. "I—this—wow." She happily sighs.

"I'm going to need more than just a wow. What would you rate this?"

A wave of nostalgia hits me out of nowhere. I'm drawn back to the memories from two years ago.

Lola briefly tenses. When she finishes her taco, she takes a sip of her drink and clears her throat.

Did it cross her mind like it did mine?

"One hundred. This"—she holds up another taco—"is perfection. Possibly the best I've ever had. If you ever meet Daisy's mom, don't tell her I said that."

The radiant smile on her face is infectious. I'm grinning just as big as she is. "I promise, I won't say anything, but I'm glad I was able to meet your expectations."

I knew she sent it by accident. The guys also found out when Saint looked over my shoulder and read the message out loud. They pretended to choke as I was drinking water and pointed out it was desperate of me to show up when she didn't mean to send it to me.

Maybe it's desperate, but I just want her to stop avoiding me. I know why she does it, and I understand, but it doesn't mean I have to like it.

My knee knocking against her leg shifts my thoughts back to her. "Sorry, I really can't help it."

A faint smile tips on her lips. "I know. I should just get used to it, huh?"

"Yeah, you should. You're stuck with me for life so..."

I'm suddenly taken back to the moment I said these exact words, two years ago.

The beach, holding hands, the agreement that we were stuck with each other for life, but that's not what we had meant. We were stuck for life until she had to go.

I have no idea how I still remember that or how after not thinking about it in a while, it resurfaces in my head as if it happened yesterday.

Is she thinking about it too?

"You know I meant that because of Phoenix. We'll always be tied to each other." I joke to ease the awkward tension, but all she does is nod.

We fall into an awkward silence until we're done with our food and we get in my car. The only time she broke the silence was to thank me for the food, the ride, and to give me directions.

The sky rumbling in the distance reflects how tonight is going.

Fuck it.

Making a split decision without thinking, I pull to the side, far enough no one would be able to hit us.

"What are you doing?"

I turn the ignition off and twist my body to look at her. I push the button to turn on the light inside the car, and I swear if looks could kill, I'd be dead.

"What are you—"

"God, I'm so fucking sorry."

Her eyes drop to my bouncing knee. I hate how embarrassed I get, but I push through my discomfort.

"I know nothing is going to change what I said, but I just want you to know that I'm fucking sorry. If I could, I'd take everything I said back. I really would."

Something sparks in her eyes, but as quick as it comes, it fizzles away. "Take me—"

Lola flinches at the thunderous roar, and flashes of bright silver streak the night sky.

She grabs my hand, gripping it hard as rain pours harshly, the drops smacking the windshield like pelts. The water obscures the road ahead, making everything look like a fuzzy blur.

It's extremely loud, but not enough to drown out the way my heart thrashes against my chest. Blood pounds in my ears.

I look at her hand and clench my teeth as her fingernails sink into my skin. It doesn't hurt, but goddamn, does it feel good.

"Looks like we can't go home."

She looks down at our hands. She retracts her hands so fast, you'd think I was on fire. Though it feels like I am.

"We could've made it if you hadn't stopped."

"We weren't going to make it."

She drags her fingers through her hair, parting it to the other side. "There was no need for you to pull over or apologize. I'm over it."

I scoff. "Clearly, you're not."

"I am over it," she says through gritted teeth.

"No, because if you were, you wouldn't act as if I didn't exist. I know you've been avoiding me on campus."

She looks surprised, like she didn't think I'd notice.

I tried to pretend like I didn't at first, but I couldn't ignore the pang in my chest every time she'd turn the other way when she'd see me.

She shakes her head. "I don't know what you want from me."

"I...I want..."

She sighs. "We don't owe each other anything. We have a baby together. We can get along, but we don't need to pretend to be friends."

"And who says I want to pretend?"

Uncertainty mars her face. Like she wants to, but she's scared.

"What will it take for you to believe that I don't want to pretend?"

"Nothing. I don't need you to—"

"Do you want me to get on my knees and apologize?" I desperately ask, my knee bouncing faster.

"Go for it—what are you doing?"

Unfastening my seat belt, I step out into the pouring rain. Within seconds, I'm drenched, my hair sticks to my forehead, my shirt clings to my chest, and my feet feel like they're deep in puddles.

Lola yells for me to get inside, but I shut my door and round the front of my G-Wagon.

I'm not a beggar. It's something I've only ever had to do once, and that was when I asked Lola if I could take her picture. I never thought I'd need to do it again, but here I am, about to get on my knees out of sheer desperation.

Wiping the water from my face, I pull her door open and sink to my knees.

"TJ, get inside. You're getting wet," she pleads, grabbing my arm, but I stay down despite the raindrops falling on my skin like tiny daggers.

"It's a little too late for that." I wipe my face again, blinking repeatedly to stop the water from getting into my eyes.

"Oh my gosh, stop being stubborn!" She shakes my arm and attempts to pull me inside. "Get inside!"

A cold shiver runs down my spine, and I shift from one knee to the other as the gravel digs into them. Despite that, I stay rooted to the ground, staring up at the pretty girl who's flipped my world upside down.

My skin prickles with goose bumps and another shudder rolls down my spine. "We're going to be in each other's lives forever. That's never going to change. So I want us to get along. I want us to be friends without pretending, or whatever it is you think I want."

I wipe my face, sweeping my hair to the side to get it away

from my eyes.

Her face softens as the ensuing silence stretches between us.

Shivers wrack my body and my teeth chatter as a strong gust of wind blows, but still, I stay rooted in my spot.

"You're frustrating, you know that?" She fists my shirt in the middle, her eyes burning with rage, but I swear there's something else there. "But we can be friends. Now get inside!"

She grumbles something under her breath that sounds like "pain in her ass" before shoving me out of the way and slamming her door shut.

It's not the time, but that was hot.

Get your head out of the gutter, TJ, you're soaking wet. I tell myself as I get up and get back in.

"What the hell were you thinking?" she scolds me, her eyes raking over every inch of me.

"Desperate times call for desperate measures," I murmur, wiping my face and hair back, shuddering as I peel off the cold, wet shirt.

I drop it on the floor of the back seat and then work my jeans down. Though they're harder to take off because they're suctioned to my legs.

"What are you doing?"

I look to my right and fight the urge to smile because she's staring at me with wide eyes. There's a tinge of pink on her cheeks. Her lips slightly part as her gaze drops to my stomach.

"What does it look like I'm doing? I'm wet, Louise. I'm taking off my clothes." I kick my shoes off and discard my jeans.

"I'm wet too and you don't see me taking off my clothes." She points to the right side of her body that's covered in water droplets.

Unfortunately, it seems like my mind is still stuck in the gutter because her innocent little statement fogs my brain.

It takes her a split second to realize what she said. A deep shade of red paints her cheeks. "That's not—you know what I—stop being a pervert."

Her flustered words cause a smile to split my face.

"Pervert? I'm not a pervert," I playfully say.

She tucks a lock of her hair behind her ear. "Well, stop looking at me like that."

"Looking at you like what?" I cock a brow.

She sucks in a breath, chest rising as she does. "Just put some clothes on."

Lola looks away, but the red never leaves her cheeks.

I'd prolong this, but I'm cold as fuck.

I'm thankful I was smart enough to carry an extra duffle in my car in case of emergencies.

I throw on my clothes and smile because she's still not looking at me. Which is funny because two years ago she saw me completely naked.

"Are you decent now?"

"I'm decent now, Peaches." I quietly chuckle, smoothing my palm over my wrinkled shirt.

She hesitates, side-eyeing me before she turns around to face me.

"Why is it so hard for you to say my name?" Any remnants of anger or frustration seep from her face, and a tiny smile cracks on her lips. "Peaches isn't even creative. I get we met over peach juice, but what if we had met over something else?"

"Like?"

She shrugs, musing over the thought. "I don't know, apple juice?"

"It doesn't suit you." I smirk when she drops her head back on the headrest, grumbling that I am a pervert under her breath.

I could tell her that *Peaches* remind me of sunsets. A vast sky with brush-like strokes of golden copper, fused with amber, and a fiery orange that makes the sky look ablaze. Maybe it's a reflection of how I felt the last day we were together, *ablaze*. Burning fiercely but nothing I didn't want to stop feeling, at least not in that moment.

"Your hair color," I reply instead.

She clicks her tongue. "That's still not very creative."

I soak in the playfulness of her voice.

"And you think you could come up with something better?"

"Yes, Lola." She beams.

For now, I'll let her think that I'm sticking with Lola. But to me, she'll always be *my* Peaches. "So are we...okay?"

Any trace of humor in her expression is long gone. "For the sake of Phoenix, we're okay, but I swear I won't put up with anything like that ever again."

It's a warning, and I know she means it. If I fuck up again, she's done with me.

"I promise it won't happen again." I raise my hand, and she stares at it with confusion. "Give me your hand."

"For what?" She hesitantly raises her hand, eyeing mine tentatively.

It's corny, but I hook my middle finger around hers. "I mean it, Lola. I promise it won't happen again."

Like a light switch, I see the spark dance in her eyes, the reminder of our promise two years ago.

"Pinky promises are overrated," I softly say.

"They are, aren't they?" Her eyes trace over our threaded fingers as I trace mine over the seam of her lips.

My heart slows, the loud beat drowning out any other sound around us as her eyes lift to my lips. It wouldn't take much. We could close the space between us. There are only a few inches.

Just one kiss. That's all it would be.

Words suspended in the air, stealing the oxygen around us, suffocating with the need to seal my lips to hers. I know she feels it. I know she's considering it. But her uncertainty ceases as a strike of lightning ghosts over the dark blue sky.

The trance we'd been stuck in is gone, along with her finger around mine, but still, I feel her warmth grip it like a vice.

"We should go." Lola's voice is a mere breathless whisper.

I glance at my finger one last time before I bring my car to life and drive off in silence.

25

LOLA

A GUST OF CHILLY OCTOBER AIR BRUSHES PAST ME, causing goose bumps to erupt all over my skin.

I should probably go back inside and put on something thicker, but I don't. I stay seated outside our small balcony, reaching blindly for my iced coffee that I've set somewhere on the ground. Once I find it and take a sip, I grimace at the watery taste. Peering inside, all the ice cubes that once floated at the top are now melted.

I wish I could say it was because of my devotion to the painting in front of me, but it'd be a lie.

While I've been able to work on the painting I promised Saint I'd paint for him, I've gotten sidetracked. I could blame it on chilly weather that numbed almost all of my body, but even the weather isn't cold enough to numb the one part I wish it would.

My thoughts.

Every so often, TJ's words from last night repeat in my head like a broken record stuck on repeat.

I don't understand why my brain has decided to obsess over his words and the way he looked at me.

The sound of the door sliding open interrupts my thoughts.

Daisy stands behind me, holding a protein shake in one hand and my phone in the other.

"Morning," she chirps.

I stare at her warily, setting my cup down as she takes a seat next to me. "What did you do?"

She's in leggings and underneath her thin pullover, she's wearing a sports bra. A thin sheen of sweat coats her flushed face, and her jet-black hair is up in a messy ponytail.

I don't have to ask to know that she just finished a workout, and that means she's been up for a while.

She sets my phone in front of me. "Don't be mad."

"What did you do?"

"TJ's here."

I cover my mouth with the back of my hand as I yawn. "I swear I thought you said that TJ's here. I think I'm sleep-deprived."

I hardly slept last night, and it has nothing to do with Phoenix. He didn't even sleep in my room last night. He slept in Cara's. And it's not because of my assignments or the few paintings I have to touch up before I deliver them to my clients.

My lack of sleep is unfortunately due to TJ. To make matters worse, I decided to get on social media yesterday. I know I shouldn't have, but I couldn't help myself. But I regret it because I got sucked into the rabbit hole of TJ's life. Not that it's necessarily a bad thing, but when I came across videos of people dissecting his "fuck boy ways"—as it was stated so many times—I couldn't help but watch.

I'm not sure how I got wrapped up in what he's been up to for the past two years, but I watched more videos about TJ than I probably should have.

Her smile tightens. "That's exactly what I said. TJ's here, and before you ask why, he asked if he could pick us up, and I said yes. Technically, *you* said yes."

I gape at her. "You did *what*?"

"Technically, it was *you*."

"Daisy fucking Diaz," I whisper-shout. "This isn't funny. Please tell me you're not serious."

I don't bother waiting for her reply; I pick up my phone. When I unlock it, the first thing I see on my screen is the conversation *I* supposedly had with him.

TJ: Morning Peaches, I know you didn't ask but if you need me to, I can pick you guys up?

Before he dropped me off last night, we'd agreed I'd go over to his house so his friends could meet Phoenix.

Me: No, it's okay. We'll drive over there.

TJ: I really don't mind.

TJ: And I'll bring coffee for everyone.

Me: You don't have to

Me: But if you really want to...

TJ: I really do.

TJ: Send me the coffee orders. I'll be there in two hours.

"What the hell? I thought you didn't like him?" I turn my phone off, pulling the clip off my hair and tossing it on the small coffee table.

"I know what I said and I still don't care for him. Trust me, it took everything in me not to slap the shit out of him, but he's going to be in your and Phoenix's lives. And I want to make an effort to get along with him."

After I came in last night, the girls were sitting on the couch, waiting for me. I told them most of what happened, but I couldn't bring myself to tell them that I was tempted to kiss him.

"Okay, well, what does that have to do with you inviting him? I thought we were driving over there."

"You know..." She stares at me, unfazed by my reaction to all of this. She's clearly not as bothered as a smile curls her lips. "I've been thinking a lot. If he really wants to make up for the shit he said, then let him work for it. It's the least he could do."

I know she's right, she typically always is, but this is the one time I was okay with moving on.

"And think about it like this. We save money. Clearly, he's not hurting for it, so why should we? It would also be good for him to see what you have to go through. You drive back and forth all the time. One day isn't going to kill him. He knows you live far and still offered to pick us up. And he offered to buy us coffee. Lo, you're stupid if you think I'm going to turn down *free* coffee. In this economy, I don't think so."

I can't argue with her logic. She's right.

"Okay."

She stands, triumphantly smiling as she chugs the remainder of her shake. "Come on, *Peaches*. TJ's waiting."

I roll my eyes and pick up my canvas, easel, and coffee cup. "You know, instead of standing there doing nothing, why don't you grab my cart and be so helpful."

"*Con gusto*." She grins, sliding the door open and pushing my cart of supplies inside.

Inhaling a long, slow breath, I step inside and release it when I see TJ standing in front of the wall in the living room that's covered in paintings. Daisy grabs her coffee and thanks TJ for it as she heads to her room. Cara and Phoenix are nowhere in sight, so I can only assume they're still sleeping.

"Morning." I set my easel down and place the painting on it.

"You amaze me."

I still for a moment before I set my cup on the dining table and close the sliding door. "What?"

"Your paintings," he explains, closing the space between us.

"They're absolutely insane. You're incredibly talented. The pictures on your Instagram don't give them enough justice."

I crane my head back, my brow rising. "You saw the pictures on my account?"

"Yeah...I saw them. I'm sure I followed you on that account and your other one, but I don't think you ever followed me back."

I remember him following me. "That's right, you did. I didn't follow you back on my personal account because it has pictures of Phoenix and I hadn't told you about him yet. As for my other account, I genuinely forgot you followed me there."

I actually hadn't thought about it until now. So much has happened since then that it just slipped my mind.

He looks caught off guard by my last response. "Oh...you don't have to follow me back, but if you want to, you can."

"Now that you know about Phoenix, I guess it doesn't matter." I unlock my phone and go to Instagram. I follow him back on my business account and then on my personal one. "Don't stalk me."

"I can't promise anything." A mischievous glint flashes in his eyes, his smile lifting higher. "By the way, here you go. I hope you like it. It's a latte with oat milk, infused with cinnamon sticks."

"Infused with cinnamon?" I get a faint whiff of cinnamon as I take the cup from him, but he doesn't let go as our fingers graze each other.

"That's what—Jesus Christ, you're freezing."

"I was just outside. They'll warm up soon." I shrug it off, despite how my body trembles.

"Here." He sets both drinks on the table and cups my hands in his palms.

"This isn't necess—"

"Don't be stubborn, Peaches," he holds my hands tighter, and tugs me closer until there's about an inch of space between us. "Let me warm you up."

"Stop calling me Peaches and I am not stubborn. This just isn't necessary."

"Yes, you are, *Peaches*. And it is. You stopped shaking." He emphasizes the nickname, giving me a pointed stare.

"I was hardly shaking, and I am not stubborn."

"You were shaking nonetheless, and stop arguing with me." He slowly strokes his thumbs over my knuckles.

I hope he doesn't pick up on the shudder that rolls down my body. And this time it has nothing to do with the cold weather.

"Why? I like to argue with you," I tease.

His thumbs briefly stop in between one of my knuckles, and he glides the pad in between the dip. "I realize that. It's what you've been doing since I met you."

I fight back a smile. "You seriously can't tell me you remember that."

It's hard to believe that he still remembers what happened two years ago. Most of what happened is still fresh in my head.

"Some of it is a little hazy, but I remember, Lola. There are just some things you *never* forget." His eyes bore into mine briefly before they drop to my lips.

My breath gets caught in my throat. My numb body becomes hot, my nerves igniting.

But the moment I hear Cara and Phoenix, I drop my hands and take a few steps back until my butt hits the table.

"Good morning." I mentally cringe at how quickly and slightly out of breath it comes out.

"M'ning," Phoenix cheerfully greets us but stops when his eyes dart to TJ. I swear I see his eyes sparkle and his smile widen. "Hi, T!"

"Hey, buddy." TJ smiles at him and then looks at Cara. "Morning."

Her eyes bounce between the two of us. I know she's tempted to say something, but she doesn't. Knowing Cara, she's going to wait until we're alone to bombard me with questions.

"Morning, I hear you brought us coffee?"

"I did." He points at the cup sitting on the island. "A large caramel macchiato, extra caramel, and oat milk."

She smiles at him. "Thank you. I'm going to go get ready."

"I guess we should get ready too." I pick Phoenix up, giving him a kiss on the check.

"Do you need any help?" TJ offers.

I contemplate letting him, but everything is in my room, and I don't trust myself to be alone with him.

"No, it's okay. I've got most of his stuff packed. We just need to change. I'll be back." I walk away before he says anything or before I can make a fool of myself.

"Holy shi—" Jayden grunts, his face twisting in pain as he looks at Landon. "Are you serious? That was unnecessary." He scowls, rubbing the side of his stomach where Landon elbowed him.

"Mate, not in front of the kid. You should know better."

"I *do* know better. I was just caught off guard. You can't tell me you're all not shocked by how much they look alike." Jayden waves his hand between TJ and Phoenix, staring at them both like he can't comprehend what he's seeing.

We just arrived at TJ's house and as soon as we set foot inside, the guys crowded us. Phoenix clutches my jacket, but surprisingly, he doesn't hide his face behind my shoulder. He rests his head on it, staring at the guys with curiosity and they do the same.

"No, I get it. The resemblance is crazy. This is literally you, TJ, but a much smaller version. He's got the curls and everything." Saint bends down until he's almost at face level with Phoenix and smiles at him tenderly. "Isn't that right? You look just like your father, you little *polpetta*."

"*Polpetta*?" I ask.

Saint's grin spreads from ear to ear. "Meatball. Just look at him. So chunky and so fuc—freaking adorable."

"Right." Jayden stands next to Saint and bends until he's at Phoenix's eye level. "I wasn't going to say anything, but he's a thick boy." He softly pinches Phoenix's chin, which causes him to giggle.

"Did you just call my son a meatball?" TJ frowns.

I stare at TJ in disbelief. I shouldn't be shocked because TJ promised he'd take responsibility, but this is not what I expected. For him to sound so...possessive.

Polly shoves the guys out of the way. She and Gabby take their place, standing in front of us.

"Don't body shame him. There's nothing wrong with a few extra rolls. Isn't that right, sweet boy?" She smiles at him, but he doesn't lift his head until Gabby caresses his cheek with the back of her hand.

"You're so cute," Gabby coos and then she looks at me, her face softening and bottom lip jutting out. "He's perfect."

"Immensely perfect." Her best friend nods in agreement.

"Of course he's perfect." Saint stands next to Gabby, bending down once again. "It's Lola's baby. He's going to be perfect."

"He's my kid too," TJ argues, but he only gets a wave of dismal from Saint.

"Congratulations. No one asked," Landon flatly states.

"Okay, we get it, he's little and chunky. A little meatball, he's just a kid, who happens to be Lola's," Jagger says from the corner of the living room, far away from all of us.

"And mine," TJ adds, exasperated.

"Don't worry about him. Kids make him nervous," Gabby whispers, shaking her head as the smile on her face grows. Even more so when Phoenix wraps his hand around her finger. "It has nothing to do with you."

"All right, stop bombarding them. They're going to be here for a few hours." TJ stands next to me, his palm going to the small of my back. I suck in a small breath as his fingers softly dig into my jacket. "Don't suffocate them or they'll never want to come back."

Everyone steps away. They all break out into conversations of their own. The girls talk amongst each other until Saint interrupts them and attempts to have a conversation with Daisy.

Attempt is the key word because she gives him a curt head nod and then ignores him. He smiles, unbothered by her lack of interest in him. He stands there, listening and smiling as they talk.

"You want to put your stuff up in my room?"

I hesitate and I know he senses it. Before I can tell him no, he grabs the strap of my purse and slips it off my shoulder and hooks it onto his.

"Stubborn, I tell you." He grins, his voice teasing, but then it softens. "I'm sorry, Lola. The last time you were here—"

I shake my head. "It's okay. We're okay now."

TJ stands in front of me, lowering his head while he strokes Phoenix's arm with the back of his fingers. The way he stands in front of me feels as if he's blocking out everyone around us.

"We're in this for life." He smiles.

I return the smile. "We are."

26

TJ

"All right!" Coach Warren blows his whistle, motioning for all of us to gather around him.

My chest rises and falls with my rapid breaths. Sweat drips down my face, making some of my curls stick to my forehead. "Fuck," I murmur under my breath, resting my hands on my hips as I try to control my heavy breathing just like everyone else is.

"Two weeks. That's all we have until the season officially begins." Coach pauses, his eyes slowly coasting around the arena as they always do, and then they fall on each and every single one of us. "I want to remind you all that last season's win and being number one in the AP poll this season doesn't mean anything. I'm glad you're all still riding that high, but one loss could change everything. So remember that every time you step foot on the court. Every point, every win counts. The effort you put in every practice and game is vital.

"Remember to submit your assignments on time, get good grades, and do *not* get into *any* trouble." His eyes land on Saint and stay there momentarily, then they move to everyone else.

"But—"

"Arlo, don't test my patience," Coach Warren cuts him off with a cold glare.

He smiles, raising his hands in surrender.

"All right, bring it in." He places a hand in the middle and we all follow suit. "Who are we?"

"Knights!" we shout in unison.

"I said, who are we?"

"Knights!" we shout again, loud enough for our voices to echo throughout the entire arena and then we part.

The guys all disperse to grab their stuff. I go to follow them, but I don't make it far when Coach calls for me. He jerks his head for me to follow him.

I falter in my steps when we get to his office. Janet sits in one of the chairs across from his desk, tapping away on her phone until she hears us. Setting it down, she stands and looks at us.

"Good, you're here. I promise to make this quick. I'm sure you're exhausted." She smiles, but the tone in her voice is far from sweet.

I tentatively step inside, closing the door behind me as Coach takes a seat in his chair behind his desk. Janet sits back down and I take a seat next to her.

"You've done exceptionally well since the news leaked." She praises, her smile growing with admiration, but it's brief as it lowers.

That's what everyone thinks, but inside, I'm panicking. Sometimes it feels like I'm going to fuck everything up.

"But only because you haven't had cameras or people asking you mindless questions. I'm here to once again remind you that it's different once the cameras are on you."

"I know."

I've been doing this for two years, going on to three. I know how relentless and aggravating some of these reporters and sports analysts can get.

"This year is different." Her voice is stern, the smile on her face completely gone. "You have a kid, TJ. That kind of news is not something anyone forgets. Everyone is curious, everyone wants answers."

I know they are. I've seen so many articles, so many posts, so many videos of people wondering whether I'll be able to balance being a father and basketball this coming season.

"I don't owe anyone anything."

"You don't, but when has anyone ever cared?" She heaves a breath. "There are people who think you deserve it. There are those who think you don't. Those who don't will purposely push buttons you didn't know existed. So I'm here to remind you to keep your cool, don't let them get to you, and *do not*"—she sits up, leaning closer to me—"do not blow up on national television."

I fight the urge to roll my eyes and stand. "That won't happen. Anything else? I need to shower."

"Yes, I've emailed you some questions that you'll most likely be asked. Use that to prepare for the pre- and post-game interviews."

"Okay." I direct my attention to Coach.

"Listen to her, TJ. This isn't only good for you but for the team. She knows what's best."

I know what they really mean to say is that they're afraid I'll fuck something up and don't trust that I'll be able to handle myself.

"Is that all?"

"That's all."

I drum my fingers along the steering wheel, gripping it tightly as I wait for the light to turn green.

The conversation with Janet plays in my head, and the longer it does, the more it fuels my agitation. I'm not sure what frustrates me the most—the lack of trust Coach and Janet have in me or the possibility that I could be set off by a stupid question.

"Help me out, TJ."

"What?" My eyes flicker from the light to my rearview mirror.

Saint, Jayden, and Jagger sit in the back of my G-Wagon, while Landon sits in the passenger seat.

On the weekends, we take turns driving to practice, except on the weekdays since we all have different schedules. Usually after practice, we grab something to eat, but now that Phoenix and Lola are in my life, I've been skipping lunch with the guys.

It's been an interesting two weeks. I've learned a few things about Phoenix, like he's potty trained, carries Winnie the Pooh everywhere he goes, likes to cuddle only when he's watching TV, and so many other things.

I still have no clue what I'm doing. Some days it feels like I've finally got the hang of it, but then Phoenix does something that throws me off the loop.

Like throwing a tantrum because he wanted ice cream instead of eating food. Lola handled it well, but I watched it happen, feeling useless because I didn't know what to do.

"Help me out with Daisy," he pleads.

The guys snicker, except for Landon. He's too focused on whatever's on his phone to pay attention to Saint.

"That's not going to happen." I shift my gaze back to the light just as it turns green.

He scoffs. "And why the fuck not?"

"You're doing the right thing, TJ. She's way too hot for him," Jagger adds, and Jayden hums in agreement.

"Too hot for me? Have you not seen Jayden? I'm better looking than him, and Cara's talking to him," Saint argues, no ounce of humor in his voice.

"We're not talking. I told you we have two classes together. We just help each other study. And I've seen myself. I'm very good-looking," Jayden replies, smug. "I can't say the same for you. Daisy doesn't even acknowledge you."

"Not right now, but that's going to change because TJ's going to help me, right?" Saint says with hope in his voice.

"I told you it's not going to happen. She hardly speaks or looks at me when I'm over at their place. I'm certain she doesn't like me. You're on your own." I pull into our driveway and park.

I don't mention the disdainful look in her eyes, the not so subtle glares that I'm sure she does on purpose, her faint scoffs when I speak that let me know how much she dislikes me.

"Come on, help me out with Daisy and I'll help you out with Lola."

For the first time since we got in my SUV, Landon briefly glances at me.

"I'm not interested," I deadpan, staring at him in the rearview mirror.

He quirks an eyebrow, smirking. "Not interested in helping me or getting Lola?"

"Get out. I need to go."

Landon gets out without a word.

"Bye, baby daddy," Jayden and Jagger singsong in unison.

I lift my middle finger as they climb out.

The only one left is Saint. He sits back, a shit-eating grin taking over his entire face. "Don't forget I'm the one she talks to every day. If you need help, you know where to find me." That's the last thing he says before he gets out, shutting the door behind him.

I don't need help getting Lola. I don't like her in that way. Even if I *did* like her like that, it's clearly not reciprocated. She's made that abundantly clear.

"Hey." Cara stands on the other side of the door, holding it open for me with a smile that catches me off guard.

Cara typically greets me with a stoic expression and a stiff 'hey.'

"Hey." I return the smile, stepping inside. I close the door behind me, then take my shoes and hoodie off.

She doesn't say anything else as she walks away and turns left, disappearing into the hall that I'm assuming leads to her room. It may not seem like much, but I'd like to think I'm making progress.

Walking into the living room, the first thing I see is the furniture pushed back and a white sheet covering the floor. There are two carts filled with brushes, paints, and some other art supplies. Three white canvases lie on the sheet next to three mason jars filled with water.

"Remember, Pooh bear doesn't like paint on him." I hear Lola's voice from behind me.

Turning my head, I see her coming out of her bedroom with Phoenix right next to her. And to no one's surprise, he's clutching the bear I gave him close to him. He's been carrying it everywhere with him since I gave it to him.

"Okay." He pouts, releasing a heavy sigh, but the sad expression on his face changes when he sees me. His eyes shine brightly and he beams as he runs toward me. "T!"

I may have absolutely no clue what I'm doing, but one thing I do know and I'm good at with all certainty is giving hugs, especially to Phoenix.

There are not enough words to describe the immense happiness I feel at this very moment or every time I come over. The serotonin that courses through my body when I see the pure joy on *my* son's face as he runs to me. It's something I never thought I'd love so much.

"Phoenix!" I spread my arms wide, quickly crouching down right as he jumps into me and winds his little arms around my neck. "Hey, buddy, how are you?"

He cheekily grins. "Good."

"How's Pooh bear?" I glance down at the bear he's still firmly holding on to, and my smile widens as I notice that he and the bear are wearing matching T-shirts.

"Good! Paint."

"Are we painting today?" I smile at him and then look at Lola. "Hey, Peaches."

Her smile falters and she stares at me, unimpressed at the nickname.

My eyes roam down the length of her body. I try not to gawk like a fucking pervert, but the jean overalls she's wearing hug her body so fucking well. They're slightly loose at her chest but tight at her hips, goddamn.

I force my gaze back to hers, and I shouldn't grin, but the threatening glare she's giving me is cute. I expect her to say something about the nickname, but instead she lets out a resigned sigh. "Hey, how was practice?"

"Good, Warren really pushed us today. I swear I can't feel my legs."

Her smile rises as if knowing I'm in pain is satisfying for her to hear. "That's a shame."

That definitely sounded sarcastic, but I don't mind it. Seeing her smile for me and not someone else makes me feel really good.

"Do you enjoy hearing that I'm in pain?"

"No, of course not." She sidesteps me. When she does, my eyes immediately drop down to her ass. Jesus fucking Christ. *Focus*. "I just said it's a shame. That's all."

I'm certain she mumbles something under her breath when she turns around. Something along the lines of, "he should have pushed you harder," but maybe it was just my imagination.

"C'mon." Phoenix squirms against me, urging me to go sit.

I snap out of it and walk over to the sheet. I sit down next to Lola and sit Phoenix on my lap, but it seems as if he's had enough of me holding him because he sits next to me instead.

"So we're painting today?"

"Yes, I thought it'd be a good way to bond with Phoenix. This is one of his favorite things to do. He loves it so much, I got him his own cart. On top of him loving it, it's educational. Right, honey?" Her eyes flicker to Phoenix, the prettiest the smile gracing her face as he nods in agreement. "Tell TJ what color that is." She points at the yellow bottle on the cart.

"Ello!" he quickly replies.

"Wow, very good, buddy. You're so smart." I ruffle his hair. "Thanks for letting me be a part of this. If it wasn't for you, I wouldn't have a single clue what I'm doing."

"Thanks for being here. For trying." Her voice is soft, like a caress to my soul. Her eyes are a deeper shade of green today, highlighting the specks of brown scattered around her iris.

"Anything for Phoenix...and for you," I say, stretching my hands at my sides, but freeze when I feel the tip of her finger graze mine.

I suck in a breath as everything comes to a standstill and those sparks from a few weeks ago return. But they slow when she moves her hand away.

"We should start painting." She picks up a few bottles from the smaller cart that has Phoenix's name on it and squirts some of the paint on each palette.

Picking up one of the palettes, I set it in front of Phoenix and set the bear next to him. "I'm going to set him here so he can watch you paint. I'm sure he would love that. What do you think?"

He nods and grins, picking up a paintbrush. "Okay."

Once he starts painting, he completely ignores Lola and me. He's too focused on his task. His tongue slightly pokes out to the side, and his brows are pinched together.

I pick up my own paintbrush and dip it in the blue paint. "You know I was thinking..." I muse, adding the paint to the canvas. "I don't know a lot about you."

She side-eyes me, her brush freezing above the canvas. "You don't know anything about me."

I dip my brush in the water, dry it on the paper towel, and dip it in the black paint. I'm not entirely sure what I'm doing, and I'm sure it's going to look like shit, but I add the paint to the canvas anyway.

"You prefer your coffee to be cold over hot. You really like wearing those colorful leggings and Converse. I'm certain your favorite colors are green and orange. You love Mexican food, and I bet if you could, you'd eat it all the time." I smile to myself, remembering how much she loved the tacos and how she's talked about eating them again.

After a beat of silence, I look up. She's already staring at me with pinched brows. It dawns on me that I probably got it all wrong and I really don't know her.

"I'm wrong, aren't I?"

"No, you're right."

27

LOLA

"How did you figure that out?"

"Your eyes, they get brighter and your smile gets bigger. I don't know how to explain it, but your expression changes when you drink cold coffee over hot. You're always wearing those colorful leggings and Converse. I figured you really like orange and green because you always wear them. And your eye makeup is always like a light peach color. And Mexican food is a given."

From my peripheral, I see his lips quirk into a small smile as he continues to paint.

I redirect my attention back to my canvas, but it's hard to focus when he's noticed something as small as the color of my eyeshadow.

"You know, I have to say I'm a big fan of the colorful leggings, and the matching Converse are the cherry on top."

My treacherous lips spread wide across my face. "Right..."

"It's not the reason you're thinking, but if I'm being honest —" He stops mid-sentence. He peers down at Phoenix and then looks at me. "It's not *kid* appropriate."

"Well, aren't you considerate," I retort sarcastically.

It's doubtful Phoenix would hear a word. He's in his own world, unbothered by our presence or conversation.

My breath hitches as TJ leans in. His warm, minty breath fans the shell of my ear. I can't see him, but I swear I feel a smirk rise on his lips. "I genuinely love the leggings, and I'd be lying if I said your ass doesn't look good in them. Although everything you wear looks really fucking good on you."

Heat rises on my neck up to my cheeks. "Thanks, that's exactly what I wanted to hear."

He resumes painting, a deep chuckle rumbling in his chest. "I'm just being honest."

"Your honesty never fails." I give him a side glance, brushing my bangs away.

"I wouldn't lie to you," he softly says.

A thought runs through my head, and I consider whether it's worth telling him or not. It's a strong possibility that he won't care, and it might make this entire moment awkward.

I shake my head, hating myself for how I'm overthinking this entire situation.

"What?"

"It's nothing." I continue painting, shoving my annoying thoughts away.

"Don't feel obligated to tell me, but we're...friends. You can tell me anything." His words are gentle, almost careful as if he doesn't want to push too much, but also as if he's extending his own version of an olive branch.

"I got depressed after I found out I was pregnant, and it got worse after I had Phoenix." I roll the brush between my thumb and forefinger, feeling the wood against the pads of my fingers. Anxiety I haven't felt in a while returns. The reminder of those dark days feels like just yesterday. "To get me out of it, Daisy thought of this *grand* idea. She thought it'd be good for me to work out with her. She said the release of endorphins would be great for my body and mental health. And Cara was the one with the idea of the Converse. I had worn out my white high-tops, and she knew how much I liked them."

I mull over the memory, remembering how Daisy and Cara

showed up unexpectedly. They both chastised me for lying in bed and doing nothing but also hugged me because they knew how much I needed it. Well, Cara did, but Daisy still supported me by hovering and occasionally putting her hand on my shoulder.

"They did that to brighten up my mood. After their unexpected visit, we started working out together on FaceTime. Eventually, talking became easier and we'd be on the phone for hours. It started off as twenty minutes, then forty, then an hour until it became hours. They saw that as a milestone and my reward was leggings and Converse."

I don't mention that my weight and stretch marks played a huge factor in my depression. I was almost fifty pounds overweight and my stretch marks were everywhere. It was hard accepting those things. It's stupid that I care so much about it, but my overthinking really killed my self-esteem.

"And that is why I have so many colorful leggings and Converse. I know it seems silly, but—"

"It's not silly," TJ cuts me off, his tone serious but soft. "It's the little things that keep us going when everything seems like it's going to shi—well, you know." He smiles apologetically and then peeks at Phoenix to make sure he didn't hear anything.

He looks back at me. "You got leggings and Converse. I got tattoos and black-out drunk. Not the smartest idea, but the tattoos I got from it were worth it."

"You got tattoos as in plural while black-out drunk?"

"Yeah, I know what you're thinking. What was I thinking? I wasn't. I was an idiot, but luckily, my friends aren't complete shi—sorry, it's a habit. Luckily, they were there to look after me. They didn't stop me from getting tattoos, but they made sure they didn't look like crap."

"You know you're going to have to show me the tattoos now." I scan every inch of visible skin, but because he's wearing sweats and a long sleeve, I can't see anything.

"I'll show you mine if you show me yours." He tilts his head to the side, his eyes slowly roaming over my body.

I raise my middle finger, smirking as his brows lift and his lips part. Despite the shocked look on his face, I see the way the corners of his mouth curve upward. When I turn my finger around, his eyes float down to the small flame inked on my skin.

"Daisy, Cara, and I got matching flame tattoos on the same finger. It's our way of always staying connected. I know it sounds cringe, but—"

"You want to talk about cringe..." He lifts the hem of his shirt, showing off part of his abs. For a moment, I get lost in the taut, tan ridges until he points at the ink on his skin. "I may have great friends, but they're still idiots. They got their names tattooed on me. Even Landon, who never joins in on anything, decided to be part of this. They call it their version of a tramp stamp."

I attempt to tame my smile, but it's hard to do when I read their names. Jayden's is the very first, followed by Jagger, and lastly Landon. "It could've been a lot worse. Unless there's worse?"

"No, this is the worst one. The other ones aren't too bad, and I have one in particular that I really like." He glances down at his covered right arm.

"Am I going to see the others?"

"Not unless you let me see yours." He cocks a brow.

I shift my attention back to my canvas and continue painting, ignoring the way his eyes burn into me. And I change the conversation. "So what do you want to know?"

A deep chuckle rumbles from his chest. "Why the name Phoenix?"

That actually gets Phoenix's attention. When he looks up at TJ, they both smile at each other, and it does something to my heart.

"Being pregnant young, everyone makes you feel like your life is over. That there's nothing to look forward to after giving birth at *such a young age*." Words from my parents and many others replay in my head as well as their disappointing and judgmental looks. "For a while, I thought they were right, until the midwife laid him on my chest. At that moment, everything felt like it was going to be okay, everything felt new. Like a Phoenix."

A stretch of silence settles between us, and I start overthinking, wondering if I said too much, or if all of this sounds too depressing. Maybe I shouldn't have said anything. What the hell was I thinking?

"You genuinely amaze me."

I grip the brush a little tighter, smiling despite the tiny ache I feel in my chest. "I shouldn't. I didn't do anything."

"I panicked when you told me and I still do..." he trails off. "If the roles were reversed, I don't think I'd be as good a parent as you."

I stopped painting. "You panic? But you look so calm...actually, you've handled this better than I expected."

He dryly laughs, raking his fingers through his curls. "I have to be honest with you. I talk to my parents at least every other day because I worry that I'm going to mess something up. It's easy to fake being okay when you're used to having all eyes on you. I've been dealing with this since freshman year. I can't say it's always been easy, but fake it till you make it, right? I know it sounds cliché, but it's what helped me get through this...and you also helped me."

For the first time, I really look at him and see the hesitation that lies in his eyes. The tightness in his face and the slight discomfort as he looks at me and then away. Almost as if he's embarrassed that he's admitted this to me.

"It's not cliché and I definitely didn't do anything." I smile at him.

"I promise, you have. I wouldn't be able to do this without you."

I hate this moment.

The way he looks at me, the way he smiles, and the sincerity behind his words. Most of all, I hate the way it feels as if time has all of a sudden come to a standstill.

Thankfully, Phoenix interrupts the moment. He slaps his

paintbrush on the palette, causing some of the paint to splatter on TJ's lap.

"Be careful, you got paint on TJ," I chide.

Phoenix leans forward, inspecting the splattered paint on TJ's sweats. He tilts his head from one side and then to the other, humming as if he's deep in thought.

"Little." He pinches his thumb and index finger.

TJ chuckles, staring down at the paint. "I guess this is the first of many pieces of artwork I'll be getting from you, huh? I bet you're going to be as artistic as your mama."

He doesn't clean the paint off. Instead, he slips his phone out of his pocket and taps on the camera app. He makes sure he gets all the specks in the frame and then he adjusts the camera's focal point and takes the picture.

"Did you just take a picture?"

"I take art very seriously and this"—TJ holds his phone in front of me, showing me the picture he took—"is a work of art," he states matter-of-factly, setting his phone next to him. "Which brings me to my next question. I'm curious to know how you do live paintings. Do you have some kind of photographic memory or something? I saw that video you posted the other night, and I can't believe you did all of that within a day. And the details? God, you're insane."

A smug smile grows on my lips at the dumbfounded expression on his face. Not only because he's staring at me like he's confused and astonished by what he saw, but because he looks kind of cute.

No...not cute. Wait, did he just say that he saw my video?

"You watched my video?" I'm sure I'm mirroring his expression, although I probably look more confused than anything. It's only a three-minute-long video, but I didn't think it's something he'd care to look at.

"It came across my feed and the second it did, I couldn't look away. The way you paint is mesmerizing."

It shouldn't mean anything and it definitely shouldn't make

me smile like an idiot. But here I am, smiling as if it was the first time someone is complimenting me.

"I don't have a photographic memory, but I do secretly take multiple pictures throughout the event and sometimes stalk my clients."

He lifts a brow, and an amused smile tugs at his lips. "Stalk?"

"Most of the time, a relative or a friend hires me, so the couple or whoever it is I'm painting has no idea what I'm doing. Before the event, I'll look through their socials, if they're not private, and get an idea of what they look like and look for anything important. Like tattoos, pets, the very minuscule details. And when I'm at the event, I take multiple pictures to make sure I get every single detail in."

"Wow, and you get the painting done that very same day?"

I deeply sigh. "I wish, but unfortunately, I'm a perfectionist and sometimes go back and make changes. I also have to do the final touches before I deliver it."

"Wow...I know I already said that, but you just—"

"Lola! Cara!" Daisy yells from the front door, slamming it shut. She runs into the living room, one hand holding a bunch of shopping bags and the other holding two boxes of pizza. She stops when her eyes fall on TJ and so does her smile. "Oh...you're here."

I don't bother to warn Daisy to be nice because she does what she wants when she wants.

"You got us pizza?" Cara takes the boxes from Daisy's hand and sets them on the counter. "And you got pineapple. Someone's in a good mood."

"I didn't order pizza and I most definitely would never order pineapple on a pizza." She grimaces, staring at the pizza topped with pineapple, bacon, and jalapeños.

"It was me. TJ just got out of practice, and Phoenix and I haven't eaten."

His eyes narrow and then something flashes in his eyes, and he shakes his head. "Thanks for the pizza. I fucking love pineapple."

Cara holds a slice of pizza an inch away from her mouth,

smirking as her eyes flicker to the jar filled with dollars and coins. "That's ten dollars in the jar."

TJ doesn't hesitate to pull out his wallet and takes out a twenty-dollar bill, handing it to me with a sheepish smile on his face. "Sorry about that."

"Don't worry about it, but it's only ten."

"Keep it. I'm sure it won't be the last time it slips."

"But—"

"Come on ,buddy, I'll help you wash the paint off." TJ dips the brush in the jar, cleaning off the paint, and does the same to Phoenix's brush.

Begrudgingly but surprisingly, he listens and TJ lifts him up, and both disappear into the bathroom.

"Hmmm..."

I look at Daisy, who's staring at me intently.

"What?" I set my brush down and stand, slipping the twenty-dollar bill in the jar. I saunter over toward the island and grab a slice of pizza.

Her lips flatten into a straight line. "I don't know, you just look...different."

"She does, doesn't she?" Cara points her half-eaten pizza in my direction.

"I've let my bangs grow out." I point at them.

"No, it's not that. There's something else I can't pinpoint." She drums her fingers along the counter but then shrugs and tosses two shopping bags at me. "Anyway, I found the perfect Halloween costume for you."

Now I narrow my eyes at her. Her smile is beaming, but the glint in her eyes is filled with mischief.

Slowly opening the bag, I pull out the costume and when I hold it out, my eyes widen and my jaw drops.

"There's no way you think I'm going to wear this?" I incredulously ask, staring at the stunning, but immensely short, strapless, red sequin dress with a long slit at the hem.

"Oh yes, you are. You'll make a killer Jessica Rabbit."

"Yes, you would." Cara nods in agreement as she grabs another slice of pizza.

"Should I remind you that Jessica Rabbit's dress is long and this"—I hold it close to my body, noticing that it's right above my mid-thigh and the slit would stop close to my hip—"is extremely short?"

"It's Halloween. It's supposed to be short and hot," she states matter-of-factly, picking up a slice of cheese pizza. "And trust me when I say this, that is going to look really good on you."

I shove the dress back in the bag as I hear the soft patter of feet against the floor and Phoenix's giggles.

"I promise you'll love pineapple," TJ says to Phoenix.

"Do not corrupt my nephew," Daisy warns, pointing a finger at him.

"I'm not corrupting him. I'm getting him to try one of the best things in the world." He grins, setting Phoenix on the counter, keeping an arm around him.

"One of the best things in the world?" She scoffs, her voice mocking. "God, the bar is set low."

I smile, handing TJ a plate. "It's really not that bad, Daisy. You haven't even tried it. How would you know it's bad?"

"I just know."

"It's okay. More for us." Cara grabs two more slices and walks toward the living room, and Daisy follows right behind her, scowling at the box of pizza filled with pineapple.

Cutting a bit off of the cheese pizza, I hand it to Phoenix, and he wastes no time eating it.

"Someone was hun—" TJ stops mid-sentence and pulls his phone out of his pocket. His fingers hover over the screen, almost as if he's contemplating whether or not he should reply to whoever texted him. But when he's going to reply, Phoenix slaps the pizza on his shirt.

"Phoenix, no." I grab his hand before he slathers more sauce all over his shirt. "That's not nice."

"It's okay. It's an old T-shirt anyway." TJ chuckles, staring amused at the tiny piece of pizza clinging to his shirt.

"I should've told you that he likes to do this kind of thing." I wet some paper towels and pump a bit of dish soap onto them and hand it to him.

"I should've known he'd do something like that." His smile widens as he attempts to wipe the sauce off, but only manages to smear it.

His phone vibrates against the counter. I glance down at it and see a text message pop up from Alexia.

Alexia: I hope you're ready for me tonight. I have something special for you.

Alexia: Just a little preview.

Alexia: 1 Image.

Averting my eyes away from black lace, I swallow thickly but struggle as tightness grips my throat and my stomach drops.

28

TJ

I REPLAY EVERY SINGLE SECOND, MINUTE, AND FUCKING hour of today with Lola to see where I went wrong, but nothing comes to mind.

Right before the pizza arrived, Lola was smiling and opening up to me, but afterward she was acting differently. She was a little quieter and her smiles were forced.

I blow a heavy breath, staring at the ceiling of my bedroom as I lie in my bed and replay the day all over again. But my thoughts are interrupted when I hear a knock at my door.

I groan, closing my eyes. "Saint, I told you I don't want to go out tonight."

He and the other guys, except for Landon, have been insistent on getting me to go out with them. I told them multiple times I didn't want to, and after a few minutes, they finally left, or at least I thought they did.

The soft click of my door opening and closing has me opening my eyes. "What part of—" I stop mid-sentence as I sit up and see Alexia, standing in front of my door, wearing nothing but black lingerie.

She smiles slyly and mischievously. "Hey, it's been a while."

"Alexia—"

She cuts me off, closing the space between us. "I figured you got a little busy with Phoenix, and that's why you didn't text me back. So I thought I'd come and surprise you. What do you think?"

I wasn't only busy with Phoenix and Lola, but I honestly forgot to text her back.

Keeping my eyes solely on her face, I drag my fingers through my hair, unsure of how to say what I'm thinking, but there's no other way around it.

"I really want to be alone tonight."

I wish I could say I feel guilty as the smile on her face drops and her eyebrows pull together. I don't doubt she's confused and hurt, but she's never shown up at my place without letting me know.

"You're seriously not going to say anything about what I'm wearing?"

I'm taken aback, but it doesn't dawn on me until a few seconds later that she's not upset or confused because I want to be alone, but because I didn't admire her fucking outfit.

"I didn't text you to come over because I forgot."

I know it makes me sound like an asshole, but I hate sugar-coating things. If there's one thing I'll never do is get someone's hopes up for my own benefit. I could word it differently, but what's the point? Sometimes it prolongs the inevitable, and there's no point for that.

"You fucking asshole! I bought this for you. I thought I'd surprise you since we haven't seen each other in a while." She clenches her jaw, her nose flaring. "You hardly reply to my messages or my calls. What the hell is going on?"

I pinch the bridge of my nose, feeling aggravated because this isn't how I expected for things to turn out. "I have a kid, Alexia. Basketball season has started. I have people on my ass all the fucking time."

"Okay? And? You've always made time for me. I've always been there, or did you forget?"

I stare at her in disbelief, but I snap out of it. It's not surprising she's somehow made this about her.

"Been there when you want to fuck." It's a shit thing to say, but it's the truth. We hang out occasionally, but in the end, we've known it's always to fuck.

Alexia breathes harshly, her eyes narrowed into slits. "You've never complained before, but now it's an issue?" Turning around, she picks up the hoodie off the floor and pulls it over her head.

Now that she's covered again, I take a good look at the hoodie. It's not even hers but someone from the football team. The only reason I know is because all athletes get custom athletic wear.

I could bitch about the fact that she's wearing some other guy's hoodie, but I genuinely don't care.

"I just want to be alone tonight." And think about where I could have gone wrong with Lola.

"Ahh," she tsks, leaning against my door with her arms crossed against her chest. She stares at me as if she's realized something and smiles wryly. "I see what this is all about. You could've just told me."

"Told you what?"

"You're with Lauren." Despite her smile softening, I hear the resentment in her voice.

I'm not an idiot to know she said the wrong name on purpose. It's childish and fucking lame. Everyone who's been keeping up with me knows Lola's name.

There is so much I could say, but it's pointless. I'm over this conversation.

Slowly inhaling, I stand and walk toward her. Her smile once again becomes sultry when I stretch my hand, but it falls flat when I wrap it around the knob and twist it.

"You need to leave."

Her jaw drops. "Are you serious? I came all the way over here for you. You're seriously going to kick me out?"

"I'm sorry I forgot to text you, but I already told you I want to be alone."

Alexia releases a shaky breath and plasters a sickeningly sweet smile on her face. "Okay, I'll leave but don't come running to me when you're bored."

I refrain from rolling my eyes as I pull the door wider. She walks out and I follow behind her until we're downstairs at the front door.

"Alexia."

She turns around. "What?"

"Her name is Louise."

Her brows draw together. "Huh?"

"The mother of my child, her name is Louise. Leave the petty shit for someone else."

She bitterly laughs, tapping her temple with her finger. "Right...Louise. Sorry, you've been with so many people it's hard to remember all their names."

I don't know what she thought she'd accomplish with that remark, but it did nothing. I'm not a saint and I've never pretended to be one. I've fucked around a lot, but so has she and I've never judged her for it and I still don't. I don't care what she does.

"Night." I smile, shutting the door behind her. "Fucking hell," I mutter, rubbing my palm over my face as I head to the kitchen. I stop at the kitchen entryway when I see Landon.

"Bloody nightmare." He leans against the counter, holding a box of cinnamon toast crunch. He dumps a few of the cinnamon sugar squares in his hand and tosses them in his mouth.

"You let her in, didn't you?" I glare at him when he does nothing but shrug.

"I wanted to test a theory."

"A theory?"

"Yes, a theory, and you proved me right." The corner of his mouth just barely lifts upward, but it lasts merely a second before his lips flatten again.

I'm not sure what pisses me off more. His condescending posh accent or the look in his eyes like he knows something I don't.

I lean against the doorway, folding my arms against my chest. "Are you not going to tell me how I proved you right?"

"No, but you'll find out...eventually." He tosses more cereal into his mouth.

Before I can say anything, the back door pushes open. Jaggers strolls in casually, grinning from ear to ear as he carries a twelve-pack of beer. My gaze strays away from him to Jay, who's grunting and cursing under his breath, but more specifically the piano he and Saint are carrying into the kitchen.

"You piece of shit! I thought you said you would help." He heaves, grunting and cursing Saint for getting him to agree to bring the piano.

"I am helping. I'm holding something really important." He flashes him a crooked grin, lifting the twelve-pack in the air. "I told you not to bring it, but you're an idiot for agreeing with that, dumbass."

"Well, this dumbass"—Saint pauses as he tries to catch his breath—"is going to make money off of this."

"How so?" I question, lifting a brow. I stare at the old wooden piano, covered in dust, that looks like it's not been played in years.

"Anyone who wants to touch it has to pay a fee. Drunk college kids will pay for anything, especially when they're told no." He proudly smiles and wipes the sweat off his forehead with the back of his arm. "When Jayden and I start making money, don't expect to get anything."

"As if you'll make anything." Jagger sets down the twelve-pack and pulls two bottles out. He tosses me one and keeps one for himself.

"And this is why you're majoring in psychology." Saint tsks, his tone arrogant. "Although it looks like you haven't learned a damn thing."

"Wait, I'm confused. Where the fuck did you get a piano from? You didn't steal it, did you?" My narrowed eyes bounce between him and Jayden.

Jay rolls his eyes, grabbing one of the bottles from the pack. "Oh my God, you're really bringing this back up? It was a mistake. Get over it."

"Mate, that wasn't a mistake. You stole a dog from someone's property. You fucking dumbarse," Landon chimes in, pushing away from the counter, and grabs a water bottle from the fridge.

"We gave it back." Saint lifts his shoulder in a half shrug. "But to answer your question, no, we didn't steal this. It was sitting on the side of the road, and it had a free sign on it. I guess it came off."

"It's true." Jagger nods, knowing we can't completely trust those two idiots.

I know they're not drunk, but I definitely know they're buzzed. When they're together and drinking, they do stupid shit. Like taking a dog off someone's porch in the middle of the night.

"Since you're all here. I'd like to increase it to one hundred," Landon states, setting his box of cereal down, and uncaps his water bottle.

"One hundred?" Jagger and Jayden ask in unison.

"Is that an issue?"

"I'm game. That makes things more interesting." Saint leans against the piano. His eyes drift to mine and then to the rest of the guys.

"No, not an issue, but your cockiness always astounds me, Taylor. You really think you're right?" Jayden questions, taking a swig of his beer.

"I'm always right."

"Wait, what do you know that we don't?" Jagger tilts his head to the side, eyeing Landon suspiciously. "You're never this sure of yourself unless you know something."

"Wait, what the hell are you guys talking about?" I stare at them, confused.

"Don't worry about it," Jagger replies, his smile smug.

"It's nothing," Jayden innocently says, though I know it's far from that.

"You know what, I don't even want to know." I take a pull of my beer. "Anyway, what are you guys doing here? I thought you were all going to be out late."

Landon and I were the only ones who decided not to go out. Although he typically doesn't like to go out to begin with. Sometimes he has other plans, but he never tells us what they are, nor does he invite us.

"Felt bad for you both. Decided to come home. Either way, we're all going out next week. No exceptions, Landon." Jagger directs his attention to him.

"I don't have a costume. I'm not going."

"I figured you wouldn't, but don't worry, I got it covered. I got the perfect costume for you." Saint grins.

Halloween is next week and we've all agreed to go out. Landon didn't officially agree, but we know Jagger will force him to come.

"No."

Saint scoffs. "You don't even know what it is."

"I don't want to know," he deadpans.

"How about we make a deal? If you don't like what it is, you don't have to come out with us, but if you like it, you have to wear everything and spend the entire night with us.

Landon takes a drink of his water, his gaze distant as he considers Saint's words. Picking up his cereal box, he dumps more squares onto his palm.

"What is it?"

He pauses, drumming his palms on the piano for dramatic effect. "Patrick Bateman."

"Who the hell is Patrick Bateman?" Jayden asks from the pantry and comes back out with two honey buns and a can of Pringles.

"American Psycho," Saint cheekily replies. "Investment banker by day, serial killer by night."

"Hmmm," Jay hums thoughtfully. "Fitting."

I nod in agreement. I've seen the movie and while Patrick Bateman and Landon don't have the same personalities, I wouldn't put it past him to be a serial killer.

I snuff a laugh. "Fitting indeed."

"Piss off." He flips us off.

"So will you wear it?" Jagger asks with hopefulness in his voice.

Landon pushes off the counter and heads to the living room, leaving us all in the kitchen. "Yeah, whatever, and wipe those grins off your faces, or I'll change my mind."

"How'd you guess he'd wear it?" Jaggers questions.

"Does he really strike you as the guy who would willingly put on something extravagant?" He snickers, shaking his head as if he's imagining Landon wearing a superhero costume or anything with too much color.

"Smart." Jagger gives him a high five and heads toward the living room, with Jayden following right behind him. Leaving Saint and me alone.

"How did it go? You were there longer than you said you'd be."

I shrug, taking a swig of my beer. "I wanted to help her bathe Phoenix as he got pizza sauce all over him. He's a messy eater." I grin, remembering how his face was covered in the tomato sauce and somehow he ended up getting it on his chest. "We also painted today and he made a bit of a mess, so I wanted to stay and help her clean up and put him to bed."

I don't mention that part of the reason I stayed longer was because I was trying to figure out what I did wrong. Then it dawns on me that maybe he might know. After all, they're *best friends*.

"You haven't, by chance, talked to Lola tonight? Have you?" I attempt to sound as nonchalant as I can, but the stupid smile on his face tells me he's not buying it.

"Maybe...why?"

"Can you not look at me like that? Also, I know you told Lola I hadn't eaten. That's not going to change anything, by the way."

While I made some improvement with Daisy today, I doubt she'll listen to a single thing I have to say.

"I'm just happy? Can I not smile? And don't worry about it. I don't need your help anyway. I'll figure it out. I always do."

I drag the pad of my finger on the cold, wet bottle, drawing an L, debating whether I should ask him again or not. I know he'll read too much into it, but fuck it, since when do I ever care what he or anyone thinks?

"So did you talk to her tonight?"

"Yeah, I did, actually, but it was cut short. Something about a date or something. I can't remember." He pushes a key on the piano, and then another.

"A...date?" I swallow, but it's a little hard. It feels as if a ball has formed in my throat, and my lungs feel a little tight. There's an odd sinking feeling in my stomach, but I push away the weird sensation.

Only it doesn't leave. It lingers.

"Something like that. She seemed excited." He pushes away from the piano and steps into the pantry, pulling out a bag of chips. "Lucky guy, am I right?"

"Yeah...lucky guy."

29

LOLA

"THANKS FOR LETTING ME KNOW ABOUT THIS."

"You don't have to keep thanking me. Just don't tell anyone or Marcos will kill me," Darius replies, winking at me from the other side of the art studio.

I met Darius on the first day of school, in our Walking Seminar class. Since we're hiking and backpacking a lot for this class, Professor Garcia paired everyone together, and she paired Darius and me.

Just like everyone else, he found out TJ and I have a kid together. The difference between him and a lot of people is that he doesn't care who Phoenix's dad is. He's openly told me he doesn't care for athletes or sports in general.

"I promise I won't, but you're seriously a life saver. I hardly have time to get my clients' paintings done at home, let alone my assignments."

Despite the lack of clients I've gotten recently, I'm still working on a few that I need to mail soon, on top of working on my assignments for school. Having TJ around, even for a few hours, has really helped, but still, I'm a perfectionist and sometimes a painting takes a little longer.

We shouldn't be in the art studio on a Saturday at 11:00

p.m., but Darius and Professor Garcia's TA, Marcos, are "extremely close." They met last year when they both signed up to be the models for a figure drawing class to make extra money. Since then, they've been *close*. They haven't necessarily put a label on their relationship, but they're only exclusive to each other.

"I seriously don't understand why you don't just become a live painter full-time. You don't need a degree to define how talented you are."

I shift on the stool, drawing my attention back to the easel. I bite the inside of my cheek, staring at my half-painted canvas until my vision blurs, and all I can manage to think about is my parents.

They had no faith I'd make anything of myself and no faith I'd ever get a degree. I know I could potentially become successful doing live paintings full time, but their belief that I was a failure motivates me to stay in school.

"It's good to have a plan B." I shrug, hoping he can't detect the strain in my voice. It's hard to keep the hurt at bay, when every time I think about them, my heart sinks. "I can't guarantee that I'll always have clients. I hardly have any as it is."

"As you should. Plan Bs are a must. If I can't get my own studio, my plan B is to sell feet pics. If all else fails, at least I know I have pretty feet."

I laugh, knowing that he's being one hundred percent serious, but I know he's too talented for something not to work out for him. Aside from being a talented painter, he's also great at sculpting.

"Let me know how that goes. I might have to join you."

I'm kidding, maybe. Even though our apartment is cheap and safe, driving an hour back and forth almost every day has gotten exhausting. That aside, I feel guilty that Cara and Daisy have to do it, only because I can't afford to move closer to campus.

"I doubt you'll have to do that. I'm confident it's all going to work out for you."

Peering over my shoulder, I find that he's already looking at me smiling. I return the smile, feeling the ache in my chest dissolve.

"Not trying to change the subject, but have you decided on what costume you'll wear next week?"

"Well..."

He cuts the space between us with his palette and brush in hand. He beams, excitement laced in his voice. "You have a costume. You have to tell me what it is."

Daisy is so adamant I wear the dress, but I'm still not sure I can pull it off. "I might have one."

"Okay, and?" he eagerly asks.

"But I'm also still looking."

Darius grumbles, scrunching his nose. "Halloween is next week. All the costumes are probably taken, unless you DIY the shit out of something."

I might just wear the costume Daisy bought. I just hope I don't regret it.

"I'm sure I'll figure something out."

"I'm sure whatever you wear, it'll be hot." He walks back to where his canvas is and sits on his stool. "So how did it go with your baby daddy today? I'm guessing good, since you were a little late getting here."

I hadn't expected TJ to stay as long as he did, considering he's meeting with Alexia tonight. Though if I had to guess, I'm sure he's already with her.

"You can just say his name," I say, but it's pointless. It seems like everyone loves to say baby daddy instead of his actual name. "And yeah, it went...good."

Good is an understatement. It was more than that. It felt as if I was talking to someone I've known for a while. Until I saw his phone and realized I'd gotten a little too comfortable and that I don't really know TJ.

I can't believe I willingly agreed to wear this.

Actually, I shouldn't be surprised that somehow Daisy convinced me to wear the dress, and Cara convinced me to wear the heels. Not that I'm against any of this, but I know we're going to be home extremely late, meaning my feet are going to be sore.

Since Daisy's parents haven't seen Phoenix since August, they decided to come by and take care of him this weekend. If it was anyone else, I wouldn't have done that, but he's grown up with them and I trust them.

"Stop that!" Cara yells into my ear due to the loud music blasting throughout Liquid. She slaps my hand away as I attempt to pull the hem of my dress down for the hundredth time tonight. "I promise, unless you bend over, no one is going to see a thing."

I give her a pointed stare. "That makes me feel a lot better."

Cara is dressed as Storm from Marvel. Even though she's wearing a black latex one-piece and her ass is practically pouring out the suit, the cape draped over her shoulders covers it.

She waves her hand dismissively, just as the bartender sets three shot glasses in front of us. "Here, drink this. It will help you loosen up." She hands me and Daisy our shots.

Daisy's dressed up as a Greek goddess. The bra and short skirt she's wearing are both covered in golden feathers that she personally made.

"Smile, Lo—I mean Jessica Rabbit." Daisy smiles, her gaze drifting down my body and back up. "I knew this would look good on you."

Despite how many times Cara and Daisy reassured me that I looked hot, I still can't help but feel a little self-conscious. My thighs are rubbing and my stomach is definitely not as flat as the real Jessica Rabbit.

"I'm smiling. I'm just trying to make sure I don't accidentally flash anyone." I give up on tugging down the dress. No matter how many times I do it, it still rides up.

"Hey, it might get us free drinks." The casualness in her tone lets me know she'd be okay if I took one for the team.

The last thing I want to do is show my ass off, but I wouldn't mind free drinks.

What the hell am I saying? Absolutely not.

"But even if anyone were to see anything, they'd all forget. Look at them." She waves at the throng of people taking up every inch of space inside Liquid. "They're all either drunk, high, or both."

"She has a point, but either way, let's not think about them. It's Halloween, you're kid-free, and you're single. We're here to have a good time and get a little drunk. Drink." Daisy takes her shot, and Cara and I follow suit, wincing as the warm liquid glides down my throat.

"That's the spirit!" A familiar voice pulls my attention away from my friends and when I spot him, I find myself relaxing and smiling.

"Hey, guys," I greet Darius and Marcos, waving my free hand at them.

"You look hot!" Darius shouts over the loud music. "I should have known it was going to be Jessica Rabbit. Of course you'd pull it off so well."

"Right!" Daisy exclaims.

"And you two." Darius stares at my two best friends in awe. "You look fucking amazing! Storm and a Greek goddess. I'm obsessed." He slightly raises his hand and bows in front of us.

We laugh, returning the gesture as we take in their costumes. They're both dressed as shirtless firefighters, with suspenders, plastic axes strapped to their backs, and yellow plastic helmets on their heads.

Darius leans in. "Hey, I gotta use the restroom. I'll be back."

"I'll come with you," I say to him and turn toward the girls. "I'll be back. I promise I won't be long."

"Okay, we'll be here." Daisy nods.

"Don't take too long or we'll go hunt you down," Cara adds, her stern expression telling me she's not playing around.

I chuckle. "I won't."

Marcos stays behind with the girls. Before Darius and I walk off, I see Daisy order another round of shots.

"You seriously look good! I'm not sure what I was expecting, but it definitely wasn't this."

"I just hope I don't regret it. It's shorter than I expected it to be."

"Who cares? Compared to what the others are wearing, your costume is pretty long." He chuckles, glancing at the couple making out in the hallway that leads to the restroom before his eyes land on the girl who's dressed as a cowgirl. She's wearing jean shorts that hardly cover her ass. "Stop stressing. Maybe you should have stayed back and had another shot or two."

I gently elbow his side. "Shut up."

"I'm messing, but seriously, stop overthinking it. You look good." He stands next to me as I get behind a group of girls waiting to use the restroom.

"Don't wait for me. It looks like I'll be here a while." I grimace, staring at the men's restroom that has no line and then back at Darius. "Don't worry, I'll probably be here when you get out."

He still doesn't move. That is until three guys walk into the restroom. "Fuck, okay, I'm going before a line starts to form, but I shouldn't take long."

"Go." I push him in that direction. "I'll be here."

When he disappears, I glance down at my dress. I'm not entirely sure if it's my friend's genuine words or the alcohol buzzing through my system, but I feel better than I did before I left the apartment.

I relish this wave of happiness before it leaves. I don't know how to explain it, but sometimes I feel this burst of excitement, like nothing can bring me down. It almost feels like a high, until it doesn't. When it wears off, I end up questioning myself and doubting things I shouldn't.

My thoughts come to a pause as the girls standing in front of me start talking about someone I shouldn't care about.

"You know, I don't care that TJ has a kid. He's still so fucking hot," one of the girls slurs. "I've always had a thing for dads. I'd be a great stepmom."

Her friend drunkenly giggles. "Jen, you're delusional and drunk."

"Drunk maybe, delusional no," her friend counters, shaking her head. "I'm just saying if he's looking, I'd be a great mom. Hell, I'd make a great stay-at-home NBA wife."

"She's definitely drunk." Another one of their friends laughs. "Good luck getting TJ to talk to you. He might sleep with you, but he's not looking for anything serious. You know what kind of guy he is."

The first friend pouts, sighing deeply. "Why must you ruin my dreams? I know he likes to fuck around, but a girl can dream."

Her friend breaks into a fit of laughter. "Just keep dreaming, Jen. It's not going to happen. I'm sure the only thing that could make TJ change his fuck boy ways is—"

A tap on my shoulder makes me jump in my spot and makes me realize just how deep I was in their conversation.

"Lauren?"

"Huh?" As soon as I turn around, I hate myself for not having a better poker face because behind me stands Alexia.

"Sorry, I thought you were someone else." Alexia chuckles, seemingly embarrassed. "You just look so much like the girl TJ hangs out with." She pauses, eyes doing a double take at my body. "Except you're so much prettier."

"Oh." Is all that I say because what else is there to say? I've never spoken to Alexia, much less ever been around her long enough to get to know her.

"God, you probably don't even know who I am." She shakes her head, pulling a black braid over her shoulder. "I'm Alexia, a really *good* friend of TJ's. You must be Lola, right?" I don't miss the subtle way she said good and what she means by that. "I've heard so much about you. You're famous."

"Yeah, I'm Lola, and I wouldn't say that I'm famous."

She scoffs, rolling her eyes almost condescendingly. "You're all anyone talks about."

I force a smile, feeling uncomfortable at the tone of her voice. "Nothing worth listening to. It's nothing good. I'm sure you've heard it all."

She shrugs. "Good or bad, it ties you to TJ. I promise it's really not a bad thing. If I were you, I'd be thriving in it. Especially since TJ has great connections and knows a lot of people. You should take advantage of it."

It takes everything not to let my smile falter or to feel annoyed at her words. "It's nothing worth taking advantage of. Being tied to TJ is not something I care for."

"No, of course not." Her smile tightens, but it softens as her eyes trail down my body. "Your costume is so cute. What are you supposed to be?" She tilts her head to one side and then the other as if she's trying to figure it out.

"Jessica Rabbit," I answer, pulling my purple glove up.

Her brows draw together. "Isn't her dress supposed to be long?"

I slowly inhale, urging myself not to feel self-conscious. "Yeah, I just decided to do something different."

"Oh." Her lips purse. "Different is...*cute*." Her eyes drop to my stomach, lingering there for a second. "The dress really looks good on you. If it were me, I'd be a little worried about how tight and short it is, but I'm sure you got it under control."

"Alexia!" a girl behind us yells. When we turn around, we see three girls standing just a few feet behind us. "We've been looking for you. Let's go. They're here."

"I'm coming!" Alexia raises her finger. "It was so good talking to you. I'll see you around."

"Yeah, see you around." I swallow, interlocking my fingers in front of my stomach.

30

TJ

"You know, I was dreading coming here, but you've just made things so much more interesting." Landon twists the ax in his hand, skimming the crowd.

I stare at him, confused. "Me?"

"We just got here and you're already looking for her." He looks at me as the strobe lights shine on the side of his face that has the fake splattered blood on it, giving him an eerie look. "Leash is tight, yeah?"

"Fuck off."

"There she is." Saint points at the bar.

My head snaps in the direction of the bar. Fortunately for me, I don't care what they think, but unfortunately, it's not Lola at the bar but her friends and a guy.

"Like a fucking dog," Landon taunts.

I refrain from rolling my eyes and flipping him off. He thrives off my annoyance, and the last thing I want is for him to say bullshit all night because I know he will.

If Jagger were here, he'd be giving me shit about it too, but he's with Gabby and Polly. He said he'd meet us here in a few.

Lola told me Phoenix is with Daisy's parents tonight. I'm happy they still help her, but I wonder if her parents wouldn't want to be with him instead. She rarely talks about them and when she does, it's always vague.

I wish I knew what she was thinking. Most of the time, I can figure someone out, or at least get an idea of what they're thinking, but with Lola, it's hard. Sometimes when I think I finally understand her, I realize how fucking wrong I am.

What I wouldn't do to know what she's thinking.

"I'm *thirsty*," Saint announces, eyes centered on the girl dressed as a Greek goddess. He walks into the crowd and toward the bar, not looking back to see if we're behind him.

"You just don't know how to give up, do you?" I hear Jayden ask Saint as he walks next to him. Landon and I follow behind them. "She doesn't want you."

"You don't..."

I tune out their conversation. I already know how tonight is going to go, and it definitely doesn't end with Saint and Daisy leaving together. I give him props for still pursuing her because she hasn't once shown an interest in him.

I look around, searching for her through the thick crowd, but she's nowhere in sight.

"Hey!" Cara is the first to greet us, a bubbly smile spreading across her face. Although I'm sure that's directed at Jayden. "Let me guess, Top Gun Pilot?"

"Yes, Miss Storm," he replies. He drags his aviator sunglasses down the bridge of his nose and blatantly checks her out. "You look *really* good, Care."

"I know Jay." She beams, flipping her white hair over her shoulder before directing her gaze on us. "Hey, guys. Whoa, Landon, I hope that's fake blood."

"Unfortunately," he begrudgingly replies and leans on the bar countertop, signaling for the bartender.

"*Ciao, Margherita*." Saint stands in between Daisy and the guy who's standing next to her, completely towering over both of them. "And her friend."

"I'm Marcos and I'll be back." He tips his half full glass at us before he disappears into the crowd.

Daisy takes her shot and spins to face us with a small smile on her face. I struggle to believe it's real because she hardly ever does that around me. But I know it's all alcohol. Her cheeks are flushed and her eyes are glossed over.

She directs her attention to Saint. "Wow, you look—"

"Amazing, devastatingly handsome, hot." He rests an elbow on the counter, a crooked grin slowly curving his lips as his eyes trail down Daisy's body.

She purses her lips, brows pinching together. "What are you supposed to be? I know TJ is dressed as someone from Money Heist and Landon is Patrick Bateman, but I can't figure what you're supposed to be."

"You can't be serious?"

"Very."

"Don't play with me, Daisy. You know exactly who I'm supposed to be."

"Not a single clue."

"I know that you know who I'm..."

I block out their conversation because something tells me she's fucking with him and he's going along with it. It's obvious Saint is dressed as Jack Sparrow.

Slowly scanning the crowd, I spot most of my teammates and a lot of other people I know. I wave and nod at them but keep searching for Lola. I keep looking until I catch sight of golden copper hair in my peripheral vision. I become confined in my spot, mesmerized, as Lola makes her way through the crowd.

She looks like a fucking dream, though it's nothing new. I've seen her in the most comfortable, casual clothing and she always looks stunning.

I swallow hard, feeling that odd stutter in my chest again. I'd never felt this feeling until recently, and it only happens when she's around.

Though the odd stutter stops when she smiles. It's not the rise of her lips that causes the air to hitch at the back of my throat. It's seeing who she's smiling at that leaves a bitter taste in my mouth.

The guy who she was with at the café walks next to her, along with the guy Daisy and Cara had been with when we got here. The annoying thing about coffee guy is that I've seen him around campus with her.

Now I wonder if she was with him last week.

She still hasn't noticed that I'm looking at her, and part of me *needs* her to look at me, but a part of me wants to look away. I look desperate as fuck, hoping she'll tilt her head just enough to find me staring at her. Hoping that she'll give me a fraction of the attention she's giving them.

I've come to realize I'm going to have to work for it because Lola doesn't give a fuck about me. She's made it clear that the only thing she cares about is me being a good father to Phoenix. Other than that, she couldn't care less about who I am and what I do.

I could look away and pretend I don't care, but I *do* care. I'm annoyed she's with the coffee guy again.

"Damn." My neck whips at the sound of a familiar whistle. Not sure when they arrived, but Jagger, Gabby, and Polly are standing next to us. "She looks good," Jagger says.

"She makes a killer Jessica Rabbit." Polly takes a pull of her drink, though I'm sure it's to hide the smirk directed at me.

"Yeah." I clear my dry throat. "Yeah, she does."

I shift my gaze back in her direction. Just when our eyes lock, Alexia stands in front of me, along with her friends.

"Hey, you're finally here." She inches forward, pressing herself against me. "I've been looking everywhere for you. I texted you earlier, but you never responded."

I take a few steps back, putting some distance between us. I look back at Lola, but her attention is focused on coffee guy.

"Yeah, sorry, I got busy with practice and Phoenix."

"Oh, that's all right, you're here now." A sly smile spreads across her face. It's the *let's go fuck* smile.

There's a reason why I haven't been texting her—I'm going to cut things off. I've been thinking about it a lot. I know it's not what I want anymore. It doesn't even feel right.

Despite wanting to end things, I'm not going to be an asshole. I won't do it here.

"Finally! I was about to go looking for you." Daisy raises her voice, walking between Alexia and me.

She smiles apologetically at her. "Sorry, the line was long."

I know I shouldn't do what I'm about to do, but fuck it.

"Hey, Mrs. Rabbit." I take a step closer to her, and surprisingly, she doesn't move away. It takes everything in me not to let my eyes linger below her neckline, crowd her personal space, or tell those two guys to fuck off.

"Hey, TJ."

"Where's Mr. Rabbit?" I arch a brow, looking both ways as if I were looking for him.

Her lips quirk up. "He doesn't exist."

"Trust me, it's so much better that way. You can do whatever you want with whoever you want. Isn't that right, TJ?" Alexia playfully nudges her elbow at my side.

I look at her, wondering what she's playing at, but she keeps her gaze glued on Lola. Before I get to reply, Saint interjects.

"I got them to send a few things to our table." Saint jerks his head in the direction of the VIP section and slings his arm around Daisy's shoulders. "Come on, you said you wouldn't talk to me until you had something to drink. I got you a little bit of everything."

Daisy doesn't protest, but she pushes his arm off her. "This doesn't mean anything."

Everyone, including Alexia, follows along. Except for Lola and Gabby. They stay behind, talking about their costumes. I don't want to say that I'm hovering, but I'm pretty much doing just that. I should give Lola her space, but I can't go the entire night or another day with her being weird around me.

"Lola, wait."

I'm not sure where Jagger comes from. He was just flirting with some girl, but now he's pulling Gabby away, leaving Lola and me alone. Or at least, as alone as we can be.

"What?" She follows behind them, not slowing down.

"Please just—just wait."

"We're in the middle of the dance floor. We need to—"

I wrap my hand around her wrist and softly tug her in the opposite direction of the VIP section, toward the wall that has water cascading down it.

We're far from being alone. There are people everywhere, but considering it's Halloween, I'm sure no one is in the right state of mind. At least not enough to know what we're talking about.

Releasing her wrist, I rake my fingers through my hair, releasing a sharp breath. "I want to know what I did wrong. I keep thinking back to last week, but nothing comes to mind. I guess I'm a dumbass because nothing is clicking, so please tell me what I did wrong. I don't want you to be mad at me."

She doesn't say anything. She stares at me and it isn't until the orange strobe light shines on her face that I see a flicker of sadness in her eyes.

"Fuck, please tell me, what did I do wrong?"

"Nothing, you didn't do anything—"

"You say that, but you've been weird around me."

"That's not—"

"I want to fix whatever I did wrong, but I can't fix it if you don't talk to me."

"I've been trying to ignore it, but it's hard to be around you when people assume you're my one-way ticket to something better. And then Alexia—you know, it doesn't even matter. I'm sorry. I thought I was fine. I thought I could get over the whispers and the looks, but I can't. I'm sorry. I'm just having a hard time adjusting to all of this. I know I should let it go because people are going to talk, but I don't know how you do it. I can't act like you. I can't act like it doesn't bother me because it does."

How do I tell her that all of this is overwhelming for me? That I thought I had life figured out, but I really don't.

How do I tell her that I can't stop thinking about her...her golden copper hair, the remnants of paint that sometimes linger on her skin, those earthy-colored eyes...

Focus!

I attempt to focus, but I fail. She's staring at me with that undecipherable look she's usually giving me. I used to think it bothered me, not being able to figure out what she's thinking, but now I like it.

"I meant it when I said I panic..." I look around, hoping that no one is listening. "I'd rather not talk about it here, but I want you to know you're not alone." I stretch my hand out, wrapping my palm around her wrist, giving it a soft squeeze. "I'm here and I don't want you to feel like you need to do this alone. When I said I wanted to be there for Phoenix, I also meant I'd be there for you."

Her gaze flickers to my hand around her wrist. "I'm sorry. I know we talked about this before, but I—"

"You don't have to apologize. It's not your fault." I smile, hoping she feels reassured, but I falter when Alexia's name resurfaces in my head. "Wait, did you say something about Alexia?"

"It's nothing important."

"Did she say something to you?"

"She—you know what? It's not worth it." She sighs, pulling her hand away. "But I do want to tell you that if you're going to be around Phoenix, just lock your phone after using it. I don't want him to see things he shouldn't."

I chuckle, taken aback. "What do you mean? I swear I've never—"

"I'm not judging you or anything. Do whatever you want to do. I just don't want Phoenix to see things he shouldn't." She looks away, her lips pursing as if she's debating something. "Last week on Saturday, you got pictures from Alexia, and your phone was close to Phoenix. I hadn't meant to look at it, but it lit up, and I accidentally saw the pictures. Just be careful about leaving your phone unlocked around him."

I think back to last week, and then it dawns on me. It never once went through my mind, but now it all makes sense.

But there's no way—she's not—there's no way Lola's jealous.

I know I should shut up, but I really can't help myself.

"Are you jealous?" I cock a brow.

"What? No—I'm not—I am *not* jealous." She aggressively huffs, folding her arms against her chest.

"Nothing happened. I know what it looks like, but I swear it's not like that."

I don't know why I feel the need to explain myself, but I don't want her to think anything happened because nothing ever did. I only looked at the picture to delete it.

She looks to the side, like she's debating whether she believes me or not.

"I want you to believe me." I draw nearer, enough to inhale her scent. It's different, it's not vanilla, but something sharp and citrusy. "You look amazing."

She cracks a small smile and rolls her eyes. I catch a shimmer of purple on her eyelids. "Yeah, okay."

"Yeah, okay, what?" I grin, inching a step closer to her.

"To both things you said."

"You don't believe either thing that I said?" I let my eyes slowly roam down the length of her body, appreciating the way the red dress clings to every inch of her skin.

She lifts a shoulder and lets it fall. "People say things all the time. Doesn't necessarily make them true."

"You want honesty? I'll give you honesty." I lick my lips, doing my best to focus on her face and not her cleavage. "I didn't ask for the pictures and I didn't sleep with her. You want to know what I did Saturday night while you were on a date? I was thinking of what I did wrong to piss you off. I was thinking about what I could do to make things better because I meant what I said. I want us to be okay, I want us to work things out. We're going to be in each other's lives for the rest of our lives, and I hope you're okay with that because I've never been more okay with anything more in *my* life."

Taking another step, I leave an inch of space in between us and continue. "And here's to more honesty because I gain nothing from lying to you. You look really fucking stunning, Peaches. It's going to take everything in me not to look at you and..."

My heart beats faster than it ever has before. I hear the loud thumping of my heart in my ears, drowning out the music in the club.

"And what?"

I almost miss her question, but the words manage to register in my head before they become muted by the erratic beat of my heart.

I hesitate to reply but decide against holding back because fuck it. I don't think I've wanted anything more than this.

"And not kiss you."

Her eyes widen a fraction and she swallows. "I—uh—I need a drink." She pivots on her heel and walks away.

31

LOLA

Something is severely wrong with me, and it has nothing to do with the alcohol I've been drinking since I've walked away from TJ. No, it has everything to do with the fact that for a second, I actually wanted to kiss him, again. And it's all I've been able to think about.

It's all I still want to do.

I shouldn't though. I should focus on making the best of this weekend, knowing Phoenix is with people I trust. And I should also be drinking more. Yeah, that's what I should be doing, drinking more.

"Hey!" I grab Daisy's wrist, pulling her closer to me so she can hear me since we're on the dance floor. "I'll be back." I lift my empty cup.

She nods, still moving along with the music. "I'll come with."

"No, it's okay. I'll be back quickly. The bar is just over there."

"Lo—"

"I won't be long. Either way, Darius and Marcos are over there." Her eyes shift to the bar and when she spots both guys, she relaxes a little. "I think they're leaving anyway, so I want to say goodbye."

"Fine, but I'll be keeping my eyes on you."

I chuckle, squeezing her wrist for reassurance, and let go as I start making my way to the bar.

"Hey!" I say to the guys just as the bartender hands Marcos his debit card back. "Are you guys calling it a night?"

"Oh no, baby, we could go all night long." Darius pushes away from the bar top but sways, almost falling in process, but Marcos manages to snake his arm around him before he faceplants the floor. "I'm good. I'm great. I'm better than ever, M. I just think...maybe...maybe I should...sit."

"You're drunk," Marcos deadpans but flashes him a ghost of a smile, staring at him as if he's the most precious thing he'd ever seen. "We're leaving."

I bite back a laugh, gabbing their helmets and axes before they're dropped on the floor. "I got it, don't worry."

"Thanks, Lola. Our Uber should already be here." Marcos tightens his grip around Darius and hauls him toward the front door.

I follow right behind, clutching everything against my chest and making sure I don't let my eyes stray off into the crowd in hopes that I'll find him. Because somehow my traitorous eyes have been trying to sneak glances despite my efforts to stay away from him.

Unfortunately, I have alcohol in my system and all rational thoughts evade my brain as I turn my head. Of course the one time I hope I don't see him, I instantly find him. And he's not alone. He's with Alexia.

I bite the inside of my cheek and look away, exiting out of the front door.

"Our Uber's here. Thanks so much, Lola, you're such a sweetheart." Marcos smiles, giving me a quick side hug.

"Yeah, no problem." Pulling back, I open the back door for him and let them both get inside.

"Bye, Lola!" Darius slurs, waving me goodbye. "Don't do something I wouldn't do." He winks, cackling.

"In that case, just be careful because there isn't anything on this earth that he wouldn't do." Marcos laughs softly as if he's remembering something.

"Duly noted. Good night, guys." I hand them their stuff and shut the door behind them, watching the Uber drive off.

I turn but stop abruptly. TJ stands a few feet behind me, leaning against the wall of the building, arms crossed against his chest, staring at the spot the Uber was just at, and then his eyes shift to me.

"You and your habit of doing things alone." He blows out a heavy breath and pushes off the wall. "Do you seriously not realize how dangerous this is?"

"I'm fine. I'm going back inside now." I make my way back in and I don't have to look back to know TJ is hovering behind me. "I don't need a bodyguard."

"Seems like you do if you're going to be making decisions that put you at risk."

"I'm not going to argue with you." I look over my shoulder, glaring at him. "Go away. I'm sure you have people looking for you."

I might have peeked at him throughout the night more than I wanted to. Anytime I did, there were always guys and girls around him.

"They can keep looking," he says, still hovering right behind me.

I let out an exasperated breath. Instead of stopping at the bar or back to the dance floor where the girls are at, I head to the VIP section. There's hardly anyone there, which means all the seats are open and I'll be able to finally take my heels off.

"Would you stop walking away from me?"

Swiftly, I turn and almost bump into his chest, but he grabs my waist, gripping it to keep me steady.

I crane my head back, staring up at him, but my traitorous eyes flicker down to his lips. I don't know if he notices or not, but he doesn't say anything about it.

"My feet hurt." I look down at my heels that no doubt broke

the back of my heels into blisters. "I want to—" I gasp, my eyes widening in shock as he bends down and lifts me up. He securely hooks his arm under my thighs and the other behind my back, pressing me close to his chest. "What are you—put me down! TJ, stop, people are looking!"

"It doesn't matter." He shrugs, staring straight ahead as he heads up the stairs.

I hold down the hem of my dress, making sure it doesn't rise up. "TJ—"

"Lola, you're looking at me. That's all that matters." It's brief, but he looks down at me before he focuses on going up the stairs.

I'm stuck on his words. I don't realize that we're already at the lounge of the VIP section. Carefully, he sets me down on one of the high stools and drags the other in front of the one I'm sitting on.

I don't say anything, although I'm not really sure what I should say. Let alone how to react to the way something so simple made me feel so...warm inside.

"I'm sorry if I crossed the line and made you feel uncomfortable earlier. That wasn't my intention."

"You didn't make me uncomfortable." I fidget with the finger of my purple glove.

"Then why have you been avoiding me? All night it's been fucking torture staring at you from a distance while you danced and talked to those guys."

"Guys?" There have been guys coming to talk to Daisy and me all night. Cara's been with us most of the night, but Jayden's been by her side. There are only two guys who were consistently with us. "Darius and Marcos?"

His jaw ticks, his hands fisting. "Them...and the others. You let every single one of them be around you while I watched from a distance." He leans back in the chair, his legs spread wide.

"It's not like that...with Darius and Marcos."

He scoffs. "Right..."

"They don't like me like that and they never will. They'd

rather take their chances on you than they would on me." TJ isn't their type, but they both admitted they find him attractive.

"Oh." He sits up, lips flattening into a straight line, recognition setting in his eyes. "*Oh.*"

"Are we done?"

"Am I really that bad that you hate being around me?"

"No, I don't hate being around you."

"Then what is it?" he asks, exasperated.

"I don't...I don't know how to feel about the things you say to me!" I blurt out. "And then you look at me like—like—" I grumble, not sure how to say what I'm feeling.

"Like I want to kiss you? Like I want to touch you? Because I do. So fucking bad."

I could blame my next words on the alcohol hindering my inhibitions, but I know what I'm about to say has nothing to do with the alcohol.

"Do it." I swallow hard. "Kiss me."

He stares at me, stunned, almost in disbelief as if he can't process what I just said.

I thought maybe distancing myself from him would clear my head, but I was wrong to believe that. Even as the alcohol runs through my buzzing body, everything sort of feels...almost quiet. The loud music, the people crowding the club, and my turbulent heart all slow down. "Are you sure? You've been drinking tonight and—"

"TJ, just—"

He stands and closes the gap between us. Everything around us evaporates into nothing as he cups my cheek, tipping my head back to stare up at him.

"Being away from you is not going to be possible." He winds his other arm around my waist and lifts me off the chair, pressing me hard against him. TJ lowers his head. His warm breath fans my lips, merely grazing mine. "It's just not fucking possible anymore."

Alcohol, it's the alcohol talking, but my mind doesn't want to focus on the reality. Instead, I pretend that he means it and relish the feel of his fingers digging into my dress, the pad of his thumb drawing soft circles on my cheek, and the hardness of his body against mine.

Standing on my tiptoes, I drape my arms around his shoulders and press my lips to his. Delicately, he returns the kiss, soft and slow, long enough for me to taste the slight bitterness of the beer on his lips, the smell of cedarwood from his cologne, and hear the pounding of my heart against my ears.

"Intoxicating," he murmurs, nipping at my bottom lip. "You are fucking intoxicating."

"Stop," I breathlessly say. "Just kiss me and let's pretend—"

He stops, still holding me as close as humanly possible. "What are we pretending?"

"Pretend that this isn't more than what it is. You don't need to say anything. So stop talking and just kiss me." I urged him.

TJ hesitates, his lips parting like he wants to say something, but then he closes them. "So you want to pretend?"

"Yeah, like we did two years ago."

"Okay." He smirks, dropping the hand on my cheek, and wraps it around my waist. "We're pretending, right?"

"Right."

"Let's *pretend* you're mine."

There's something mischievous about the way he looks at me, something possessive about the way holds me, and something controlling about the way he says it.

"TJ, that's not—"

"Peaches, we're pretending." He dips his head again, his lips just above mine as his fingers faintly stroke my back, causing me to shudder. Goose bumps break across my skin. "Just like we did two years ago. Let's pretend, yeah?"

I nod, but that's all I manage to do as he closes the gap and tugs my bottom lip between his teeth. He then sucks it hard and sinks his teeth into it. It hurts, but the pain fades away and a wave of pleasure takes me under.

And if the searing heat coursing through my body isn't enough, a needy moan claws its way from the back of my throat. Somehow it feels as if that's exactly what TJ needed to hear because he stops toying with my lip and slips his tongue into my mouth.

He fervently kisses me, his tongue intertwining with mine with a desperation that makes me moan harder. I'm breathless and dizzy, and it's not from the lack of oxygen but from how fucking hot and full of want he kisses me.

I should stop this right now. There's no way I can pretend like this doesn't affect me. Like my thong isn't wet, my nipples aren't hard, and my clit isn't pulsing. I should stop because this is more than me just feeling hot. This is—is my back against the wall?

He breaks our kiss, leaving me panting, chest rising hard, and frantically wanting more. I should be embarrassed at the sound of my deprived whimper.

"Say you're mine," he huskily demands. His hands slowly creep down the curve of my waist and glide across to my hips.

"No, kiss me." I urge, leaning closer to him.

"Not until you say it."

I blow a harsh breath. "You're frustrating, you know that?"

"Yeah, I know." He flashes me a crooked grin. "Say it."

This feels like we're overstepping a boundary. Tiptoeing over the imaginary line between pretend and reality. I should be careful because one wrong step, and I'll be screwing myself over, but it's only one night.

Just one night of pretending. In the morning, it won't mean a thing.

"Beg for it."

His lips hover over mine, his hands descending to my ass. "Lola." The gruffness of his voice has me sucking in my breath, but I hold it as he roughly cups my butt and presses me against his hard erection. "*Please* just say it. Please say you're mine. Just—"

"Hey—oh shit, sorry!" Jayden says loud enough for me to

sober up for a moment, making me realize where we are. "I just wanted to let you both know we're all going back to the house."

"We're coming too, Lola!" Cara giggles, her words slurred.

Peering around TJ's arm, I see Cara and Jayden standing just a few feet away from us. Thankfully, they're not focused on us but on each other. His arm is around her waist and she holds on to him like she's afraid she's going to fall.

There's no doubt they're both either almost drunk or already drunk as they sway from side and side and laugh at whatever they're saying to each other.

"We're going." TJ breathes harshly, glancing down at his erection pressed against my stomach.

I bite my bottom lip, doing my best not to smile, but it's hard as he groans.

"Look at what you do to me."

"That looks like a personal problem." I hold back my smile, and unapologetically shrug as I slip from his hold.

32

LOLA

"*MARGHERITA*, I DEDICATE THIS TO YOU." SAINT points the microphone he's holding at Daisy.

Everyone came back to the guys' house, including most of the basketball players and a number of girls. Some of the guys and girls are in the kitchen playing beer pong, while the rest of us are in the living room doing karaoke.

"Locked Out of Heaven" by Bruno Mars appears on the flat screen TV mounted on the wall.

Saint tosses the microphone in the air and almost drops it but manages to catch it before it falls. "Hit it, Gabby!" he says, mimicking Jack Sparrow's voice. He even walks like him, but that may just be because he's drunk.

As soon as the music starts playing, Daisy sinks into the couch, hiding her face behind her red plastic cup. "Please don't let him do this," she pleads, eyes begging with desperation.

I stifle a laugh, looking away as she looks at me with a murderous glare, but her harsh stare is no match for Saint's singing.

"Stop being dramatic. It's not that...bad."

I lied. It's bad. He might be immensely good-looking, but his singing is horrible. Though no one cares because they're all too drunk to care that he sounds terrible, and we all sound just as bad.

"The last thing I need is for anyone to think we're sleeping together." She hisses. "Do you not realize what this song means?"

TJ leans in, brushing his shoulder against mine. Invading my space again, like he has the past hour that we've been here. If he's not touching my shoulder, then his leg is rubbing up against mine, and if he's not doing that, then he's twirling a lock of my hair around his finger like he's doing now. His arm is draped along the back of the couch and a lock of my hair is laced around his finger.

It's the alcohol and all pretend, I keep telling myself for what seems like the thousandth time.

"It could be worse." He smiles, amused by the look of horror on her face. "Oh, come on, what's better than Jack Sparrow serenading you?"

"Fuck you, Theodore," she says in the most patronizing way, plastering a big smile on her face.

"Oh, come one, it could've been Shark Boy singing to you."

Jagger dressed up as Shark boy to match with Gabby, who dressed as Lava girl. His rendition of the lullaby that Shark boy sings in the movie is probably the most iconic and comical thing I've seen all night.

"You know I liked senior week TJ better."

"But you didn't know me. I'm pretty sure we said about two words to each other."

"Exactly." Daisy's face softens, her smile becoming genuine as she leans back on the couch, chugging half of whatever's in her cup. "I guess it's one song, but we never speak of this again."

"She's a ray of sunshine," TJ sarcastically retorts.

"I'm in a really good mood, so I'm going to pretend I didn't hear that, but call me sunshine again and I'll stab you with my heel."

"And she means it. Don't fuck with Daisy when she's drunk," I whisper.

Drunk Daisy is fun and wild, but she's also unpredictable.

"Got it," he whispers back, smiling, though it slips as his eyes connect to mine.

Suddenly, it feels like we're back at the club, the music and voices drowned out by the crackle of hot energy that binds us.

We haven't talked about the kiss or the fact he was begging me to say I was his. I've stuck with pretending I wasn't close to saying exactly what he wanted to hear.

He's so close to me, hovering and invading whatever little space I have. I should push him away. I shouldn't like this. I shouldn't keep thinking of him touching me, his tongue...

"I'll be back." I quickly stand, blowing a shaky breath as I make my way to the kitchen, but regret it instantly as a hard body crashes against me, causing their drink to spill all over me.

"Fuck, sorry. I didn't see you," one of TJ's teammates, Wyatt, says, though it seems like he's far from apologetic as his eyes drop down to my chest and linger there. "If it makes you feel better, you look really goo—" He snaps his mouth shut and stares at me remorsefully.

TJ stands next to me, cocking a brow, staring at him with a blank expression. "You were saying?"

"That I should be getting her some paper towels. I'll be back." He quickly scurries off.

"Fucking idiot," TJ mutters under his breath as he turns around. His eyes drop down to my dress before quickly shifting away. "Let me give you something to change into."

"It's fine. I should get going."

"I really hope you don't think I'm letting you leave this house wet."

Something tells me he didn't mean for it to sound that way, but as we lock eyes, I'm certain I know what he's thinking about because I'm thinking it too.

"I don't think that would be a good idea."

"Why? It's just a shirt."

"Because you and I know it's more than just a shirt."

A coy smile curves on his face. "It's just a shirt."

I arch a disbelieving brow. "Just a shirt?"

"Just a shirt."

Feeling the liquid seep into the dress, I decide against arguing with him and follow him up to his room. He keeps me close to him, shielding my body with his as we pass the living room that seems more packed than it was a few minutes ago.

Once we're in his room, he slips into his closet and I stand in front of the painting still hanging on his wall.

Memories of senior week and the night I told him about Phoenix resurface in my head. They fade away when I feel him stand right next to me.

"Can I ask you something?" I pull my gloves off.

"Anything."

"If you could, would you take senior week back?"

He doesn't hesitate as he answers. "No. Taking it all back would mean not meeting you, and not meeting you would mean no Phoenix, and a world without Phoenix is a world I can't imagine."

My heart sputters out of control.

He looks at me just as I look at him. When our eyes connect, I know I fucked up coming here.

"Here." TJ stretches his hand out, holding the shirt for me.

"Thanks." As I grab the shirt, my fingers brush against his and once again my heart goes crazy. *It's minimal contact. Calm. Down.* I tell myself. "I promise to give it back."

"Don't worry about it."

We both still hold on to the shirt, neither one of us letting it go. I need to change and get out of here before I do something I regret, but I can't bring myself to move.

"Lola?"

"Hmmm?"

"Are we still pretending?"

"I...I don't know what we're doing." I lick my lips, giving him a half shrug.

"Do you want to stop?"

I should nod, but instead, I shake my head. "No, I don't want to stop."

TJ takes the shirt and lets it fall to the ground. "I've not forgotten where we left off. Say it."

I roll my eyes. "No, I'm not going to say that."

He grabs my waist, squeezing it softly as he guides me backward until my butt touches his desk. "Why are you so stubborn?"

"Why are you insistent? None of this is real," I counter, tilting my head to the side.

Letting go of my waist, he rests his palms on the dresser and bows down. "So this isn't real?"

One hand stays on the dresser while the other toys with a lock of my hair and then he pulls on it. "Still not real?"

I blow a shaky breath, shaking my head.

His grip loosens and his hand descends down the curve of my hip, and once they're at the hem, he stops.

"What about now?"

I swallow, feeling my throat become dry. I use all my willpower to not rub my thighs together. "No."

A smirk rises on his face as he lets go of the hem and his hand slips under my dress. "Come on, Peaches, you can't tell me this isn't real?"

This is way too real, if my wet thong isn't an indication of it, but I refuse to admit that. "It's not. Especially because my name isn't Peaches. We've been over this."

"Have we?" TJ feigns ignorance, lifting his fingers on the outside of my thigh, teasing my skin, and leaving a small trail of fire.

I clear my throat, refraining from letting a moan escape. "You're frustrating, you know that?"

A deep chuckle rumbles against his chest. "So I've heard, but you know what's really frustrating?"

"What?" I hate the way I sound breathless.

"That you think this isn't real because you and I know once I touch you, my fingers will be so fucking wet." His lips are so close, I'd hardly have to move to touch them.

I roll my eyes. "You're so full of yourself."

"Yeah, occasionally." I'd hate how smug his tone is if only I didn't find it hot. "But this isn't about me. We're talking about you. Just accept this is real, and I'll be happy to move my fingers exactly where you want them to be."

I suck in a breath, gripping the edge of his desk as his fingers move to the inside of my thigh. "This isn't—" I gasp, feeling a single finger graze between my folds through the lace material. It's meticulous and dizzying the way he drags it purposely slow.

My fingernails dig into the wood, breathing harshly as I feel the material of my thong graze against my clit, adding just the smallest pressure, but it's enough to make my legs quiver.

"It's real. Say it. Beg for it," he demands, repeating my words from earlier.

The last bit of my restraint fizzles into nothing as he adds more pressure and another finger. I completely lose myself when he finally touches my aching bundle of nerves.

"It's real," I whimper, biting my lip hard as I grind shamelessly against his fingers, feeling the fabric stick between my folds. "This is real."

"Beg for it, Lola," he gruffly whispers against my lips.

"Please, TJ..."

The rest of my words get lodged in the back of my throat as he lifts me up, pushes whatever's on it, and sets me down on his dresser. "Spread your legs for me."

The possessiveness in his voice does something to me I can't explain, and I spread my legs, hiking my dress up to my waist.

"So fucking wet," he rasps, nipping my jaw while his fingers push the drenched lace to the side.

I exhale a shaky breath, dropping my head back as he drags two fingers up and down my folds, but when his fingers find my clit, a loud moan escapes my lips. I'd be embarrassed if I wasn't desperate to find my release.

"Don't stop," I beg, arching my back as his thumb circles the little bud, and his other finger glides down my pussy. And then, in a split second, the first orgasm wracks through me.

It's embarrassing how fast it happens, but I don't have time to process it as he thrusts two fingers inside of me.

"Ahhh," I whimper, clenching around his fingers as he thrusts them in and out while his thumb is still on my clit.

"Deeper?" he asks next to the pulse ricocheting against my throat.

"Yes...deeper," I needily say, nodding desperately.

I'm not sure how he manages to get his fingers in so deep, but they get a spot I've never gotten to before. He thrusts his fingers, fucking me with them rapidly, all while I'm gaping and begging for him not to stop.

I'm so close, every inch of my body burns and shakes in anticipation. When I open my eyes for a brief moment, I catch a glimpse of TJ's and my reflection in his mirror. I don't know what's wrong with me, but the sound of his slick fingers, seeing the position we're in, me grinding against him, and his fingers working in and out of me, I orgasm hard and my entire body spasms.

I shut my eyes tight, breathing hard as I buck my hips against him. My pussy throbs as the orgasm ripples throughout my entire body.

When I finally catch my breath and open my eyes, I realize that my dress lifted higher and TJ's staring down at my stomach covered in stretch marks.

That's enough to bring me back to reality. I push him away and hop off his dresser, pulling my dress.

"Lola, I—"

"It's pretty late. I should get going." I interlock my fingers in front of my stomach, a wave of overwhelming emotions crashing against me. "I'll, uh..." God, why am I so awkward? "I'll see you later."

I make my way to the door, ready to make a run for it, but before I can grab the doorknob, TJ's words halt me in my tracks.

"Do you want to spend the night?"

It takes a second for the words to fully register in my head, but even when they do, I feel like somehow I still didn't hear him correctly.

"What?"

"Do you want to spend the night?"

Because my poker face is shit, I know I probably look like a deer caught in the headlights, wide-eyed and lips parted, staring agape at his question.

"I promise it's not like that," he says before I get to say anything. "I just think it'd be better if we waited until morning to take you home. With all the parties going on and everyone drinking, it's just safe for you to stay here."

I tuck my hair behind my ear, crossing my arms against my chest. A debate plays in my head as I contemplate what I want to do. I wasn't even supposed to be here tonight, especially in his room of all places.

"I have to get back to my friends. I'll just call an Uber, and we'll come pick up the car in the morning if that's all right with you and the guys."

TJ looks at me like he's realized that I didn't come alone. He smiles and nods understandingly. "I'm not letting you take an Uber. I'll drive you all home."

"You don't have to—"

"Either I take you home or you stay here. I'm not going to argue with you."

"Okay, you can take us home."

33
TJ

I'VE FANTASIZED A LOT ABOUT LOLA.

It was innocent at first. She was just there, smiling and laughing so beautifully. That's how it always started, but then something shifted and her smiles turned into parted lips, and laughs turned into breathy moans.

It wasn't just parted lips and breathy moans. She'd be naked in different positions. So many different ways to be fucked.

All I could do in my dreams was stare at her. And when I was awake, I fantasized about the way she would sound and feel.

All I wanted was to get her out of my system, just once and for all. I wanted to be able to stand in front of her and not have the desire to kiss, touch, and hold her.

I'm really a dumbass for thinking it was going to work. Thinking I'd be able to stand in front of her and still not have that same desire. I shouldn't call it that, not anymore. The best way to describe the way she left me feeling was consumed.

Consumed in her touch, her laughs, her smiles, her whimpers, her delicate hands.

I'm so consumed in her, red golden copper hair and dry paint fucking cloud my vision.

I can't begin to explain how the hell it happened or how to make it stop, but I'm not sure if I want to.

I sigh. I'm not sure how many times I've tossed and turned, but I give up. No matter how hard I try, I can't fall asleep because the one person I can't stop thinking about is sleeping in my bedroom.

Lola had no choice but to sleep over because Cara fell asleep in Jayden's room and Daisy fell asleep on the couch. I knew she felt awkward about staying over, so I offered to sleep on the couch so they could take my room.

It's not a big deal. I've slept on the couch a few times when I was too drunk to make it upstairs. The problem is that every few minutes, I think about my fingers inside her soaked, tight pussy. I think about how wet she was, how well she took them, how she fucking begged, how she moaned, and her cheeks burned red. And every time I think about it, I get hard.

Like right now.

"Jesus Christ," I mumble.

Sitting up, I brace my elbows on my knees, covering my face with my palms. That is until I hear the stairs creaking.

"Sorry, did I wake you?"

I only see her silhouette because of how dark it is, but Lola stands in the middle of the staircase, not moving.

"No, I've been awake." God, I don't know what she's doing to me, but my heart is racing so goddamn fast. "Can't sleep?"

"No. I'm sorry, I should probably head ba—"

"Do you want some coffee?" I offer, cringing at how quick those words leave my mouth. I should be embarrassed at how badly I'm starting to crave her presence, but is it really a bad thing to *want* to be near her...all the time?

"Right now?" she whispers.

"Right now," I affirm.

The silence between us lingers and for a moment, I think she's going to head back upstairs, but she takes the last remaining steps down.

Standing, I quickly adjust my pajama pants, thankful that I'm only semi-hard and it's dark.

"Be ready to be impressed. This is going to be better than any coffee you've ever had."

"Oh? Is that so?"

"Yes." I cut the distance, blindly reaching for her hand. She stiffens when I wrap my palm over her hand, but she doesn't pull away. "Sorry, I just don't want you to trip over anything."

I could turn the light on, but the last thing I want is for anyone to wake up. It's not because I selfishly only want to be with Lola.

Her stiff hand eases against mine. "Okay, lead the way."

Guiding her to the kitchen, I hold her hand firmly and somewhere along the way, we interlock fingers. And it makes me realize that nothing has ever felt so right.

And now I'm not sure how I'll be able to let go, and I don't mean just physically.

When we get to the kitchen, I turn on the range hood light. It's dim, but it emits enough light for us to be able to see each other.

I glance from my peripheral but have to do a double take because she's wearing my shirt.

I've seen thousands of people wearing a jersey or shirt with my number or last name on it, but no one has ever looked as good as Lola looks right now. Her hair is slightly disheveled, her eyes mesmerizing like the universe, her lips stained red, and my shirt engulfs her perfect body, stopping right at her thighs.

"Yo-you-you're wearing my shirt." Did I just fucking stutter?

"My dress wasn't too comfortable and it's still wet. I hope it's all right that I'm wearing it." She shyly says.

I'm smiling like an idiot but fuck it. "Yeah, it's okay with me. You can wear any of my shirts...whenever you want."

"Thanks." She returns the smile, but it slips as if she realized she shouldn't have been doing that and pulls her hand away from mine. "So about this coffee."

"Right." I step over to the counter where the brand-new coffee machine sits. "Be prepared to be impressed. I've worked my ass off to perfect the perfect cup of coffee."

Lola leans her hip against the counter. "I hope you know what you're getting yourself into. My expectations are extremely high now and I'm going to be a harsh critique if the coffee isn't *perfect.*"

I open the cabinet doors above the coffee machine and grab two mugs. "I spent too much money on this for it not to be perfect."

"Did you just buy the machine?"

"Uh...yeah." I sheepishly smile, setting the mugs down. "I just thought I could make coffee whenever you and Phoenix come over."

"Oh." Lola stands straighter and I think she flushes.

"I would grind the coffee beans for you, but I'd hate to wake everyone else up."

She smiles and it's not the small, forced, trying to be nice kind of smile. It's the special kind I've seen her reserve for Phoenix, her best friends, and unfortunately...Saint.

I need to stop obsessing over her smile or everyone will be up before the coffee is ready.

"Ready to be amazed?" I ask as I grab everything to make the coffee.

"Amaze me."

I work on making our coffees, all while she watches me attentively and when I hand her the mug, she inhales the hot steam like she typically does. She softly moans, and I wish she hadn't because memories of her on my dresser flash through my head. But it's not just on my dresser, but in the kitchen. In my fantasies, she's naked, bent over the counter, screaming.

Fuck is wrong with me?

"Wow, I'm sorry I doubted you."

I can't even gloat or feel smug because I'm doing everything in my power not to get hard, but I'm weak.

I'm a weak man for Lola Larson.

"Told you." Is all I manage to say in a strained voice.

She blows the hot steam away before she takes a slow sip, and this time only a content sigh escapes her lips. "You know you're going to regret buying this. I might just come here every single day."

"Then I'll just make sure I have enough of everything." I make a mental note to make sure I go out and buy more coffee beans, milk, and creamer.

She brings the mug to cover her mouth, but I see the corners of her lips rising. "I'm kidding."

"I'm not. You and Phoenix can come whenever you want."

Lowering the mug, Lola's eyes lock with mine. "But what if you're not here?"

Setting my mug down, I walk to the other side of the counter, pulling the drawer that holds our car keys. Grabbing mine, I unclip the key ring from the other ring.

"What are—" She stops halfway, her brows rising and eyes flicking down to my palm. "You're not serious."

"I'm very serious." I hold the key ring in front of her.

"TJ, no." Shaking her head, she pushes my hand away and takes a step back as if she were putting some distance between herself and the key.

"Lola, yes."

"I'm not going to take it. What about the guys?"

I cock a brow. "What about the guys?"

"What will they think if I randomly show up? I'm sure they wouldn't like it if I did, and let me tell you, Phoenix isn't a very quiet kid. You've met him. What if they're trying to rest and he's loud?" Her attempt to reason with me is cute but pointless.

"They won't care. Jagger might be a bit weird around him. He's not very good with kids, but he'll be all right." And that's putting it lightly. Jagger is a mess around kids, and so painfully fucking awkward. "Landon is always in his room or never home, so you'll never have to worry about him. And Jayden and Saint like kids, so it's not an issue with them. Either way, now that the season has started, they'll hardly be home."

Lola nervously bites on her bottom lip, her fingers drumming along the side of the mug. "I can't take it. I'd hate to bother anyone or for Phoenix to break something. You know how curious he is. He likes to get into everything."

I drop the key on the counter as the realization hits me. I inch forward, watching her closely to make sure I'm not overstepping. When she doesn't pull back, I get closer and slowly raise my hand to cup her neck. Grazing my thumb gently against her cheek, I drown in the universe that is her eyes.

"You and Phoenix are part of my life, and that's never going to change. They all know that and understand how present I want to be in his life as I do in yours." With my free hand, I blindly reach for the key on the counter. "Phoenix is important and so are you. If you're happy, then I know he's happy, and that's all I want."

Taking Lola's free hand, I place the key on her palm and curl her fingers over it, encasing her hand with mine.

"You don't have to come for coffee, but just use it in case of an emergency."

"An emergency?" She cocks her head to the side, deep in thought. Probably wondering what kind of emergency would make her have to stop by.

"A raging storm. You definitely don't need to be driving through that." Unease settles inside of me at the thought of her driving through a storm. "Matter of fact, I'll just pick you up unless I'm at an away game."

"I don't need a chauffeur." She sweetly smiles up at me. "*If* there's an emergency, I'll use it. And maybe, just maybe, if I need a little pick-me-up, I'll stop by for a cup of coffee. Now you should probably drink your coffee or it's going to get cold."

Her eyes flick to the mug I've yet to drink from.

There I go again, losing track of time. And again, it happened because of her. *Accept it*, my subconscious tells me.

"So..." I trail off, shifting my thoughts because I'm teetering over the edge of no return, and I know once I fall, there's no going back. Though I'm just not sure how much of a bad thing that is anymore. "Now that Halloween is over, I've been meaning to talk to you about something."

"Oh?" She licks her lips, catching a stray drop that clings to the seam of her bottom lip.

Lucky drop.

"With Thanksgiving coming soon, my parents were wondering if you and your parents would like to get together and do something? We can't actually meet on Thanksgiving because I have a game, so it'd have to be on the weekend. But my parents are more than willing to come here or meet anywhere. They've been dying to meet Phoenix, and they'd really like to meet you and your parents."

The curve of her lips falls downward and her once vivid eyes dim. Lola looks away, her gaze getting lost in the distance as she exhales a heavy sigh.

"If you're not ready for my parents to meet Phoenix, I completely understand. Don't worry, I can—"

"No, I'd love for your parents to meet him." She plasters what has to be the fakest smile I've ever seen on her face. "They just won't be able to meet my parents. They, uh—they didn't take the pregnancy well. They had a solution for my *problem*, but I ended up not going through with it. So they kicked me out, and I haven't spoken to them since." Her lips tremble, but she somehow manages to keep her smile intact.

"They kicked you out?" My words are hushed, full of disbelief.

The further her words sink into my brain, the further the guilt sinks into the pit of my stomach.

What the fuck? They kicked her out?

Despite the huge smile she plasters on her face, she shifts uncomfortably from one foot to the other. "Yeah...it's not a big deal."

"Not a big deal?" I seethe, bile rising up my throat. "You're their only daughter and they kicked you out?"

I've fucked up more times than I can count. I'm sure there has been a time or two Mom and Dad considered whooping my ass, but despite my many fuckups, they've always been by my side.

I can't imagine not having them, especially now with Phoenix. They're part of the reason why I'm able to stay sane.

How could they do that to her? Their only daughter.

She shrugs, her smile never wavering.

"Lola, don't smile like everything's okay. You don't have to pretend to be okay with this." My heart squeezes painfully for her.

"I...I," she sniffles, looking away. "I don't want to talk about this anymore. I think I'm going to go to bed."

"Wait." I wrap my hand around her wrist, begging for those pretty eyes to look my way. "We don't have to talk or we can. We can talk about anything you want. Just let me be with you."

"I don't need your pity." She scowls.

"No, this is not what that is. I just want to be with you."

It's the truth. As mad as I am, this has nothing to do with me feeling bad for her and everything to do with the fact that I like being next to her.

Her silence stretches for what feels like an eternity, and despite that, I cling to her presence and grasp onto her wrist because any second, she's going to pull away.

"Okay, I'll stay." A sad smile graces her face as she pulls her wrist away from my hand.

For a while we stand in the kitchen, drinking our coffees until streaks of sunlight pour from the window, announcing that it's daytime.

34

TJ

THERE'S NOTHING LIKE STARTING THE SEASON AT home.

The crowd, the music, the chants, and the lights are unlike any other. I won't deny the nerves that wrack inside of me, but despite them, I thrive in the energy that buzzes throughout the entire arena.

"This is going to be one hell of a game." Grasping his ankle, Saint bends his knee and pulls his heel toward his butt.

We're all waiting in the tunnel that leads to the court for the announcer to call us out.

Not only is it our first game of the season, but we're playing Baylor, who recruited five-star, Xavier Foster. On top of being ranked number two in the nation, his stats are fucking great. Everyone has and still is talking about him being the one to knock me off *my throne*. I get it, he's a freshman, only eighteen years old, while I'm twenty-one, not to mention he's never been injured, and he's a point guard like me.

Sure, he's the one I should watch out for, but they somehow forget that I'm playing with the number one player in the nation, Saint. I'm not worried or stressed. We don't even play the same position, but if I *was* worried or focused on who'd knock me off my throne, it'd be him.

"It's just like any other game." Jagger paces back and forth, his head bobbing to nothing.

"Just hope you all play that way," Saint says, getting everyone to look at him, except Landon. He's leaning against the wall, arms crossed against his chest, head bent down.

He smiles like he usually does, but no one misses his sharp tone.

"Aside from playing Xavier." He rolls his eyes. "We're also playing Landon's brother, Ashton, and TJ has a kid."

Xavier and Saint have beef with each other. We're not sure why. All we know is that they grew up together.

"Your point is?" Jayden asks.

"Everyone's going to talk a lot of shit."

"*Step*-brother." Landon grimaces. "If any of you are too worried about what anyone has to say tonight, don't bother setting foot on the court. We'll be better off without you."

"So inspirational. You just know how to hype us all up," Saint sarcastically remarks.

"You're the one who brought this shit up," Jayden accuses.

He shrugs, smiling. "Just making sure we're all on the same page."

I roll my eyes, not commenting on his lack of awareness or indifference in reading the room. We're all confident in our ability to play tonight. We wouldn't be here if we didn't think we were. But it doesn't mean we're not all feeling the pressure of what's at stake tonight.

Saint stands next to me. Leaning in, he whispers, "You good?"

"Why wouldn't I be?"

I expect his signature shit-eating grin and a random-ass joke, but for the first time, he does none. "We know what they're all saying, but we've got your back, okay." It's not a question, but a reassured statement so that I don't second-guess him or any of my teammates and their support toward me.

Giving him a curt nod, I look in the direction that leads toward the court. AP poll and championship set aside, me having a baby has been the team's center of attention.

The news was leaked at the end of September. We're now in the beginning of November. I had hoped that everyone would've let it go by now, but they're all set on talking about it every chance they can.

"We got this," he says, holding his fist up.

"We got this," I repeat, tapping my knuckles against his.

One point. We won by one point.

We were doing great in the first half, up by twenty points, but in the second half, they were able to make a comeback. There's no excuse other than we fucked up because we weren't playing cohesive as a team. It didn't help that Xavier and Ashton were taunting the hell out of Saint and Landon.

I heard comments being made about Lola and me, but I was able to shut those out. Until now.

"Are you tired?"

"Come again?" I glance in the direction of one of the many reporters standing in front of me in the locker room.

Derik smiles wryly. He and many other reporters hold their phones and cameras close to my face to ask post-game questions. Something I've been dreading since the shot clock went off.

"It's no surprise that you're a father. Congratulations, by the way."

He's always been a condescending piece of shit, I remind myself as I force the friendliest smile I can muster and nod.

"So with that being said, is he keeping you up? Because you seemed a *bit* tired out there."

In other words, *you're the reason why your team did so fucking horrible.*

Thankfully, Janet had me practice for these stupid questions. I guess it wasn't so useless after all.

"No, he's not keeping me up. I'm sleeping just fine."

"TJ." Another interviewer waves his hand, pulling my attention to him. "I can't imagine what it's been like since you found out you became a father a month ago. How are you handling the stress of having a baby and being an athlete?"

Gripping the ends of the towel draped around my neck, I take in a deep breath. "Handling it the same way any professional athlete has been for years."

"But *they're* professionals. *They're* not in college, still doing homework. What I'm trying to ask is, your team seemed overwhelmed on the court. Do you think they're a reflection of how you've been feeling recently?"

I grit my teeth, feeling my cheeks ache at how hard I'm smiling. I'm sure my knuckles are white from how firm I'm holding on to the towel, but I don't look. Keeping my eyes locked on the interviewer, I fucking smile despite the anger that boils inside of me.

"I admit we could've been more cohesive. There's no excuse for it. We had enough training to prepare us for the season, but one game won't define us. We made mistakes, but we'll learn from them and be prepared for the next game."

"Thanks, TJ, good chatting with you."

"How did you feel..."

And the questions continued, one after the other. I dreaded each one.

"Drink this." Jayden hands me a cup filled to the brim.

Hesitantly, I take the cup, inspecting it closely before I sniff it. I scrunch my nose, handing it back to him. "Jesus fuck, Jay, did you pour the entire bottle of tequila?"

A sly smile stretches across his face, pushing the drink back.

"Don't ask questions Kingston. Just drink."

"Hey..." Saint pauses, his eyes falling to the very full cup in my hand. "Why aren't you drinking?"

"That's what I'm saying. Drink." He encourages, taking a drink out of his own cup.

Jagger stands next to me, wrapping his arm around my shoulders. "TJ takes pictures of—why aren't you drinking?"

I roll my eyes at their insistence but most importantly at myself. Not too long ago, I wouldn't have given it a second thought and chugged the drink in seconds, but now I can't bring myself to do it. Or bring myself to enjoy the party the guys decided to throw in honor of our first game of the season. The whole team is here, except Landon, which is nothing new.

Despite the shitshow of a game we had and the post-game interviews, there are only two people I'm thinking about and they're an hour away from me.

"Maybe I'm not trying to die tonight."

Jagger clicks his tongue. "That's a bit dramatic, Teddy. Sure, it'll get you fucked up but look at the bright side."

"There's no bright side when you're looking *inside* a toilet bowl first thing in the morning. No, thanks, I'm not in the mood."

"We know, but it'll help you clear your head from...everything."

By everything, they not only mean the games or questions, but the negative onslaught of posts and comments I'm getting tagged in on social media. No one has wasted a second to remind me just how badly *I* did. They won't talk about how dirty Baylor played, but they'll talk about how shitty *I* did.

Maybe I do need this.

"Fine, but just one and that's it. Just because we're not having practice tomorrow doesn't mean I want to get shitfaced." I take a large drink but immediately regret it as it burns my throat. I shudder, shaking my head as the drink settles in the pit of my stomach. "Holy fuck, what's in this?"

"The good stuff." Jayden lazily smiles at Saint, taking a drink of his own.

"That's the spirit, Teddy." Jagger slaps my back hard, causing most of the drink to spill on me. "Oops, sorry."

I groan, staring down at my camera hanging from my neck, and my shirt and jeans. They're not drenched but wet enough that I need to change. "Way to go." I grunt, pushing his arm off my shoulder. "I'll be back."

"Hurry! I want you to take some pictures of me," Jagger yells as I make my way up the stairs.

Once I'm in my room, I change out of my wet clothes, but before I head back, bright purple catches my eye.

Lola's gloves lie on my desk. I've been meaning to give them back, but I can't bring myself to part with them.

They're not only a reminder of the night I made her come but also of how sad the night ended. I can't get the look on her face, the sound of her voice, the quiver of her lip out of my head.

I can't change the shit her parents made her go through, but I can change how everything plays from here on out. Because I want nothing more than for Phoenix and Lola to be happy. They deserve it all.

"Hey." A soft voice drags my gaze away from the gloves to my door. Alexia stands in front of the door with a look I know all too well. "I've been looking for you."

"Alexia—"

"Just listen, okay." She saunters toward me, and as she does, I take a few steps back, making sure there's enough space in between us. Though she doesn't care because she takes another step forward, leaving hardly any space between us.

"Can you take a step back?"

Her stunned expression morphs into hurt. "Really? You used to not mind me being this close to you. Should I remind you of the many times you and I—"

"Stop. I don't want to do this." The weight of everything slowly starts to pile on top of my head. I feel a sharp pulse hammer around my head. "I don't want to argue. I told you I'm done."

She puffs an aggravated breath. "But I don't want things to end between us. We have something really good going for us."

I ended things. Granted, I shouldn't have done it at the club during Halloween, but she desperately wanted to know why I wouldn't touch her anymore. I told her it wasn't the time or place, but she wouldn't stop following and bombarding me with questions.

"We can be friends, nothing more." I offer, repeating the same thing I did last week.

"Look." She takes another step, placing her hand on my bicep. "I know you're stressed and have a lot going on, but I can help you. Take it out on me."

A triumphant smile spreads across her face when I wrap my hand around her wrist, but it plummets when I drop it and sidestep her.

"It's not about the stress or whatever it is you're thinking. I just don't want you to feel like I'm leading you on."

She sits on top of my desk, crossing her leg over the other. "Then tell me what it is because I don't understand how we went from fucking for two years, to you deciding you don't want me anymore."

I will in all my patience and hope to God I don't go off. I've learned my lesson with Lola, and the last thing I want is to be a dick.

"Don't do this. We're done. Let's move on."

"We're done? Just like that, huh?" She pouts, eyes glossing over. "What does *she* have that I don't?"

Wiping my palm over my face, I release a weary breath. "Don't bring Lola into this."

She stands, laughing sardonically. "You've known her for hardly three months, just three fucking months!" she bitterly spits out. "While you've known me for two fucking years, TJ. I don't get it or understand what difference she made that I didn't?

Because for the past two years, I was the one sucking your dick, not her. Not to mention every other bitch, but regardless of them, I was here! Not her!"

I grind my teeth. "I don't want to do this."

"I'm not leaving until you tell me!" she demands. "I don't understand how you chose three months over two years."

I tried so hard, I really did, but I can't do this anymore. The conversation is spiraling out of control and I'm seconds away from losing my shit. I know she doesn't like me romantically; this is just another way to get what she wants.

Sucking in a breath, I ignore my throbbing headache and say exactly what I should've said from the beginning. Something I wish I had realized sooner.

"You really want the truth?"

"Yes."

"I'm able to see a future with her, but with you, I don't see anything."

Her laugh is dry and humorless. "Of course you have to. It's not like you have any other choice. You have a fucking child with her!"

I breathe a sigh. "When I first met Lola, there was this *insignificant* spark. I thought it was something fueled by the moment, a thrill." But she's always been more than that. Lola's a rush of adrenaline that never stops. She's far more exciting than anything life could ever offer. "It was so unexpected meeting her but so fucking amazing." I pause, contemplating whether I want to continue, but fuck it, I'm going to make sure I get my point across. "Meeting you was never like that."

From the very beginning, my soul collided with hers, and it's never been able to let go.

"Oh," Alexia says, her voice feeble. There's a flash of sadness on her face, but it's replaced with a cunning smile. "Well, good luck getting her to believe that. You're going to need it." She stalks past me, slamming the door behind her.

35

LOLA

My stomach grumbles loud, but I ignore it and glance at Phoenix. He's playing in his playpen, while simultaneously watching *Nemo*. He shouldn't be up right now. It's way past his bedtime, but tonight he decided he didn't want to sleep. I typically wouldn't allow this, but I've been so busy with work and school assignments, I forgot I'm supposed to deliver a painting by Sunday.

It might have not slipped my mind if I hadn't been too busy thinking about everything that occurred last week.

I keep overthinking every glance, every touch, every spoken word between us. It doesn't help that he bought a coffee machine and gave me his house key. My thoughts are diverted to my phone buzzing on the coffee table but completely come to a standstill when I see the name on the caller ID.

TJ

Setting my palette and paintbrush down, I contemplate whether I should answer it. What if he's drunk and accidentally called me? Or what if he butt dialed me and I answer and hear another girl's voice?

No, I'm sure it's nothing, but what if...*stop it, Lola*.

Before I can let myself overthink the endless possibilities, I answer.

"Peaches, hey."

"Hey...is everything all right?" I hesitantly ask.

"Yeah, everything's all right. You weren't sleeping, were you? Fuck, that's kind of an idiotic question. Of course you probably were. It's almost midnight. This is a really bad time, isn't it?"

"Sleep, what's sleep?" I snuff a laugh, staring at the painting of the newlywed couple I'm supposed to ship by Sunday.

He chuckles in return. "I'll take that as a no."

"Wait, are you drunk?"

He breathes a sigh of relief. "No, fortunately not."

Placing my phone between my shoulder and ear, I stand from my stool, stretching my arms over my head until I hear two pops. "What's that supposed to mean?"

"The guys, they—you know, it doesn't matter. Is this a bad time?"

I pause, noting the tension in his voice and the lack of noise in the background. It's completely and utterly silent.

"No, not at all. I'm just working on something." I step away from the canvas, peeping at Phoenix one more time before I saunter over to the kitchen. "Are you okay?"

"I'm...yeah, I'm okay." I hear the smile in his voice, but his response feels far from it. "Are you going to bed anytime soon?"

"Not anytime soon. Phoenix decided he's not going to bed tonight."

"I thought I heard him in the background." The shift in his voice sounds lighter and happier than a second ago. "Would you like some help putting him to bed?"

I smile at the insinuation of his question. "You want to help me put him to bed?"

"I do."

"You'd be here close to one in the morning. You're really going to drive an hour away?"

"What if I told you I already did?"

"You're here?" There's a sharp spike in my heart rate, sending an electric flutter to spread across my body. "Stop lying. I don't believe you."

"Open your door."

My eyes rapidly jump to the door, staring at it like he'll appear any second.

"Come on, Peaches, open the door. It's cold out here."

I stay grounded in place, finding it hard to believe that TJ willingly left a party, drove an hour away, and is now here. But I quickly realize that he's not lying as three soft knocks echo around the entryway.

"I probably deserve to freeze, but come on, have some mercy on me."

His words drag me out of my stupor and before I know it, I'm at the door. I take a quick look at my outfit, cringing at my oversized and very old paint-stained shirt and sweatpants. There are patches of new and old paint on them, and some holes that have accumulated over the years.

I look tragically messy, but who cares? I'm not going to overthink it.

"You don't have to open the door, but I just wanted to hear your voice," he says as I open the door.

I open my mouth to say something, but nothing comes out. *It doesn't mean anything*. I remind myself.

"We're not pretending anymore," I say, hanging up the call.

"I know."

I shoot him a quizzical look. "Then don't say things like that."

Because we've both been so busy, we haven't really seen or talked to each other. Thankfully, the girls have been helping me with Phoenix, meeting TJ halfway so that he can spend some time with him.

They don't know what happened and I don't plan on telling them. TJ and I had agreed it was a night of pretend. I'm certainly pretending he didn't make me come on his fingers, or that I wanted things to go further.

"I'm not pretending right now. I just wanted to hear your voice." His words are wistful and the corners of his lips lift into a small, sad smile. "I promise it wasn't pretend. I meant it. I *mean* it."

The chilly breeze that passes reminds me I'm not breathing and he's still standing outside.

I ignore the whirl of emotions taking over my heart and mind and step to the side, gesturing for him to come in. The last thing I want is to let words that mean nothing to distract me. Even if they might sound sincere and make my heart spaz out.

"Were you really that bored?"

He steps inside and shuts the door behind him. "Bored?"

"It's Friday night, close to midnight, and you came here. Saint sent me videos," I explain and that little information is enough for TJ to know what I'm talking about. "He wanted me to convince Daisy to go, but she's working tonight."

Even if she didn't have to, she wouldn't have gone.

TJ takes his sneakers off, and when his eyes settle on my clothes, he smiles.

"Stop looking at me like that. I know I look messy."

"You don't, but that's not what I'm looking at. You just have some paint right here. Can I?" He raises his hand, waiting for my approval.

I know I have more paint on other parts of my body, but still, I nod.

He raises his hand and gently rubs the pad of his thumb down the side of my neck, slowly working his way down.

I stand as still as I can, reminding myself to breathe and hope that he can't feel how heavy my heart is thrashing and or say anything about the goose bumps emerging.

"So was it really that boring?"

He cocks a brow, his eyes attentively trained on the paint on my neck. "Boring?"

"You just won your first game of the season. I thought you'd be celebrating with the rest of the guys. Congratulations, by the way."

His thumb pauses, burning into my skin as it stays in the same spot. "Did you watch the game?"

"Just a little. The TV was on in the break room," I admit, omitting the part that I was too distracted by watching him play that my thirty-minute break became forty-five minutes.

"Good thing you didn't watch the entire thing. It was a complete shitshow," he dryly replies and resumes rubbing the paint away.

I was too focused on my tumultuous emotions and hadn't noticed the tension in his eyes, the strain in his voice, and the tightness in his shoulders.

"Is everything all right?"

He shrugs, not saying anything.

I may not have watched the entire thing, but I know they won by one point and some people haven't been saying the nicest things.

"I'm here if you want to talk." I softly smile at him.

TJ doesn't reply instantly. The silence lingers, but when he speaks up, I feel his thumb skim over my collarbone. "The party wasn't boring. I just needed fresh air."

"You drove an hour for fresh air? Doesn't that seem like a waste of gas?"

Shifting his gaze up, his lips curve into a small smile. "No, it's not a waste if it's worth it."

I swallow, my hands becoming clammy at my sides. "Was it?"

"Yeah, it's *just what I needed.*" His hooded eyes flick down to my lips, and I can't help but lick them.

I drum my fingers along my thigh, wondering if I'm about to make a mistake, but it's pointless because my feet have a mind of their own. I step closer, standing on my tiptoes as his hands cup the side of my neck, guiding me closer to him.

Just as I'm about to lose myself in him, Phoenix calls for me. "Ma!"

We break apart, and I blink, the daze I'd been in fading away.

"I really need to put him to bed." I turn around, blowing a shaky breath.

"Is he always up at this time?" he asks, following behind me.

"Not always, but sometimes."

When we step into the living room, we both chuckle at the sight of Phoenix. He's standing, his face pressed against the mesh wall of the playpen.

He gasps and pushes away from the wall, jumping and smilingly giddy when he spots TJ behind me. "T!"

"Hey, little bear," TJ greets as Phoenix raises his arms, impatiently and excitedly begging to be picked up. "Why are you still awake, huh?" He bends over the playpen and scoops him up, tickling him in the process. "It's way past your bedtime."

"Memo, ish."

"You're watching *Nemo*?" He tenderly smiles at him. "Do you like the fish?"

"Yes!"

The wave of emotions returns, gripping my heart in a way I've never felt before. Kind of like a warm embrace, but much more intense, sort of feels like—no, no, no, absolutely not.

Sure, he gave Phoenix a really cute nickname, and he's holding him like he doesn't want to let go. So what if Phoenix stares at TJ like he's the world and feels extremely comfortable with him?

"I think someone is ready to go to bed." TJ's voice interrupts my flustered thoughts. He glances down at Phoenix as he rubs his eyes and yawns.

My thoughts are way past flustered. They're chaotic but in a good way and I hate it. I want them to stop, but as I stare at Phoenix cuddled against TJ's chest, his arms draped around his neck, and TJ slowly rubbing his back with his palm, I fucking melt.

"I'll take it from here." I go to take him, but I'm taken aback when Phoenix grips TJ's shirt tightly and shakes his head.

"No," he sleepily murmurs, digging his face against his chest.

"Come on, you'll be more comfortable in your bed." I try again, but still, he doesn't budge. "You can't sleep on your dad. He's tired too. Aren't you—what?"

TJ's lips turn upward and his eyes soften. "Nothing...I'm not tired."

"But you just—"

"I'm good. I don't mind staying as long as you don't mind."

"It's pretty late." I hesitate, looking at Phoenix. His eyes flutter, but as if he can sense that I'm lingering, he holds on to TJ's shirt like his life depends on it.

"Not really. It's pretty early, actually."

"TJ—"

"You can kick me out once he's completely fallen asleep, but I'm not leaving. It wouldn't be fair to you, and just look how comfortable he is."

He's not lying. Phoenix looks so cozy, I'd hate to move him. And I don't have it in me to tell him no. I really need to finish the painting.

"Okay, thanks." I smile at him.

"Don't thank me. I'm just doing what I should have done from the beginning."

A month ago, I would've found his words hard to believe. Then again, a month ago, I would've found anything that had to do with TJ hard to believe. But I don't feel the way I did then, and the thought unnerves me more than it should.

"So what are you working on?" Thankfully, he shifts the conversation and my thoughts. He carefully walks toward my canvas as if he's afraid that he'll wake up Phoenix, and once he's standing in front of it, his eyebrows skyrocket and his lips part open. "Wow."

Standing next to him, I peer up at him as he's absorbing the painting. As his eyes coast over the canvas, he shakes his head, repeating wow every time he focuses on a certain detail.

"The details are insane. You're just—" He stops mid-sentence and stares down at me, the same way he was staring at the painting a second ago. He inhales a sharp breath and smiles. "You're extraordinary. I swear you will never stop amazing me."

A heat rises on my cheeks as I pick up my brush. "Thanks. I, uh, have to finish this. I just have a few more things to add to it and then I'll be done."

Taking a few steps back, he playfully says, "Don't worry. I promise I won't bother you. Just pretend I'm not here."

True to his word, TJ doesn't bother me. In retrospect, it doesn't matter because pretending he isn't here is hard.

He's been pacing back and forth in my living room, all while Phoenix sleeps soundly on his chest. His steps are light, hardly audible, so it's not a problem.

But I wish they were heavy and loud like I'd anticipated so I could have an excuse to kick him out, but they aren't. His height and pacing aren't what is hard to ignore. It's how hyperaware my body is to him. The feeling is overwhelming. I made two mistakes with the painting because I couldn't focus.

Looking over my shoulder, I spot TJ standing in front of my wall of paintings, still holding Phoenix.

That sight shouldn't do things to certain parts of my body, but it does.

"Do you not want to lay him down?"

I've asked about four times now, but every time he looks at me and says, "Can I hold him for a little longer?"

And those words, God, those words shouldn't make me feel a certain way. "You can hold him for as long as you want. I just thought you'd want to let your arms rest. As much as I love Phoenix, he's a little heavy."

His lips quirk up. "He's pretty light, actually. Weighs probably as much as a loaf of bread."

"Loaf of bread?" I hold back my smile, turning around, and pick up the varnish and paintbrush.

"It's something Jayden said. He's always thinking about food." I hear his amused voice and his footsteps get closer until I feel him behind me.

Sucking in a steady breath, I pour some of the varnish into a different pallet and dip my brush. "That's what Cara said. He really likes food, huh?"

"No, he *loves* food."

I quietly chuckle as I drag the wet bristles across the canvas.

"What's that?"

"It's varnish. It helps enhance and protect the painting. Making it look ten times better than it already does." I may not be the most confident person in the world, but one thing I'm not only confident but proud of is my art.

TJ hums. "Mesmerizing."

"It is, isn't it?" I tilt my head back to look up at him but find that he's already looking down at me.

"What? Do I have paint on my face?"

"No, I—" He pauses when my stomach embarrassingly growls. His eyes flicker to my hands covered in dry and wet paint and then to the canvas. When they shift back to me, there's concern etched on his face. "You've been working on that painting for a while?"

"A few hours. I would've been done sooner, but I had to make sure the crystals on the veil—" I stop, my lips tightening as my stomach grumbles again.

"Let me get you something to eat."

"No, it's okay."

"Lo—"

"It's late." I glance at the time on my phone. "And I'm certain everything is either closed or closing."

"I'm sure I can find something that's open." He persists.

"No, really, it's okay. I can make something here."

His eyes shift in every direction, almost as if he's hesitating for something. After a few seconds of contemplation, they land back on me. “I can help you. I, uh, don’t know how to cook, but I’m sure I can figure it out.”

“You don’t have—you don’t know how to cook?”

“I’ve never had the need to know how. I tried a few times and the last time that I...well, let’s just say the fire department had to be called.”

“That bad?”

“That bad.”

I fight back the urge to smile. “Well, I’ll show you, but you have to promise not to burn my kitchen down. I’d really love to get my security deposit back.”

“I promise to do my best not to burn it down.” He holds his palm up, a grin spreading across his face. “So what are we making?”

36

TJ

My Friday nights have always consisted of parties, my bedroom, or a hotel room when I'm at away games. Never in my wildest dreams would I have thought that I'd be learning how to make blueberry pancakes with the mother of my child at two in the morning.

It's kind of wild but all in a good way, and I hope to God this isn't a dream because waking up is going to suck.

Coming here was the best decision I could've ever made.

After Alexia left, I had no desire to head back downstairs and pretend like everything was okay because I felt drained. Not physically but mentally. The post-game interview and the onslaught of negative comments I've seen about me on social media are fucking with my head. It's the first game of the season. I shouldn't have let that get to me.

Though the drained feeling was the least of my worries because of the new realization of what I feel toward Lola. It scares the shit out of me.

It sounds ridiculous to be afraid of what I feel, but I've never wanted anyone as much as I want her. I crave to hear her laugh, to see her smile, to have her eyes on me and *only* on me. I'd be anything she wanted me to be if she'd let me.

Feeling suffocated and overwhelmed, I left the house and drove off with no destination in mind. I just needed to get out until I was consumed again with the thought of Phoenix and Lola. Before I knew it, I was outside of her apartment, hoping to God she would be awake.

Now I hope I feel the same way about wanting to learn how to make pancakes.

I mean, how hard could this be?

We stand side by side, staring down at the ingredients sitting on the counter in front of us.

Phoenix is in her room, sound asleep. Thank God for that because I'm not sure how I'd be able to watch him and pay attention to her at the same time. Multitasking with a kid is a job of its own. I praise all the parents who do it.

As she picks up the boxed pancake mix, she looks up at me.

"Before we get started, I just want you to know that I'm horrible at following directions. I just pour and stir until my heart feels content."

"Pour and stir until my heart feels content, got it." I grin, giving her a thumbs-up.

Lola turns, but I see the corner of her lip twitch. She pulls the tab on the side of the box and pours the powder into the bowl.

"I personally like using milk over water because it makes them fluffier," Lola explains as she pours milk into the bowl. Then proceeds to mix the ingredients with a whisk and once she gets it to a consistency she likes, she grabs a handful of blueberries and drops them in the batter. "And remember to keep it on medium heat."

She gives me a side glance, her lips tilting upward at the reminder I had the heat on high.

"Are you mocking me?"

"No, of course not." She shakes her head, her lips lifting higher. "It's just a reminder, that's all."

I narrow my eyes, holding back a smile. "Right, a reminder."

A full-blown smile spreads across her face, making it hard for me not to smile. And when she peers up at me, I can't help but let my lips ease into a smile that mirrors hers.

"Grab the butter and coat the griddle," she instructs.

I do as she says and then pick up the bowl, pouring some of the batter. I do my best to make them round, but they're ovals at best.

"Okay, this isn't too bad."

"Easy, right. Now all you have to do is wait until the bubbles appear and then you flip it."

Keeping my eyes locked on the pancakes, I patiently wait for the bubbles and, once they appear, I flip them. I release a breath I hadn't realized I was holding when I see how perfectly golden they are.

"Holy shit. I didn't burn it."

Lola quietly giggles. "Now all you have to do is give it a minute, and then you can take a peek to make sure that side is golden brown too. If it is, you can take it off."

I do just that and repeat the process all over again without Lola helping. She must have a lot of confidence in me because she steps away for a moment to retrieve what looks like a large notebook.

After giving my pancakes a once-over, I watch her flip through the pages and realize it's a planner. A small crease forms between her brows and her eyes grow in size as she brings it closer to her face.

"Damn it," she mumbles under her breath as she grabs her phone. Her eyes bounce between the screen and the pages as if she was trying to confirm something. She exhales a harsh breath as she sets both things down and drums her fingers along the counter.

"Is everything okay?"

"Yes—No. Phoenix got into my things the other day and found my planner." She flips it around, showing me the tattered and colored pages.

I wince at just how bad it looks because it's hardly legible.

"I was going to get a new one, but I've been putting it off. So I just transferred all of my dates to the calendar on my phone." She laughs to herself, but it's humorless. "Somehow I overlooked a wedding I booked for next Saturday and didn't add it to my phone. I don't have a sitter..."

"I'll watch Phoenix."

"But you have an away game the night before. I can't ask you to do that."

"We'll be home first thing in the morning."

I don't mention that I have practice that afternoon, but she already looks stressed as it is and the last thing I want to add is more of that. I don't know how the hell I'm going to manage or how I'm not going to be stressed myself. I've never taken care of Phoenix by myself. Hell, I've never been more than a minute or two alone with him.

This could potentially be a disaster, but I got this. I think.

She muses, drumming her fingers. "Are you sure?"

"Yes, I'm sure. Please don't stress. Either way, this was bound to happen," I say, hoping to relieve the tension.

Slowly, I see her stiff body relax and the drumming stops. "Are you sure?"

Am I positive I won't fuck this up? Absolutely not.

"I'm sure."

"Okay." She exhales a small breath as her lips curl up and taps her fingers away on the screen. Probably adding the date on her calendar.

It's small, but that smile is so goddamn worth it.

"Can I ask you something?" after removing the last pancake off the griddle, I turn the heat off.

"Yeah, anything." She sets her phone down, directing all of her attention to me.

"This might sound like a stupid question. You're already working as a live painter, but you're going to school to major in art. Why?"

"It's my plan B. Just in case being a live painter doesn't work out. And it's stupid but..." She pauses, hesitating. "I'm trying to prove my parents wrong, even though they'll never know."

It takes everything in me not to close the space between us and encase her in a hug.

Knowing what I know now, I feel like a bigger piece of shit than I did before. Knowing her parents kicked her out because she got pregnant has been running through my mind since she told me. If I didn't feel guilty before, I definitely feel guilty now. I know I had no control in that matter, but it doesn't make me feel any better knowing she had to figure it out all on her own.

"I'm sorry. I shouldn't have brought that up."

"No, don't be sorry." I hope to God what I'm about to say isn't going to make this worse because I have absolutely no idea what I'm doing. "Remember when I said we're going to be in each other's lives forever? That means that if you ever need me, I'll be there. If you need to talk or if you need a hug or anything at all, I'll be there. I'll *always* be a text or call away."

Lola stares at me, crestfallen. A small, sad smile slowly rises on her lips. "When I told my parents I was pregnant, they were mad but surprisingly not as mad as I first thought they would be. But only because they thought it was Matt's, my ex-boyfriend's. When I told them it wasn't his, that's when everything changed. They gave me an ultimatum. I either get an abortion and we pretend like nothing ever happened, or I keep the baby and leave the house. Well, it was more like keep the baby, but you'll never be welcomed here. You'll be nothing to us.

"There were a few more words, but it's honestly pointless to repeat. I thought about it. So many times I thought about getting the abortion because it would make everything so much easier for them. All that time, I thought about them, but I never thought about me. *They* never thought about me. I know *I* fucked up. It was my fault because *I* wasn't safe enough, *I* wasn't cautious enough. I just wasn't...*enough*."

Her bottom lip quivers and her eyes become glassy, but despite that, she wears a smile like she fucking means it. And I hate it, not her smile, but knowing that she feels like she needs to prove something to someone who doesn't mean anything.

As a lone tear trails down her face, she quickly wipes it away and shakes her head. "I'm sorry, this is stupid."

"Don't apologize and it's not stupid."

I do my best to rein in my anger and think through what I want to say, but the word *abortion* keeps repeating in my head. Ultimately, the choice would've been hers and I would've supported her no matter what, but knowing now that that was an ultimatum her parents gave her makes me feel sick. Because it wouldn't have been a benefit for her but for them.

"It is, feeling this way over someone who doesn't mean anything. I know what you're thinking. It's wrong to want to prove them wrong when they'll never know. But you should have seen the way they looked when I ran into them and told them about my business, about changing my majors." The smile on her face fades, and she sniffles. "'Of course you'd choose something easy that'll never get you anywhere. You're nothing but a failure,' they said."

When a second tear rolls down her cheek, I decide to close the gap, enveloping her in an embrace.

She melts into my arms, releasing a dejected sigh. "Maybe they're right. Maybe I am a failure. I hardly get clients now..."

Cupping her neck, I tilt her chin up with my thumb to meet her somber eyes. "I refuse to let you talk about yourself like that. I've not known you for a long time, but I can tell you I've never met anyone as resilient as you are. You don't just amaze me because you're talented but because you kept pushing despite everything that's happened. You're so extraordinary. Please don't ever let anyone make you believe otherwise."

Another tear springs from her eyes, and before she gets to it, I wipe it away with my other hand and then tuck her loose strands of hair behind her ear.

"I'm sorry," she croaks.

"You have nothing to be sorry for."

"I'm supposed to teach you how to make pancakes, not make this night depressing. God, I'm a mess." She lets her head fall on my chest, mumbling, "This is embarrassing."

I snake one arm around her shoulders and rub my palm along her back in slow circles. "You did teach me successfully. I didn't burn your kitchen down, so you'll definitely be getting the deposit back."

It's faint, but I hear her giggle.

"And you didn't make the night depressing." I stop rubbing her back and tuck my fingers underneath her chin, tilting it back to look down at her.

Lola's so fucking beautiful and she doesn't even realize it. She says she's messy, but she's like a work of art. She's sort of chaotic, magnetizing, and covered in the colors of the universe. I don't mean that because she has paint on her skin. No, it's the coalition of amber and green in her eyes, her golden copper hair, the tinge of red that sometimes coats her cheeks...

"I know it wasn't easy and you didn't have to tell me, but you did, so thank you. And I already told you this, but if you ever need to talk or need a hug, I'm here." I smile at her.

She returns the smile. It's nowhere near as bright as it typically is, but one thing is for certain. It's definitely not fake.

Baby steps.

"Thank you."

"No, thank you."

"For what? I'm the one who cried on your shirt."

I chuckle. "For giving me a chance, for letting me be a part of Phoenix's life. For not getting the abortion."

Since I've met him, I can't imagine my life without him. It's hard to believe a world where Phoenix doesn't exist. I don't and can't begin to describe the unconditional love I have for him.

Her lips rise a little, but slowly, the smile withers away as her gaze drops down to my lips. Dragging the pad of my thumb down the column of her throat, I feel her swallow, and when I raise it and let my fingers linger below her jaw, I feel her erratic pulse.

Or it could be mine, or it could be that I feel both of our pulses come together as one.

I wait for her to pull away when I wrap my entire hand around her throat and meet her heated eyes. I wait for any sign of hesitation that she doesn't want this. I wait for her to voice it and when she doesn't, I ask. Because the last thing I want is to misread the signs and screw everything up.

"Can I kiss you?"

"Yeah," she breathlessly says.

I feel so fucking alive in this moment. I brush my lips against hers and inhale the faint scent of vanilla. I know that nothing will ever feel as invigorating as this.

I close the space between us, swiping my tongue across her bottom lip, feeling how soft it is. I wind my other arm around her waist and bring her as close as I possibly can while I tighten my grip on her throat.

She takes me by surprise as she wraps her arms around my shoulders, but what really does it is the light moan that vibrates against my tongue.

I should add desperation to the list of things I'm willing to do because I'd do anything just to hear it again.

Just as I deepen the kiss, Lola jumps, pulling away from me as we hear keys jangling and clatter to the ground.

Daisy stands by the entrance, staring at us wide-eyed. "Sorry, I'm just going to—" She points her thumb over her shoulder, walking backward, but stops as her eyes fall on the stack of pancakes we've yet to touch. "Wait, did you guys just make those?"

"Uh, yeah," we both reply, out of breath.

"Thank fuck, I'm starving." She grabs two and turns around, but before she walks away, she says, "If you're about to do what I think you're going to do, wrap it. And if you do it on the counter, wipe it off. Night."

37

TJ

I'M LATE.

Holy fucking shit, I'm thirty-five minutes late.

I'm never late, ever!

No, let me rephrase that. I've never been punctual to doctor's appointments, classes, parties, and many other things, but one thing I can proudly say I've never been late to is practice. In fact, I'm always the first to arrive and the last to leave.

People say there's always a first for everything, but this is the one thing I never wanted to have a first in. The moment I step foot on the court, Coach is going to chew my ass out.

If there's one thing Frank Warren hates more than losing games, it's tardiness. He always goes into spiels about how inconsiderate people are toward his time and how they don't deserve it if they're going to waste it. And that's just the condensed version of it because the real version isn't as nice.

"Excuse me!" I hurriedly say, almost crashing into the group of people I assume are taking a tour of the arena.

I catch a quick glance of their shocked expressions as I look over my shoulder to apologize. I'm not sure if they're staring at me because I'm running like a fucking maniac or because I'm gripping Phoenix like my life depends on it while his bag and my duffle hang from my shoulder.

"Fucking hell," I groan as more people come into view. I quickly sidestep them before I trample over them.

"Fuck!"

My eyes triple in size. "No, Phoenix. Don't say that."

He giggles, clearly finding this amusing. "Fu—"

I softly clamp his mouth shut with my hand. I stop to catch my breath and eye him sternly. "Your mom is going to kill me. Don't say that. I'm really trying to get on her good side."

If Coach Warren doesn't kill me, I know Lola will.

Phoenix tilts his head, clutching his bear. His dark brown curls dangle with the movement. He beams, no doubt having no idea what the hell I'm talking about.

"Just be a good boy, Little Bear." I lightly tap his nose and the bear's.

I know he understands that much because he nods, eyes crinkling at the corners with happiness at the nickname I've given him.

Pushing past the door that leads into the locker room, I set him on the rolling chair in front of my locker and crouch down to his eye level.

This is probably going to be pointless. I have no idea how much he'll understand or if he'll listen, but I'm going to try it anyway.

"I'm going to need you to behave. Your mommy isn't here and I'm going to be playing basketball, okay?"

His eyes glitter with excitement. "B-ball?"

"Yeah, ball." I smile at him.

"TV b-ball?"

I stare at him, confused. "TV?"

"Throw ball." He throws his hands in the air and that's when it hits me. He watched me play on television. Lola didn't tell me that.

Now I'm smiling big. "You're going to behave, okay?"

"Kay." He nods. I'm not sure if he really understood me, but I'll take it.

After quickly changing out of my clothes, I throw everything in my locker, grab his bear, and sprint to the arena.

As I approach the court, fear seizes my body. I've never dreaded practice, but I guess there really is a first for everything.

I'd be here on time, but I couldn't figure out how to buckle Phoenix in. I didn't realize how fucking tricky that shit was. Though the buckle was the least of my worries, somehow Phoenix got into Landon's room, drew on his wall, and got ahold of the yogurt Lola packed and got it all over him and me.

Now I truly understand what Lola meant when she said not to turn my back on him, not even for ten seconds because that's all it took for him to cover himself in the vanilla yogurt.

Swallowing the hard lump in my throat, I blow a shaky breath, hating how my heart is hammering. It's so fucking loud, I can hardly hear the sneakers squeaking against the hardwood floor, the stretches being called out, or Coach Warren's loud voice echoing throughout the arena.

Fuck it, I say, forcing myself to go in.

Everyone's attention draws to me and then their eyes dip to Phoenix clinging to my side. They stare at me, wide-eyed. Except for Coach. He's the only one whose back is facing me.

"Theodore Jackson Kingston!"

"Hey, Coach," I awkwardly reply.

"You're late." His voice is clipped. "I don't want to hear nor care about the excuse. You are so fuc—"

He stops mid-sentence, eyes flicking down to my son. Snapping his mouth shut, eyes blinking repeatedly—but I look at him equally shocked because this is the first time I've ever seen him too stunned to speak.

"I know I'm late. I'm sorry. Lola had to work today and we didn't have a sitter."

Coach nods slowly, like he's still trying to process what I just said. But he sobers up and faces the guys. "Did I tell anyone to stop? What the f—heck are you guys doing? Get to it!"

He leans into Reggie, the assistant coach, whispers something in his ear, then they look back at me.

Coach Warren approaches me and as he does, he tips his head in the direction of the tunnel, motioning for me to follow behind him.

I mentally prepare for whatever punishment he's about to lay on me. I'd apologize, but I know it's pointless. He doesn't care about apologies, just actions.

"TJ, you've done some really stupid, questionable things..." He rubs his chin, deep in thought. And I hate it because his prolonged silence unnerves me. "But I'm proud of you."

I'm taken aback because that's the last thing I expected to hear.

"Ah, thanks?"

The scowl on his face softens. And it shocks me because *the* Frank Warren is anything but soft.

"I know things haven't been easy and trying to manage everything with being a parent has been hard. I can only imagine it as a parent myself, but I want you to know how proud I am of you for stepping up. I know parenthood isn't easy, but I can promise you it's worth it. You being here for that little one will mean more to him than you can ever imagine."

He smiles tenderly at Phoenix then back at me, but it only lasts for a mere second before his face becomes serious.

"Thanks, Coach, it means a lot." I smile, feeling the weight on my shoulders lift off.

"Now give me the kid and go warm up. You've already wasted enough time." He motions with his hands to pass him Phoenix.

I nod and attempt to hand him over, but Phoenix clutches my shirt and stiffens.

Smiling, I peer down at him, ruffling his hair. "You're going to be okay. This is Coach Warren, and he's going to take care of you while I play ball, okay?"

Phoenix eyes him up and down, still not convinced if he should trust him.

I'm unsure of what to do until I ask myself what Lola would do, and I know exactly what. Bringing his bear to my ear, I pretend like he's whispering and nod.

"Did you hear that?"

Phoenix shakes his head, so I bring the bear to his ear.

"Do you hear it now? Pooh bear wants to go with him and boss the others around. Do you want to boss the others around too?"

As I hand the bear to Coach Warren, Phoenix loosens his hold on my shirt and peeks at him with curiosity.

"Come on, little man." Coach bears a wide smile that spreads across his face, earning a small, sheepish smile in return from my son. "Let's go boss them around. I promise you'll have lots of fun. I'll even give you your own whistle like mine." He dangles the whistle that's strapped around his neck.

That's all it takes for Phoenix's nerves to wither away. Coach takes the sign and takes him from my arms.

I smile at Phoenix, ruffling his hair one last time.

"TJ," Coach says before I walk off.

"Yeah?"

"I meant it when I said I'm here for you. That means next time you reach out to me if something like this happens again. We'll help you out."

I nod. "I definitely will. Thanks."

"Oh, and, TJ."

"Yes?"

"Next time you're late, with or without your son, there will be consequences."

I swallow. "Yes, Coach."

Meeting my teammates on the court, they stare at me with utter disbelief, not able to believe that I got away with it. Quite frankly, I'm still shocked. Granted, it's a one-time thing, but still, he doesn't give passes to anyone.

"Listen up." Coach Warren's voice reverberates throughout the arena. It's loud enough to get everyone's attention but not loud enough to scare Phoenix. Though he's too busy playing with the whistle and his bear to notice. "We have a guest, a very small guest, with us today. That being said, watch your language."

His eyes narrow threateningly, coasting over each and every person in here, making it clear there will be consequences.

But of course, there's always that one dumbass who likes to test the waters, and that dumbass happens to be Saint.

"What if it's in another language? It's not like he'll understand anyways." Saint *innocently* smiles.

Some of the other guys look at the ground, pressing their lips together or covering their mouths with their hands.

Coach Warren mirrors his same smile. "I'm so glad you find this amusing, Arlo, and because you do, wall sits, now."

His smile falls flat. "But—"

"I am *not* messing around," he snaps. Those who were smiling aren't anymore. "Watch your language or else. I don't care what language it's in, just don't say it. Are we clear?"

"Yes, Coach," we say in unison.

"Wall," he grunts at Saint. "The rest of you, transition drills. TJ, form shooting."

"*Figlio di puttana*," Saint mutters under his breath.

"Add five more minutes to that." Coach doesn't glance at Saint, but he doesn't have to because his words are enough to let him know that he heard him. And even though none of us know what that means, he knows it wasn't something *nice*.

The guys cackle, watching Saint press his back against the pad that surrounds the basketball pole. There are no walls here, so Coach uses it as one.

Something tells me Saint won't be the only one doing wall sits.

"All right, everyone, gather around." Coach circles his index finger in the air.

"Does that include me?" Jagger asks, eyes desperate, legs shaking, and face drenched in sweat.

Coach glances at the watch on his wrist. "You have thirty more seconds, Spears." He scans the arena, a satisfied grin on his face. "I hope you have all learned a lesson or two."

Groans, mutters, and heavy breathing are heard all around, but they're all suppressed by Jagger's loud, "thank God," as he slowly stands.

I know he's dying to let himself fall to the ground, but Coach Warren's penetrating stare encourages him to push away from the pad and make his way over to us.

"Good job!" Phoenix raises his tiny hand, waiting for Jagger to give him a high five.

"You're the reason I got in trouble." He glares at him, but his face softens after a beat and taps his hand.

Before practice ended, Coach told Phoenix to go around and tell the guys good job and to give them high fives. And now that he's finished with his task, he stands next to me, showing me his whistle.

"This is what I like to see, and this is what I better see at our next game. Don't get cocky because we've won the past three games. We can easily lose if you get distracted and that's easy to do with everything going on. With that being said, I'm extremely proud of all of you for keeping level-headed." He pridefully smiles. "Keep up the good work, get lots of rest, and stay sober for those of you who are over twenty-one."

He glares at half of the team, particularly the ones under twenty-one. "I don't want to get a call that any of you are in jail because if you're in jail, then I'm going to jail." His eyes lock with Saint's.

Saint scoffs, placing a hand over his heart. "I can't believe you think that low of me. You really think I'm capable of doing anything bad?"

"Yes," we all answer for him.

"I'm appalled and feel attacked." Feigned disappointment takes over his face. "I'm a literal saint. I mean, come on, it's my literal name."

"Far from it," Coach grumbles.

Saint dramatically scoffs. "Far from it? What happened to innocent until proven guilty?" He can't believe the words coming out of his mouth as he laughs. "Come on now, it was a one-time thing. You can't tell me if the opportunity arose to go crowd surfing, you wouldn't do it."

"No, and don't act like it was *just* crowd surfing."

"Okay, so maybe I got dru—"

"Saint Arlo, do not finish that sentence. You are not twenty-one." He shakes his head, running an exasperated palm down his face. "Everyone hit the showers."

I go to pick up Phoenix, but Coach stops me.

"Absolutely not. Go shower."

"Thanks so much." I ruffle Phoenix's hair before I make my way to the shower room.

The guys surround Saint, who's holding Phoenix when I return to the arena.

"That's right, I'm the godfather," he proudly states and doesn't backtrack when our eyes connect. "Isn't that right, TJ?"

He decided to proclaim himself as Phoenix's godfather a while ago. If it had been anyone else, I would've said no, but it seemed Lola was okay with it, and I can tell he genuinely cares for him.

Before I get to say anything, Coach stands in front of me.

"I know it's too early to say this, but I think someone might be following in your footsteps. His eyes were completely trained on you the entire time. Even tried to mimic some of the things you were doing," he says with a grin. "Keep up the good work, now more than ever. You have someone very important looking up to you." He pats my shoulder and walks away.

There's a feeling I can't explain growing in my chest, and I don't even realize how hard I'm smiling until I'm standing in front of the guys.

"TJ, he looks so much like you. It's freaking ridiculous. I know he's your kid, but Jesus, the resemblance is uncanny." Q gapes, bending down in front of Phoenix.

"Were you this chunky? Gosh, look at the rolls. Nix, buddy, we need to cut back on the puffs." Jayden snorts, poking them.

"Doesn't look one bit like Lola." Landon tilts his head to the side, assessing him as if he's trying to find one trait that might resemble her.

There is one; it's the shape of his brows. It's not the first thing anyone notices, but I do. How can I not? It's hard not to notice anything about her.

"Wait, did you just call him Nix?" I ask.

"Yeah, what do you think? We all have nicknames, so why shouldn't he? Plus, he's pretty much part of the team," Jayden says, making funny faces at my son. "Isn't that right, Nix?"

I smile, nodding in agreement.

"I hope you all learned something valuable today," Coach says from behind us. "Just because you use condoms doesn't mean they're always effective. Do whatever you want with that information." He and Reggie laugh as if a joke was said and only they got it.

"You better believe I'm keeping a plan B with me everywhere I go," Jagger states, looking mortified.

38

TJ

"So when is Lola supposed to be back?" Jagger asks.

"I, uh, I'm not sure."

Jagger's head whips in my direction. "What do you mean, you're not sure?"

"Well..." I rub the nape of my neck.

I had every intention of asking Lola questions. I even made a note in my phone so I wouldn't forget, but as soon as I got to her apartment, I got distracted.

I swear I wasn't trying to be a creep, but Lola was running around in nothing but a towel while soaking wet. She was in the midst of getting ready for the event when I got there.

Any rational thoughts slipped my mind. While she got ready, I played with Phoenix and thought of every possible disgusting thing while I tried not to get hard.

I'm very aware of how pathetic that sounds.

"I just sort of forgot."

"You forgot? What if she never comes back?" Jagger gapes, rubbing the nape of his neck.

"You dumba—idiot. Of course she's coming back." Jayden slaps him upside the head.

"She's going to be here a little later. I know that much. The wedding was a bit of a drive," I explain.

"So what do we do now?" Jay questions.

We stand in front of the couch, crowding around Phoenix, staring down at him. He's sitting on the couch, playing with his bear and his whistle.

"There're a few parties on frat row. We could—I don't know, take him? He looks like he likes to have a good time," Jagger suggests.

It takes everything in me not to slap him.

"Sure, I'm just going to take my son to a house filled with every drug you can think of. Lola's going to love to hear that *our* son was around pill poppers and coke heads," I sarcastically remark.

Saint shakes his head disapprovingly. For once, he's not smiling. He's looking at Jagger like he wants to slap some sense into him. "W. T. F. is wrong with you?"

"Jagger, you're an idiot." Jayden slaps him again, and this time he glances at me, letting me know he did that for me.

"It was merely a sugg—"

Landon cuts him with a cold glare. "You twat. When was the last time the kid ate?" He glances at Nix.

As if he could feel his daunting stare, he tilts his head back to stare at Landon. A big, giddy grin splits across his face, and surprisingly, it's enough to soften Landon's hardened stare.

"I gave him a snack before practice. I'm sure he's hungry now."

"Well, let's grab him something to eat before we have to explain to Lola why her child starved to death."

Jay snorts, bending down to pick him off the couch. "Have you seen these rolls? I'm sure he'll be all right."

Nix has no idea what he's talking about, but he giggles as Jayden pokes his belly.

"So what does he eat?" Landon asks.

"Mac and cheese."

He's obsessed with it. I'm sure if he could, he'd drown himself in a bucket of the cheese sauce. At least that's what Lola said.

God, I miss her. *You just saw her this morning.* My subconscious mocks me.

"Oh, we're going to Benny's." Jayden decides, already making his way to the front door with Saint in tow.

Benny's is a small hole-in-the-wall run-down diner just ten minutes from here, but despite its appearance, it has some of the best fast food around. To top it off, it's not usually crowded with college students like every other restaurant.

As I walk out, locking the door behind me, I send Lola a few messages, updating her once again. She's busy, so I don't expect a reply back, but I keep telling myself that she'll really appreciate it. And I'm desperately craving her attention.

Me: Going to Benny's with the guys. Phoenix is going to love it there. They have the best mac and cheese.

I also snap a picture of Saint and Jayden playing with Phoenix and his bear and send it to her.

Me: Jayden came up with a nickname for Phoenix. Nix, what do you think?

Me: Also Phoenix is pretty much part of the team now, so he's obligated to come to games and practices.

I don't expect a reply in return, but I'm surprised when I get a picture.

Peaches: Attached: 1 image.

It's a selfie of her, smiling with the painting of the couple who's getting married in the background.

She looks so fucking heavenly, it's unreal. And her smile, goddamn, I love that smile.

I got the chance to see what she was wearing before she left for the wedding, and it took everything in me not to take a picture. Mainly because it would make me look like a creep.

Me: I think about you so much it's unhealthy, and then you go and send me this picture.

I type out, but because I'm a chickenshit, I don't send it. As I'm about to delete it, Jayden calls my name.

"TJ, are you ready to go? We're starving out here!"

"Yeah, I'm go—" I look down at the screen, realizing that somehow I sent the message.

Fuck.

I can't stop staring at the message I sent Lola two hours ago. She probably hasn't seen it, but there's this nagging, pathetic voice in my head telling me she did and doesn't care.

Especially because she hasn't brought up Halloween or the kiss from last week. I've tried to talk about it, but she always shuts it down and it's driving me insane. I can't stop replaying the kiss in my head and how badly I want to do it again.

"I think I f'ed up." Saint's voice disrupts my thoughts.

Tucking my phone in my pocket, I lift my head. "What do you mean, you think you—"

"It's stuck on me." He aggressively pulls on the baby carrier strapped to his chest.

"How did you manage to do that?" I snicker.

"I don't know. I was just trying it on because—that doesn't matter. Help me take it off."

"Where are the guys?" I prop Phoenix on my hip and attempt to take it off with my free hand.

After Benny's, the plan was to hang out at the house until Lola arrived, but then Saint pointed out that the house isn't "kid-friendly."

What university house is kid-friendly? We have a box filled with shit people have left at the parties we've hosted. There are also two blow-up dolls somewhere and one or two boxes of condoms lying around. And we have alcohol, lots of it.

We didn't plan what we wanted to buy. All I know is that Jayden grabbed a shopping cart and disappeared with Landon and Jagger an hour ago. And that was after Saint said to get whatever and that it was on him. I told him I'd pay for it, but he said, "as the godfather, it's my job to spoil him."

"They said they were going to get something that's going to be beneficial to Phoenix's learning—mental—fuck if I know. They said a lot of things."

I shouldn't call him out considering his situation, but I really can't help myself. "That's ten dollars in the jar."

Lola's money jar gave me the idea of getting one for my house. There's currently a hundred dollars in it.

He grumbles something under his breath that sounds a lot like Italian. I may not speak it, but I'm sure he cussed me out.

"This is really stuck on you." I fail miserably and laugh, watching him struggle to get it off.

"Great, I guess I better make good use of this. Come here, *Polpetta*." He snatches Nix from me and puts him inside the carrier. "You might as well make yourself useful and put those photography skills to use and take my picture."

Arching a brow but not questioning it, I take a picture. I grin at Phoenix. He's happily hanging from the carrier, holding his bear. He's so unbothered and so giddy, my smile grows wider.

"Now send it to Lola and tell her to send it to Daisy."

"Why?"

"Because most girls love it when guys are good with kids. Especially if it's kids they're related too. And Daisy loves Nix more than anything in this world, so if she loves him, she'll love me for loving him."

If that doesn't scream delusional, I don't know what will.

"It's been what? A few months and she still hasn't shown you signs of interest. I'm impressed with your persistence. It's never going to happen, but I applaud you for your determination."

"You say that now, but she smiled at me the other day," he states so seriously, I don't know whether to laugh or not.

My lip twitches. "A smile?"

"Don't look at me like that. I know what you're thinking, but it's progress."

"Right, *progress.*"

"More than you've ever made with Lola."

I narrow my eyes. "What do you know about Lola and me?"

A sly smile curves his lips. "More than you think."

My smile drops and before I get to ask him anything, he walks off. I follow him, my thoughts going rampant at the thought of Lola saying something to him about us.

"What do you know? Has she said anything to you?"

He stops in front of the toddler toys, skimming over the colorful ones. He points at some, asking Phoenix which one is his favorite.

"Saint."

"That's my name."

"Stop playing. Did she say anything to you about me?"

He shrugs. "Possibly."

I blow an aggravated breath. "What did she say?"

"I can't say. I've been sworn into secrecy." He pretends to zip his lips.

You've got to be fucking kidding me. "Secrecy?"

"We're part of the OCC. It's in our oath."

I blink. "OCC? Oath?"

"Only Child's Club. We don't have siblings, so we rely on each other, that kind of thing." He grabs a blue dog that Phoenix is pointing at and presses its paw. I recognize the dog from a show he recently started watching and has now become obsessed with.

I stare at him, unblinking. "Rely on each other? You've known Lola for almost three months. When did you guys get so...close?"

There's something *green* and disgusting piercing in my chest, invoking a bitter taste in my mouth.

"I don't know. It just happened," he replies with all the nonchalance in the world. "We have class together, so occasionally, we meet up, drink coffee, and discuss things."

I swear my right eye is twitching. "Discuss things?"

He looks at me, chuckling while Phoenix becomes preoccupied with the blue dog.

"Things that don't pertain to you." He cheekily smiles.

Because he's pissing me off and I'm an asshole, I smile, doing my best not to let that ugly, green *thing* make an appearance again.

"You may have gotten a smile, but Daisy talks to me now, and I'm at her apartment all the time."

That's right, Daisy and I are at a different level in our...*friendship*. She doesn't look at me like she wants to stab me in the knees anymore. And she talks to me more now, like makes actual conversation with me.

I hoped that would rile him up, but he inhales a sharp breath and the smile on his face grows wider. "And one day that will be me."

"I can't stand you."

"You love me. And I love you."

He goes to pinch my cheek, but I swat his hand away.

"There you are." We turn at Jagger's voice.

My gaze drops down to the cart filled to the top with all sorts of things.

"Jesus Christ, did you grab the entire store?" I gape. Scanning the cart, I see things that I know Phoenix is not old enough to use or eat. "What do you need an Oculus for?"

"This is all for his developmental growth. If there's a zombie outbreak, this will really prepare Nix."

"And a Nintendo serves what purpose?" I hold the Mario game up.

"This is Mario we're talking about. He can't have a childhood if he doesn't play it." Landon snatches it from my hand.

I stare at them, bewildered. "None of this stuff is necessary. We're only getting what we need."

"God, you sound like such a dad." Jayden snorts a laugh.

"Don't worry, it's like taking a dollar or two from my bank account. I won't notice it's gone and neither will you." Saint's signature happy-go-lucky smile appears on his face.

I guess it doesn't matter because he gets a hefty allowance every month. I do too. I won't downplay how great I got it. My parents not only set a trust fund up for my siblings and me, but we get allowances every month, except for Ben now, who has a job.

Despite how much I get, it's nowhere in comparison to what he gets.

"And don't worry, we got everything you told us to get." Jayden points at the outlet covers, cabinet locks, a baby gate for the stairs, and a few other things I told them we needed.

Jagger drapes his arm over my shoulder, guiding me in the direction of check-out. "Now stop stressing, baby daddy, and let's go home."

Never in my wildest dreams did I imagine spending a Saturday night with my friends drinking juice—that's right, juice. We're with *my* son, playing with his toys, and drinking toddler-sized juices.

"All right, Little Bear, it's time to go to sleep."

It's crazy how fast time went by. One moment, we're unloading everything from the cars, unpacking it, and making sure there isn't anything small for Phoenix to put in his mouth. Next, we're playing with his toys, making bets, and losing money.

It all started with the beehive toy Phoenix picked out. It's the size of a basketball with a hole on top. Its purpose is to get as many bees inside before time runs out. It started with me teaching Phoenix how to play, and it was supposed to be fun until Saint made a bet.

None of us could resist, and we agreed. It was simple at first, laying the hive on the ground and throwing the bees in it. But because we're all competitive as fuck, we made it harder, placing it far away from us. Setting it at the bottom of the stairs while we were at the top, and many other places.

I'm not ashamed to admit we've been playing with it for over an hour, but I'm ashamed to admit that Landon beat us all.

"Well, this was fun." A faint smile ghosts Landon's face.

"But?" Jayden looks at him.

"But what?"

"Shouldn't you say better luck next time?"

He blankly stares at us. "No. This isn't luck. I'm just better."

"Whatever." We roll our eyes.

Picking up Phoenix from the couch, I take the maple-flavored puff snacks Lola packed him and stuff them in his diaper bag. If he could, he'd eat the whole damn thing.

I take out a change of clothes and everything I need and get him ready for bed while the guys clean up. Once he's ready, I sit on the recliner and rock him, but a few minutes pass by and still he moves around, talking gibberish to his bear.

"How is he not tired? I feel exhausted." Jagger yawns.

"I have an idea." Landon stands from the couch, and before I question him, he goes upstairs and comes back in a flash with his guitar. "Cover the kid's ears," he instructs.

I stare at him, confused, but cover them regardless. "Why do you—"

"If any of you dumb fucks record me or make a single comment, I will make your pitiful lives miserable for the rest of the year. And do not fucking test me." His eyes bounce between all of us, making sure we understand that it's not a threat but a promise.

We don't say anything. Not only because we know he'd make good on his promises, but because we're all shocked that he's going to play in front of us. For as long as we've lived with him, we've never heard him sing. Occasionally, we'll hear him play but never sing.

Landon sits on the floor and leans against the wall as he sets up his guitar. He clears his throat and strums his fingers along the strings until a soft and slow melody dances around the room.

I'm lost in his deep, melodic voice. I register a second later that he's playing "Beautiful Boy" by John Lennon.

We stare at each other, speechless and awe-stricken as he continues to sing. Except for Jagger, which isn't surprising since he's known him the longest and they're the closest.

Peeking down at Phoenix, I smile as his eyes flutter and he snuggles deeper against my chest. I kiss the top of his head, reveling in the song, and count down the minutes until I see Lola again.

39

LOLA

Cara: You need to get on Instagram! Now!

Daisy: Get on your business one now!

Me: Why? Is it really important? I'm almost home.

I'm at the store buying the last things we need for our Friendsgiving. Since I won't be with Daisy and her family for Thanksgiving this year, the girls and I decided to do something together. We also invited Gabby, Polly, and Juls over.

Daisy: Yes it's important!

Me: Oh God please don't tell me it's something bad?

Cara: No, it's really good! Just check it right now!

Even though they said it's not bad, I can't help but feel anxious.

Social media and I are in a love-hate relationship. Sometimes great things come out of it, like getting new clients and getting sweet comments about my art. Other times it's a reminder that people are shit, and it takes a toll on my mental health.

Lately, it's been neither and while it's great that people aren't sending me hateful messages or leaving me nasty comments, I'd love to get new clients. Unfortunately, it's been immensely slow. Too slow that I'll only be working at the museum until I miraculously get new clients.

Opening the app, I switch over to my business account. I swear my jaw hits the floor and if they could, my eyes would pop out of their sockets. Last time I checked my account, I barely had a thousand followers, but now I'm close to four thousand and they still keep coming. If that isn't enough to shock me, I'm even more floored when I see the reason for the increase in my following and influx of messages is due to the post TJ tagged me in.

I'm not sure when he took the pictures of my wall, or him standing in front of my paintings. He's brought his camera over a few times, but I didn't think much of it. I thought he was working on homework.

Cara: He asked me to take a picture. Now it all makes sense.

Daisy: Damn he's really trying to redeem himself. Still on my shit list, but he's definitely not number one anymore.

Cara: Not only is he trying to redeem himself, but he's trying to prove something...

Daisy: I'm so glad you're thinking what I'm thinking.

Me: Stop it.

Daisy: Stop what? It's so obvious!

Me: No. We're not going there.

Cara: Yes we are! He's so obvious about it, how are you still not seeing it?

Me: I'm done with this conversation.

Daisy: We're not! And since we're on the subject, we need to discuss the MASSIVE sexual tension.

Me: *rolling eyes emoji*

Me: Do you guys need anything from the store?

Cara: Aw look at you. Denial at its finest.

Daisy: Get something to celebrate!

I drop my phone in my purse, attempting to keep my smile at bay, but it's hard to tame it down when the reason behind it is hours away.

The basketball team is away for the Invitational and this year it's in Las Vegas. They've been gone since last Wednesday and won't return until tomorrow, the day before Thanksgiving. The same day he gets back, we'll be taking off to Florida. I'm nervous. I'll be meeting his family for the first time, and I'll be there for four days.

I keep overthinking. It wasn't bad at first, but then my thoughts spiraled out of control. What if they're not as nice as they sound? What if they're like my parents? What if they realize they regret inviting me over and kick me out? What if they think I'm trying to use TJ for attention and money?

It's ridiculous to think that considering they paid for my plane ticket, despite me telling TJ I could pay for it.

Oh God, what if I made a mistake? Trepidation smacks me hard across the face.

"Hey." A cheery voice snaps me out of my thoughts,

reminding me that I'm at the grocery store, panicking in the middle of the chip aisle.

I've come to recognize that voice. With dread, I turn, plastering a smile on my face. "Hey."

"How are you? It's been a while." Alexia smiles, tossing her silky black hair over her shoulder.

"Yeah, it has."

Last time we saw each other was on Halloween. I've seen her around campus, but it's always just passing by.

Her gaze sweeps over my body, stopping on the patches of dry paint on my jean overalls. "I had no idea you were so *talented*. I saw your work on TJ's account and I'm impressed. It's *actually* really good."

There's something about the way she says it, but I tell myself not to overthink. Maybe she's just being nice.

"Thanks." I ease the tight smile on my face.

"I also saw that your following grew since TJ mentioned you. You were at what? Eight hundred and twenty or something?"

I nod, wanting to ask how she knows the exact number, but before I get the chance, she speaks.

"I told you it's great to have someone like TJ on your side. Knowing him is going to open up so many doors for you. Telling him to post you was smart."

"I didn't tell him to do anything," I reply, doing my best to keep my smile from dropping.

"Oh." Her brows rise like she's genuinely surprised he did that without me having to ask. "You should definitely tell him to post you more often so that way people don't forget who you are."

Alexia stands straighter, shoulders squared and smile wide and bright. Her gaze feels patronizing and almost like she's trying to size me up.

I hate confrontation. While Cara and Daisy thrive in it, I don't. My palms get cold and clammy, and my heart always feels like it's going to implode. And I hate the aftermath of it because I overthink everything I said. It's a cycle I hate going through, which is why I rarely do it.

But right now is the exception.

"I know there's something going on between you and TJ, and whatever it is, I don't want any part of it."

She bitterly chuckles. "I'm only trying to be nice to you. This has nothing to do with the fact that TJ and I *fuck*. If you have a problem with me, then I'm afraid to tell you that you're going to have a problem with half of the female population at the university."

She enunciates *fuck* like she wants me to see the clear image of them two together, and she succeeds.

"Right, nice. Although it seems like you're the one with the issues. I don't care what he does, but it seems like you do since you're bringing it up."

Her jaw ticks, but she plasters a haughty smirk on her face.

"You don't have to believe anything I say, but TJ doesn't do commitment nor monogamy. I would know. He's fucked me and every other girl for two years. Don't think you're special just because you have a kid with him. Just wait until he gets drafted. I've seen what girls are willing to do just to get a small fraction of his attention. Just imagine what they'll do once he's making millions. Do with that information what you will."

"This is probably the greatest thing, besides giving you Phoenix, that TJ could have ever done." Cara stares down at the screen of her phone, a pleased smile gracing her face. "The numbers just don't stop going up."

"It's really sweet that he did that." I swear if Gabby could, she'd melt on the spot as her bright brown eyes soften and her bottom lip juts out.

"Twenty people have already emailed her asking what—make that twenty-one." Daisy grins, staring at my email on my laptop.

"Twenty-one people have emailed her wanting to book for an event or to see if they can get a painting done before Christmas."

"It was smart of TJ to post this now. Think of all the people who have yet to buy Christmas presents," Polly excitedly adds.

"This is so exciting. I'm so happy for you." Julianna beams from the floor where she's playing with Phoenix.

I wish I could share their excitement, but I can't stop thinking about what Alexia said. It's been plaguing my mind since I got home, throughout dinner, and the game. It doesn't help that my traitorous eyes seem to follow his every move. And don't get me started on the number of times my ears have perked up at the sound of his name. Which is a lot because TJ seems to be the commentators' favorite topic of discussion.

Occasionally, they'll talk about his other teammates or USC, the other team they're playing, but the topic always strays back to him. I can't say I blame them. He's killing it tonight. I haven't seen him play much, but I don't have to, to know he's that good.

"I mean, are you kidding me? This is the TJ we all fell in love with freshman year!" the sports analyst, Gary Woods, eagerly exclaims. "He comes at them and keeps coming at them, and he doesn't stop. You can't help but root for the kid. He's unstoppable, he's fierce, he's—"

"Determined," the other sports analyst, Johnny Williams, adds. "Like he's trying to prove something to the world and let me tell you, he's doing exactly that. I mean, with three minutes left of the game, he's scored thirty points and has twelve rebounds, not to mention he's made all ten free throws."

"He's driving the offense aggressively but playing so fluidly. It really is an awe watching Kingston play."

"And let me not get started on Saint Arlo..."

I tune them out, hating myself for how invested I am anytime they have something to say about him.

Because you miss him.

"Lola?"

Daisy waves her hand in front of my face, dragging my attention away from the TV to her.

"Sorry, what?"

She sets my laptop on my lap, pointing at the incoming emails.

"This is wild. Look how many people have emailed you already."

"Yeah." I don't bother to hide how unenthusiastic I feel about it.

"What's wrong?"

"Nothing, I just wish he hadn't posted anything. Sure, it's great, but the last thing I need is for people to think I'm using him."

Though I'm not sure if it matters because they assume that already.

All eyes snap in my direction, but it's Daisy and Cara who eye me intently like they can see right through me.

"Who said it?" Daisy asks, her words sharp and body stiff as if she's mentally preparing to throw hands.

"No one said anything. I just don't want nor need his help."

A small, understanding smile lifts on Cara's lips. "I love you and support that you want to do this on your own, but if any of us have learned a thing or two from social media is the power of influence, and TJ has that."

I can't help but roll my eyes at that. "Of course he does because he's TJ freaking Kingston."

Daisy shuts my laptop and sets it on the coffee table. "Tell me who said it or I'll find out myself."

I should just drop it and not ruin the night with my shitty mood, but I can't let go of Alexia's words.

It's unfortunate that my brain only wants to remember the things that hurt me.

"I ran into Alexia at the store and—"

"That fucking bi—" Polly slaps her palm over her mouth, eyes flicking down to Phoenix. She winces and drops her hand. "Sorry, Lola, that female dog," she whispers.

Cara snaps her fingers as if she's trying to remember who she is. "Alexia? Who's Alexia again?"

Juls eyes me warily, lips parting but closing like she doesn't want to say what she's thinking. "She's uh, she's the girl TJ's sleeping with."

"Was," Polly corrects. "The girl TJ *was* sleeping with, up until two months ago."

She sits up, shocked and curious. "Past tense, as in—"

"As in, he's not messing around with her anymore, or anyone for that matter. He officially cut things off on Halloween, but he stopped sleeping with her before then."

"How do you know?" Cara questions.

"Jag told me, but don't tell him I told you, or he won't tell me anything anymore. I can't ask Landon because he likes to *mind his business.*" She uses air quotes around the three words. "Boring."

"Right, mind his business." Sarcasm drips from Julianna's voice, but it's so faint the girls don't hear it.

"Look, whatever she told you, don't listen to her. She's just bitter and jealous because TJ cut things off." Polly rolls her eyes, shaking her head. "You should've seen the way she was chasing him down on Halloween. He didn't want to cut things off there, but she gave him no choice because she was insistent. I should've known she wouldn't take it well."

"I guess I don't blame her. They've been messing around since freshman year. Surely she developed feelings. I mean, who wouldn't?"

I would know. I have this hapless infatuation toward him.

She lays her hand on top of mine, squeezing it as if she were trying to reassure me. "Don't feel bad. I promise she doesn't deserve your empathy."

"I mean, can you imagine messing around with someone for that long and not falling for them?"

"Well, then she probably has feelings for some of the guys on the football and hockey team."

My brows lift. "What?"

"TJ and Alexia were never"—she pauses, wincing like she feels bad for what she's about to say—"exclusive to each other. It was mutual because neither one was looking for anything serious. Just a good time. If she ever developed feelings for him, she never made it known because when she wasn't with TJ, she was with someone."

"Oh..."

"Alexia's a pretty girl. She can get attention on her own, but she gets it more when she's with someone like TJ, or Eli the QB, or Brooks the captain of the hockey team. Especially when she posts them on Instagram, people eat it up. Girls want to be her, and guys want to be with her. It's just how social media works and she knows how to use it in her favor. She's subtle about it, but she makes sure you know she *knows* them."

She pauses as if she were trying to remember something and then she nods.

"This is the one thing I can tell you that she said word for word, 'can you imagine having someone who everyone wants? Because I can.' You should've seen the deranged look on her face. That's how I know she doesn't like him. She likes the idea of wanting someone who no one else can have."

"Some of the girls in my sorority are friends with her, and I can attest that that's true," Julianna adds.

"And now *you* have the one person she can't have." Polly smirks, pointing at me.

"No, I don't have anyone. He's not mine." I quickly shut down any ideas playing in their heads. "Nor do I want him to be mine."

Lies. Lies. And more lies.

"Does he know that?"

"Why would he? We're nothing more than friends, who happen to have a kid together."

I look down at Phoenix, smiling as he plays with the small basketball TJ bought him the night he took care of him. But I regret thinking of that night because I'm reminded of the text message he sent me.

I think about you so much it's unhealthy, and then you go and send me this picture.

Since he hasn't brought it up, I pretend like I never saw it. I just wish my mind would get the memo because I think about it more than I should.

"She's in the denial phase." Cara chuckles.

"I am not."

"Yes, you are."

"There's no phase. Stop trying to look for something that's not there."

"Really now?" A sly smile lifts on Daisy's face. "Are we going to pretend like his toothbrush isn't in your bathroom? Or that you emptied a drawer in your dresser for his clothes because he's been staying over *a lot*. And let me not forget the two-thousand-dollar coffee machine he brought the other night."

Simultaneously, their jaws drop.

So maybe he's slept over more than once, but I felt bad making him drive back to his house because he always stayed so late. And the other night he brought the coffee machine from his house. He said it's more useful having it in my apartment so I can make coffee whenever I want.

"He bought the fancy machine that's on your counter?" Gabby gapes, her face brightening.

I look down, trying to hide the way my traitorous lips lift upward. "Yeah...but it's not a big deal. He just knows how much I love coffee."

"Not a big deal?" I hear the giddiness in her voice. "He paid two thousand dollars and it's not a big deal? Does she hear herself?"

"Oh my gosh!" Julianna smiles and her eyes glitter like she's heard the most glorious thing. "Are you guys—"

"He sleeps on the floor," I cut her off, glaring at Daisy. Who seems like she can't shut her mouth. "Get any ideas out of your heads. *We* are nothing more than friends. I don't see TJ like that and he doesn't see me like that."

I lie, but it's better than admitting out loud how I feel about him.

Gabby sighs. "I'm so jealous of you."

"There's nothing to be jealous about."

"I mean, I'm jealous too because, how oblivious must you be to not notice how obvious he is?" Polly chuckles.

"Right! He's so obvious and he doesn't even try to hide it." Cara nods in agreement.

"I swear I thought I was seeing things. I've noticed the look in his eyes."

"He's got it bad."

"Really bad."

"He's throwing so many signs."

"So many."

"And—"

I cut Gabby off, "Okay, that's enough. How did we go from talking about Alexia to this?"

"Oh, Lola." Daisy smiles, her tone patronizing.

"I'm done with this conversation. Look, we missed the last few minutes of the game." I feign a disappointed groan, drawing my attention back to the screen.

"We knew they were going to win. They were up by twenty anyway."

I know because Coach Warren only sits TJ the last few minutes of a game if they're up by so many points.

Daisy says something, but once again my eyes lock on TJ. He stands near the tunnel, talking to one of the reporters, Shannon. Fans linger in the background, leaning over the railing, stretching their hands out for a chance to get a high five or get their jerseys signed by him and any player passing by.

I wish I could say it's the questions the reporter is asking that I find so fascinating, but I can't stop looking at the sweat that coats his skin and jersey. How it trickles down the side of his face, neck, and onto his chest. How his jersey clings to his taut and impressively defined torso.

His hands are at his hips, but every so often, he lifts his hand to move the damp curls sticking to his forehead. I swear my mouth waters at the sight of his biceps flexing.

I'm so focused on his arms, I don't hear the question until I register one very familiar word.

"—Peaches."

"Really, peaches?" The reporter hums, seemingly impressed with his answer. "It makes sense because you played phenomenal tonight."

The screen splits in half, he and Shannon on one side, and the other a replay of all the baskets he made tonight.

"Thank you. You have no idea how energizing it is to have a peach. I had one earlier today, and it was all I needed to give me that extra boost. I swear the benefits are insane." His cheek twitches.

"Thanks for the boost," he said earlier today when we spoke on FaceTime.

She smiles. "Well, I guess I should have one myself."

He brings his bottom lip in between his teeth, releasing a deep chuckle. "Yeah, the good ones are hard to find, but I swear when you find the right one, it's worth it."

"You all right?"

I blink, looking at Daisy.

"What?"

"You all right...*Peaches*?" she whispers, making sure no one else is listening, but I know Cara is.

"Shut up." I press my lips together, attempting to hold back the smile threatening to rise. "It means nothing."

"That was live. You can't tell me it means nothing."

"It doesn't." It's a weak reply and she knows it.

The harder I try to push my feelings away, the harder they push back.

40

TJ

"SAINT, HURRY UP." I PEEK AT MY PHONE AS IT VIBRATES in my hand. A notification appears from my Uber letting me know it's here.

"I told you I'm fine home alone."

"And I told you I'm not leaving you alone, but I do need you to hurry the fuck up."

He peers over his shoulder, flashing me a grin. "So you can see your Peaches?"

I eye the little dagger on his desk but opt for the pen instead and throw it at him. It smacks him in the ear and falls to the ground with a soft clank. "Don't call her that again."

He rubs his ear, dramatically wincing in pain. "Why are you so aggressive? You could have cut me or worse, stabbed me. These are million-dollar ears, *stronzo*. All I asked was if you were ready to see your—" The so-called pain diminishes from his face and he laughs. "Okay, fine, I won't call her that."

"You won't call her that *again*."

He raises his hands in surrender. "I won't call her that *again*."

I'm more than ready to see Phoenix and Lola. It's only been a week since I last saw them, but I swear it feels longer than that. During the three back-to-back games, I was focused, my mind only on my teammates and winning, but before and after was a different story. They were constantly on my mind. There wasn't a day I didn't go without thinking of them, and every small thing reminded me of them.

It's why I packed ahead of time. I wanted to have everything ready so that once I got home, I'd be ready to go. I would've left already, but as I was leaving, I saw Saint lying in bed reading a book.

He was supposed to visit his grandmother but said the plans changed. He didn't tell me why and I didn't pry. I could tell he didn't want to talk about it. But I did grab his duffle and told him to pack enough for a few days. He was reluctant but eventually agreed, but now he's becoming a pain in my ass. I'm tempted to say fuck it and leave him if he doesn't hurry up.

"Seriously, hurry up. I don't understand why it's taking you so long to pick a damn book. Who needs that many books anyway?"

There are two books in his duffle, and he's currently holding one in each hand, debating which one he wants to take.

"I don't know what mood I'll be in."

"Mood? Does it even matter? It's a book. Let's go."

He whips his head in my direction, staring at me like I've offended him. "God, you know nothing. I can't just take any book. I have to have options."

My gaze drops to his duffle, staring at a very familiar and worn book. "Didn't you already read that one?"

"It's called a comfort read. If I can't get into any of these, I'll just reread this one." He tosses the book in his left hand in his bag and places the other back on his book shelf. "All right, I'm ready to go."

"About fucking time. Let's go." I walk out of his room and head down the stairs.

Saint snorts, following behind me.

"What?"

"So are you and Lola going to continue this weird foreplay you got going on, or are you guys going to make it official?"

"There's no weird foreplay."

We step out of the house, lock it behind us, and get in the Uber.

"The back and forth eye fucking is insane. And don't get me started on the *not* so subtle touches. You make it so painfully obvious you want her, I don't know why you don't just go for it."

"I don't know what you're talking about."

"So are we going to pretend like you didn't threaten to waterboard us in our sleep if we checked Lola out? Or that *you accidentally* misplaced Quiton's car keys because you overheard him talking about Lola's ass? Which he's currently still looking for." He holds up his phone, showing me the text messages Q sent the team group chat, asking if anyone has seen his car keys.

My teammates weren't only checking her out but talking about her ass.

I can't blame them because Lola has a double take ass. I understand how wrong that sounds, but she has the kind of ass people break their necks for. I would know, I've done it, I've seen random people do it, and I've seen my friends do it. It's always so quick they think I don't notice, but I do.

I can't control what anyone thinks or says about her, but I refuse to hear or see it. So if I need to be petty to get my point across, I will. I'm also not a violent person, but if I need to, I won't hesitate to knock someone out.

"Maybe he shouldn't have been running his mouth." I shrug.

The corners of his mouth quirk up. "Where?"

"The arena."

I could've been an asshole and accidentally dropped them in the trash, but I accidentally threw them across the arena. I'm not entirely sure where they landed, but they're up there somewhere. There are only twenty-one thousand, two hundred, and eighty seats. He'll find them.

"You can't tell me I'm seeing things."

"You're not seeing this." My heart speeds up, warning me that it's pumping more than it should. If that isn't warning enough to stop talking, my fucking palms become wet. For some reason, I can't stop the rest of the words from spilling out of my mouth like a broken dam. "I like her a lot. I like her so goddamn much, I don't just physically want her, I need her. Everything she has, I want. But the problem is I don't think she wants what I want. Anytime I try to bring us up, she shuts me down. Like she can't bear the thought of being with me."

That feels like a punch to my stomach, knocking all the air out of me with the ugly truth that she's not into me as much as I'm into her.

I don't know when it all happened, when I fell so fucking hard for her, but all I know is that I *want* to be with Lola.

"Hmm..." he hums.

"Hmm what?"

"Just talk to her."

"Did you not hear the part where I said—"

He thumps me in the forehead. "What the hell is wrong with you?"

"What?" I slap his hand away.

"You've always been cocky as shit and so full of yourself, I don't understand why you're hesitating when you haven't even talked to her."

I mull over his words. Debating on what I should do. I know what I want, but the fear of getting rejected is too fucking real. I know how arrogant it's going to sound, but I've never been rejected. Anything I've ever wanted, I've always had. It doesn't matter what is, I've always known that no matter what, I'd get it. But for the first time ever, the fear of rejection is freaking me out because I've never wanted anything or anyone as much as I want Lola.

Those soft little laughs, the infectious smiles, middle finger promises, those hazel eyes that look like the earth, dainty paint-covered hands, and everything else.

"The worst she could say is that she's not interested." He beams, lifting a shoulder in a half shrug.

I glare at him. "That's exactly what I wanted to hear."

"You have to mentally prepare in case she turns you down. And if she does, you use your cocky as shit charm to make her fall in love with you."

"You make it sound like it's that simple." I blow a heavy breath.

"I never said it was."

"You weren't kidding about Lola living so far away." Saint gapes out the window, looking in the direction we came from and then at Lola's apartment. "You're telling me you've been driving an hour back and forth every single day? How the hell do you do it?"

It's exhausting, but every mile is worth seeing the two people who've become so important in my life.

We hop out of the Uber and saunter over to her apartment. "I just do. Plus, I don't have the right to complain. Lola does it all the time."

"You should have her move in with us. Lola can stay with you, Cara with Jayden, and Daisy with me," he jokes, wiggling his brows.

I know he's just messing around, but the joke fuels an idea in my head. But I store it in the back of my head as her door opens and she steps out.

Lola comes out with a suitcase, a book bag strapped on her shoulders, her purse hanging on one shoulder, and Phoenix attached to her hip, all while holding a sippy cup, her keys, and phone in her other hand.

Even with everything she's carrying, she still looks effortless and so fucking stunning. She's wearing an oversized corduroy jacket, a black tank top underneath that sticks to her like a second skin, and it's tucked underneath light denim jeans that hug her hips and thighs so nicely. And the whole outfit is paired with black Dr. Martens.

Her eyes meet mine, but it's only brief before they train on Saint.

I hate that they're not on me longer, and I hate that I want nothing more than to pull her in my arms, but I don't. I stay rooted in my spot, taking her in.

"Hey, I didn't know you were coming." She smiles, hugging him.

"I wasn't, but TJ just can't bear the thought of being without me. I took pity on his desperation and alas, here I am."

She stifles a laugh when I give him a less than impressed stare. "You know I can still change my mind."

"You love me too much. You wouldn't dare."

"I'm tempted."

He rolls his eyes, bending down at Phoenix's eye level, a goofy smile spreading across his lips. "Hey, *Polpetta*."

"Ant!" He smiles excitedly. They've only met a few times, but Phoenix has gotten really comfortable around him.

Saint looks taken aback. "Ant?"

"Leave him alone. He's trying," I say. "Hey, Little bear." I ruffle his hair, tapping his and the bear's noses.

"Mm, we'll work on that. You'll also have to learn Italian." he states in a grave tone, as if my son is supposed to understand what that means.

"Let him learn English first before we try to teach him another language. He hardly understands Spanish and he grew up around it," she says.

"We'll work on it," he says nonetheless and plucks Phoenix out of Lola's arm. "He really looks nothing like you."

She pouts, rolling her eyes, and I have to look away because images of the same expression in certain positions cross my mind.

I don't know what's wrong with me. Sure, I haven't had sex in a while, but I'm fantasizing something extremely perverse over a pout and an eye roll.

I snap out of my fantasy and grab the rest of her stuff from her full hands.

"Thanks." She swallows, her gaze dropping to my hand on top of hers. I wait for her to move it away, but she doesn't.

I try to stop the thought, but all I can think of is my hand around her delicate throat.

Sucking in a breath, I pull my hand away.

"We should get going. We don't want to miss the flight. My parents will kill me if they don't get to meet their grandson today," I say as we make our way to the Uber. "They promised to disown me if I mess anything up."

She tucks a lock of her wavy hair behind her ear. "They're excited, huh?"

"That's an understatement." When we're out of earshot from Saint and Phoenix, I grab her wrist, stopping her from going any farther. "I'm really happy that you decided to come."

"Well, I know how excited your parents are to meet Phoenix."

I don't miss the sadness that lingers in her voice and hate the reason behind it. But I try not to dwell on those pieces of shit.

"I mean, I'm happy my parents are going to meet him, but I meant that *I'm* really happy you decided to come," I reiterate, making sure she understands what I'm trying to say. "I missed you."

Her eyes grow a tad, like she can't believe I said that. I can't believe it either, but I don't regret it.

A beat of silence passes between us before a tentative smile grows on her face. "I, uh, I missed you too."

"I've never been in first class before." A sated smile stretches across Lola's face.

Saint snorts a laugh. "You were hardly in there before you fell asleep."

"I got about three hours of sleep last night, thanks to him."

She tightens her grip on Nix as we get on the escalator to go down.

"You know, I'm glad you guys had a kid," Saint muses, eyes floating between Lola and me and then at our son. "*Now* more than ever I'm going to be safe."

"You do know Lola and I used a condom when she got pregnant?" I cock a brow, smirking as his smile slips and Lola's cheeks turn a bright pink shade.

He looks at us in mortification. "You're not serious, are you?"

"Oh, I'm serious."

He drags his fingers through his hair. "Fuck."

"Language," I warn him again. I'd been doing that since we picked them up.

"You two used a condom and you still got pregnant?"

"But I wasn't on birth control," she adds with a sheepish smile.

Wasn't as in past tense? Meaning she's on it now...and she's probably...

"Hmmm." He looks thoughtful and then he smiles mischievously. The kind of smile that tells me he's about to make a dumbass comment. "You know...you really should bring him over to the house more. The guys could really use this as *their* form of birth control. Could you imagine Jagger with a kid?"

I laugh because I can't imagine Jagger Spears with a child.

"We should get a girl to—" A familiar voice interrupts my very brilliant plan as we step off the escalator.

I'm met with three pairs of familiar eyes, but none of them are focused on me. They're focused on the little boy in Lola's arms.

My parents blew up my phone, reminding me to let them know as soon as we arrived. I told them the time we'd be here, though Mom should know since she booked the flights. Of course she said, "what if the plane gets delayed or something happens, and we don't make it at the planned time."

We meet my parents in the middle, and when I place my hand on the small of her back again, Lola's entire body becomes stiff.

I lean into her and quietly say so only she can hear me, "I promise everything's going to be all right. I wouldn't bring you here if I didn't think so."

She doesn't look at me, but I see her lips rise slightly.

"I'm so glad you're all finally here." Mom opens her arms and wraps them around me, and then pulls away and hugs Saint next.

"Sorry, this was all last minute. TJ insisted I come," he says, his voice unsure.

"No, we're glad you came." Mom's voice is soft and loving, squeezing him a little tighter before she finally releases him. "You're welcome anytime."

"We're happy to have you over. Don't ever hesitate to come. You don't even have to ask," Dad assures him, giving him a small pat on the back.

Saint nods, his smile tight and awkward, but then it softens into his usual laid-back one.

"Lola." Mom clasps her hands in front of her chest as she looks down at Phoenix, who has his cheek pressed firmly against her chest, eyeing everyone curiously. "Thank you so much for coming," she quietly says, emotion lacing her voice.

A small, apprehensive smile curls at her lips. "Thank you for inviting me. *Us*."

There's a moment of silence where no one says anything. I know they have so much to say, so much to ask, but they don't know where to begin.

I see a wave of emotions flash through Dad's eyes, but I know he won't act upon them. Not the way that Mom is because her eyes are watering, and I know she's dying to hold and hug him. Even Dad looks like he wants to approach him, but they both hesitate in their spot. I'm sure they don't want to crowd or make them uncomfortable.

"Jesus, the Kingston genes run strong." Hazel breaks the silence, stepping forward. "It's good to finally meet you. I can see why my brother knocked you up." She eyes Lola from head to toe.

"Hazel!" Mom and Dad chide.

"What?" She innocently smiles, raising her hands up. "I'm just being honest." She looks at Saint for backup, but I glare at him. His lips flatten, but his cheek twitches.

"I hope you're all hungry." Dad changes the conversation. "TJ found a Mexican restaurant not too far from here that we could eat at."

"I just know how much you love Mexican food. I hope it doesn't disappoint."

The apprehension wavers off and a soft smile takes over her face. "I'm sure it won't."

I breathe a breath of relief, feeling the stiffness in her back ease and the tension subside.

41

LOLA

I CAN'T SLEEP.

I've closed my eyes multiple times, counted to twenty, put on soothing music, got on my phone and answered emails and messages regarding my prices and availability. I even showered again with steaming hot water in hopes that it would relax me. I've done everything I can think of to fall asleep, but nothing has helped. I keep tossing and turning, hoping sleep will sneak up on me, but tonight it's decided it doesn't want to come.

Though I'm sure it would if I could stop feeling guilty for dreading my decision to come here.

I started mentally preparing for the worst the moment I agreed to come with TJ. I kept waiting for the inevitable, thinking they'd be the opposite of what TJ made them out to be. It wasn't until we sat down and got to know each other that I realized they're nothing like my parents.

I feel stupid now, assuming they'd be anything like them. They weren't only interested in getting to know Phoenix, but they were interested in me too. They asked me about school, my job, my business, and other things. And not once did they bring up my parents. I can only assume that was TJ's doing.

But it wasn't just their words of kindness that made me feel this way.

They redecorated an entire room just for Phoenix. It literally looks like a Winnie the Pooh wonderland, with a few other things that he's recently fallen in love with. Like Nemo, Bluey, and basketball.

Who puts that much effort if they don't care?

There's still this little voice in the back of my head, warning me to tread lightly in case everything goes to shit. It's stupid to feel that way because my son doesn't only seem to be having the time of his life, but I can tell he feels comfortable. So much so he wanted to sleep in his bedroom tonight.

Did it break my heart? Just a little because that means he's growing up. It's inevitable, but it makes me so emotional to think that one day he won't need me anymore.

Pushing that depressing thought aside, another thought I tried to push away comes barreling in.

What I feel for TJ is not just a hapless infatuation. And I have to stop lying and telling myself that I don't miss him because I do, I really do.

With him being around more, I started getting used to his presence. Buying me random coffee, his attempt at blueberry pancakes and other foods, teaching Phoenix how to throw a basketball, and staying up with me despite fighting every night for his life to stay awake until I go to bed.

We created this little routine, and I didn't realize how much I missed it and him until I saw him again this morning.

Deciding that I can't lie down anymore because I'll literally go crazy in my own head, I grab my phone from my nightstand and pad over to Phoenix's bedroom.

Who would have ever thought I'd be saying that?

I smile at that and push his door open but stop at the doorway. TJ's sitting on the recliner, legs sprawled wide, arms folded against his chest, with an iPad propped on the armrest.

"Hey." I awkwardly wave, still rooted in my spot.

He taps the screen, pausing whatever he's watching. "Can't sleep?"

"No, and I tried everything. Figured I could come in here and do some work." I step inside, standing next to Phoenix's crib, and gently caress the side of his cheek with the back of my fingers.

"Same." He flips the iPad over, showing me a still image of the last game he played at the Las Vegas Invitational. "Figured I could come in here and do some work." He grins, repeating my words.

I smile, dropping my hand. "Work?"

"I'm looking for mistakes I made, things that worked and didn't. And a few other things," he explains.

I nod, understanding what he means. I watched Sebastian, Daisy's brother, do the same thing—for baseball and soccer—when I lived with them.

"I hate to admit this, but you're pretty good."

"Hate to admit it? Just *pretty* good?" He gasps dramatically and cocks a brow, exaggerating on the word with feigned offense in his voice.

"I thought I'd help you out."

"How so?"

"I have to humble you. If I don't, you'll let your big ego get to your head, and you won't play as good as you do."

I can tell he's trying to keep his expression stoic, but I see the twitch at the corner of his lip and the gleam that flashes through his eyes. "Wow, thank you. I certainly feel humbled now. It's exactly what I needed."

"You're welcome. Glad I could be of service." I salute him.

The smile he was trying to tame spreads across his face and he quietly chuckles. "Maybe I should stop watching film and bring you with me at all times. I'd definitely be on top of my game if I had you to humble me at all times."

"Not sure your coach would appreciate my services."

"He wouldn't, but *I* would."

I don't miss the double meaning behind it or the way his eyes become heated as they sweep over me. Is it wrong to say that I don't hate the way he said it or looks at me? Is it wrong to say that I can picture myself doing things I probably shouldn't?

"Having me around too much could possibly be your downfall."

"Or the best thing to ever happen to me."

My heart stops for a millisecond but then picks up. It goes too fast and I feel like it's going to break out of my chest.

My lips part, but for some reason, I can't bring myself to say anything. Thankfully, TJ speaks up.

"Did you watch the entire game?"

"I did and I heard something very interesting."

He leans back, resting his elbow on the armrest, and props his chin on his knuckles. "Oh yeah? What did you hear?"

I take a step forward, folding my arms over my chest. "Something about the great benefits of peaches."

His cheek twitches. "You know, I heard the same thing too. I actually had one that day before the game. Really gave me a boost and everything."

"And everything?" I grin.

"And everything," he confirms. We say nothing but smile at each other, letting the silence linger, but after a beat, he stands. "I've been thinking a lot, and there's something I really want to get off my chest."

"Yeah?"

TJ blows a breath, rubbing the back of his neck with his palm. Does he...does he look nervous?

"I've been thinking a lot about us and—"

He clamps his lips as Phoenix stirs in his sleep. He rolls to his other side, murmuring something as he does. We both still, our eyes locking on him, hoping with every fiber in our being that he doesn't wake up because we both know he won't go back to sleep if he does.

Once he stops moving and murmuring, we let out a sigh of relief and look at each other. Neither one of us has to say out loud what we're thinking.

"Let's get out of here before he wakes up."

We slowly and quietly creep out of his bedroom, closing the door behind us.

"That was close." I quietly chuckle. "So you were saying?"

"I, uh, are you sleepy?"

"No, I think I'm more awake now than I was earlier. Why?"

"How are your pool skills?"

"No fucking way. You lied to me." TJ's mouth is agape, brows pinched together, expression full of disbelief as he watches at the 8 ball smoothly sink into the pocket.

I try to act indifferent about winning for the second time, but I can't help the smug smile on my face. "How so?"

TJ sits on the edge of the table, crossing his arms against his chest. "I asked you how your pool skills were and you said, 'I'm okay, I'm really not that good'." He repeats my words, mimicking my voice. "No, of course you're not *good*. You're fucking great."

After we left Phoenix's room, TJ brought me down to his pool house. Where he not only has a pool table but a few other games, a small—I'm not sure I should even call it that since it's almost the size of the kitchen inside their house—kitchen and living room. The tiny house is just as pretty as his actual house.

It's insane to think that he spent his whole life here, living his best life.

I scoff. "I don't sound like that, and that's the truth. I'm just okay."

"Okay my ass. You beat me twice and that never happens."

"I wouldn't have if you hadn't gone so easy on me."

"I didn't—"

I cut him off with a pointed stare. "Yes, you did."

His lips tighten, raising his hands in surrender. "Okay, so maybe I was in the beginning."

"See—wait, was? I beat you twice. Just admit you were being

easy on me, so we can do this again and I can beat your fair and square."

"I did. I went easy on you in the beginning, but the second time around, I didn't."

"You're so frustrating, you know that?" I poke his hard stomach with the tip of the pool cue, leaving the chalk residue on his shirt. "Just admit it, or are you afraid I'll beat you again?" I arch a brow, still poking him until he wraps his hand around the top of the pool cue and firmly holds it in place.

The carefree, playful expression on his face is replaced with a grave one, and his whiskey eyes darken. "Trust me, you don't want me to be honest, and I'm done. Let's play something else."

Because I'm stubborn, I push the cue against his chest again. "No, I don't want to play anything else, not until you're honest."

TJ sinks his teeth into his bottom lip, shaking his head, releasing a harsh breath. "Fine." This time it's him who tugs the cue under his arm, pulling me along with it. "I was honest when I said I went easy on you the first round, but the second time I got distracted." He tugs it again, and still, I don't do anything to stop it. "And because you want nothing but the truth, I won't downplay my thoughts."

I nod, not being able to breathe from how thick and hot the air feels.

"I was distracted because every time you'd bend over, I was trying my hardest not to look at your ass and get turned on." His eyes brazenly coast down my body before they rise back up. "I was doing my goddamn best not to imagine how I'd *fuck* you against this pool table." He pulls the cue until there's hardly any space between us.

My hands become slick with sweat, and my thighs clench as his words paint a very dirty picture in my head.

"So no, I wasn't going easy on you. I was too distracted thinking of the many ways I'd like to fuck you, Lola."

My face burns at the image that plays in my head, and somehow that ignites a spark to spread and a fire to erupt throughout my entire body. I'm too hot. I can't stop my thighs from clenching again as my clit throbs, but it only throbs harder.

He stands at his full height, towering over me, and with one final pull, the pool cue slips from my hands. From my peripheral, I see him set it on the table, and I vaguely hear a faint smack on the floor before my gaze draws back to him. TJ winds an arm around my waist and his other grabs the back of my neck.

My thoughts are so chaotic, but I've never been more sure as two words slip out of my mouth in a rushed whisper. "Show me."

TJ doesn't hesitate to crash his lips against mine, swiping his tongue against my bottom lip as if he's asking for permission and once my lips part, he shoves his tongue inside my mouth. It's rough, desperate, and so demanding. I struggle to catch up, but I can't help but revel in the need.

He bites my lip, but I can't bring myself to focus on the pain because my body burns with need and my thoughts fixate on how he feels against me. I'm too consumed by him, so I allow myself not to think for once as he lifts me up. I circle my legs around his waist and my arms around his neck. He turns us around and sits me on top of the table.

He drags me to the edge until my ass is almost hanging off the table and presses me against him.

I moan into his mouth as his erection digs right where I want it the most. I thread my fingers through his hair at the nape of his neck and shamelessly grind myself against him until my core tightens with anticipation. My mind becomes muddled, numb almost when he cups my ass and squeezes it hard, pushing me closer to my impending orgasm.

I breathlessly gasp, eyes fluttering as he helps me roll my hips to add more friction.

"Don't stop." His voice is gruff against my lips. "Don't fucking stop."

I grind faster against him, biting the inside of my cheek to hold back the moans that threaten to claw their way out of my mouth.

"Let me hear you." It's not a question but a demand. "Don't worry, they won't hear you. No one will. So let me fucking hear you."

And instinctively, soft whimpers slip from my lips, but it's not enough for him. He dips his head and latches his mouth on the side of my neck where my erratic pulse is hammering. He licks and nips my heated skin, but I groan loud, dropping my head back as he bites hard and sucks forcefully until my eyes are rolling to the back.

I feel it. I'm so close, teetering over a blissful edge with no care if I don't return. My toes curl and just as I'm about to come undone, TJ stops sucking, his lips hover, and warm breath fans over my ear.

"You should see how wet you are. Soaked right through." He grips my ass tighter, voice thick and gravelly like he's doing his best to control himself. "Look at yourself and look at what I do to you, what you do to me."

I lick my dry lips, blowing a shaky breath as I look down. Sure enough, there's a wet spot in between my thighs, my arousal soaking through my panties and the thin material of my olive green pajamas. I'd be embarrassed, but I don't have time to process it because my eyes lock on the outline of his hard dick tenting his pajama bottoms. It's massive and thick, straining against them.

His erection pushes against the wet patch between my thighs, sending electric jolts to shoot up to my core. I want to look up at him, but I can't bring myself to because I'm stuck on what we'd look like if we didn't have clothes on.

"I know what you're thinking about."

I blink out of the daze, lifting my head to meet his dark, hooded eyes. "I—"

"Keep your eyes on us."

I don't argue with him and drop my gaze to us and where we're only separated by thin fabric.

"Look at you and how fucking responsive your needy pussy

begs to be fucked." He rasps. Even if I wanted to deny it, the wet spot between my thighs grows. "You can see it, can't you? My cock filling you."

"Yes," I pant, feeling dizzy at how intoxicating he feels and sounds.

"Come on, Peaches, show me how badly you want to be fucked. Show me how badly *you* want it." I wish I could say I hate how arrogant his voice sounds right now, but it has the opposite effect on my body. It thrives and burns at his words and how deep and throaty they sound.

"Please." I'm shocked at the guttural moan that falls from my lips, or how I hook my legs around his waist and not let go once I have his erection right where I want it.

"Good fucking girl." He groans in my ear. "Now come."

Two words, like a snap of a finger, have me coming undone. I'm thrashing against him, moaning and panting loudly, begging him to make sure my orgasm never stops.

And God, he doesn't stop. He holds me firmly against him, as if knowing that keeping the pressure on my clit is all I need for it not to stop.

"TJ, please don't stop," I beg, dropping my forehead against his chest.

There's another wave of pleasure that sweeps over my body and just as I feel it, my legs tremble and untangle, but before they collapse, he grabs my ankles and locks them in place.

"You're doing so good. Don't let go." He keeps his hand still at my ankles and the other at my hip. He holds me in place, watching me as I whimper and relentlessly grind myself faster against him until I see a white, bright, blinding light as a second orgasm wrecks through my body.

"Oh fuck." I squeeze my eyes shut, digging my fingers into his back. I shudder. A hot shiver shoots down my spine and despite me finally coming down from it, TJ holds me. Like he knows that he can still wrench another one out of me, and I'm sure he could because there's a faint pulse between my legs.

"Lola?" he says after I catch my breath.

"Hmm?"

"Do you want to stop?"

I wait for doubt or any semblance of what I felt on Halloween to appear, but it never comes. When I crane my head back to look up at him, I feel confident when I reply.

"No."

42

TJ

I've never seen anything more fucking breathtaking than the sated look on Lola's face. Her lips are swollen and red, cheeks flushed, and eyes heated with lust. She's a dream come true, and despite having her here right in front of me, it all feels unreal. Like if I blink, she'll disappear and I'll wake up.

"What?" She clears her hoarse voice, tucking the wayward strands of hair that have slipped past her ponytail holder, behind her ear.

The words, *I like you*, hang on the tip of my tongue, but this isn't where I want to tell her. The last thing I want is for her to think that I'm only telling her because I have her in this position. I've noticed she's an overthinker and needs reassurance.

Instead of saying what I want to say, I settle with, "I don't want you to think that this doesn't mean anything."

I keep it short and simple because there's so much I need to say, but I decide against it. I'll tell her, just not today.

I hook my fingers underneath the waistband of her bottoms, gliding my finger along the crinkled fabric. "Are you sure you don't want to stop? Because I'm close to ripping your clothes off and bending you over."

She sits up straighter. Her arms draped around my shoulders tighten. "I'm sure."

Those two words of confirmation are everything I need as I grab the hem of her shirt. But before I get the chance to pull it over her head, she places her hand on top of mine to stop me.

"No, don't take my shirt off."

"Hey." I tuck my finger under her chin, tilting her head back so that I can see those pretty, earthy eyes. "Don't do that."

"I just—" She timidly smiles. "Trust me, it's best if I leave it on."

"And trust me, it's best if we take it off. I want to see every inch of you. Your stretch marks aren't going to deter me from appreciating your body the way I'm supposed to."

Her eyebrows rise. "It doesn't bother you?"

I realized after Halloween why she was quick to lower her dress and noticed the way she always had her hands in front of her stomach.

"Bother me? Lola." I drop my hand from the hem and chin and cup her jaw with both hands. "You had our son. You brought life into the world. They're proof once again of how astoundingly resilient you are. Please, for the love of God, don't ever feel like you need to feel embarrassed or hide them from me or anyone else. They're part of something beautiful that you and I created."

Something about my last statement feels like déjà vu, and I think she feels it too by the way she looks at me. I can't pinpoint why it sounds so familiar, but I don't dwell on it and focus on the girl who drives me wild.

"If you don't want to take off your shirt, I completely understand and respect your decision, but I hope that one day you can come to love those lines as much as I like y—them."

Goddamn, TJ, way to be smooth. Dumbass.

"Okay." She breathes.

I drop my hands as she slowly tugs her shirt over her head and lets it fall behind her on the table.

A sheepish smile curves her lips as I brazenly drag my gaze

over her almost naked top half. I let them linger on the faded lines that mark her light ivory skin. They're spread across her stomach, aimlessly. Some are small and others a little longer.

"You're so beautiful," I softly say, grabbing her waist, and steadily let the pad of my thumb drift over her skin. "Don't ever let this make you feel any less."

The sheepish smile replaced with one a little more confident. Hesitation lingers in her eyes, like she's unsure, but regardless, she doesn't stop my wandering fingers from touching her.

I stop, not wanting to push too much, and shift my attention to her face, although it falters as I see her chest rise.

My dick painfully throbs as I stare at her supple breasts that almost spill out of the thin lace bra she's wearing. I'm not even sure it's a bra, but it doesn't matter because I'm glued on her pebbled nipples and how they're straining, begging to come out.

"I want to come over these," I say without thinking but don't let myself mull over my words. Cupping her breast, I pinch the tight bud between my fingers.

The softest whimper echoes throughout the room, and I know she's doing her damnedest not to be loud, worried that someone will hear, but I know they won't.

I pinch the nipple harder, twirling and tugging it until her thighs are rubbing, and I see the wet patch between her thighs grow.

Hmm.

"Does the thought of me coming all over your tits turn you on? Or the possibility of someone catching us? Or is it watching me play with you?"

She bites her lip as another moan expels from them and keeps her eyes on my fingers as they move to the other nipple.

"Or is it all three things?"

I stop my assault and grab the lace, tugging it down with one hard pull until her breasts spill out and fall in a bounce.

Goose bumps circle her dusty rose nipples and spread across her chest.

Pecking her lips, I make my way down, peppering kisses and nipping her skin until I get to the big, round, pink-purplish bruise beneath her jaw. I know she's going to hate me when she sees it, but God, do I fucking love it. The color is a huge contrast to her skin tone. I contemplate covering her body with more, but the last thing I want is for her to never let me do it again, so I continue to descend. I lick the line of her collarbone, relishing the way her body writhes beneath me.

When I reach the top of her breast, I look up at her to make sure she's looking, and sure enough, she is.

I smirk at the way her cheeks heat up as if she were embarrassed, but she doesn't look away.

"Stop looking at me like that." She huffs loudly, almost breathlessly.

"How am I looking at you?" I tease, dragging my tongue down the swell of her breast but stop above the tight bud waiting to be sucked.

Lola heaves a sigh. "I...I don't know but just stop."

"You do know, say it."

I play with her other nipple, pinching, pulling, rolling it between my fingers as I drag the tip of my tongue around it, enjoying how her thighs clench again.

"TJ," she urges, pushing her chest out.

"Peaches," I tease.

Her fingers tangle in my hair, harshly pulling as she blows an aggravated breath. "Like you're enjoying this too much."

I hiss, wincing in pain as she tugs with no remorse, but damn, does it feel good.

"I can't stop looking at you like this because *I am* enjoying this way too much. Don't ever ask me to stop because as long as I get to see you like this, I'll never stop enjoying it. Not until I have every inch of you memorized."

I let her soak in my words before I drag and twirl my tongue across and around her sensitive nipple. Over and over, I repeat the motion until she's panting and whimpering, and ragged breaths filled with, "yes, like that," echo.

But when I suck hard and bite down on it, her back arches and the "yes" is replaced with, "I want more..."

"More?" I let go of it, licking my way to the side of her tit, and suck on it hard until the same pink-purplish bruise is coloring her skin.

"Yes...bend me over." Her plea is timid, catching me off guard because the look on her face is far from timid.

My cock jerks and I feel the pre-cum stick to my boxers, making it uncomfortable to move, but every heated thought comes to a screeching halt at an ugly realization.

"I don't have any condoms."

"It's okay, we can stop." Disappointment laces her voice.

An idea so perverse springs to mind. I don't know how she'll feel about it, but something tells me she might enjoy it.

"Do you trust me?"

She doesn't hesitate when she replies, "Yes."

I grab her elbow and jerk her to her feet, then spin her around and pin her down on the table.

"Anytime you want to stop, just let me know. We only do what you're comfortable with."

Peeking over her shoulder, she nods, and eagerness grows in her dark, dilated eyes.

I hook my fingers under the band of her pajama bottoms and panties, then drag them down, letting them pool around her feet.

"Fuck," I mutter, swallowing hard at the sight of her ass. The dreams I always have are nothing in comparison to what it looks like now. "Goddamn, Lola," I palm her ass cheek before I bring my hand back and slap it hard. I groan as it bounces and she yelps, sitting up, but soon after moans.

"Spread your legs and prop one on top of the table." The deep tenor in my voice shocks me because I'm far too excited to sound like that.

She kicks her clothes to the side, and like I instructed, raises her leg, propping the inside of her knee on top of the pool table.

"Now bend over and let me see how wet you are."

I take a step back to ingrain the image of Lola bent over, ass in the air, and soaking wet pussy out on display for me and me only.

I palm myself over my pants, rubbing myself. I haven't done anything, but I just know that no matter how cold my shower is, I'll never not get hard at the image of Lola like this. It's really a shame I don't have my camera, not that it matters because I'm sure she wouldn't let me take her pictures, but the things I'd do to be able to.

Dropping my hand, I grab her hips, squeezing them hard, and kneel right in front of her. "I wish you could see yourself. Your pussy is so fucking wet. I know it's going to drench my face, and I bet you're going to taste so damn good."

She looks over her shoulder. Her eyes meet mine momentarily before they flick to my lips.

I flash her a crooked grin before training my attention to her ass. I drag my palms to her thick thighs and slide them over to her hamstrings. I grip them, pushing her up until she's standing on her tiptoes.

"Stay just like this."

I inhale sharply, clenching my jaw as I bring my fingers to her pussy. She's so wet, they become slick with her arousal and the inside of her thighs glistens and coats with it.

"Mmmm..." Lola moans, and I faintly hear the pop of her knuckles.

I glide my fingers along her slit before I slowly sink them inside of her. The deeper I get them in her, the more she pushes her ass and arches her back.

Despite her being so wet, she's so tight, I can feel her walls contracting against my fingers. I can only imagine how good it'd feel if it were my cock inside of her.

"You're so fucking tight."

"It's been a while..."

"You mean—"

Lifting my head, I look up at her, but she's not looking at me this time.

"I haven't been with anyone since you. I mean, I have but—what I'm trying to say is that I'm not experienced. We can stop if you want."

Fuck that. I don't know where the sudden urge of possessiveness comes from, but I don't fight it.

"If I say anything right now, I'll sound like a possessive asshole."

She finally looks down at me, eyebrows pinched together. "Like what?"

"Nothing." I push my fingers deeper but slower this time. "You don't want me to say what I'm thinking. I want nothing more than to taste you."

"I do want to know what you're thinking...ahhh." She moans a little louder as I find her clit with my other hand.

"I don't want anyone to see you like this." I circle the little bundle of nerves and stare in awe at how well her cunt takes my fingers. I imagine fucking her from behind, watching her ass bounce against me. "I *never* want anyone to see you like this."

"Ohhh," she groans, pushing up on her toes as her thighs start to tremble. "Please don't stop."

"I mean it, Lola." I pick up the pace, thrusting my fingers in and out, and when she starts squirming, her breathing becoming erratic, I curl my fingers and scissor them inside of her.

"I—oh God!" she cries out, her orgasm breaking through. She spasms, moaning at the top of her lungs as I continue to finger fuck her pussy. And when I feel like she's coming down from it, I replace my fingers with my mouth and plunge my tongue inside of her. I eat her out like my life depends on it while I stroke her clit with my finger over and over again.

I groan, reveling in the way she rides my face. She rolls her ass, meeting every thrust until she stills and her body constricts.

"TJ, T—" My name flies out of her mouth like a prayer of

cries and she shakes uncontrollably against me, her clit pulsing haphazardly, walls clenching around my tongue.

Her legs are still quivering by the time she comes down, and her breaths are ragged. "TJ, I'm too...sensitive," she all but whimpers, legs begging to collapse beneath her, but I grip her thigh, letting her know that I won't let that happen.

Removing my tongue from inside of her, I drop my finger from her clit as I kiss the inside of her thigh.

"Come on, just one more."

With one final kiss, I bring my mouth to her swollen clit and switch between sucking and flicking my tongue across it. While I use my other free hand to drag it along her slick folds, gathering some of her arousal on my fingers. When I know they're good and wet, I trail them up to her asshole. She stiffens and I wait for her to tell me not to touch her there, but she doesn't.

Her body shudders as she humps my face. "That—that feels good." It's a meek whisper, like she's embarrassed to say it.

"Yeah?" I rasp, drinking her in, enjoying how sweet she tastes and how tight her asshole feels.

I circle my finger around it, and when she's not too tense, I slowly sink one finger inside of her.

"Fuck," she bucks her hips, groaning and almost sitting up as I continue to push inside of her.

"I'm almost there. You're doing so good, Lola." I encourage, digging my fingers into her delicate skin.

When I'm finally knuckle deep, I pull it out and slowly thrust it in again, drawing her clit into my mouth again and sucking hard. It doesn't take long before she's coming again, her hole puckering around my finger as she comes hard, crying and begging with unintelligible words.

"Oh my God," she croaks, the leg resting on top of the table falling slack.

Pulling my finger out, I lick her arousal off my lips and hover over her. Her eyes are closed, lips parted like she's still trying to catch her breath, and hair clings to her damp forehead.

I smile, leaning over her, and kiss her bare shoulder. "Come to bed with me."

Her eyes pop open, and slowly, she stands, fixing her bra in the process. "Do you not want me to..." Her gaze flicks down to my hard dick.

There's nothing more that I want than to see her swollen lips wrapped around me, but I can see the sleep in her eyes and the yawn she's trying to stifle.

"Don't worry about it." I will most definitely be taking care of this in the shower. "So will you come to bed with me?"

"You want me to sleep in your room?"

"Yes." I hold my breath as I hand her back her shirt.

I've played in front of thousands of people. In front of crowds that are always either praying for our downfall or hoping we can get another win under our belt. Sometimes I feel a little anxious, but nothing feels as nerve-racking as I wait for her reply.

She finishes dressing and then a small, radiant smile takes over her face. "Okay."

"Let's go to bed." I take her hand in mine, interlocking our fingers together.

43

LOLA

I HAVE NO IDEA WHAT TIME IT IS, BUT I DON'T CARE because this has possibly been the best sleep I've had in a while. I can't remember the last time I didn't wake feeling groggy or disoriented.

Wait a minute.

My alarms didn't go off, and they should've because I already had them set.

There's no way I slept through all six.

I must still be reeling from the post orgasm to have slept this good for a few hours. Not to mention TJ's mattress is the comfiest I've ever slept on.

That realization has my eyes peeling open at the sudden reminder of where I'm at. Rays of sunshine pour through the glass, blanketing the entire room with brightness.

When I pat the side of the bed, I realize TJ isn't lying next to me. His side is messy but empty.

Sitting up, I grab my phone from the nightstand and my eyes nearly bug out when I look at the time: 11:10 a.m.

How did I sleep past my alarms? Oh God, Phoenix!

Shoving the duvet off my body, I jump out of bed and leave

TJ's bedroom. Before I make it to Phoenix's room, I bump into a soft chest, but it's me who almost falls to the ground.

"Whoa there." A soft hand wraps around my forearm, steadying me and holding me in place before I can fall on my butt. "Are you all right?"

"Sorry, I wasn't paying attention." I apologetically stare up at Hazel.

She's not as tall as her brother but definitely taller than me. I do want to point out that I'm average height, five-foot-five, despite my best friends reminding me that I'm the shortest in the group.

"It's okay, no harm done." She waves a dismissive hand, a friendly smile curling her lips before it turns sly as her eyes focus on my neck. "Hmm...do you wear foundation? Concealer maybe?"

I know that I'm not the prettiest thing in the world first thing in the morning but damn. "Uh, yeah, why?"

"Good." Her lips twitch, as if she were trying to tame her smile. "You might want to use them to cover"—she points to my neck—"that up."

My hands immediately cover the spot right below my jaw, where TJ's mouth had been last night.

My face feels hot, embarrassment coiling in the pit of my stomach. Now I understand her comment. "I, uh, this is, we—"

"Don't worry, you don't need to explain yourself to me, and I'd like to not hear the details."

"Right, sorry." My lips tighten into a forced smile.

God, just take me now.

"Anyway, I'm really glad you came. My parents were a little worried, but I knew you'd come."

"Really?"

"Yeah, even TJ was a little worried, but I promised I'd be on my best behavior."

I smile, feeling the embarrassment fade away.

"Why did you have to promise to be on your best behavior?"

"Because I tend to say things I shouldn't. I promise I'm working on it, but sometimes I just can't help myself." Mischief glints in her eyes. "The world would be too boring if I didn't add a little chaos into it."

She sounds too proud and a little arrogant at her statement, leaving no doubt that she's TJ's sister. Plus, she has dark brown curls, the eyes, and height.

I stare at her, amused. "Chaos is good sometimes."

She reminds me of Daisy but a much more bubblier version.

"Right, thank you for appreciating it. My family doesn't always." She clicks her tongue, rolling her eyes. "You know, two years ago, I knew you'd be amazing, and I've been proven right."

"Two years ago? But we didn't know each other then."

"TJ's a creature of habit. He likes to sleep his life away, arrogant just to be, and has no sense of direction in the kitchen."

I have no idea where she's going with this, but I listen anyway.

"But you must have made one hell of an impression because he went out of his way for someone he didn't know. He knew he'd get grounded but still took Dad's yacht without permission to impress you. Mind you, it was brand new when he took it."

Faint images of that day play in my head. I haven't thought about that day in a while, but somehow it rolls in my head like a film and plays as clear as day.

"It's okay. I'm just glad you didn't stand me up."

"I wouldn't do that to you, Peaches. I'm in too deep and I can't go back now, figuratively and literally speaking."

Oh my God.

She takes my silence as approval to continue.

"And to top it off, he goes and christens the bed."

I open my mouth to speak, but nothing comes out.

"Don't worry, he got grounded for three weeks and all was well." She shrugs.

"Oh my gosh. How am I going to look at your parents now?"

I attempt to hide my internal panic, but it seeps out of me like an uncontrollable flood.

"They were angry at first, but it doesn't matter now. You guys gave them a grandson. It was a shock to us all, but you should see how happy they were once it wore off. Especially Mom. She's gone overboard with shopping for Phoenix, but I guess you really can't blame her. He's the only grandchild. My reign as the youngest is now over, but I don't mind it. He's just too cute, and those cheeks," she coos.

My heart painfully constricts and shrivels, knowing that that's what I wish my parents had done.

"Anyway, let me shut up or I'll talk your ear off. If you're looking for TJ and Phoenix, they're on the court playing with Saint."

The sadness dwindles away. "How long have they been there? I set my alarm, but I guess I slept through it."

"Not too long, maybe thirty minutes or so, and I'm not sure what alarm you're talking about, but I didn't hear anything."

"You didn't hear all six alarms?"

"Six?" She gapes, expression perplexed. "No, I didn't, but if TJ asks, tell him that you woke up on your own."

"Why would he ask that?"

"Because I tend to be a little loud and he was afraid I'd wake you up. Anyhow, I'm going to get ready before the rest of the family starts showing up." She flashes me a smile before she walks in the opposite direction of TJ's bedroom.

In the matter of seconds she disappears, but I still stand in my spot, feeling stupefied.

I know it was all in the heat of the moment, but I swear I'm going to kill TJ. Before I looked in the mirror, I expected something small and faint on my neck. But it's the opposite of that. It's huge, bright red, and his teeth marks have indented my skin.

I've never put so much concealer in one place ever, and still it wasn't enough to cover it. Some of the red bled through the concealer, and awkward little patches of it still covered my neck.

"Maybe they won't see it." It's what I keep telling myself as I make sure my hair is covering the spot.

Wiping my clammy hands on my leggings, I stroll over to the court where everyone is at.

TJ gave Saint and me a tour of his house yesterday, but it was pretty late when he did. Now that I'm outside in broad daylight, I really take in the exterior, marveling at the large pristine pool, the palm trees, the large rectangular table that could sit about twelve people, the huge fire pit that's sunken into the ground, a basketball court to the left and the pool house to the right next to it.

It astounds me to know that people live like this. My parents weren't wealthy, per se, but they had enough to live comfortably.

I smile at the sight before me. TJ's parents are sitting on a bench, cheering Phoenix on as he runs with the mini basketball in his hands to the miniature net they bought him. Saint pretends to block him and lets Phoenix knock him over. He falls onto the polymeric rubber dramatically, holding his nose with one hand while the other is fisted into the air.

"Flagrant foul! Flagrant foul! Flagrant foul on the *Polpetta*!"

"It's not a flagrant foul. It's not his fault you tripped on your own feet," TJ argues.

Phoenix is so unbothered, he runs to the basket and just like TJ has been showing him, dunks the ball. Ever since TJ showed him that, he's been obsessed with dunking the ball and nothing else.

He raises both arms in the air, jumping up and down, his curls bouncing along with him.

"That doesn't count. He should be ejected. He better hope my nose isn't broken, or I'll sue him." Saint sticks to pretending to be hurt as he groans loudly and dramatically. "I'll make sure I take every last maple puff, and I'll sell his bears to pay for my surgery."

"Come here, buddy." TJ waves his hand over and Phoenix happily does. Once he's standing next to him, TJ bends down and motions for our son to follow along whatever he's doing. They both cup their hands, placing it behind their ears.

I know what he's doing because I've seen him do it at games after a win and I asked him once about it. With all the arrogance in the world, he said, "It's a big fuck you to everyone running their mouths. I want them to know I hear them, but I don't give a single flying fuck."

A wicked smirk curves TJ's lips. "What's that? What's that? We don't care! You still suck!"

I laugh, watching Saint stand and chase Phoenix around. Granted, Saint is walking because one step for him is like ten or so steps for Phoenix.

Eyes turn in my direction, but it's TJ who jogs toward me. With every step, his smile widens and when he's finally standing in front of me, every single second of last night replays in my head.

I was bent over on his pool table, while his tongue and fingers were simultaneously on me. Which reminds me.

"Wipe that smile off your face," I whisper.

His smile falls, his gaze sweeping over me with worry. "What's wrong?"

I lift my hair slightly, showing him the hickey. "What the hell is this? How am I supposed to be around your parents with this on my neck?"

He infuriatingly smirks. "It's called a hickey, and don't worry, they won't notice. If by chance they do, they won't care."

I scowl. "Stop being a smart-ass. How do you know they won't care? They're going to know something happened last night."

"And so what if they were to know? How do they think Phoenix was brought into this world?"

"We're—we're not together." I hate how bitter the words taste in my mouth, but it's better to say them out loud than to pretend last night was anything more than just something done in the heat of the moment. "And they know that. What I'm trying to say is that—"

"You're afraid of what they'll think of you." He finishes off for me.

I cast my glance down. It's stupid to care about what they'll think, but there's doubt that lingers at the back of my head. What if they change their minds about me? What if they turn out to be like everyone else? What if—

"I meant what I said last night." TJ takes my hand in his. "I told you not to think it didn't mean anything because it—"

"What's poppin'! Where's my nephew?"

A loud voice comes from behind us, but before I can turn around, TJ squeezes my hand, urging me to look at him.

"There's something I've been meaning to talk to you about, but I'd rather not do it here. I promise once I get the chance, I'll tell you." He squeezes my hand one last time, letting it go as the loud voice approaches us.

"Nice meeting the girl my brother got grounded for." A guy just as tall as TJ stands next to him, sporting the same sly smile Hazel had earlier.

Even if he hadn't said brother, I would've known they're related. Their features are strikingly familiar, with a few differences.

"Ben, shut up," TJ deadpans.

Ben slings an arm around him, putting him in a headlock. While they wrestle, a girl stands in front of me, and I also recognize her from the pictures. Glowing dark brown skin, a radiant smile, and legs for days.

I may or may not have found out that she's Ben's wife and they met through basketball when they were in college.

"Hey, I'm Mariah, and that doofus over there is my husband, Ben." She points a thumb over her shoulder where Ben is now in a headlock.

I stifle a chuckle, grinning at her. "Hey, it's good to meet you. I'm—"

"The one and only Lola. We've heard so much about you, and I do not mean on social media."

I stare at her quizzically, but she doesn't explain. She just smiles at me sweetly like I'm supposed to know what that means.

"Sorry about that. I had some unfinished business with that one." Ben's arm is draped around TJ's shoulder, ruffling his hair as if he were a little kid.

TJ swats his hand away, smiling despite the roll of his eyes. "There was no—"

"Benjamin and Theodore," Charlotte huffs, walking toward us along with Phillip, Saint, and Phoenix. "Not in front of Lola! Let her get acquainted first, or she'll never want to come back."

Ben shoves TJ out of the way and envelops his mom in a hug. "She got acquainted on the yacht just fine."

"Benjamin!" Charlotte goes to slap his shoulder, but he moves just in time.

If my face could melt off due to how hot it is, I'm sure it would. And I'm certain my jaw dislocated from how hard it dropped to the ground.

TJ mentioned his brother didn't have a filter. I prepared for it but not well enough.

"I'm sorry. I just had to break the ice."

"The same way you broke Dad's—"

"That shouldn't have been the way I broke the ice. I'm sorry, Lola," Ben immediately cuts TJ off, a sheepish smile on his face as Phillip narrows his gaze at him. "Sup, Arlo." He gives Saint a quick head nod before bending a little down in front of him, holding Phoenix. "Let me take a look at my nephew."

Phoenix grips Saint's shirt, covering half of his face against his chest, timidly staring up at him.

TJ grabs the back of his shirt, hauling him back. "You're scaring my son with your ugly face."

"First of all, dipshit—"

"Language!" everyone but me says.

TJ smacks the back of his head. "That's going to be ten dollars in the jar."

"Ten dollars? For what?"

Mariah laughs, shaking her head. "You're an idiot. You need to watch your language in front of him. Isn't that right, little man?" She steps a little closer but leaves enough space so he doesn't feel overwhelmed. "So pay baby P."

My heart warms at the nickname.

Phoenix takes a peek at her. A small, tentative smile grows on his lips.

"I was just going to say that I'm not ugly," he mutters under his breath, pulling out his wallet, and slips out a bill. "I only have a fifty."

"That will do." TJ gingerly snatches it out of his brother's hand and stuffs it in the pocket of his shorts.

Ben doesn't argue with him and bends at Phoenix's eye level again. "I'm sorry, baby P, and I'm sorry that you look so much like your father." He hooks his index finger under his chin, gently caressing it. "God, you got the cheeks, the eyes, and the curls. Are you even the mother?" He looks up at me, staring at me skeptically.

"H-he looks like me." I weakly defend.

They all look at Phoenix, then at me, then back at Phoenix, and then at TJ. They don't have to say a thing for me to know who they think he looks like.

"Maybe in a different lifetime he did," Saint says.

44

TJ

"He's so cute," Hazel coos, clasping her hands at her chin.

"He's a Kingston, of course he's cute," Ben pridefully says, shoving Hazel out of the way so he can get a closer look at Phoenix.

"Can you both shut up? He's going to wake up," I whisper-yell, pushing them both away from his crib. "And I swear, if he does, you're both staying up until he falls back to sleep."

A few hours ago, we got through Thanksgiving dinner, and afterward we played ball with Nix. And not too long after that, he started yawning. Lola was going to bathe and put him to bed, but I told her I'd take care of it while she got ready for bed. I was doing a good job until my siblings decided to come in and crowd him as if he were a zoo animal.

"We get him for one more day. I'll take my chances." Hazel shrugs but still keeps her distance, respecting the boundaries.

"Look at you, being a good father," Ben teases, his voice much softer than before.

"I hope I am."

"Hey." Ben jabs my side with his elbow, the teasing in his

voice gone. "You're a good father. Don't let those assholes get in your head."

"It's not about them," I honestly reply.

I know he's talking about the idiots online who have a lot of negative things to say about me, but it's not them I care about.

I'm more confident than I was before about my parenting skills, but I'm still afraid to fuck this up. The last thing I want to do is disappoint Lola and Phoenix. Those are the only people whose opinions matter.

"Then—oh," I hear the smile in his voice without looking at him. "I know *she* thinks so too."

"I hope so."

"She does. If she didn't, she wouldn't have trusted you to get him ready for bed alone," Hazel adds, standing next to me. "Trust me, she knows and we know. You're a good dad, TJ. I'm so proud of you." She engulfs me in a hug.

"I guess we're doing this, huh?" He loops his arms around us, squeezing us tightly.

"Look at us, so fucking adorable. If Mom sees this, she's going to lose her shit." I grin, hoping it can mask the emotions I feel overwhelming me.

"Oh, I'm sorry."

We twist our heads in the direction of the door. Lola stands outside Nix's bedroom, bashfully smiling.

"No worries, we were just bonding and shit," Ben casually says, dropping his arms from around us, and Hazel follows suit. "But we're leaving now. I know you both have a busy day tomorrow."

I side-eye Ben, giving him a *what the fuck* look. To which he gives me the *shit, I didn't know* look.

I've made plans for tomorrow afternoon that Lola has no idea about, and I intend to keep it that way. I had no intentions of letting my siblings know, especially Hazel, but they overheard Dad and me talking. I'd have no issues sharing said plans if I knew they could keep their mouths shut. And it's not that I don't trust them, but Ben will run his mouth just to fuck with me, and Hazel overshares when she's excited.

"I meant because Hazel will drag you all around Miami. So be prepared and wear comfortable shoes, and don't be afraid to tell her to shut up. She'll talk your ear off if you let her," he quickly supplies.

Hazel rolls her eyes dramatically, playing the part of being offended. Thankfully, Lola doesn't question it and nods with a smile.

"Anyway, we'll leave before we wake baby P," Hazel says, giving me a quick side hug before she walks over to Lola. As they get lost in conversation, Ben directs his attention to me.

"I can't imagine how overwhelming this has been for you, but you're really doing a good job." His words are sincere as he pats my shoulder, giving it a firm squeeze. "I'm glad you stepped up. Not many people do it, and I couldn't be any more proud of you."

There's nothing playful or teasing about his words, and it shocks me but all in a good way.

Ben is the most unserious person—besides Saint—I've ever met. It's why he didn't follow in Dad's footsteps and go into the NBA. He said he'd get canceled before his career ever started because he doesn't know when to shut his mouth. He also doesn't like to *follow rules.* He said it's just not in his blood. That's why he's his own boss, working as a private basketball instructor for extremely wealthy families who are willing to pay hundreds.

"Thanks." I smile at him.

He draws me in for a hug, whispering, "Fuck the world and fuck anyone who thinks otherwise."

I nod as we break apart.

"All right, well, good night to both of you. Have fun tomorrow and thanks for taking one for the team." A mischief gleam glitters in his eyes.

I can't say I'm surprised by whatever's going to come out of his mouth.

Lola's brows furrow. "What?"

"You gave Mom her first grandson. Mariah and I gave her a dog, but poor Cash, our golden retriever just wasn't enough," he somberly explains, but I see the twitch in his cheek as he steps out of the room as Lola slips inside. Looking over his shoulder, he smirks, his eyes locking to her neck. "Anyhow, be safe. There's something in the Miami air that makes people do *wild* things."

Lola's eyes slightly widen and her cheeks redden.

"Welcome to the family, Lola." He chuckles, walking away.

"Your brother is something else." She stands in front of the crib, gently stroking Nix's cheek with the back of fingers.

"That's Ben for you." I stand next to her, placing my hands on top of the railing next to hers.

The red on her cheeks becomes a faint pink, and her sheepish smile relaxes into a softer one. "Thanks for putting him to bed."

"I told you to stop thanking me. I'm just fulfilling my dad duties."

"Sorry, force of habit." Her damp hair falls like a curtain, covering the side of her face.

Lifting my hand, I tuck her hair behind her ear. I should've stopped there, but I see the deep red bruise covering the side of her neck. Satisfaction washes over me as I wrap my fingers on the back of her neck and brush my thumb over the mark.

"Come to bed with me."

Her pulse spikes against my thumb. "You want me to sleep with you again?"

"Yeah. I want you to sleep with me again," I assure, my voice low and husky.

She shifts her gaze to Nix, her fingers drumming against the bar. "I don't know if that would be a good idea."

"Why's that?"

"Your bed is too comfortable, and I'll end up oversleeping again."

"You didn't oversleep. I turned your alarms off."

Her brows shoot up. "You did?"

"I hope that was all right? I just thought you'd enjoy sleeping in. I know I haven't been able to help you much, but I promised you I'd do my best anytime I could."

It's been hard trying to help Lola with Nix in the mornings because if I'm not at basketball practices, I'm at away games. But I told myself that once I had the chance, I would help her, even though it takes every inch of my willpower to get up.

"Thank—" Her lips curl upward and she closes them when I cock my brow.

"If you want to thank me, you can come to bed with me." I drop my hand from her neck and take her hand in mine, pulling her out of Nix's bedroom and guiding her to mine.

"I never agreed." Lola attempts to sound serious, but I hear the playfulness in her voice.

"No, but your toothbrush is in my room, and my bed is much more comfortable than the one in the guest bedroom," I say, instead of pointing out that she easily let me lead her to my room. She doesn't hesitate or stop me, and even as I shut the door behind us, she keeps her hand in mine.

"What if your parents find out? Won't they get mad?"

"I don't know, it depends..." I smirk.

"On what?"

I shouldn't, but I really can't help myself. "Are we going to be sleeping or are we going to be loud?"

Her jaw drops and those light ivory cheeks burn red. "That's not—we're not—you're so frustrating."

"You keep saying that, but I don't think you mean it." I grip her hips, walking her backward until her back is pressed against the wall.

"I do mean it." There's no conviction in her voice, only a tremor as I slip my hand underneath her pajama bottoms and panties. "We really shouldn't do this...not again...not here."

Her eyes flutter, a tiny moan slipping past her lips as I drag two fingers between her folds that become wet with every stroke.

She heaves a sigh, gripping my arm. "TJ..."

"Yeah?" I rasp, leaning down to kiss her jaw as my fingers continue to glide across her.

"We should stop." Her fingernails dig into my skin, and she spreads her legs, pushing my hand down as my fingers tease her.

I revel in her shaky gasp as I slip my middle finger inside of her. "We should, shouldn't we?"

"Yeah, we really—"

A soft knock to my door pulls us out of the lusty haze, but still, I don't move my fingers unlike Lola, who's trying to push me away.

"TJ?"

"Yeah, Mom?"

Looking down at her, I pull my finger out slightly and add another one. I whisper, "Don't be loud."

Lola's jaw tightens, her nails digging deeper into my arm as I slowly pump in and out of her.

"I'm going to bed now, but I just wanted to say that I'm so happy Phoenix and Lola came over. Hopefully, your brother didn't deter Lola from coming again."

"No, Mom, I'm sure Lola will definitely *come* again." I pull my fingers out and shove them back in, slapping the heel of my palm hard against her clit. Her thighs clench, squeezing my hand as her lips part. The faintest gasp manages to tumble out of her mouth right before I cover it with my other free hand. "Shhhh," I softly say, pecking her forehead before I do it again.

"Good," she replies, sounding pleased with my response. "I'm going to bed now. Good night, Teddy. I love you."

"Night, Mom, love you too."

I drop my hand as the sound of her footsteps fades away.

"So where were we?"

"I can't believe..." she whimpers, squeezing her eyes tight as I quicken my pace. "I can't believe you did that. We need to stop or..." she moans. "Or they'll hear us."

I shove two fingers inside her mouth as I scissor my fingers inside her. "Problem solved. Now suck and stay quiet, or like you said"—I lean down and my lips hover over the shell of her ear, whispering—"they'll hear us."

I hear the sharp intake of her breath, and for a moment, I think she'll push me away, but she sucks my fingers deeper into her mouth and tentatively rolls her tongue around them. But I realize how bad of an idea this is because now I'm extremely hard. My dick is throbbing, pressing against my boxers and sweats, wanting nothing more than to be taken out.

Seems like I'll be taking another cold shower tonight.

Pushing that thought away, I focus on Lola and how needy she becomes as she grinds against my hand and sucks faster on my fingers.

"You're doing so good. Sucking my fingers like that, sucking them like you're pretending it's my cock." Her pussy clenches around my fingers and I swear she becomes wetter, and she grinds faster, urging me with her other hand to fuck her faster.

She whines, mumbling something that sounds like, "why," against my fingers when I pull out slightly.

"Take a deep breath for me," I command and without a beat of hesitation, she does, and I add a third finger inside of her. "That's why." I kiss her temple, enjoying the garbled sounds that mix with her moans as she drops her head to my chest.

She stills and tenses, groaning as I drive my fingers deeper inside of her. She's so tight, her pussy clenches with every push and when I'm knuckles deep, she pulses around them. But goddamn, does her cunt stretch and become slicker.

"Come on, suck," I grit, pushing my fingers deeper into her throat until she gags. It takes her a second, but after she catches her breath, she twirls her tongue around my fingers and sucks them. "Now ride my hand, Lola."

She peers up, heavy-lidded eyes in a daze. It takes every bit of self-restraint not to remove my fingers and fuck her against the wall because seeing her mouth and pussy filled with my fingers has altered the state of my fucking chemistry.

Nothing will ever look as mesmerizing as having Lola at my

mercy.

"Come here." I quickly remove my fingers and drag her to our bed.

"What are you—"

If I can't have her ride my dick, then my face will do. "Sit on my face," I rasp.

"You want me to—"

"Yes, unless you're not okay with it." I'm too turned on. My dick is painfully hard. I didn't think if she'd be comfortable enough to do that. "I'm sorry, forget it. I wasn't—"

"Take your clothes off."

It's not a question but a demand, giving me whiplash from how those four words caught me off guard. She shifts from one foot to the other. A small, tentative smile grows on her lips, and fingers nervously drum her at her side.

"Stop looking at me like that. I just think it's only fair if I return the favor."

"You want to..." I'm pretty certain I've gone to heaven because this feels unreal, far from reality. Lola can't be insinuating what I think she is. "Are you sure? Don't feel—"

My mouth dries as I watch her strip out of her clothes. She stands naked in front of me, and despite the crimson red that blossoms on her cheeks, the determination on her face doesn't waver.

"TJ, take your clothes off."

In record breaking time, I'm naked.

"Bed, now." She licks her lips, fingers drumming against the side of her thigh.

No questions. No hesitation. No what-ifs.

I get on the bed, lie on my back, and follow her every move like a hawk. She climbs on the bed and I suck in a breath, heart ready to burst as she straddles my face, and bends over until I feel her warm breath fan the head of my dick.

I'm still stuck in whatever daze she's pulled me in until she swipes her hot, wet tongue across the seam and I snap out of it.

I fight the urge to moan and hook my arms under her legs. I cup her ass and spread her cheeks but pause when she takes me into her mouth, and the soft vibrations of her moans have me feeling drunk.

"Goddamn." I roll my eyes, releasing a harsh breath before I pin her pussy to my mouth, and pull her pulsing clit into my mouth. I alternate between sucking and flicking my tongue on it, pausing in between as she sucks me off. I'm struggling to focus because with every suction, moan, and vibration, I lose myself.

I'm not sure how, but I manage to pull myself out of the fog. In one long, languid swipe, I drag my tongue down the little bud to the entrance of her pussy and I thrust inside of her.

Her body jerks, but I keep her in place as I drive quickly into her, tasting her, feasting the fuck out of her. She fervently rolls her hips, blubbering incoherent mumbles on my dick, and then she stills, her back arching. She sits up as her pussy convulses against my tongue.

I stop what I'm doing when I hear the faintest cry leave her lips. I move one hand from her leg to her back and push her back down.

"Put your mouth on my cock, baby."

Her tight body shakes uncontrollably, and tiny mewls slip from her mouth every so often.

"Lola, baby, suck."

I lick the inside of her thigh and on the very same spot, I bite her until she gasps. That manages to pull her out of it and she takes me in her mouth, sucking me off until I feel her saliva trickle down my balls.

"Just like that." I blow a harsh breath as she works on me. The soft suctions of her mouth mingle with her moans, dragging me back to the fog.

I clench my teeth, forcing myself to focus on her again. Lazily and slowly, I lick her up to her asshole. She tenses and sits up. Our eyes lock when she looks over her shoulder down at me.

"Do you want me to stop?"

She pulls her bottom lip in between her teeth and she shakes her head.

"Do you want to watch?"

"Yeah."

I spread her cheeks farther apart, and with eyes locked on each other, I lick her. With every stroke, her asshole pulses on my tongue as she slowly rolls her hips. She softly pants, whispering indiscernible words, and she tips her head back, her hair swaying against her back.

I'm not sure what I'm more desperate for, getting off or having her eyes on me. And somehow she must've read my mind because she glances down at me one last time before she lowers herself and continues where she left off.

She twirls her tongue around my shaft and when I feel it completely immersed in her saliva, she pulls it into her mouth and sucks me off.

I try to focus on her, but I can't anymore because my body tenses and my cock swells. I feel like I've been set off by a live wire. Every fiber in me goes off like fucking fireworks and I come hard inside her mouth.

I tip my head back, clenching my jaw hard. I grip her hips until I come off the high that continuously rolls off my body.

I don't know how long it lasts, but when I finally come off, I'm spent and feel lightheaded.

"Wow." I clear my throat, blowing a ragged breath as Lola lies next to me. A few beads of cum linger on her chin.

"Was that okay?"

I wipe them off with my thumb. "Okay? I can't even begin to describe how phenomenal that was."

She smiles, not saying anything else, and like last night, I stretch my arm out and she nuzzles against me.

"Good night, Peaches." I kiss the top of her head and pull the duvet over our naked bodies.

"I can't believe we're here again." Warm, earthy eyes slowly roam over the yacht, soaking in the exterior before they drift to the ocean.

The once clear blue water is now a mirror of the sky. Searing red, deep vibrant orange, and golden yellow tumultuously and painstakingly painted across the sky. It seems as if someone had started blending the colors so beautifully, but toward the end finished the painting in a frenzy.

Reminding me of the painting Lola and I saw at the museum two years ago.

Despite the state of the sky, it's still hypnotic to see as the colors bleed into the water. If it weren't for the sun setting on the horizon, illuminating the last little bit of the day before it disappears for the next few hours, it would be hard to tell where the sky and sea meet.

Standing at the bow of the yacht, she leans over the railing, holding the cup of coffee we stopped by to get before we came here, close to her chest. I stare, mesmerized, as the corners of her lips rise slowly. She hasn't said anything, but I can see the flashback playing in her mind, as it does for me.

"So it's just us?" she asks, her eyes still set on the sea.

"Just us."

I'm not sure if this is over the top, if I should be doing more, or if this is okay, but I thought the best place to talk to Lola is where it all started. Just Phoenix, her, and me. Granted, Nix is asleep in the room, exhausted after Hazel gave them and Saint a tour of Miami. Which I'm completely okay with. I want Lola's complete and undivided attention on me.

"You didn't take it without permission this time, did you?" She takes a sip of her drink, her smile hiding behind the cup.

Of course Hazel would let it slip, and now not only Lola knows but Saint knows.

"Not this time, but even if I had, it would have been for a great cause."

"A great cause?"

"The first time I took it was because I was trying to impress my girlfriend."

"Your girlfriend...was she impressed?"

"I'd like to believe she was." I stare at the bracelet wrapped around my wrist and suck in a breath, inhaling the salty air. Finding comfort and ease at the nostalgic feeling about this moment. "Maybe that's what I'm trying to do, again."

Her hand freezes in the air, the cup of coffee just a few centimeters away from her parted lips. "And what's that?"

I blow a breath and everything comes to a standstill.

"I've been thinking a lot, trying to figure out how to put my thoughts into words. If I'm being honest, I'm afraid to fuck this up because I have yet to figure out how I want to tell you how I feel without it sounding stupid."

The shock on her face wavers, but she doesn't say anything and I take that as my cue to continue.

"I..." I pause, contemplating what I want to say because whatever comes out of my mouth is either going to sound corny or not enough. Fuck it. "I think about you a lot. So much that you've permanently cemented yourself in my dreams and my thoughts. I think about you so much, it's probably become unhealthy because I obsess over having your attention on me. "

Breathe, dumbass. Breathe.

"I hate when you give any fraction of your attention to any guy while I desperately seek it all the time. I hate when they flirt and look at you as if they have a chance with you. It pisses me off, Lola. I can't go another day and look at you and not fall any deeper. Every single day, I fall, and I swear I've tried to stop." I anxiously rake my fingers through my hair, hating how they tremble and my breath sounds labored. *Breathe.* "I've tried to control what I feel because sometimes it's too much and my heart feels too tight. But it's stupid and I should know fighting the inevitable is pointless. I like you a lot, and I can't stop feeling what I feel for you, not unless you tell me to stop."

Even then, I'm not sure if I'd be able to.

Lola's the embodiment of a sunset. Something you always look forward to even though you know it's going to appear every day, around the same time. Because you know that it's not always going to be the same colors. Sometimes you get a cotton candy sky that brings peace to your mind and sometimes you get a blazing sky that sets your soul on fire. And sometimes on special days you get a coalescence of both.

Lola stares at me, unblinking, like she's not grasping my words or reality. Her cup is now dangling from her hand at her side.

"Please say something."

She swallows hard. And then she looks at me with an expression I know all too well and my stomach sinks.

"I'm sorry, but I—"

"You don't feel the same way." My heart squeezes painfully in my chest, but I suck it up and plaster a smile on my face.

"TJ—"

"No, it's okay. I just wanted to tell you how I—"

"Can you shut up and listen?" She scowls, but I see the faint tinge of red on her cheeks. Then I notice her drumming her fingers along the cup and she blows a shaky breath. "I didn't want to admit this because it scares me, if I'm being honest, but I also like you a lot."

I hold my breath, waiting for the *but* despite how fucking elated I feel right now.

"But you and I know it's not going to work."

"What makes you think that? We haven't even given it a try. Why are you so quick to shut it down?" My words tumble too quickly out of my mouth. I should be embarrassed at how desperate I sound, but I can't bring myself to care.

"It just wouldn't." Her voice is low and filled with discomfort. Her eyes don't even meet mine.

"Don't give me that. Be honest. I'm always honest with you," I say, wanting nothing more than to reach out and touch her, but I don't.

She looks at me like it pains her to say it. "I'm not looking for something short term. I'm finally getting the stability I need in my life, and I can't be with someone who might not give me that."

I don't know what I expected, but it wasn't this. "Short term? You think I want short term?"

A sad smile slips on her lips. "Why kid ourselves? You're leaving next year, and I'm staying here. We'll be miles away from each other, and I'm sure you'll meet a lot of people along the way."

I understand her words loud and clear. She doesn't think I'd be faithful. I don't know if I should be upset that she doesn't trust me or happy that she's considered us being in a relationship.

"Contrary to what you believe, I wouldn't go out of my way to date you if I was going to cheat on you. I may be a lot of things but cheater isn't one of them. I know my words probably mean shit, but I swear to you I'd never hurt you." This time, I take a step forward, reaching my hand for hers, and hook my middle finger around hers. "If you don't want to take my word for it, you can ask my last girlfriend about the kind of guy I am. We dated for three days about two years ago, but I swear I was the best boyfriend."

Her cheek twitches, but still, she looks at me like she's in pain, like she's unsure of what to do.

"I just want to be *yours*, like I want *you* to be mine." Desperation pours from my mouth. "It doesn't matter how many miles and people are between us. It's only you and me." I unhook my finger, interlocking my fingers between her slender ones. "Give me a chance and let me prove it to you. Please, Lola, please."

She blows a breath, nodding, and the sad smile morphs into something a little brighter. "Okay, I'm going to trust you."

Breathe. "Yeah?"

"Yeah." Her smile sets my heart ablaze and I know that fire will never be put out.

There's so much we need to talk about, but for now, I hold her tight, knowing I'm never going to let go.

45

LOLA

"I KNOW YOU'D RATHER BE ANYWHERE BUT HERE, BUT thanks for coming."

The crowd is extremely loud, but I still manage to hear the "yeah, yeah" from Daisy.

Cara drapes an arm around her shoulder, her lips stretching into a playful grin. "Calm down. I know you're excited, but tone your enthusiasm down just a little."

I laugh at Cara's sarcasm.

We came to our first NCU basketball game, and Daisy's not thrilled to be here. She's never cared enough about the game to understand it. It's why she's never attended one, but after some begging, she caved in and came.

"They better win or I want my money back." She flicks the nonexistent piece of lint off her light blue crop top.

"You didn't pay for your ticket." I snort, adjusting the noise cancellation earmuffs on Phoenix.

The earmuffs keep coming off because he's too excited and keeps bouncing on my lap. He's immersed in the buzzing crowd, the marching band, the sea of black, white, and light blue colors representing the school, the two knight mascots, and the cheerleaders.

"No, but they'll need to pay an inconvenience fee for wasting my time," she says, her tone grave.

"Hey, I'm so happy you guys came!" Gabby beams, waving at us from the court. She stands in front of the row of chairs that are placed for the team.

Thanks to Gabby, we were able to get in for free. She's working as a media coordinator intern for the team, taking pictures and uploading them on Instagram and their other social media accounts. I'm not entirely sure how she got the tickets, but all she said was that being an intern and having two best friends on the team has its perks.

"Thanks for getting us the tickets," I reply, returning the smile. "I know it was all last minute but—"

"Don't worry about it. The look on TJ's face is going to be worth it. You guys look so cute." Glittering brown eyes flicker to the jersey I'm wearing with TJ's number before moving to Nix, who's wearing the same jersey. "Can I please take a picture?"

Before TJ and I started dating, I had considered coming to a game, but my work schedule always clashed with the basketball schedule. That's until I got back from Miami a few days ago and found out I didn't have to work today. One idea led to another and now we're here.

I asked Darius and Marcos to come, but they had to work. Polly's here, but she's on a date with someone. And Juls, well, she said hell had to freeze over before she ever stepped foot in the arena and watch Satan's spawn play. Her words, not mine.

I didn't tell TJ I was coming because I wanted to surprise him, but now I can't stop myself from overthinking. We started dating a few days ago, and now I'm here at his game wearing his jersey. It's stupid that I'm putting too much thought into it, but I can't help myself.

"Yeah." I stand, adjusting Nix on my hip, making sure his jersey is on display for the camera.

She snaps a few pictures and then gives us a thumbs-up. "I gotta go, but you guys are so adorable."

I grin, waving her goodbye before she saunters to the tunnel. But before I can sit down, someone taps my shoulder.

I'm met with four smiling faces when I turn around. I don't know much about sororities, but I know these girls are in them. They proudly wear the button pin with the Greek symbol of their sorority on their tops.

"Sorry to bother you, but are you Lola?" one of the girls asks.

"Uh, yeah, I'm Lola." I tentatively smile, pretending I didn't hear one of the girls not so discreetly whisper, "I told you" to her other friend.

"And he's"—her eyes dart to Nix—"TJ's son?"

"Yeah, he's *our* son."

It's hard to gauge their expressions. Sometimes I can tell when someone's being fake. Other times they mask it so well it's hard to tell.

But I feel at ease when the corners of their lips rise higher into genuine smiles.

"Oh my gosh." They all break out into fits of squeals and coos.

"He looks so much like TJ."

"He's so cute, and he has the curls."

"And you two are wearing matching jerseys to match TJ. Please, this is so cute."

They say a few more things until they finally leave, but that isn't the end of it. Other people, not just students, stop by and all ask the same questions.

Are you Lola?

Is that TJ's son?

As soon as I said yes, they talked to me as if I were some sort of long-lost friend they had lost contact with.

"*Pinches metiches,*" Daisy mutters under her breath as a couple that spoke to me the longest walks away. "Are you all right?"

I nod, taking my seat and sitting Phoenix on my lap. "I'm all right. That was...that was a lot."

I thought I understood how popular TJ is, but I really underestimated it. He's nowhere near celebrity famous, but he's popular enough.

"Don't mind them. You know people just love to be nosey," Cara supplies, rolling her eyes. "This is the first time you come to a game with Phoenix. The girls want to know *the* person who took NCU's biggest fuck boy off the market, and the parents just want something to talk about."

Daisy smirks, bringing her fisted hand to her lips, pretending it's a microphone. "Please, Lo, do tell. How does it feel to have the most desired guy on campus?"

She holds her hand close to my lips, but I swat it away.

"Shut up." I bite back a smile. "You're never going to let it go, huh?"

"How can she? Our Louise leaves for Miami single and comes back with a boyfriend and a hickey." A sly grin pops on Cara's face. "So much for *not* having feelings for him. Good thing we saw it coming."

"I just..."

"We know." An understanding smile lifts on Daisy's lips.

Sometimes doubt lingers, and I worry about the what-ifs, but I think back to what TJ said.

"I wouldn't go out of my way to date you if I was going to cheat on you. I may be a lot of things but cheater is not one of them."

The announcer's voice pulls me out of my thoughts, shifting my focus to the guys as they come running out of the tunnel to the court.

The arena gets louder and the crowd loses it, cheering, clapping, and stomping their feet. As the announcer calls out the players' names, they stand in front of the chairs lined up for them.

Manic butterflies roam in my stomach when I lock eyes with TJ. I've seen him play on TV, but physically being here and seeing him in his uniform is different.

"They look good, huh?" Cara smirks, her perfectly styled brow arching high.

My face warms. "Yeah, they really do."

He still hasn't seen me, and I doubt he will, at least not until the game is over. We're sitting pretty close to the team, but because we're all wearing the same colors, we blend in with the crowd.

I could try to get his attention, but I don't. I watch and admire the way his muscles bulge and flex with every movement. And the way he laughs and shakes his head at whatever Saint says to him.

TJ's eyes coast over the crowd, soaking it all in as he always does. When his eyes slide over the section we're in, they immediately dart back to me until our eyes connect.

He blinks a few times, eyebrows pinching together and head slightly tilting as if he can't believe we're here. When I smile and wave at him, the confusion dissipates and the crease between his brows smooths out. He leans into Saint and says something to him, and then makes his way to us.

Coach Warren yells at him, but he ignores him. His eyes focus on us, determined as he rounds the row of chairs and runs up the steps to us.

My eyes grow, not shocked because of what he's doing but worried because of the look on his coach's face.

"What are you—" My words get cut off as he pulls us in for a hug, but he doesn't squeeze me too hard since Phoenix is in between us. Pulling away, he looks down at me, still keeping one hand on my back.

"Hey, buddy." TJ grazes his finger under Phoenix's chin, earning a cute giggle from him.

"T!" our son excitedly says.

His ecstatic smile erases all the doubt clouding my head.

"You came."

"Surprise." I smile.

"Consider me very surprised." Something shifts in his eyes as they flicker down to my jersey. TJ squeezes my waist, his Adam's apple rising and falling. He leans down, his lips at my ear. "How am I supposed to concentrate when you're wearing my jersey and you look...you look really fucking good."

"Just pretend I'm not here."

"It wasn't possible before and it's definitely not going to be possible now."

"I might reward you *if* you win..." I crane my head back, meeting his eyes that are now dark, his lips now lifted into a smirk that almost looks daunting.

He kisses my forehead, but his lips linger there. "I hope my reward is you bent over in nothing but the jersey."

"Oh, come on! Are you serious?" Daisy yells, cupping her hands around her mouth. "Number nine, this isn't soccer. Get your ass up!"

Kentucky's player, number nine, Deion Lowry just fell out of nowhere. Not only is it a bullshit fall, but he's clutching his nose with both hands. Screaming, might I add.

I know his nose isn't hurt, but I really wish it were.

All night, he and his teammates have been ganging up on TJ, and only him. I know it's part of the game, but I've seen enough basketball in my life to know they're trying to intimidate him. Though it's past intimidation now.

I've lost count of how many times they've accidentally elbowed, pushed, shoved, and tripped him. All while wearing those stupid smug smiles on their faces.

As angry as I am, I don't let myself show it because I'm holding Phoenix. For almost being two years old, he's extremely attentive and in tune to whatever TJ's doing and whatever is happening to him. Anytime something happens, he'll stare back at me as if he's asking for reassurance that his dad is okay.

"I swear I'm going to punch somebody." Daisy fists her hand, clenching her jaw.

Cara and I look at each other, refraining from making a

comment about how much she's enjoying this. She swore she was going to be bored and was most likely going to be on her phone all night. From the moment the game started, she's been on her feet more than any of us, shouting when Kentucky does something stupid and cheering when NCU makes a basket.

She's *definitely* not having fun.

"Phoenix, I think you and I are going to have to show them how it's done." She takes the small basketball TJ got him and shows him how to throw it. It's comical to watch because Daisy has no idea what she's talking about and is using soccer terms. "Maybe one day that will be you up there."

All my anger disappears at the thought of Phoenix following in TJ's footsteps. We're still miles away from that ever happening, but I can picture it. I've seen how Nix listens when TJ's showing him how to shoot the ball into his little tots basket or how focused he is when he's watching film with his dad. He'll explain what's going on, and despite Phoenix not having a clue what he's talking about, he stares at TJ like he's the world.

Pushing the thoughts of the future to the side, I draw my focus to the game that's now resumed.

Kentucky seems to have calmed down, which is surprising considering we're in the second half, up by eight points, with only four minutes left.

There's an anxious buzzing energy floating around the arena, everyone counting down the seconds as they tick by before the buzzer goes off. We all know three minutes and a half is still a long time before the game ends. Anything can happen.

Like Dieon shooting a smooth three-pointer, leaving Kentucky just five points behind.

"It's okay." Cara lets out a shaky breath. "Just three more minutes. That's all we have. We got this."

I hold my breath, keeping my eyes trained on TJ as Jayden passes him the ball and dribbles it down the court. Right as he sidesteps one of the players and jumps, releasing the ball in the air, another slaps him and somehow manages to elbow him, causing him to fall back, slamming hard against the floor.

"What the fuck?" I stand on my feet, throwing my hand in the air.

Everyone's over Kentucky's shit, but more so the players. Especially Landon. He doesn't care as he not only bumps his chest against the chest who hurt TJ, but then proceeds to shove the offending player hard, causing him to fall and slide across the floor.

Another one of Kentucky's players pushes Landon, but Jagger comes from behind, shoving him back. Everything happens too fast. Players from each side start shoving each other while others are pulling their teammates back. The coaches are yelling and the referees are blowing their whistles, but it's pointless because there's only so much it can do.

I shift my attention away from the chaotic scene to TJ. He sits on the floor, talking to the athletic trainer as he assesses him and every so often, he talks to Saint and Jayden, who stand next to him. My heart hammers hard as I notice red spots on his jersey.

I hadn't realized I was holding my breath until the athletic trainer moves, giving me a better view of TJ. As our eyes connect, I swear for a split second I hate him. His bloody lip lifts into a tantalizing smirk and he winks at me.

Jesus Christ, Theodore. Only you.

His friends help him up while the AT continues to talk to him. He nods multiple times, eyes still on me, and his smirk never slipping from his face.

The chaotic scene that unfolded before us has now calmed down. Each player is on their respective side, their coaches yelling, and the referees talk amongst each other.

TJ gets pats on the back from his teammates and then it's his coach who stands in front of him, gripping his chin, moving it from side to side.

"Fucking Nash," he snarls, his lip twisting in disgust as he rolls his eyes. "Kingston, are you good? Or do you—"

"I'm *peachy*, Coach," he replies nonchalantly and licks his bruised lip.

"Atta boy!" He pridefully smiles, patting his shoulder.

The rest of the game flies by and we win despite Landon being ejected for pushing Nash. He also got ejected and nothing felt more gratifying than hearing the entire arena boo him as they led Nash to the tunnel.

As soon as the guys break from their huddle and head to the tunnel, TJ makes his way to us. He smiles and nods at the people who congratulate him and beg for his attention, but he never stops until he's standing in front of me.

"Are you okay?" I glance at the gash on his bottom lip. It's a little swollen and cracked with dry blood.

It's wrong I'm thinking this, but somehow that adds more to his appeal. His face is flushed, a wet sheen coating every inch of him. Beads of sweat roll from the side of his face down to his neck and chest, making his jersey cling to his torso.

I've never paid attention to shoulders, but they're broad and muscular, and I can't help the way my eyes travel down over them. I follow the slight indent on his inked bicep, but I don't make it far before a deep chuckle rumbles between us.

"I'm peachy. Are you?"

46

TJ

"ARE YOU SURE? THERE'S NO GOING BACK."

"I'm sure, Peaches." Reaching behind me, I grab the neck of my shirt and pull it over my head, then let it fall. I drop to the floor and lie flat on my stomach on top of the white sheet she laid down, staring up at her. "Come on, use me as your canvas."

I'm trying not to feel smug, but I love how she looks at me and the way her eyes dilate.

"Don't be so cocky." Lola looks away, dropping to the ground next to me, straddling me. She sits right below my ass, her paint stuff already set up, ready to be used.

I chuckle, folding my arm over the other, resting the side of my face on top of them. "You're making it hard not to."

"I don't want to hear it," she playfully chides.

"That you were checking me out? Don't be embarrassed, Lola, you can check me out as much as you want."

"And feed your ego? I don't think so."

I close my eyes, inhaling a breath as I feel the cold, wet brush filled with paint on my skin. I don't mind it, though. It's a great distraction from getting hard.

Lola is wearing nothing but my jersey and panties. So really, if anyone is struggling here, it's me.

The last time we were physical was when we were in Miami. It's only been a few days, but it feels like forever ago.

"But I love it when you feed into my ego." I prop my elbow on the floor, resting my chin on my palm, and stare back at her. But it's a big mistake and I regret it instantly.

My dick twitches and I have to urge myself not to get hard. And not to imagine what she'd look like if I were lying on my back instead.

A breathtaking smile stretches wide across her face. Half of her hair splays over one shoulder, cascading down in waves. While the other half is tucked behind her ear. My jersey is bunched around her hips, exposing every inch of her thick thighs. And when I look between them, I get a peek at her black panties.

I swallow hard, slowly dragging my gaze upward, appreciating all of her before my eyes do a double take on her chest. Her nipples are hard, pressing against the fabric.

"Stop moving and turn back around. I don't want to mess up."

Her eyes don't meet mine. They're intently focused on the brush in her hand as she twirls it around the palette, mixing the paint.

I'd call her out on the way she looks flushed and the slight clench of her thighs, but I don't. I'm struggling as it is and Phoenix is asleep in his crib.

Turning around back to my same position, I close my eyes, focusing on the way the brush glides on my back.

After the game, the guys decided to throw a party at the house. Since it was all last minute, we didn't have a sitter. Lola insisted I stay, but I didn't care to be somewhere she wasn't.

Even if I had stayed, I would've dwelled on the shit show post-game interview and drunk until I forgot about it. It's something I do from time to time when I feel too wired to sit still or drive. It's an unhealthy coping mechanism, but at the moment, it always feels great. That's until Lola came back into my life.

"TJ?" Lola nudges me with the end of the paintbrush, making me realize I had zoned out.

"Sorry, what?"

"I know this isn't fun and probably not how you want to spend your Saturday night. I seriously don't mind if you go. I have a painting I have to finish and mail soon and school assignments to do."

She goes to get up, but I grab her ankle, keeping a firm grip around it.

"I'm not going anywhere, and I don't want you to either." I smile up at her, hoping to reassure her. "I just got a little...lost in my thoughts, but I swear it's nothing important. I'm sorry I gave you the impression I didn't want to be here because there's nowhere I'd rather be."

Lola nods, returning the smile, but it wavers. She stares at me like she's figured out everything I'm thinking.

Her body eases as I let go of her ankle, and she settles back down. "Are you okay?"

"I..." I turn back around, resting my chin on top of my crossed arms, and cross my ankle over the other to stop it from bouncing.

"You can talk to me. I'm here," she softly says before she resumes painting.

I revel in the silence, absorbing her warmth and basking in the scent of her vanilla perfume.

"When I first got hurt my freshman year, I thought it was all over. I thought I was never going to recover. It sounds dramatic, but at that moment, I swear I thought it was." I whisper the words I'd been afraid of saying out loud. She doesn't say anything nor stops the bristles from sliding over my skin. Giving me the courage to continue talking. "Getting hurt was eye-opening and scary as fuck. I know I came back better than ever, but sometimes the fear of getting hurt again fucks with my head. And then I think about the shit people say."

The comments, the post-game highlights, the interviews, the

questions, and everything that happened since then trigger a cold shiver to run down my spine.

"I used to not care, but sometimes I get in over my head because of what's being said about me as if their words are going to determine my future. It's ridiculous, but sometimes it feels like their words hold some sort of truth. Like I'm going to peak in college and not make anything of myself. Or that I'll make it but realize that whatever talent I have doesn't compare to others. I know comparison is a thief of joy, and I'm doing better, but sometimes I have my moments. And then there are those stupid interviews. God, I hate those."

The weight of those words lifts off my chest, making it easier to breathe for the first time in a long time.

I feel her lean in, hovering just slightly over me. She plays with the hair at the nape of my neck, her finger twirling around one curl. I'm overdue for a haircut, but I know how much she loves to play with my hair and I love it too.

"They love to antagonize you because you're hard to get a reaction out of. You give them nothing but solid answers despite the questions they throw at you. But sometimes because you are you, your replies come off arrogant. It's slightly annoying at times, but I know you mean no harm. They just don't see that and they don't care. But you shouldn't change anything to appease them. After all, you are *the invincible*."

My head perks up. I look over my shoulder at her. "You stalked me."

"I don't want to hear it." She sits up, picking up the brush she set down.

I can't help the smug smile on my face. "You've watched and read about me."

"Seriously? Out of everything I said, that's what you got?"

"Just admit. It will make me feel better." I feign sadness in my voice.

There's a twitch at the corner of her lip, but she gives me a deadpan stare. "You're not that important. I didn't stalk you."

"I did."

The brush suspends above my back, and her eyes meet mine. "That was a waste of time."

"Nothing about you is a waste of time."

Lola pulls her bottom lip in between her lips as if she were trying to suppress her smile but fails as the corners rise upward. "Turn around or I'll never finish."

I smile, turning around.

"It's why they love to antagonize you because they desperately want to find a flaw. And if that means getting a reaction out of you, they will." She proceeds to paint. "I know it's easier said than done, but you have to find your happy. Once you do, I think it'll be easier for you to get through the interviews."

I muse over her words, though I don't need to because she's right. It's something Coach Warren has been preaching about during our one-on-one monthly meetings. "Finding your happy," he says. I want to joke about it, but the longer I sit on her words, I realize I've already found my happy as I twist the extremely worn out leather bracelet.

"Do you still have it?"

"Have what?"

"The bracelet that matches mine? Do you still have it?" I impatiently ask.

"Why?" I hear the smile in her voice.

"Because what better way than to say you're taken than wearing *my* name on your wrist. So do you?"

"That sounds a bit possessive."

"Because I am. What kind of boyfriend would I be if I wasn't?" I attempt to sound like I'm joking, but there's nothing inside of me that feels playful. "So do you have it?"

"It might be in my jewelry box."

"Can you get up for a second?"

She stifles a laugh. "Not yet. I'm almost done." I wiggle in place, getting a few quiet laughs from her. "TJ, stop being so impatient. I'm almost done."

I attempt to push up, but Lola holds me down with one hand on my shoulder. I could easily flip us over, but I don't want to mess up whatever she's done.

"Stay still," she demands, still keeping one hand on my shoulder.

"I am." I raise my hands in surrender. "Are you going to tell me what you're painting?"

"Not yet." She lifts her hand from my shoulder and when I hear the brush swish in the mason jar filled with water, I take the chance to push up and twist my body. A small gasp escapes her as she lands right above my dick.

I didn't think this through and it's a big mistake because I feel myself becoming hard at the sight of her straddling me.

There's a sharp intake of her breath. "You're going to ruin it."

My palms rest behind me, holding my weight. "I promise I'm not."

I tell myself to get up, but I can't bring myself to do it. Not when she's staring at me with heated eyes and I feel her thighs clench around me.

Her eyes flicker down to my lips and slowly, she leans in as I do. I close my eyes, ready to feel her lips against mine, but they shoot back open as I feel the brush on my cheek.

A haughty smirk lifts on her lips as she swipes the brush down my cheek to my neck and chest. "I told you to stop moving." Her eyes twinkle with mischief and quickly, she stands up, dropping the brush right next to me as she makes a run for it.

"Why are you running, hmm?" I stand up, slowly stalking toward her. With every step I take, she takes two back.

It feels as if we're playing a game of cat and mouse. She stands on the opposite side of the couch, keeping as much distance as she can from me. All while she tries her hardest not to laugh because as much fun as we're having, we're both very aware that if we get too loud, we'll wake Nix up.

"Wash your hand first and I'll stop." Her eyes descend to my fingers covered in paint.

"Come here."

She shakes her head. "No."

"Lola, come here. Now," I gravely demand.

A spark of challenge ignites her eyes as a coy smile perks on her lips. "No. Not until you wash your hand."

"Okay, fine." I turn on my heel, heading to the kitchen. From my peripheral vision, I see her slowly approach me and that's when I take my chance and turn back around, running toward her.

A muffled squeal slips past her lips as she tries to run away, but I manage to grab her waist.

"TJ, stop." She laughs, attempting to pull away, but it's pointless. I tighten my grip around her waist and press her to my body. "No, don't. Don't do—" Her jaw drops as I cradle her cheek with my paint-covered fingers.

"Sorry, what was that? I didn't hear you." I kiss her forehead, dragging my palm from her cheek down to her neck, wrapping it around her throat.

I let my impulsive thoughts get the best of me because I squeeze her throat. My fingers lightly dig into her skin, feeling the steady pace of her pulse pick up. I should drop my hand and push my filthy thoughts away because Nix is just a few feet away. The only thing separating us is the closed door.

Lola's already looking up at me when I look down at her. The playfulness is gone, morphed into something darker and...hesitation?

I don't get to wonder what she could possibly be thinking about before she sinks down to her knees in front of me.

The air catches in my lungs. I've fantasized about Lola on her knees in front of me. But those fantasies don't come close to reality.

"You don't have to do this." I swallow thickly, though it's impossible because my throat has become too dry. "You really don't have to—"

"Do you *really* want me to stop?" Her fingers hook under my sweats and boxers, but she doesn't pull them down.

I once said I was a weak man for her and I meant that. I *am* a weak man for Lola.

Clearing my throat, I shake my head. "No, I don't want you to stop."

My hard dick throbs with anticipation. I watch eagerly as she pulls my sweats and boxers down in one swift movement until they're pooling at my ankles.

We were moving so fast, I didn't focus on her expression in Miami, but now that I really take it in, I smirk. Her smile is meek, and her wide eyes trail up and down my body like she's unsure if she should look at my dick or not.

I'm the hardest I've probably ever been, and my pre-cum is not only coating the tip, but it's leaking down the side of my dick.

"I—wow."

"You're feeding into my ego."

She rolls her eyes.

"I'm going to choke you with my cock if you do that again."

She stares up at me, looking at me dead in the eye, and does it again.

"I mean it."

"Me too." Her voice is soft, almost low, that if I wasn't listening closely, I wouldn't have heard it.

Lola blows a shaky breath, wrapping her hand around the base, and leans forward. Her tongue pokes out, flicking the tip, smearing the pre-cum all over her tongue as if she were tasting it.

My eyes flutter closed, head tilting back, but the air in my lungs almost seizes when her entire mouth takes the head. I groan, clenching my jaw, feeling her hot, wet tongue circle around me, but my eyes roll back when she sucks it.

"Fuck," I murmur, looking down at her.

Her hair has fallen in front of her face like a curtain, and I fist it because the last thing I want to miss is the look on her face when she gags on me.

"Spit on it," I rasp, inhaling a breath as she glides her palm down.

She pulls her mouth back and spits twice on me. A string of saliva clings to her bottom lip, dripping down her chin. Lola doesn't lick it off, her gaze focused on her hand as it slowly works its way up and down my cock.

"Open your mouth and suck."

Leaning forward, parting her lips, she engulfs the head and takes me in as deep as she can before she gags and pulls back.

"Don't stop." I push her head back, getting her to gag.

I shouldn't enjoy that sound, enjoy the way her eyes water and fingernails dig into my thighs. God, I shouldn't fucking enjoy it as much as I do, but Jesus fucking Christ, I do.

So I do. I push her head again, keeping it there until I feel salvia seep out of her mouth.

"I told you I'd make you choke on it," I grunt, easing my hold on her head but not her hair.

She pants hard, chest rising and falling rapidly. Despite the tears running down her cheeks and the saliva trailing down her chin, she sheepishly smiles and licks her lips. "I deserved that. Now let me congratulate you like you deserve."

Lola takes me into her mouth until I hit the back of her throat. She pulls back and does it again but faster. I'm breathing hard, closing my eyes as I bask in her wet mouth suctioning my dick.

"Fuck, Lola." She pulls me out of her mouth and swipes her tongue along the seam of my tip. She then trails it down my length until her mouth is at my balls, and when she pulls them into her mouth and sucks, I moan. "Holy shit, just like that." I encourage as she slides her closed palm on my shaft back and forth, the saliva around it helping her hand pump me as she continues to suck my balls.

When I open my eyes, I find her eyes already on me, filled with a satisfied glint.

"Fuck, don't stop," I hoarsely whisper when her tongue glides back up and brings my dick into her mouth.

The vibrations from her moans send hot, electric zaps to shoot down the base of my spine. My breaths become ragged and I grunt low "fucks" as her cheeks hollow every time she sucks in.

My jaw drops and I have to restrain whatever noise is trying to claw its way out of my mouth as my entire soul ceases to exist. I come inside her mouth hard, holding her head in place.

It takes me a few seconds to get my shit together and once I do, I pull her up to her feet. I take in her swollen lips, the cum and saliva dripping down her chin, and the deep color of her eyes.

"I—" My lips part, but I don't say anything because I genuinely feel speechless like I did when we were in Miami.

"Stay right here. Don't move." I grab my boxers and put them on. I quietly pad over to her bedroom, taking a quick glance at Nix to make sure he's still sleeping, and grab what I need before I slip out.

Standing in front of her, I wipe her chin clean and toss the wipes on the ground on top of the sheet.

"I could have done that," she sleepily murmurs.

"My mess, my responsibility." I grab her wrist and strap the leather bracelet around it. "Possessive, obsessive, and clingy as fuck. I hope you're okay with that."

She smiles, staring down at my name engraved on the brown leather. "I'm okay with it."

I snake my arms around her back, hauling her close to my body, and kiss her forehead.

Softly she exhales, wrapping her arms around me. "A chaotic sunset is what I painted. They make me think of you."

47

LOLA

"YOU'RE AMAZING. THANK YOU SO MUCH FOR DOING this."

"I know. I usually get called brilliant, but amazing will do," Daisy says with a smug smile on her face.

I'd hug her because she managed to get TJ's gift for me in time, but I know she'd feel awkward if I did, so I settle with sarcasm.

"Your arrogance never fails to astound me."

She shrugs. "Good. Never let it stop."

I'd roll my eyes at her if I wasn't already nervous and amped with too many emotions. My heart palpitates are hard as I open TJ's Christmas gift and look over it, making sure everything looks right.

"What do you think?" I chew on my bottom lip, anxiously waiting for her reply or an expression. "I know it seems too fast, and maybe it is, but I wanted to do this. I think it's fitting, and no matter what happens between us, I—"

Daisy gently squeezes my arm, stopping my word vomit. "You don't need to explain yourself to me or anyone. As long as you're happy, then I'm happy." Relief fills me, watching her smile as she takes the gift from my hands and skims it delicately. "How do you feel?"

"I feel good. Excited. Nervous." Nerves settle inside of me. I drum my fingers on top of my lap. "Feels like an end to an era, but a necessary one. I don't know if that makes sense, but—"

"No, I get it." She hands me back the gift. "A lot has happened since you found out you were pregnant, and a lot has changed this past month."

A lot has changed since TJ and I started dating a month ago. Even though we hardly see each other because of our busy schedules, things have been steady and nothing less than amazing. There's the occasional overthinking, but I always remind myself that I promised I'd trust him.

Getting up, I walk over to the walk-in closet that's going to be Daisy's for the next few days and set the gift on the top shelf. We were supposed to be celebrating Christmas at her house, but her family is currently in Europe because her brother, Sebastian, got called up for a soccer trial. Since they left during exam week and are still not sure when they'll be back, she didn't go.

So we're in Miami, spending Christmas with TJ's family and Saint. Although Saint and TJ aren't here because they're in Atlanta, Georgia, for the CBS Sports Classic and won't be here until tomorrow, Christmas Eve.

We wanted to go but didn't because of work.

It's a little weird being here without TJ, but his family accepted us with arms wide open and have been nothing but welcoming. They didn't hesitate to let Daisy stay and insisted on picking us up from the airport, so we wouldn't have to come in the Uber. And TJ's mom asked if she could have Nix while Daisy and I got settled in.

Sitting back on the bed, I let myself fall back, as does Daisy, and we stare at the ceiling in silence for a moment.

"Say it."

"I wasn't thinking about anything," I lied.

She elbows my arm. "Come on, it's me you're talking to."

I contemplate whether or not I should say anything, but she's right. This is Daisy I'm speaking to, my best friend.

"Sometimes...things feel too good to be true. Like shit's going to hit the fan because I'm getting too...comfortable. Am I horrible for thinking that?"

I trust TJ, I do, but every so often there's this feeling in my chest that won't go away. It feels heavy and suffocating. I don't know why and I can't shake it off. No matter what I do, it always comes back.

She shifts to her side, propping her head on her shoulder as she looks down at me. "You're not horrible for thinking that. It's understandable considering TJ's...past, but believe when I say that I know he genuinely likes you." She grabs a lock of my hair and twirls it around her finger. "You know what I always say—"

"*El amor es para pendejos*," I say for her. She's said it so much, I can say it almost perfectly, but I can't roll my Rs as beautifully as she does.

"It is, but it's not like that for you guys. He stares at you like if he doesn't look at you every five seconds, you're going to vanish into thin air. *Poof*." She waves her hand in the air, emphasizing on the word. "He looks at you the way delusional people wish to be looked at."

I grin. "Delusional people?"

"The lovesick fools who wish for those bullshit fairy-tale romances."

I chuckle softly, staring back up at the ceiling. "I know I'm just overthinking everything and I need to chill out."

48

TJ

Our winning streak is over and it's all my fault.

I'm always good about blocking everything out, but when a player from Kansas, Keegan Rucker, started talking about Lola last night, I lost my shit.

At first, I was able to ignore him because I knew he was only taunting me, baiting me to go off.

Everything was fine until he brought up her business and said he had booked her for a *"one-on-one special."* I tried hard to ignore how that made me feel, but then he pushed me over the edge and asked if she'd wear her Jessica Rabbit costume.

"Do you think she'll wear the Jessica Rabbit costume? I saw the pictures, but I'm sure she looks better in person. She just looks so goddamn fuckable, I know you know. When you're done with her, can I have her next?"

I shouldn't have elbowed him hard in the stomach, knocking the air out of him, but he shouldn't have been running his mouth.

As much as I hate that we lost and hate that I'm the reason for it, it was worth it as I stood over him, watching the agonizing look on his face as he tried to catch his breath. And nothing was more satisfying than seeing the Kansas fans lose their shit because I wasn't ejected.

How did that not happen? I genuinely don't know, but I'm not questioning it.

Typically, I'd muse over tonight's outcome, but losses are inevitable. I do feel guilty for letting my emotions get the best of me and letting my teammates down, but I don't regret what I did.

I quietly slip into my room, but I stop at the doorway, just as Lola steps out of my bathroom.

I asked her to sleep in my room, but she said she'd think about it. I know she's worried about what my parents would think, but they couldn't care less. They know she's my girlfriend—I'm obsessed with how good that sounds—and we have a kid together.

Lola seemed so unsure, I thought she was going to sleep in the guest room with Daisy, but she's here.

Dropping my stuff on the floor, I close the gap between us and take her in my arms. Having her in my arms, everything stills. I'm submerged in her warmth and vanilla scent.

"I've fucking missed you."

A breathtaking smile spreads across her face. "You saw me a few days ago."

I cup her neck and tip her head back, kissing her forehead. "A few days too long."

She rests her head against my chest. "I missed you too."

It's been a few days since I've seen her and Nix. We Face-Timed and texted every chance we could get, but still, nothing feels better than physically having her in front of me.

I don't know if it's normal, but I *always* miss her. I genuinely hate whenever we're not together and hate every time I have to say goodbye.

The draft has been on my mind a lot these days because if I get drafted, the Toronto Raptors might have the first pick. That means if I'm the first in the draft, I'd be moving to Canada without Nix and Lola.

Never in a million years would I have thought something like that would sound so depressing.

We haven't talked about our future together. I've been

meaning to, but with our busy schedules, it's not something I want to do over the phone. I've also not been sure when the right time to talk about *our* future would be. Even though we've only been together for a month, I know Lola is and will always be it for me.

Aside from basketball, I've never been more sure about anything in my life, and Lola is a sure thing.

"What are you doing up so early?"

She cranes her head, looking up at me. "I woke up an hour ago and couldn't go back to sleep. Figured since Nix is going to wake up in an hour or two, I'd go ahead and get ready for the day."

Slowly and lazily, I drag my palm on her back. "Go back to sleep. I'll keep an eye on him."

"It's okay. I know you're exhausted." Her eyes flutter and body shudders at the motion.

"Not really. I feel wide awake."

"Are you okay?"

"Yeah..." I trail off, but the look she's giving me tells me she can see right through my bullshit. "Just feeling a bit anxious, but I swear it's nothing. It'll wear off, eventually."

A small, sad smile slips on her face, but it's not a pitiful one, but one that feels like she understands how I feel. It doesn't last long on her face as it's replaced with a more cheerful one.

"You want to go somewhere?"

"I'll go wherever you want."

I breathe in deeply, inhaling the salty air, feeling another weight lift off my shoulders.

It's been years since I last woke up to see the sunrise. I'm certain the last time, I was in middle school. Mom and Hazel always tried to get me to go with them, but I could never be bothered to wake up early enough to see it.

It's somewhat dark out, but in the distance, the crown of the sun barely peeks from the horizon, and the rest hides behind it. There's a hue of light red that encapsulates the golden sphere and a pale yellow that illuminates just above it.

Glancing at my side, I smile, staring at the wonderstruck look on Lola's face as she takes in the almost desolate beach. We brought Nix with us because he woke up early, and Daisy and Saint decided to tag along. Aside from us, there are a few joggers running along the shoreline.

Raising my camera, I capture the look on her face before it disappears.

She smiles as she takes a small sip of her cold brew that we stopped to get before we got here. It's not too cold outside, despite it being the end of December, but there's still a chilly breeze. Still, I'm sure we could be in the negative degrees and Lola would still drink something cold.

"You should be taking a picture of this instead." She waves her hand across the beach.

"Okay," I say, standing a few feet behind her. "Turn around."

"I said take a picture of the beach, not of me."

"I am." I grin. "Lola?"

"Yeah?"

"Smile, golden girl."

An ethereal smile takes over, as it always does when I say that to her. I realize how different her smiles are whenever I say that rather than just saying, "smile." They're always more vibrant, softer, making her face glow like it is now.

I said it just to tease her at first. She got gold paint on herself one day, and I didn't notice until we were outside watching the sunset. The golden streaks bathed her, giving away the patch below her jaw, and trapping her in a shower of sunlight.

Though the sun doesn't have to cover her like a veil to get the effect because even in the darkness the same glow envelops her.

Quickly, I snap the picture as I hear our friends' voices come closer.

"He just loves me more," Saint taunts Daisy, carrying Nix on his shoulders.

"You bribed him with ice cream. That's the only reason why he chose you."

"Nah, he would have chosen me regardless. Isn't that right, *Polpetta*?" He pokes Nix's belly a few times, getting him to giggle.

"Keep telling yourself that."

Saint lifts Phoenix from his shoulders and hands him to me. I happily take him, adjusting him on my hip as Lola and Daisy step a few feet away from us.

I'm not sure what that's about, but I take my chance to talk to Saint.

"What do you think you're doing?"

A big, goofy grin splits across his face. "What are you talking about?"

"Taunting Daisy, pissing her off. I thought you were trying to win her over?"

"Oh, I still am. I just decided to change my tactics."

"Tactics?" I chuckle. "And how's that working out?"

He tiredly sighs. "It's...a work in progress."

"I'm not sure if I should applaud you for being a delusional optimist or for your commitment."

It's been three months and she has yet to show any ounce of interest. But I commend him for his persistent dedication. No one does it better than Saint Arlo.

He shrugs, smirking as his eyes drift to hers. Funnily enough, it's as if she heard us because her eyes connect with his and she glares at him.

"She's just playing hard to get. She definitely wants me."

I play along with his delusion. "Right, she *definitely* wants you."

"Why can't you have faith in me? I had faith you and Lola would end up together. It's why I bet so much mone—" He snaps his mouth shut.

"You did what?"

He wears an innocent expression. "Nothing, I did nothing."

I narrow my eyes and before I can interrogate him, the girls come back.

"Arlo." Daisy jerks her head, gesturing for him to follow her.

"Going, Diaz." He saunters toward her but looks over his shoulder and mouths, "she wants me" as Lola makes her way back to me.

I laugh, shaking my head at him.

"What's that about?" Lola asks, her eyes bouncing between me and Saint.

"Saint just being Saint."

"Ahhh." She gives me an understanding smile.

As they walk off along the shoreline, Lola stretches the beach blanket on top of the sand. She digs out the toys she brought Nix to play with from her tote, setting them down next to the blanket, along with the Christmas present she got me.

I told her not to get me anything, but just like me, she was insistent because I also got her something. I've been thinking about this gift for a while, and I know it's going to be extremely helpful for her.

We were going to wait to open presents tonight at midnight once it was officially Christmas, but she said she couldn't wait anymore to give me mine.

Setting her gift down, we both take a seat and watch Nix get to work. He grabs the tiny shovel and scoops the soft, cool sand into the just as tiny plastic bucket.

As he busies himself, I take a few pictures of him and then let my camera hang from the strap around my neck.

We bask in the silence, staring at the foaming waves as they steadily roll toward the shore and then fizzle away as they're pulled back. They come in layers, softly roaring and crashing about all while the sun slowly ascends without a hurry.

Closing my eyes for a second, I breathe in the salty air and relish the soft grunts of my son as he scoops the sand, Lola praising him for how much he managed to get, and the waves that rock back and forth.

My life has always been fast-paced, and it'll always be like that, but being here with them, it always seems to slow down. The chaos in my life ceases, letting me catch up and appreciate every second I spend with them.

When I open my eyes and look down at the people who have become my everything, *my family*, I realize they're *all I need*.

A realization settles deep inside of me and it baffles me.

How can we go our entire lives and miss the chance of meeting the best people in the world? The thought of never meeting Lola and never having Phoenix really fucks with my head more than my injury ever did.

The thought unsettles me because I don't want to be anywhere they're not.

"What?" Lola smiles.

Someone once said, *"When you know, you know."*

I always thought it was unrealistic and corny because how does one know? How does one ever feel it? It's not something that constantly runs through my head, but on an extremely rare occasion, I've thought about it.

And today those rare questions have been answered because *I know*.

"I..." The anxiety that gripped me earlier is nowhere in comparison to the overwhelming way my heart races or the way my thoughts spiral for the girl sitting next to me. I should say something, but I chicken out and decide against it, at least for now. "I want you to open your gift."

I hand it to her, hating the way my palms have become sweaty and shaky. Why the hell am I so nervous?

"You really shouldn't have." She shyly smiles and pulls out the box covered in forest green wrapping paper with gold snowflakes all over it from the gift bag.

"I really wanted to. It was time for an upgrade."

Lola's brows pull, a deep crease forming between them as

confusion takes over her face. "Upgrade for"—her eyes grow triple in size, and her lips part as she tears off the wrapping paper—"an iPad?"

"Before you start to argue with me and decide you can't accept it because you like to be stubborn and fight with me." I give her a pointed stare before she can say anything. "You're such a busy woman, and I thought you should have something dependable, something Phoenix won't be able to rip apart."

"This is too much. I can't take this," she softly says.

"You will." I grab the bag from her lap, pull out the pencil I also got, and hand it to her. "Watching you still use that joke of a planner not only stresses you out, but it stresses me out."

Her chin wobbles and I don't miss the way she blinks repeatedly to stop the tears that flood her eyes. She sets everything to the side and gets on her knees, then wraps her arms around my neck. "You seriously didn't have to do that, but thank you. I promise I'm going to use it all the time."

"I know you are." I tuck the lock of hair that managed to escape her messy bun behind her ear.

But we pull away when we hear a soft smack followed by another. Nix cheekily smiles, slamming his shovel against the iPad box.

"Phoenix, don't do that. We have to be careful, okay?" Lola picks it up and stores it back in the bag. "Just like we're careful with Pooh bear."

He listens to his mom as she explains to him what she's going to use the iPad for. I capture the moment on my camera and snap a few more with the ocean behind them.

The tangerine sun has risen halfway, but it hides behind fluffy, pillow-like clouds that stretch along the horizon. Still, the rays manage to seep through them, refusing to stay hidden. Rose gold spotlights permeate across the sky and ocean. Blending with the remnants of the blue night sky in an ombré effect. The transition from night to day is slow, but the wait is worth it.

Especially as every second that passes by, the colors shine on Lola and Nix.

As if she were reading my mind, she bends down and connects our lips. The kiss is brief, but I still feel her lips on mine even after she's pulled away.

She releases a shaky breath, holding the present she got me. "I hope you like this. It's nothing expensive but—"

"It could be socks and I'd still love it," I joke, taking the bag.

Though I know it's not socks because the bag is extremely light, and as I take the gift out, I see how thin it is. She tentatively smiles, but still, she encourages me to unwrap it.

I quizzically stare at the Priority Mail envelope. It's been opened, but it's fastened by a single piece of clear tape. Peeling it off, I peer inside, only to see a single sheet of paper and nothing else.

"Is this one of those ticket-like gifts where you let me do whatever I want? Hazel once gave me—" Pulling it out, my heart beats dangerously inside my chest as I read the big bold black letters.

Birth Certificate
Phoenix Kingston

I reread the name over and over again, not breathing every time that I do.

"Holy shit." My voice is barely a hoarse whisper. I know my son is right in front of me. I shouldn't have said that, but I couldn't stop the words from leaving my lips. Or stop the stinging at the bridge of my nose or the way my eyes blur with tears. "Is... this...is this real?"

I reread the paper, wiping the mist underneath my eyelash.

"If he's going to look like you, he might as well have your last name." I hear the smile in her voice, but I don't dare look at her because I'm close to losing my shit. And I'm certain I heard her voice crack, so if she cries, I'm definitely going to lose it.

Sniffling, I slip the certificate back in the envelope and set it back in the bag. And then I pull Lola into a crushing hug.

"You have no idea how much this means to me." I press a kiss to the crown of her head, but I don't move away. Not until Nix grabs my forearm, like he's letting us know that he doesn't want to be left out.

I quietly laugh, blinking a few times before I let go of her and lift him up.

"Please don't let this go to your head," she teases, knowing it's what we both need.

"Oh, you better believe it will." My cheeks ache from how hard I'm smiling, but I can't stop. "Phoenix Kingston, that sounds good. Doesn't it?"

"Yeah, it does."

The elated look on her face is all I needed for the last bit of weight on my shoulders to completely dissolve.

We walk to the shoreline, our feet sinking in the cool, wet sand as the sun continues to rise. We stop to let Phoenix marvel at the birds that fly over us and because he loves to keep us on our toes, he makes a run for it.

Lola and I briefly look at each other, smiling before we chase after him.

I've never felt more at peace than I do now.

49

TJ

"LANDON, *AMICO*," SAINT SLURS, HIS SMILE LOPSIDED AS he slings his arm around Landon's shoulder, tugging him to his body. "Smile, it's New Year's Eve."

"No." He shoves Saint off, his upper lip curling in disgust.

I take a swig of my beer, hiding my smile behind it.

Like every college student who isn't at frat row or home celebrating New Year's Eve, we're at Liquid, waiting for the clock to strike twelve.

I don't know how Jagger convinced him to come because Landon was dead set on staying home. But he's here, still unapproachable as ever, but he's here. He didn't even crack a smile when two girls approached him and asked if he was up for a good time. And they weren't the only ones who tried.

Any other guy wouldn't have hesitated to escort them home, but Landon couldn't be bothered.

Saint rolls his eyes, but he doesn't let that deter the smile on his face. "You'll have the best time of your life before the night ends. I'll make sure of it."

"Don't bother. Just be happy he came and hasn't left." Jagger chuckles, just as buzzed as Saint and Jayden.

Saint sidles next to me, slinking his arm around my neck and clinking the neck of his bottle against the corner of my phone. "Stop looking at it. She'll be here soon."

My eyes instinctively flicker to the dark screen of my phone, hoping that Lola would reply already, but she hasn't. She had to work tonight but said she'd be here along with her friends as soon as she got done.

While she worked, I had Nix with me until my parents arrived and took over.

Ever since I posted her on my Instagram, a lot of people have reached out for paintings. But it doubled when Saint posted the painting Lola gave him a few weeks ago. Since he has a bigger following, she's gotten more requests.

While I'm all for her business growing, I hate that I hardly see her. She'll be gone almost an entire day when she does a live painting for a wedding. She says those take the longest, but they pay the most.

"If I knew you'd be this obsessed, I would've bet more money," Jayden grumbles, though the loud music quickly drowns it out.

"Bet? What bet?" I ask, tucking my phone in my pocket.

"Did I say bet? I meant—"

"You know exactly what you meant. Matter of fact, if I recall correctly, you"—I narrow my eyes at Saint—"also said something about a bet."

Cheeky smiles rise on their faces, except for Landon's.

"We played the let's-see-how-long-TJ-can-be-in-denial-before-he-asks-Lola-out. It was just for fun at first, but then Landon made things interesting and turned the game into a bet," Jagger explains and scrunches his nose.

I want to say I'm surprised, but I'm not. I'm friends with a bunch of idiots.

"I'm assuming you didn't win?"

"They didn't, but I did." For the first time since we got here, the corner of Landon's lip twitches, and for a brief second, he sounds alive.

"How did you—"

"Know? Mate, you were so obvious."

"I really wish I hadn't bet so much money." Jagger blows a harsh breath, taking a large drink of his beer.

"And you're studying Psychology?" Landon clicks his tongue, his tone condescending. "You should consider changing your—oh, fuck off."

"What are you..." I follow his line of sight, wondering what could've set him off, but I stop at the girl who drives me fucking wild.

Lola's already smiling, but it grows wider when our eyes meet. Though I can hardly keep them on hers long before they stray down the length of her body.

It's hard to look or focus on anything else because she's wearing a short, shimmering gold dress that molds to her body like it was specifically made for her. A thin gold chain wraps around her neck a few times, holding the dress in place at the top of her breasts.

I'm struggling with everything in me to shift my gaze away from them, but the plunging cowl neckline does little to hide her tits.

The gold dress clings at her waist but then flows right below her mid-thigh. And with every movement, the hem rises up dangerously but somehow manages to stay in place.

I'm all for Lola wearing whatever she wants and makes her feel comfortable, but this is the one time I really wish she were wearing anything but that damn dress.

I need to stop gawking at my girlfriend because I can feel blood rushing to my dick. The last thing I need is a hard-on, but I'm so fucking weak for her.

"Lola, I knew you had bad tastes in guys, but friends..." Landon's words bring me out of my horny haze.

Shifting my gaze, I realize that Lola has other company besides her best friends and Polly and Gabby. I recognize the blonde,

Julianna Sparks. She's in one of the sororities, but I don't know who the other one is.

"Lola." Julianna pins her with a glare. "I thought you said that *thing* wasn't coming."

"I didn't know he—"

"Well, if it isn't the human equivalent to the bubonic plague," Landon cuts her off, eyes burning into Julianna.

"Careful, I'll kill you." A haughty smirk curls her lips.

"If that means putting me out of the misery you seem to dreadfully carry everywhere you go, I'll gladly accept death."

"You two know each other." Gabby's sweet, friendly voice cuts between the animosity emanating from them.

"Unfortunately," they reply in unison.

"It's close to midnight. Shouldn't you be off hiding in a cave, sacrificing some poor soul or talking to the devil?"

Someone needs to say something, but it's like watching a car accident happen in slow motion. We see it coming, we know how bad it's going to be, but there's really nothing we can do to stop it.

"I've tried, but in order for the sacrifice to work, the person must have a soul. And you, Hollywood, do not." He clicks his tongue in disappointment. "But don't worry, I'm sure they have a special place for you somewhere."

Her lips tighten into a straight line. "Thanks for the invite, but I'm leaving before I say or do something I'll regret."

"Please do. Your presence is exhausting and underwhelming."

"Fuck you."

"No, thank you. I'd rather choke on vomit," he replies dryly.

"As if I'd ever let you touch me." She stared at him as if he were the most disgusting thing she'd ever seen. "Bye, everyone." She waves at us and before she walks away, flips Landon off without sparing him a glance. The girl who came with them follows suit.

"What the fuck just happened?" Daisy's voice snaps us all out of our trance.

"That was...intense." Gabby awkwardly laughs.

"Just another day." Jagger half shrugs with exasperation in his voice. "That was actually the most civil I've seen them."

Cara cocks a brow. "The most civil?"

"That was entertaining," Saint snorts a laugh.

As everyone falls into conversation, forgetting all about what just happened, Lola saunters toward me as I do to her, but Jagger steps in front me right before I can grab her.

I sidestep him just as he lazily drapes his arm around her shoulder. A wicked glint shines through his eyes and he smirks.

"Little Red, whenever you get tired of this dumbass and want a real man, I got you." He winks at her. "I may not have much *dad* material, but I sure as hell have a lot of *daddy* material."

"For fuck's sake." I push Jagger's arm away from Lola and wrap my own around her waist, pulling her to my chest. "Fuck off, Jagger."

I know he's only messing, but what kind of boyfriend would I be if I wasn't as possessive as I'd promised Lola I'd be. The last thing I want is to cheat her out of getting the total boyfriend package.

"Don't be jealous, Teddy."

I scoff, giving him a quick once-over. "I promise you there's nothing to be jealous about."

"Little Red, if you change your mind, you have my number." He winks at her before he gathers around everyone else.

I shift her body so that she's facing me, grip her chin, and tip her head back. "You have to delete his number."

"Don't be jealous, Teddy." She giggles, repeating and lowering her voice like Jag.

My lips hover over hers, getting a faint smell of peaches and whiskey from her breath.

"I can't help it. Especially when you're dressed like this..." I trail off, my mind becoming drunk and hazy as I feel the smooth skin at the small of her back.

I'm too stunned to speak as I idly drag my palm over her

completely exposed back. Occasionally, the golden chain that acts as a support to hold her dress up, tickles my hand.

"I get a little jealous of anyone looking at you the way I look at you." I close the gap, connecting her lips with mine.

She smiles against my lips. "You shouldn't."

"I told you, I can't help it," I huskily say.

"So how is it that you look at me?"

I know what she's doing. A tantalizing smirk curls her lips, and her eyes shine with mischief.

"For the sake of me not getting hard in the middle of Liquid, use your imagination."

She purses her lips as if she's holding back from smiling.

"You're really living up to the golden girl name, huh?" I drag the pads of my fingers one by one down her spine, reveling in the way she shudders against me. "You look really fucking good."

Before she responds, Daisy and Cara haul her away from me.

"We're getting drinks. We'll bring her back!" Cara yells over her shoulder at me.

"It's going to be a long night." Jayden stands next to me, blowing a ragged breath. His eyes train on Cara until she and the girls blend into the drunken crowd.

"A long fucking night." I chug the rest of my beer, wondering how the hell I'm going to make it till midnight and not drag Lola out of here.

It's been a...night.

Everyone's having a good time, but I'm close to losing my shit.

It sounds dramatic, even for me, but that's what happens when your girlfriend has an insane body, wearing a dress that makes her look like a goddess, and is dancing so erotically.

At least to me it is because from my point of view, the way she rolls her hips, shakes her ass, and wickedly smiles does things to me. Makes filthy images play in my head and tempts me every so often to say fuck it and drag her out of here.

Instead of doing what my brain and dick desperately want me to do, I stay put and watch her from a distance, letting her enjoy her time with her best friends. She doesn't let loose often, and even when she does, she's constantly thinking about Nix.

Tonight, I made sure the only thing on her mind is having fun. To keep her overworking mind at peace, I've already texted my parents multiple times to ask how he's doing and asked for pictures.

Especially because this is the first time they're babysitting him.

The DJ lowers the music, announcing there are ten minutes left until the new year, and the huge screen behind him illuminates the time in big bold white letters.

Before I get the chance to make my way to Lola, she's already making her way to me.

I spread my legs wide, beckoning for her to stand in between them. As she does, I take her in, smiling at her flushed chest, glassy eyes, and the lopsided smile on her face.

Gripping her waist with one hand, I rest the other on the back of her thigh. "Having fun?"

She sways, snaking her arms around my neck, and lets them dangle over my shoulders. "I am, but I'll have more fun if you come join me."

"I have joined you."

There's no way in hell I wasn't, but after almost embarrassingly getting hard after she decided to grind her ass against me, I called it quits.

Her fingernails softly dig into my back as her glassy eyes morph into something dark, lust-filled, and that bottom plump lip juts out into a pout. "But I wanted you to stay."

I inhale a sharp breath, ignoring how heavy my heart careens inside my chest or how the blood rushes to my dick, causing it to throb.

"Stop looking at me like that," I beg.

How the tables have turned. A month ago, she had asked me the same thing, and now it's me. I'm the one pleading with every inch of me for her to stop looking at me like she wants me to fuck her.

Or maybe I'm just reading too much into it because it's been a while since I had sex, and I'm desperate. To bend her over, pull her dress over her ass, and fuck her until she's soaking my dick with her arousal.

"Like what?" An alluring smile spreads across her face, giving the illusions that those two words are supposed to be nothing but an innocent question.

But I hear past the sweetness that drips from her voice and feel her legs slightly spread.

"Like you're hoping I'll touch you right now."

Fire ignites in her eyes as they dip down to my lips. "Maybe... that's what I want."

"You've been drinking." It's the only reason why she would suggest I touch her *in* public.

Not that anyone would see us, at least I don't think because they're all drunk or lost in their own world.

No one would ever notice if I slipped my hand under her dress.

"Just a little, but I'm not drunk. I'm giving you consent, TJ." Her voice is so meek, I almost don't hear it.

"We could get caught..." Slowly, I drag my palm up her thigh until I feel the hem of her dress tickle the top of my hand.

She licks her lips, eyes drifting to the left and right and then back at me. "Yeah...we could."

I slip my hand under her dress and drag my middle finger under the curve of her smooth ass and then I cup it, squeezing it hard. Her lips part and if the music wasn't too loud, I'm sure I'd hear her gasp.

"We would get kicked out." I release her cheek and slap it before I slide my hand over her hip, feeling the lace that wraps around her skin beneath the pads of my fingers.

"Or maybe not. Maybe we'll get lucky."

"Someone could be recording us. You know how people are."

I take a quick peek, making sure no one is looking, and they're not. There're just a few more minutes till midnight. No one is in their right mind right now, and even if they are, they couldn't care less about what we're doing.

Her eyes widen for a fraction, and then she drops her gaze to my hand between her thighs. I figured that would freak her out and make her pull away, but it does the opposite as she steps a little closer.

My mouth goes dry, but my dick instantly hardens, not holding back anymore.

"You would like that? Wouldn't you?" I bring my hand to the lace that covers her pussy, relishing how wet it is as it clings to her. Dragging two fingers down her slit, she shifts from one foot to the other, and her fingers grip my shoulders for support. "Answer me."

She doesn't, though. It seems like she's become shy again, but that's going to change right now.

Shoving the lace to the side, I drag my finger over her swollen clit, flicking it over and over until her lips part and her chest haphazardly rises and falls.

I grip her waist hard with my other hand. "Fucking answer me."

"I...*ahh*," she pants, eyes glazing over with need, lips parting wider with every flick. Lola looks away, teeth sinking into her bottom lip before she releases. "Yes...I'd like that."

I'm not sure if coming from doing absolutely nothing is possible, but I swear I could right now.

"Look at me," I demand and like the obedient girl that she is, she does. I remove my finger from her clit and drag it down her slit, slipping two fingers inside of her. She jerks, but I keep her grounded with my other hand.

Lola's eyes flutter, and her thighs squeeze my hand as I pump my fingers in and out of her. She's so wet, she stretches with ease, accommodating my fingers and taking them so well until my knuckles are buried deep inside of her.

"Look at me, Lola," I rasp, feeling her walls clench. "We don't want anyone to know what we're doing. So smile and *act* like we're doing nothing but talking and having a good time. Okay?"

She stiffly nods. Her lips rise, but her smile is weak at best.

"Say it." I quicken the pace of my fingers, hitting her clit with the heel of my palm.

"Okay," she breathlessly says. She's extremely tense, her body almost shaking, but somehow she manages to genuinely smile.

"Now fucking come so we can go home."

Her body stiffens and her lips part just an inch as her pussy spasms in waves and clenches my fingers. I don't relent, not when she hides her face in the crook of my neck. I continue to thrust my fingers inside her, smirking at the choked up breaths and stifled moans that slip past those pretty lips.

Her fingers dig into the side of my neck. I'm not sure when she moved them, but I relish the pain they bring.

"I got you." I hold her in place, still pumping my fingers in and out of her, and lessen my pace until her body isn't trembling against me anymore.

As I remove my fingers, the entire club erupts loudly, shouting Happy New Year at the tops of their lungs. Confetti, streamers, champagne, and God knows what else rains down on us.

"Happy New Year, Louise." I keep her pressed to me as I pull my head back and kiss her forehead. "Now let's go home."

50

TJ

I've never hated Saint more than I do now.

Any other day, I wouldn't care that he got drunk, but today of all the days, he had to get fucking plastered.

Landon's typically pretty good about taking care of these things, but sometime during the middle of the night, he disappeared. I couldn't ask Jagger for help because he went home with two sorority girls, and Jayden went to Cara's, so I was left to take care of him.

Helping him isn't the issue because I've taken care of my friends plenty of times. The problem is that it took two hours to get him to go to sleep. He was all over the place, insisted he needed to smoke, and when I wouldn't let him, he tried to hit me.

Lola offered to help, but I refused. I told her to wait in our room, but for as long as she had to wait, I'm certain she fell asleep.

Rubbing my hand over my face, I defeatedly step into my room, expecting to see Lola sleeping, but I'm pleasantly surprised to see that she's not.

She's lying on her stomach, her knees bent, legs in the air, and an ankle crossed over the other. She's too busy looking at the pictures in my camera, she hasn't realized that I'm here. But that quickly snaps me out of my stupor, realizing that she's using the camera I never let anyone touch.

In quick strides, I plop it out of her hands and shut it off. "You're not supposed to be looking at that."

Her brows pinch together, and a small crease forms between them. "Why not?"

Lola can look through my phone, my socials, anything she wants, but this is the one thing I didn't want her to look through. At least not yet.

"Because..." There's no malicious intent behind these pictures, but I don't know how she'll react. Some of the pictures I got permission to take, others I didn't.

"Those are pictures of me."

Setting the camera on my dresser next to the others, I lean against it, resting my palms behind me on the edge, and cross my ankle over the other.

"They are."

The corner of her lips tugs upward. "Why do you have pictures of me? It seems obsessive of you."

"It's not what you think." I smile, feeling relieved that she's not upset about it. "It's for a project."

"A project? Are you going to continue being cryptic, or are you going to tell me?"

"At the start of the semester, we were asked to pick something that empowers us. The pictures are supposed to convey what we feel. They're supposed to speak for us as they should speak to anyone who sees them."

Lola sits up, the smile slipping from her face. She stares at me, taken aback. "I empower you?"

"You do."

A disbelieving chuckle tumbles from her mouth. "How? I've done nothing to do that."

"Your resilience. The way you just push through life despite everything that's happened. You genuinely amaze me and give me so much purpose. I can't remember the last time anything ever made me feel the way you do."

I could ramble on and on about the way she makes me feel, the way she makes me look at life, how to take on life, but I don't think I'd ever find the right words. But the pictures, they describe how I see her and how she makes me feel empowered.

A tender, radiant smile extends across her face, and a rosy hue coats her cheeks. She stands and closes the space between us. Her heels click, her dress swishing with every movement.

I spread my arms and unhook my ankles, welcoming her in my space. I embrace her, wrapping my arms around her shoulders as she slips hers around my waist.

"I did nothing."

"You did everything."

Everything I'd never be able to do if it wasn't for her.

She tips her head back, glassy eyes filled with unshed tears. "You're making me emotional."

"I tend to have that effect on people." I grin, twirling the cool metal chain around my finger.

Lola rolls her eyes.

"Roll your eyes again."

She peers up at me, stares me dead in the eye, and rolls her eyes with so much fucking sass.

I smile, kissing her forehead. "You're cute when you get bratty."

"I'm not brat—" She gasps as I spin us around and then twist her, pinning her chest against the top of my dresser.

I rest my palm next to her head, bracing my weight as I hover over her, my lips to her ear as I absentmindedly grab one of my cameras. Her breaths are shallow and uneven, and her eyes track my movements. I adjust the camera to make sure it'll capture both of us, but I don't turn it on.

"I won't press the button until you tell me to, and if you've changed your mind and don't want to do this anymore, that's fine as long as you're comfortable."

She heaves a shaky breath, her gaze fixed on the camera. "Turn it on."

Those three words trigger something inside of me like a switch. My finger works fast, turning the camera on, and I press the button to record. My dick jerks up, tenting my jeans and nudging her ass.

"Stay quiet. I'd really hate to wake up Saint."

I couldn't care less if he did, but I'm sure he's not because he's completely knocked out.

Aside from watching us, nothing turns her on more and gives her a thrill than the possibility of us getting caught, and the way she fights the urge not to moan.

Pulling away from her, I wrap my palm around the nape of her neck, keeping her pinned to the dresser, and with my other hand, I raise the hem of her dress above her perfectly round ass, letting it bunch at her hips.

I swallow a groan, clenching my teeth, staring down at the nude thong she's wearing. I don't know if I'm really punishing her or myself. My plan is to edge her on, but I don't know if I'll be able to do that.

Fuck. Focus.

"Just remember I warned you not to roll your eyes at me."

"That wasn't a warn—" The rest of her words are cut off, her breath hitches, and she jolts, but I keep my palm firmly on her neck.

Her ass bounces and a red handprint decorates one cheek. "So fucking perfect," I murmur, sliding my hand between her slick thighs, cupping her pussy through her thong. "You're wet but not wet enough. I know you can do better than that. Can't you?"

"Yeah..." She fists her hand, pressing her lips together to muffle a moan.

I draw my hand away and swing it back before I slap the other cheek, smiling in appreciation at the red handprint that now coats it.

Lola squirms, rubbing her thighs together, and digs her nails into the wood. "I'm wet enough." Her voice is low, almost drowned out by her soft pants, but I hear it.

I unfasten the button on my jeans and pull my zipper down, but I don't pull it out, not yet. I just need to give it space to breathe, but I'm close to coming and I haven't been inside her yet.

Slipping my hand between her thighs again, she's right. A wet, sticky patch seeps through the thin fabric, making it cling between her pussy lips.

I can't help the wicked smirk that curves my lips. "You are, aren't you?" I drag my middle finger up and down her slit, enjoying the way she shifts from one foot to the other, writhing beneath my touch, and pants like she's close to coming. "And you're also close, aren't you? Your body feels so goddamn tight, your thong is soaked through, you're wetting my hand, and you're rubbing your thighs, desperately seeking it."

"Yes, yes, yes." She bites back a moan, closing her eyes as she rolls her hips and humps my hand. "I'm so close."

"I know." I dryly chuckle, removing my hand. I curl the string between her ass around my finger and slide the drenched fabric between her slit.

"TJ!" She jerks up, but I push her back down. "What the hell are you doing?"

"Punishing you, of course."

She turns to look at me, anger swirling in those dilated hazel eyes, nose flaring, and jaw clenching. "Are you serious?"

"Very." I wink at her, my smile smug.

Using my foot, I spread her legs wider apart, pulling the string upward to graze her clit.

"That's not—" Her lips part, but the more I pull on the string, the farther her lips part.

I've never done this, never this slow, but ever since Halloween, I've had this desire to completely own her, to control her. And there's no doubt in my mind that she likes this. Otherwise, she wouldn't be pushing her ass against me or soaking my hand.

"Oh," Lola mewls, her back arching, almost lifting off the

dresser. "Like that. Right there. Don't stop," she breathlessly whines, knuckles turning white as she clenches them tight.

I yank the string and then move it from side to side, grazing the spot that's driving her wild.

Moving my hand from her neck, I thread my fingers through her hair, taking a fistful. I lift her head slightly as I let go of the string and cup her pussy. "Ride my hand like you do so well, baby."

I push my finger to her clit, adding more pressure as she rapidly rolls her hips in circular motion. I keep my eyes glued below her waist, staring hypnotized as her butt bounces.

Lola frantically humps my hand. The moans she's trying so hard to hold back slip from her lips in breathy cries as her body becomes taut and rigid. "Oh my God." She sinks back down, her moans strained and low as she comes.

"TJ?" she says after she catches her breath.

"Lola?" Letting go of her hair and pussy, I kiss the top of her bare shoulder as I work on getting the chain off.

"Fuck me."

I stop, lifting my gaze, meeting her dark hooded eyes and crimson cheeks. "Yeah?"

She nods. "Yeah."

Dropping my hands, I spin her around and crash my lips against hers, forcing my tongue inside her mouth. She meets me with fervent need, her mouth and tongue just as desperate as mine. And when she moans into my mouth, the vibrations of it send a searing heat down my spine. I bend my knees, keeping my mouth on hers, and cup her ass, lifting her up, and she circles her legs around me.

I walk to my bed, never breaking our kiss until I lay Lola on her back and then I stand over her. She looks beautiful, flushed cheeks, skin glistening, hair splayed across my duvet, and dress bunched at her hips, exposing how wet she is between her thighs.

Reaching over my head, I grab the neck of my shirt and take it off, letting it fall to the floor as I kick my shoes to the side. I drop my jeans and boxers next, fighting back the urge not to smirk as she props herself on her elbows and her eyes drift down until they stop at my painfully hard dick.

She blinks and looks back up at me. She can pretend like she's not affected, but her eyes are wild and shot with unfiltered heat.

"Shut up." She moves a wayward strand of hair away from her lash.

"I didn't say anything," I innocently say. Reaching for the drawer in my nightstand, I grab a condom and set it next to her.

"Your stupid smirk says it all."

I crawl over her and settle between her thighs. She spreads them wider apart, bending her knees.

"What does it say?" I whisper, pecking the corner of her lip, and work my way down to her jaw. I latch onto her warm skin and suck hard, eliciting more breathy moans.

She lies back down, fisting the duvet as if she's needing something to hold on to and then my name leaves her mouth in a needy plea. "TJ."

Drawing back, I stare with satisfaction at the dark shade of red that flares on her throat.

"Red really looks good on you." I swipe my thumb over the spot, feeling the heaviness of her pulse against the pad.

"I'm not even going to ask how big it is."

"It's good that you don't." My cheek twitches. "This dress needs to come off."

I give her some space to take it off, and when she does, she brings her hands to her stomach.

"Don't do that." I move them to the side and lower myself to her stomach. "This"—I softly brush my lips across her stretch marks—"shows how strong you are." I kiss one end of her stomach. "How amazing you are." I kiss the middle of her stomach. "How beautiful you are." I kiss the other end of her stomach and then sit up, hovering over her. "I love everything about you. Stretch marks and all." I smile down at her, pulling her in for a soft kiss.

I feel the tension ease from her body when I sit back up and hook my fingers under her thong and slide it down.

"And my heels?"

"We're keeping those on." I grab the condom, rip the foil off, and slip it over my cock. "Ready?"

"Yeah." She sucks in a sharp breath as I drag it up and down her soaked pussy. I tease her entrance a few times before I raise it up to her sensitive clit and lazily glide over it.

"*Oh...*" She shuts her eyes when I bring it back down and slip the tip into her entrance. I push a little more inside and suck in a tense breath at how tight she feels.

"Relax," I grit, kiss her forehead, and hope to God I don't come from barely being inside of her. "I'm not even halfway in yet."

She raises her head, propping herself on her elbows, and looks at where we're connected.

Slowly and teasingly, I take my time thrusting inside of her, knowing how much she's enjoying this. It's agonizing for me because I just want to thrust inside of her, but she's getting turned on by us. She's wetter than she was before and with every push, her pussy clamps down on me.

But I only hold out for so long because her whimpers and moans echo around the silent room, and when she spreads her legs farther apart, I thrust completely inside of her.

"Holy fuck," we both groan.

"Goddamn, Lola, you feel so damn good." I drop my head, heaving a breath.

She hooks her legs around me, her heels digging into my back. "Don't slow down."

I hiss in pain, grinding down as her thighs clench around me, adding friction.

"Faster," she demands, her head lolling, but her eyes are still laser focused below our waists. "Harder."

I thrust hard and fast, my balls slapping her slick pussy, the sound mixing with her moans and my groans. The noises encourage me to fuck her rougher because nothing sounds more erotic and euphoric than the way we sound. It's raw and so fucking animalistic.

"This pussy is mine and only mine," I huskily say.

"Yes!" she cries out, bucking her hips up and throwing her head back. "Only yours."

I pull out but linger at her entrance. "Look at us."

We both stare at my dick, completely covered in her arousal. She watches as I grab the base and slide it into her, completely disappearing until I pull it back out and repeat the motion.

Never in my life would I have thought something would be this mesmerizing, this erotic, but I can't look away. I'm completely transfixed by the way the head disappears inside of her and soon her hot pussy swallows my dick. It clenches every time I'm about to pull out, and every time I do, we moan.

Pulling out, I sit up on my knees. I grab her hips and lift her slightly, aligning myself at her entrance. And then I pull her forward and quickly thrust inside of her.

"TJ..." She gasps, crying out loudly as I roughly drive deeper inside. "Please don't stop."

I lick my lips, drawing my eyes to her breasts as they bounce. "So fucking beautiful."

Not feeling like I'm deep inside of her, I sit on my ass and scoot back until my back is pressed against the headboard with me still inside of her. Her hands snake around my neck as I grab her ass and keep her grounded to my dick.

I pinch her chin and make her look at me. "I swear I can't get enough of you. Nothing will ever be enough. I need to drown in you." I'm breathing harshly, my soul burning and yearning for her. She closes the gap between our lips and kisses me, but in between them, I say, "But even if I did, I don't think it'd ever be enough. I'm so in l—" I grit and hold her down as her pussy chokes the fuck out of my dick.

It takes everything in me not to come as she takes control,

catching me off guard. She not only grabs onto the headboard but switches between bouncing on me and rocking back and forth.

"God, like that, Lola. Don't fucking stop." I moan, dropping my head back.

Lola rides me until she comes. Her body jerks and suddenly stills for a tense second before she spasms and cries out my name. She wraps her arms around my shoulders, holding me tight as her hot cunt grips me. I lose myself for a moment, relishing the feeling until I lift her up and push her down.

She lies on her back, chest heaving, skin flushed and covered in a sheen of sweat, and strands of hair stick to her face.

Leaning over her, I line myself and drive into her. Her back arches, fingernails digging into my arms. "TJ, I'm going to come again."

"Good, come with me." I buck my hips faster, harder, rougher until my balls tighten, my back goes rigid, and an electric shock shoots down my spine. I come just as she does.

I drop my head, shuddering as I release inside the condom. It takes me a moment to get off her because I swear it just keeps coming.

I pant harshly and finally pull out of her and discard the condom while she goes to the bathroom.

When she comes back, we lie next to each other, extremely spent, sweaty, and exhausted.

"Wow, that was..."

"Yeah..." I trail off, brushing the hair that sticks to her damp forehead to the side, and I kiss it.

"Happy New Year to us."

I smile, hugging her tight. "Happy New Year to us."

The three words I've been hanging onto since Christmas cling to the tip of my tongue. I should say something, and my lips part to say them, but nothing comes out.

I'll tell her...just not right now.

51

TJ

"This is so fucking weird."

"I still can't believe this is happening."

"I bet he got in Saint's box."

"He doesn't look high to me."

"I would know if he got in my box."

"Well, he has to be on something because what the actual fuck?"

"Or maybe we're all just high? In some kind of derealization state."

"Love really makes you do wild things because past TJ would never."

"Past TJ would have burnt the house down."

"Past TJ would *not* be using seasonings."

"Or limes."

"We're fucked. The world is ending. That's the only explanation for this."

"Do any of you not have anything better to do?" I shift my gaze away from the skirt steak on the cast iron to my dumbass friends staring at me like I'm a fucking unicorn.

"No," they simultaneously reply just as Landon steps into the kitchen but comes to a quick halt. His usual vacant face is now a perplexed one.

"Mate, are you..." he trails off, eyes fixed on the tongs in my hand. "Cooking?"

"Yes, I'm cooking. Yes, I bought groceries. Yes, I know what salt is."

Saint jokingly asked when he saw me pick up the salt shaker. Though now that I think of it, I don't think he was joking.

If it wasn't for the steak sizzling, the kitchen would be nothing but silent.

Landon's brows skyrocket. "You bought groceries?"

"Get your jokes out and leave." Turning my back to them, I bring my attention to what matters, and that's making sure I don't burn the food. The last thing I want is to serve Lola burnt tacos.

I've worked too hard for all of this to go to shit. I got the steak yesterday and left it marinating overnight. Gabby made the salsa for me. I bought her favorite Mexican drink and homemade tortillas from the local Hispanic market because I wasn't confident those would come out good.

I may have figured out how much salt I need to use and not burn the kitchen down, but I'm still not one hundred percent confident in my cooking skills.

Even if I were, I'm trying to keep it simple. I want to focus all my attention on Lola and Nix as soon as they arrive, and cleaning is going to be the last thing on my mind.

We're nearing the end of January and I've hardly gotten to see her. Our schedules have been chaotic since the year started. Aside from games and practices, there's a month and a half left until March Madness begins and on top of that, I've been preparing for the NBA draft.

I still make time to see Nix, but seeing Lola has been hard. Any free time I have, she's working and when she's free, I'm at an away game or practice. And when we're finally together, she's busy and I'm with Nix.

Not seeing each other brought an idea to mind and I don't see how she wouldn't agree. It's why I decided to have dinner in and not out.

"So domesticated." Jagger snuffs a laugh.

"I'll stand by in case we need to call nine-one-one." Jayden cackles along with the other guys who sit around the dining table. Landon, though, he leans against the wall, his eyes burning my back.

I say nothing but flip them off as I transfer the steak to the cutting board.

They talk amongst themselves, but their eyes follow my every movement. Until we hear the front door open and soft footsteps pad along the floor.

Nix comes barreling in, curls and cheeks bouncing, and his smile giddy and beaming, with Lola right behind him.

He runs past the guys as I crouch down, spreading my arms wide open to catch him as he jumps on me. "Hey, Little Bear."

"Hi, Da!"

"Hey, Lo—" My head whips back to Phoenix. "What? What did you just call me?"

"Da—" He pauses, brows pinching together, looking to the side as if he's deep in thought. "Da-Daddy." He smiles, clapping his hands, proud of himself.

"Did you just call me—" My eyes flicker to Lola, who's already staring at me with the same giddy smile he's sporting. "He just called me daddy."

"We've been practicing." She beams, almost bouncing in her spot.

My heart swells and a thick wave of emotions washes over me. The same wholesome feeling I felt when I saw Phoenix's new birth certificate returns. I never thought something as simple as Phoenix calling me dad would elicit an overwhelming flood of emotions.

I love my parents and siblings. I love basketball. But nothing compares to the immense love I have for Phoenix and Lola. I've never felt empty in my life. I've always had what I wanted, but now I have everything I need.

My friends stare at me, and I can already see the gears in their heads turning. I can only imagine the jokes formulating in their heads about me on the verge of tears. Surprisingly, they don't come. At least I don't think they will now.

Saint and Jayden are too childish not to say something, but they will eventually.

Jag snaps his fingers, pointing at Lola. "Now I know where I know you from."

We all share the same confused look. Not knowing what the hell he's talking about.

"I thought I was going crazy." He shakes his head, laughing to himself. He studies Lola like he finally found the missing puzzle piece. "But I knew, I knew you from somewhere."

"I promise we've never met," Lola supplies, but still, he shakes his head, refusing to believe what she said.

"It wasn't that we met, but I'd seen a picture of you. And your face is tattooed on TJ's arm."

Her wide eyes drop to my arm, though she doesn't see it because I'm wearing a long sleeve. "No way."

"Yes way." He grins. "Long story short, freshman year, he lost a bet and had to get one of the guys on the football team tattoo something on him. TJ may have been drunk, but it was your face he wanted on his arm."

Jayden nods, snapping his finger. "Now I remember."

"It was about time you all caught on," Landon says.

"Wait, you knew?" Jagger asks.

"Of course I knew."

Saint huffs. "I feel so left out."

As the guys start talking about that night and reminisce freshman year, Lola stands next to me. She doesn't say it, but I know she wants to see it, so I prop Nix on my hip and push my sleeve as far as it will go.

"There you are." I point to the mermaid inked on my skin.

Her eyes grow in size and her jaw falls slack. "He wasn't kidding. A mermaid?"

"I didn't pick the mermaid, but he asked who I wanted it to resemble."

She studies it, and her delicate fingers trace over her face down to the tail. "Obsessed much?"

"You have no idea." I wink at her.

"Lola." Jayden clears his throat, pulling her attention to him. "I want to warn you that TJ cooked, and that's a rare and I mean *extremely* rare phenomenon. So, if I were you, I'd chew with caution and have nine-one-one on standby."

Her lips twitch. "I don't think that'll be necessary. I like TJ's cooking."

Everyone does a double take, staring at her like she's lost her mind.

"Blink twice if he coerced you to say that," Saint slowly says in a quiet voice as if I'm not standing a few feet away from him.

"He didn't but—"

Jagger cuts her off, looking taken aback. "I know he's your boyfriend, but you don't need to say that to make him feel good about himself. Lord knows he'll let that go to his head."

Landon also chimes in, "Whatever he's paying you, I promise it's not worth lying for. That gargantuan ego of his can take it."

I flash them a smug smile. "I'm not sorry to burst your bubbles, but my ego will always thrive."

"Cocky little sh—" Landon stops himself, eyes flicking to my son. "I still don't know what you see in him, Lola."

"Don't you all have somewhere to be?"

I'm not entirely sure what their plans are tonight, but it's the weekend, so surely they have something to do. I know Saint has a date or a scheduled fuck, or something along those lines.

He finally stopped pursuing Daisy after she verbally told him she'd never be interested and that he was too young for her. Even though there's only a two-year age gap. But it was enough to kill whatever infatuation he had toward her.

Since he stopped pursuing her, he's been hooking up with random girls, bringing them home, even bringing two at a time.

They all finally get the hint but still make jokes as they walk out of the kitchen.

Nix squirms against me, letting me know he's had enough of being carried. "Da, I want down."

I don't think I'll get over hearing that.

I set him down and he scurries off into the living room.

Lola circles her arms around my waist as I bring mine around her shoulders. She tilts her head back, looking up at me.

"I hope you're hungry."

"Starving." She licks her lips, gaze flickering to mine.

I know what the looks means, and if Nix weren't here, I'd say fuck the food, but that's not the case.

Pushing that thought away, I kiss her forehead and unhook my arms from her. "Let's eat. I have something I want to talk to you about."

"I'm so full." Lola softly groans, placing her hands on top of her stomach. "That was so good."

My girlfriend, the mother of my child, just said *my* food is good. There are many things I've accomplished and still want to accomplish, but if I never do, hearing those four words will be enough for the rest of my life.

I'm tempted to tell her to repeat them just so I can record her and send it to the group chat. I'm sure they'd lose their shit, and nothing would be more satisfying if they did, but there's something important I need to say.

"Did you really like it?" I sit next to her on the couch, relishing on the sated look on her face.

I'd be lying if I said I wasn't a bit worried. It was my first attempt at making tacos. All I had going for me were the YouTube videos I watched and the directions Gabby gave.

"I really did. Everything was a ten out of ten." She twists her body to face me, flashing me with one of those pretty smiles. "So what's so important you wanted to wait until we were done eating?"

Glancing over at Nix, making sure he's still distracted with his bear and basketball, I direct my attention to Lola.

"With the upcoming draft, I've been thinking a lot about our future."

She sits up, her body becoming stiff. "Okay?"

I take her hand in mine before she can drum it along her lap. "Nothing is guaranteed once I enter the draft, not until the draft combine in May. Even then there is no certainty what pick I'll be, but from what I'm hearing, I could be in the top four. And if that's true, I could be drafted to Canada, Texas, Washington, or Michigan." I blow a breath, rubbing the top of her hand with my thumb. It could still change, but those are the projected picks. "I don't know where I'll end up, but no matter where that's at, I want you and Phoenix to be there with me."

She doesn't instantly reply. Which is fine. I sort of expected her to be shocked, but I'm hoping it's a good kind of shock.

Her hands become clammy against mine. "I can't."

"You're kidding, right?"

"No, I'm not kidding. I can't go with you."

I wait a beat for her to tell me she's messing with me. I wait for her to tell me she'd love nothing more than to come with me, but the longer I wait, the longer the silence stretches between us.

"Why can't you come with me?"

"Because..." she trails off, looking away.

And then it dawns on me.

"You're trying to prove a point to people who aren't in your life anymore. Am I right?"

Lola pulls her hand away from mine, head hanging as she drums her fingers along her thighs. "You don't understand."

"What's there to understand? These people abandoned you

when you needed them the most. Their opinion about you should be the least of your worries."

"Who said it was just their opinion?" When her eyes meet mine, I don't see the same brightness in them from just a few minutes ago. "Do you not see what people say about me online? I'm still an opportunist jersey chaser. Anytime I'm seen with the guys, I'm a homie hopper. The only reason why I even have a career is because of you. I'm only *remotely* interesting because I'm dating you. Should I continue? Because there are many more comments just like that. Can you imagine what they'll say if I drop out of college to be with you?"

"Who cares? No matter what you do, people are always going to talk."

She scoffs. "Right, it's easy for you to say."

"Easy for me?" I let out a humorless laugh. "Should I remind you what they're saying about me right now?" We've lost a total of four games, and we've moved down in the AP poll. We lost our last game at home by ten points. *You're a washed out junior with no game. You're an embarrassment to the program,* is possibly the nicest message I got this week. "But it's pointless because I've found my happy place, and I thought you did too."

Never thought I'd find it easy to face the comments and interviews, but since I've found my happy place—Lola and Phoenix—it's been easier to deal with.

"I've tried, but it's not easy pretending like it doesn't bother me. I can't be you."

My knee bounces and anxiety looms over me, but I try to tame it.

"I don't need you to be me. I just need you to be you. I just need you and Phoenix to be there because I don't want to be anywhere you guys aren't."

I don't care how desperate it sounds. I just need her to understand it, but the look on her face tells me she doesn't understand my desperation.

So when she doesn't say anything, I do.

"You're really going to let random people on the internet influence your decision? After everything we've been through, their opinions matter so much more than us?"

"Don't do that," she says quietly.

"Do what? Say it how it is? Because that's exactly what you're doing. Not only are you too worried about what random people have to say. Random people who don't know jack shit about you, but you still give a damn about *two people* who don't."

I immediately regret the words as they leave my mouth and hate how she looks at me like I've slapped her.

"Lola, I shouldn't have—"

"It's fine," she curtly says. "We'll figure out a way for you to see Phoenix, but I'm going to stay until I graduate."

Blowing a resigned breath, I take her hand in mine, rubbing over her paint-covered knuckles. There's more I want to say, but I'm afraid I'm going to fuck it up and say the wrong thing.

I force a smile. "Okay, we'll figure something out."

Past me would have said fuck it and argued with her until she'd agreed to come with me, but I've learned a lot and I know I'd only push her away. The last thing I want is to be a dick or force her to do something she doesn't want.

Even if it's killing me inside, knowing I'll be miles away from the people I need the most.

52

LOLA

"This is so hard to watch." Gabby winces, resting her elbows on the table, interlocked fingers underneath her chin.

The team is currently losing by twenty-five against the University of Florida and there are only three minutes left until the game is over.

It's been stressful watching them play. They've had too many turnovers, missed half of their free throws, and their defense is lacking.

Since they're playing in Florida, the girls, Gabby, Polly, and Darius came to The Lucky Jersey bar to watch the game. Just like many other NCU students, who are crowding the bar.

Nix is with the sitter. There's no way I would've brought him here.

Within the past three hours, the ambience has significantly changed. Everyone who came in to root for the team with hopeful spirits either looks upset or downright pissed off.

Though most of those who are pissed are the guys. There's a specific group by the bar that I'm certain are just a bunch of frat guys running their mouths.

I ignored them at first, but it's been hard as the night has progressed. Especially when one of them said, "TJ was doing good until he got one pussy. She's not even worth it." That got the rest of his friends to agree and add their own opinions that didn't stray off from what he said.

"Hey, look at me." Cara moves her head, blocking the group of guys from my field of vision. "Don't listen to them. They're just a bunch of drunk idiots."

"A bunch of nobodies," Polly chimes with disdain in her voice. "It's always those khaki loafer loving assholes who love to run their mouths. Seriously, don't listen to them. They're probably on edge because they lost whatever money they bet."

I smile and nod, shifting my attention to one of the many flat-screen TVs hanging from the ceiling.

They only have a minute left and they've managed to score five points, but they're still behind by twenty. It doesn't take long before the game is over and the players are shaking hands with the other team. Their heads hang low as they head to the tunnel, not sparing the Florida fans a look as they cheer and chant their team's win.

"Well, it could've been worse." Daisy shrugs as she picks up her pint glass and chugs the remaining liquid.

Darius cocks a brow, staring at her, amused. "Worse? They lost by twenty points."

Daisy may understand basketball a little more and watch it now without complaining, but she's not extremely invested.

"Everyone has bad games and this is NCU's fifth loss of the *entire* season. Have you seen Florida's stats and how many times they've lost since the season started?" She chuckles, her tone patronizing. "They have more losses than wins and the season is almost over. Donut they'll play in March Madness."

Or at least I thought she wasn't invested. Cara and I look at each other. Neither one of us says what we're both thinking.

I muse over her statement, knowing she has a point. I know the people online won't agree. They'll have a lot to say, but why should it even matter?

That's something I've been asking myself since TJ asked me to move with him.

"I'll be back. I'm going to the restroom." I slide out of the booth and stand at the edge of the table. No one says they need to go, so I push past the crowd and step inside.

But I almost walk back out when I spot Alexia standing in front of the mirror above the sink. We don't typically run into each other, but when we do, she always has something to say. She's never mean, but she always sounds snarky.

Before I can take a step backward, her eyes lock with mine in the mirror. A deep smile stretches across her face and she spins.

"Hey, how are you doing?" Her bubbly smile throws me off, but then I notice the glassy look in her eyes and rosy cheeks.

"Hey, I'm doing good. How are you?" I'm so painfully awkward, I internally cringe.

"I'm doing great."

"Well...it was good talking to you." I turn left to walk to one of the stalls but stop in my tracks when she speaks again.

"I knew him for two years, and that still didn't stop him from messing around."

I turn back around, huffing in frustration. "Look—"

"You really think he's taking the loss well tonight? You don't know him like *I* do. You haven't been there for the past two years like *I* have. You know what he does after a loss? He finds someone to fuck, and I can guarantee you that's exactly what he's doing tonight."

I pinch the bridge of my nose, groaning at this nonsense. A few months ago, I'd considered that possibility. I'd overthink what TJ would be doing, but he's done nothing to break my trust.

And while that may have been what TJ did after a loss, that was before me. I'm not going to contemplate or overthink what he may be doing tonight because he hasn't given me a reason to doubt him.

"You really are miserable, aren't you?"

She stares at me, offended. "Excuse me?"

"Every time I've run into you, you always have something to

fucking say. I don't understand what your issue is."

"Issue? I don't have an issue. I'm just trying to look out for you."

"You're not trying to look out for me. All you've done is talk shit from the moment I met you. I don't even know you."

Her nose flares, lips tighten, and cheeks redden. "You act like you know him, but you don't. I was the one who was there for two years and then he threw me to the side like I didn't matter. You think he won't do that to you? Well, you just watch because he'll discard you like fucking trash when he finds someone better."

I could argue and get upset, but I know I'd be wasting my time. I also just don't care what she has to say. I'm done with the bullshit and letting people get under my skin.

"Then why didn't you do something about it? You had two years. What stopped you?"

She hesitates, blowing a ragged breath and her eyes water. "Because he was always busy fucking around. Surely you've seen how much attention he gets. How many girls message him, check him out, go up and talk to him. Surely you're not that naive and oblivious. He loves the attention, loves the girls who throw themselves at him. I don't know what kind of bullshit lie he told you, but he's not going to stay faithful. Guys like him never do. And if you don't believe me, check his phone. Although I bet he won't let you do that." She aggressively wipes the tears that run down her cheek.

Little does she know that I know all his passwords, and he's notorious for leaving his phone everywhere. If I ever need his phone for anything, he never hesitates to give it to me.

And I'm not worried about the girls. Yeah, they still try to flirt with him, but he never entertains them.

I trust him, but his friends like to tease him in front of me, especially Jagger. He said whenever girls ask for pictures, he'll keep a distance between them and have his fingers interlocked behind his back.

I don't know what to say. I'm sorry things didn't work out between you two?

"You're not special." She bitterly laughs, eyes raking over me.

"But you are?" I don't mean to let that slip, but I'm tired of her bullshit. "I mean—" Why am I even backpedaling? "I don't even know you and I'd rather keep it that way."

"I should've kept my mouth shut. The news would have never —" She quickly clamps her mouth shut, eyes growing wide.

"It was you? You're the reason—"

"What does it even matter? You won. You have him." She aggressively pushes past me, huffing loudly as she opens the door. "When he screws you over, don't be surprised because that's going to be all on you."

Alexia stalks out of the bathroom, letting the door slam behind her.

I wait for any lingering thoughts of doubt to come, but for the first time in a long time, I don't feel anything.

Surprisingly, I feel good despite how the conversation ended.

"Why are you so quiet?" Cara's voice drags me out of my thoughts.

"You're still not thinking about what Alexia said? Are you?" Daisy arches a brow.

"No." It's the truth because my mind has been preoccupied with TJ.

We didn't talk much last night after his game. Though we haven't talked a lot since our conversation two weeks ago.

I was upset at first, but as I thought about what he said, the more I knew he wasn't wrong.

I was.

"TJ asked me to move with him after the draft."

Astonishment takes over their faces. They push everything aside and direct their attention to me.

"When did he ask you?" they ask in unison, shock lacing their voices.

"When would you guys be leaving?"

"Where would you guys be leaving to?"

"Oh my gosh, you're going to be an NBA milf!"

"I'm going to miss you and Nix, but I'm so happy for you!"

"You're going to have to send us lots of pictures and FaceTime us."

"We need to let the front office know we're not going to renew our lease."

"We need to—"

"Whoa, wait, stop," I cut them off from making any more comments or asking any more questions. "I told him I wasn't going."

"You're not going?" they simultaneously ask, confusion etched on their faces.

I sigh and tell them what happened and everything that was said.

I take a drink of my coffee but grimace because it's gotten cold now. I knew I should've stuck with making cold brew. Setting the mug down on the coffee table, I sit back and watch Phoenix play with his toys as I twist the leather bracelet on my wrist.

I regret making it seem like TJ didn't understand what I was going through. Like it was only hard for me to deal with the negative comments when he deals with it on a daily basis.

Last night is a prime example of it because the comments were horrible. Despite having an almost perfect season, the fans didn't care because they wanted the win. They act as if the guys didn't want it just as bad.

"I shouldn't have said what I said, but when he brought up my parents, it hurt. I know more than anyone how little they care about me." Though little is an overstatement because they don't care at all. "They kicked me out and didn't look back."

"It was wrong the way he said it, but he's not wrong." Daisy sits closer to me. She pulls my hair out of my bun and starts to intertwine three locks into a braid. "The losers online are always going to run their mouths. That's never going to change. Its social media. They'll voice their opinions just because they can."

"Yeah..."

Cara studies me like she's figured something out. "But you don't really care about that anymore, do you?"

"I mean, it hurts when I come across something about me." It sucks, but I stopped caring a while ago. Just like I stopped caring about what Alexia had to say.

Once Daisy's done braiding my hair, she loosens my hair and starts over again. "But that's not the reason why you're so adamant you need to finish school, is it?"

I'd lie, but we've been friends for so long, they'll see right through me.

"No, it's not." I stare at the canvas on the easel by the glass sliding door. I finished the painting this morning. I'm just waiting for it to dry so I can send it off to the happy couple who got married last week. "My parents said an art degree would get me nowhere and that I'd be wasting my time. If I left, I'd be proving them right. I don't want all the money I spent, the loans I've gotten, the early mornings, late nights, and the driving back and forth to be for nothing. Not to mention you guys had to put up with living an hour away from campus, when you both could have certainly moved closer, just to help me. It wouldn't be fair. Remember the plan is to finish school together. That's why we got this apartment."

"Oh, Louise."

I anxiously drum my fingers. It's been a long time since Cara called me by my legal name.

"I love you, but just no." She clicks her tongue, shaking her head disapprovingly. "I get where you're coming from, but remember the degree was always your plan B if becoming a live painter didn't work out. And we all know it's really working out for you."

"It's going so well, you've had to put people on a wait list. I mean, come on, when in your wildest dreams did you think that would ever happen? A freaking wait list!" Daisy excitedly exclaims.

They aren't lying. My degree has always been my plan B if all else fails, and a wait list isn't something I imagined would happen. I've booked so many people, I've made enough money to move closer to campus and buy new and better supplies. Though I don't need to because TJ already did.

A package showed up at my door when he was at an away game last week. I'd only mentioned I needed better supplies once, and that was late one night. I didn't think he'd remember because he was exhausted and on the verge of falling asleep.

"And yes, we did agree on living together until we graduated, but that was before TJ. I promise Daisy and I will be okay. We're not going to be upset that you're choosing what makes you happy. We *know* he makes you happy."

"He does make me very happy." My nose stings at the bridge and my eyes water. "I know it sounds ridiculous, but I just wanted to prove them wrong. I wanted them to know that despite what they thought, I could do it."

"And you did, *you* did it. Not *them*," Cara says.

"And who cares what they think. If they couldn't be there at your lowest, they don't deserve to be there at your highest." Daisy lets go of my hair and hugs me, making the tears I was trying to hold back roll down my cheeks. "If anything, you could always do online classes, but do what makes you happy, Lo. No matter what, we'll support whatever you decide to do."

Cara wraps her arms around us. "But I swear, if you move, we'll need to be able to talk to Phoenix."

Nix raises his head and stares at us with curiosity and then stands and walks to us. "I want up."

"Come here." As the girls let me go, I lift him up and hold him for as long as he lets me.

As we cuddle, I make up my mind, knowing it's the best decision for Phoenix and me.

53

TJ

There aren't many people who intimidate me, but if there's anyone who can successfully unnerve me, it's Coach Warren.

The easygoing smile and laid-back posture he greeted me with when I stepped into his office are nowhere in sight. His lips are in a tight line, shoulders rigid, and his eyes bore deep into my soul.

Exhaling a sharp breath, he stands from the other side of his desk and walks to his door, shutting it completely closed. He sits across from me, perching his elbows on his desk, pinching the bridge of his nose.

"Okay, you're going to have to repeat yourself because I don't think I heard you correctly."

"I'm not going to declare for the draft. I've decided I'm going to wait until next year."

Basketball has been my whole life.

Anything I've ever done was always for basketball. The university I picked, the reason why I wake up at the ass crack of dawn, reviewing film when I could be doing anything else, and prioritizing it over anyone.

Everything I ever did was for basketball, but now that Phoenix and Lola are in my life, anything I do, I do it for them.

I still want to play in the NBA. That's my goal, but now it's not my life's purpose. That's why I can't declare this year. I can't leave knowing the people I love are staying behind.

I already spoke to my parents, and they said they one hundred percent back me up on whatever I decide to do. Having their support means so much to me because I know I made the right decision.

Leaning forward on his elbows, a deep crease settles between his brows, concern etched on his face. "Are you in *trouble*?"

"Uh, trouble, no?"

"Did someone *coerce* you?" he cautiously asks.

"Coerce?"

"TJ, son, did someone threaten, manipulate, or force you not to declare? With everything going on, I could see why someone would—"

"No, it's my decision."

The leather chair squeaks as he leans back and folds his arms against his chest. His eyes narrow, studying me with a scrutinizing stare.

After a beat of silence, he asks, "Did you smoke something? Snort something? I swear to God if you're tripping out right now—"

I bite back a laugh, quickly shaking my head. "No, I swear I'm clean. You can test me."

He rubs his temples, closing his eyes for a brief moment before they pop back open. "Okay, then what the hell is going on? You haven't stopped talking about declaring since your freshman year, and now you don't want to do it? Is the media getting to you? I know it's overwhelming, but you've handled yourself well."

"It's not about the media." Which I couldn't truly give two fucks about. They can talk all the shit they want. I'm over the bullshit. I know my worth. "If I wait until next year, I'll be able to graduate."

He gives me a disbelieving look. "Don't bullshit me,

Theodore. I may be twice your age, but I'm not an idiot. Do I look like an idiot to you?"

It's rhetorical, but regardless, he wants me to answer. "No, sir, you don't look like an idiot to me."

"So let's try this again. Why do you all of a sudden not want to do something you've been working your whole life for? Something you never shut up about. Something you've been counting down the days for?"

"My family." I was going to leave it at that, but for some reason, I can't keep the rest of the words from leaving my mouth. I don't owe anyone anything, but he of all people deserves to know.

"My son and girlfriend are here. It wouldn't be right to leave after everything that happened. And I don't want to miss out on Phoenix's life any more than I already have. I missed his birth, his first steps, his first birthday, and so many other things. I know there's nothing I could've done because I didn't know Lola was pregnant, but I can do something about it now. I know it's inevitable to miss out on certain things, but if I can prevent it, I'm going to. And Lola, I don't ever want her to feel like she has to do anything alone."

I played out our conversation multiple times in my head, wondering what I should've said to get her to agree to move with me. But as I thought about it, I realized how fucked up it had been for me to make her give up everything she had worked hard for.

Also bringing up her parents was a shitty thing. I'll never know what it feels like to be abandoned by the people who should be there for you the most. But what I will do is spend the rest of my life making sure she never feels that way again.

A smile stretches across his face, and his serious expression softens. He stares at me the way he did when I brought Nix to practice.

"Lola must mean a hell of a lot to you if you've already made up your mind on something you've wanted all your life."

My *need* for her is more than a want.

"She means a lot to me. She's the mother of my child."

"If this is what you really want, then I support your decision. You know you can count on me for anything you need. And I guess...I won't mind having you another year."

I grin at the feigned disdain in his voice. "Thanks, Coach, I really appreciate your support."

"No, thank you for being man enough to take responsibility. It's not easy, nothing ever is, but I can promise it's all worth it. Especially the unexpected things."

That's what meeting Lola was, unexpected. We didn't plan anything. It just happened.

Just like I didn't expect to fall in love with her, it just happened. I hadn't realized how deep I was until I figured if it's not her, it's not anyone else.

Every moment I spend with her leaves me wanting more of her.

There's not one moment that feels less than another because I crave everything that revolves around her. From the loud to the quiet moments. Spending our time in the kitchen as she teaches me how to cook. Seeing her at my games wearing my jersey. The laughter that bubbles out of her anytime I attempt to paint. Trying new coffee while we make blueberry pancakes in the middle of the night. And my attempts to keep my eyes open until she's content with her paintings.

If it's not her, then what's the point?

"If you change your mind, the deadline is April 26." He raises his palm, letting me know he's not done. "Just think about it. I support your decision, but a lot can change from here until then."

Even though that's two months away, I've made up my mind. I've also done something that I can't go back.

"Thanks, Coach, for everything."

"As long as you're not doing anything illegal, I'll always support you and the rest of the guys." He stands, rounding his desk and opening his door. "Now get out there. I need you focused. March Madness is just a few weeks away, and I need you at your best."

"Yes, sir." I smile, standing from the chair and walking out of his office.

Jagger: I swear you'll never see me pussy whipped.

Jayden: We know.

No one adds anything else to that because we all couldn't agree more with Jay.

Jagger: Fuck all of you. I'm capable of being boyfriend material.

Saint: How the hell are you going to say you're never going to be pussy whipped, but then say you're capable of being boyfriend material?

Jayden: Make it make sense.

Jagger: What I'm saying is that I'll never be pussy whipped, but if I was a boyfriend, I'd be a damn good one.

No one replies to that message because we all know he wouldn't make a good one. Not because he's a terrible guy or anything, but he doesn't care about monogamy or being tied down. At least that's what he said.

And the idea of Jagger with a girlfriend seems...illogical.

Jagger: Wow! Really? Landon, you aren't going to back me up?

Landon: Leave me out of this.

Landon left the conversation.

Saint added Landon to the conversation.

Jagger: I bet none of you thought TJ was good boyfriend material, but here we are.

Saint: You're right, we didn't, but like you said, here we are. TJ's not going to declare because he wants to stay with his little peach.

Aside from my parents, siblings, and Coach, I also told my friends. They've been there and supportive from day one, and they still continue to do so. They were shocked but understood why I'm doing it. Except Jagger. He still supports me but said I was a better man because he could never.

Me: I've told you NOT to call her that.

Landon: Peach...fitting.

If he were here, I'd punch him, but he's who knows where, and I'm at the museum, waiting for Lola. She doesn't know that I'm here. She was having car trouble, so Cara dropped her off. I told Cara not to worry about picking her up and not to tell her because I've also booked one of her museum tours.

I had to improvise because I hardly see her as it is. So if it means I'll book appointments to see her, then I will.

Me: Saint stop adding him back to the chat.

Landon: I think I'll stay a little longer.

Me: *middle finger emoji*

Jagger: Anyway, FUCK YOU ALL for thinking I wouldn't be boyfriend material. You'll all see the day I become one, it's over for you bitches!

Saint: *skull emoji*

Jayden: Sure Jag.

Me: Right...

Landon: K.

Jagger: TJ I can't wait for the day Lola comes to her senses and realizes you're not worth it and leaves your ass. When she does, daddy will be right here to console her.

Me: Please don't ever call yourself that again.

As my phone vibrates in my hand, letting me know I got another message, Lola's voice drags my attention away from the screen to her.

The nerves from earlier come back again as I think through what I want to say. I already know what I need to say, but I keep repeating them to make sure they still sound okay.

Her back is to me as she talks to the receptionist, so she hasn't noticed that I'm here. And that's more than okay for me because I let my eyes drag down the length of her body.

Her outfit is nothing but simple and professional. She's wearing a white long-sleeved satin top, the sleeves rolled up right below her elbows, and a brown satin skirt that stops at the mid of her calf, and a knot at her waist that holds the skirt up. The heels she's wearing aren't too tall but add a little more to her height. Her usual wavy hair is straight this time and cascades down her back.

Before my mind drifts to perverse thoughts, I shove them away for a later day and stand, striding to her before she turns around. I stand a few feet away from her, and when she turns, it takes everything in me not to hug and kiss the hell out of her.

The small, professional smile on her face cracks and a sweet, pretty one takes over. Lola's eyes double in size as she takes a step closer but doesn't close the space between us. I see her hand lift, but she quickly drops it and twists the brown leather bracelet on her wrist. I know what she's thinking because I'm thinking the same thing, but neither one of us acts on it because she's still working and needs to be professional.

"You're here."

"I'm here."

"Wait, are you my eight o'clock appointment?"

"I am." I take another step as she does and I lean down, as discreetly as I can, to whisper in her ear, "I'd love to schedule another appointment. Do you work after hours?"

She looks up at me, tilting her head back just enough. The practiced, professional smile is back on her face, but I see the playful gleam in her eyes.

"I'd have to check my schedule. I am a very busy woman."

"Surely you can fit me in. I promise I won't take up a lot of your time." I eye the button that's tight at her chest, ready to be popped off.

She hums. "In that case, I think I can fit you in."

"I *know* you can." My gaze flickers to her mouth as hers drifts below my waist.

I know she's trying hard, but those gorgeous lips I'd love to fuck grow and spread wide.

She sidesteps me and looks over her shoulder. "Come on, we should get started."

Side by side, we start at the front of the museum and slowly make our way around. She tells me about the piece of artwork and the artist. It's not until our fourth stop, a statue of an angel with a bow in his hand but the arrow right through his heart, that she doesn't say anything.

"Lo—"

"I'm sorry." Lola looks up at me. The same eyes that greeted me with warmth are now melancholic and her lips are cast downward. "I'm sorry for diminishing your feelings and acting like you don't understand, when no one better than you understands how shitty social media is."

My hands flex at my side, wanting nothing more than to hug her, but instead of acting upon what I want to do, I tuck them in my pockets. She needs to be professional, and the last thing I want is to get her in trouble.

"You don't have to apologize. You weren't necessarily wrong."

"I was, I—"

I can't wrap my arms around her like I want to, but I'll be damned if I can't touch her. Slipping one hand out of my pocket, I lace my middle fingers around hers.

"It's easy for me to say what I said because I've had to deal with it for almost three years. Not to mention, I was in therapy for it, and then you and Nix came along and I found my happy place." I smile, squeezing her finger, earning a tiny smile from her. "But you, you got thrown into this and I really wish you hadn't. I wish I could make it all go away. I really fucking wish I could, Lola. But even though I can't, just know that I'm always going to be here. If I need to cuss someone out online, then I will. I'll even find out where they live if I need to."

A faint chuckle slips past her lips, and the smile I had seen earlier returns. "Please don't do that. The last thing I need is for you to get arrested."

"For you, I would." I grin, lacing another finger around hers. "I'm sorry for what I said about your parents. I shouldn't have brought it up and said that."

"You weren't wrong. I just...I wanted to prove them wrong so badly, but it's dumb to fixate on it because knowing them, they still wouldn't care. Deep down, I always knew that, but part of me always...hoped. I know it's stupid but—"

"It's not stupid. I *hoped* you'd forgive and here we are. I *hoped* you'd like me back. I *hoped* you wanted me as much as I wanted you. I *hoped* you'd think about me the way I think about you."

"You're making it hard for me not to kiss you."

I flash her a grin. "I know."

She softly swats her hand at my shoulder, and when her eyes flick to the side, she releases her intertwined fingers from mine.

She plasters a professional smile and takes a few steps back. I don't realize until she does that just how close we were and neither one of us noticed.

I turn to see who she's smiling at and recognize the person on the other side of the room. It's her boss and she's giving Lola a look I know all too well. It's the same look Coach Warren gives Saint when he's doing something he shouldn't be doing.

"I really want to kiss you right now,"

"Don't say that to me when you know I can't," she chides, blowing a harsh breath. "We should continue with your tour, so you can get your money's worth."

"Oh, I am." I shamelessly let my eyes trail down her body. "My tour guide is hot."

She rolls her eyes, but I see the amusement on her face as she turns around and continues to the next piece of art.

I fall into step next to her, but before she can carry on with the rest of the tour, I say, "You know, you amaze me."

"You've said that before."

"I wanted to remind you again."

She looks up at me and smiles as I smile down at her.

For the next two hours, she gives me an entire tour of the museum. We could've finished an hour ago, but we kept messing around. Though it worked out in our favor because almost everyone is gone. There are just a few people lingering here and there, but not in the room we're in.

We stand in front of the last painting, and now that she's done telling me about it, she turns to face me, and a cheeky grin splits across her face. "So what are your thoughts on your tour guide?"

There are so many thoughts running through my head, but there's one that's constant. One that reminds me over and over again that Lola is a sure thing, and if it's not her, it's no one else.

"My thoughts are that I'm in love with my tour guide."

Her smile falters and she stares at me with a blank expression, like she's not registering my words.

This probably isn't the best place to tell her, but I couldn't wait anymore. I've held onto these words for so long, and now that I've said them, I regret not saying them sooner.

Nerves eat at me when she still hasn't said anything, but I know I need to confirm what I said. I need to reassure her because that's what she needs.

"Louise, I love you. This"—I grab her hand, placing it on my chest right where my heart beats wildly for her—"this is yours, it's all yours, and will always be yours. I want you to know that you own every part of me, and no one, absolutely no one will ever have this because it's all for you, my love, my happy, my everything, only for you."

When her eyes become glossy and when her bottom lip quivers, I panic, wondering where I could have gone wrong.

"You love me?" Her softened eyes search mine.

"Louise, I *fucking* love you."

She blows a shaky breath, smiling despite the way her bottom lip trembles. "And I love you."

Such simple words, but I swear they ignite every inch of me.

I shouldn't, but I can't help it anymore. I close the space between us and connect my lips to hers. I relish the softness before I pull her bottom lip between my lips and slip my tongue into her mouth. I wrap my arms around her waist as she snakes her arms around my shoulders. Her fingers tangle through my curls at the base of my neck, eliciting goose bumps that always break out whenever she touches me.

Nothing has ever felt better. I want to stay in this moment, but then I'm reminded where we're at and I'm sure she does too because she pulls away.

"Never been more thankful for peach juice in my life."

Lola giggles, but then she becomes serious. Her gaze strays from side to side and then something flares in her eyes like she's made up her mind.

"What?"

"My shift is over, but I'm willing to work after hours."

54

LOLA

I'M AWARE OF THE TROUBLE WE COULD BOTH GET IN IF we're caught, but I can't bring myself to fixate on the hypotheticals.

I brought us to the one room in the museum that no one ever comes to but Juls and me. It's storage that holds all the holiday decorations and other random stuff.

We come here on our breaks when we want to take a nap because there's an upholstered backless bench. Or when we want to take pictures because of the stunning opulent wall mirror with a golden frame and top arc.

Tonight, I don't have to worry about Juls showing up because she's not working, or anyone else, for that matter. Everyone's mostly gone but security. Though I don't have to worry about him because he never wanders to the second floor of the museum.

The moment I shut the door behind us and lock it, he forcefully presses me against his chest and pushes our bodies until my back hits the wall.

He closes the remaining gap and encases my lips in his, kissing me fervently. It's rough and dominant, pulling and sucking on my bottom lip hard, leaving me panting and gasping for air. I part my lips just a sliver to catch my breath, but TJ forces his tongue inside my mouth. When our tongues collide, I forget the need to breathe, and I let his mouth consume me, the way his hand tightens around my waist, and his hard erection digs into my stomach.

I lose myself with the force of his mouth, not thinking of anything else until he breaks the kiss, resting his forehead against mine.

"Fuck," he mutters breathlessly. "I don't have a condom."

My shoulders deflate with disappointment, but I'm desperate, hot, and have run out of fucks to give.

I'm so desperate, a thought comes to mind, and I should have immediately shut it down. I should have extinguished it, but my need for him is stronger than my will.

And it's been so long, I want this.

"Okay, and?" It's a rash, breathless response, but I don't think too much into it.

He lifts his head, staring down at me incredulously. "Are you sure?"

"Yeah, I'm sure."

As if he had never stopped, he resumes kissing me with or if not more intensity than before. All while his hands untuck my shirt from underneath my skirt and undo the buttons of my shirt in a frenzy.

"Fuck," he groans into my mouth, and in his feverish, impatient haste, he grabs my shirt from the middle on each side and jerks it outward, causing the remaining buttons to pop off and fall to the ground in a soft clatter.

They bounce and scatter on the ground, getting lost behind the boxes. "TJ, what the hell?"

"I'll buy you another one. Just take the fucking shirt off," he gruffly orders, and his hardened stare doesn't leave room for me to argue or question him.

That shouldn't have sounded as hot as it did, but it does. I like it when he's cocky and smug. And when he's serious like this, it turns me on.

I shrug it off, letting it fall to the ground as he pulls his shirt over his head and throws it somewhere.

His eyes drop to my chest and I don't wait for him to tell me to take off my bra. I reach behind and unfasten the clasps, letting the straps slide off my shoulder and fall off me. My nipples become taut and goose bumps from the cool air break across my breasts.

I see the tick in his jaw before he closes the space in between us, devouring my mouth as he bends and hooks his hands underneath my thighs. I instinctively wind my legs around his torso and he slams me against the cool wall.

Pulling his mouth away from mine, he peppers wet kisses from my cheek down to my jaw and latches onto my hammering pulse. I drop my head back, softly moaning at the warmth that floods my system. I should tell him to stop because when he does this, he always leaves the biggest hickeys and my makeup only covers so much. But I really can't bring myself to care.

"Mmmm..." I thread my fingers through his hair at the base of his neck, biting my lip as he sucks harder and my clit throbs heavily.

When he's done, he kisses the spot, but his lips linger. His warm breath fans the now cool spot, despite how it burns on the inside.

"Whenever you look in the mirror, I want you to look at this and remind yourself who *owns* you," he gravely murmurs against the spot. "Remind yourself that you're fucking mine."

My breath hitches when our eyes connect because the whiskey color in his irises darkens into two pools of molten amber.

He grips my chin with his thumb and forefinger and moves my head up and down. "Say yes, TJ."

Oh God, why is that so hot?

"Yes, TJ," I breathe.

As soon as I reply, he lets go of my chin and lowers his head to my pebbled nipple. He pulls the tight bud into his mouth, his teeth holding it down as his tongue flicks over it.

I attempt to hold back the moans, but as he continues his assault, I can't stop them. They force their way out, echoing around the room.

He hisses when I pull on his hair, but that seems to only encourage him because he sucks, bites, and flicks my nipples harder.

"I love you." He kisses the slope of my breast before he lifts his head.

"I love you too." I loosen my hold on his hair, feeling bad for how hard I was pulling on it.

"I meant your tits, but I love you too."

The guilt instantly fizzles away. "You're annoying."

"But I'm *your* annoying person." He smirks, pecking my lips.

I roll my eyes at the arrogant look on his face. I may love it at times, but sometimes it's infuriating.

"I love it when you roll your eyes," he says, the grip on my thighs tightening as he carries me away from the wall, and stops when we're at the olive green bench. "Gives me more reason to fuck the sass out of you."

I swallow hard, clenching my thighs as my clit needily throbs again.

"Do it then."

Something sparks in his eyes and he sets me back down on my feet. He rests his hands on my hips and spins me around so that my back is facing his front. Our eyes lock in the mirror and another smirk tugs on his lips. But I don't let my gaze linger on his because I take a look at myself.

My cheeks are flushed, my lips are swollen, my once straight hair is now a frizzy mess, an eye-catching hickey colors the side of my neck, and nipples are extremely taut that they ache.

I already look like I was fucked, and he's barely touched me.

I snap out of my thoughts when I hear the sound of his zipper being pulled down. From the mirror, I see he's already taken off his shoes, and then my eyes flick to his jeans as he slides them down his long legs along with his boxers.

TJ stands in his naked glory behind, and when I go to turn around, his hands grip my hips again. "Stay like this. I want you to keep looking at yourself."

My heart heavily hammers, and fingers flex at my sides as I watch him take a seat. He slides his hands back and then I feel him tug the knot that holds my skirt together. He pulls the straps until I feel it loosen at my waist, and the silky material falls, pooling around my feet. He then hooks his fingers under the waistband of my panties and pulls them down.

I wasn't going to wear the skirt because we're in the middle of February, and it's still freezing out, but I'm really glad I did.

"Goddamn." He heaves a sigh. "You're perfect."

Far from it. Stretch marks spread across my stomach, the side of my hips, rounding to my butt, and on the inside of my thighs. And I have cellulite.

"I'm no—" I yelp at the hot sting on my ass cheek.

"We can agree to disagree on many things, but this is not one of those things that we'll disagree on. You. Are. Perfect." His eyes lock on mine, any form of amusement gone from them as he enunciates each word. "And I want you to believe it too because it's true. Say it."

"I...I'm perfect," I quietly say.

"Louder, Louise."

"I'm perfect."

"You are. Every inch of you. Every part of you. Every microscopic thing is nothing but perfection. I won't let you believe otherwise."

And I believe him. The way his eyes burn into mine and his voice is velvety soft despite the slight rough edge, I know he means it.

I smile and nod. He eyes me like he's making sure I believe it and after a lingering beat of silence, he breaks it.

"Now turn around and get on your knees."

The sweet moment morphs into something electric. I feel it singe every nerve inside me.

My body acts on his command and I do as he says, turning around and dropping to my knees. I swallow, staring at his hand wrapped around his dick. It's huge, thick, and imposing, leaking with pre-cum.

Nerves work their way inside of me because I've given him two blowjobs, and still the thought of having him in my mouth is daunting.

"You did such a good job last time," he praises. "Come here." I lean closer and with his other free hand, he takes a fistful of my hair. "And I know you'll do a good job again. Won't you?"

"Yes."

"Good girl."

Never in my life would I have thought two words would sound so validating. Especially *those* two words that do something wild inside of me, and I crave to hear them again.

Licking my lips, I part them and stick my tongue out, licking the tip. He groans in appreciation as I drag my tongue along the seam and then twirl it, tasting his pre-cum.

Looking up at him, I find his eyes already on me. Dark and hooded, jaw tight, and nose flaring.

The way he stares at me encourages me to part my lips wider and suck the head of his dick. He blows a sharp breath when I draw him in deeper until I can't go any farther.

"That's it, Lola, you're doing so good, filling your mouth with my cock." His voice is strained, like he's losing every bit of his self-control. "Now fucking suck."

I do just that.

I suck him off and replace the hand on his shaft with mine. Alternating between my hand and mouth.

"Shit," he moans, the word barely slipping past his mouth.

I grin, the dazed look on his face satisfying. Doubt that had clouded my mind disappears, leaving me feeling nothing but confident.

Picking up on speed, I suck faster and harder as I'm pumping, my cheeks hollowing and saliva trickling down the side of my chin. I feel the specks on my breasts, and something about it makes me feel hot and wanton.

I suck him in deeper, despite how my throat reacts to having something that thick shoved deep inside of me. My eyes prick with tears and my jaw burns with the rapid suction, but I don't relent because the noises sputtering out of TJ are so worth it.

He moans and mutters strained words. I look up at him again, but he's not looking at me. He's looking at the mirror.

"Your ass looks so fucking good," he grits, his jaw tense as he groans again. His grip on my hair is slight of a dull pain as he pulls on it, but something about the pain feels good. "I need you to sit on my face again."

I rub my thighs, remembering the position we had been in in Miami. If I didn't feel hot before, I definitely do now.

His entire body tenses and before I can continue, he lets go of my hair and pulls me up.

"Why did you—"

"If I come, I'm going to come inside of you."

Everything happens too fast, he turns me around, my back to him. I take in my reflection, noting how my lips are puffy, swollen, glistening with my saliva.

"Mmm, you look like a fucking dream," he says, hands around my thighs and his lips at the curve of my spine. He kisses me, leaving a trail of goose bumps as he works his way down until his lips are right above my butt.

I hear the sharp intake of his breath before he presses a kiss on each cheek and pulls me back.

"Spread your legs for me."

I lift a brow with uncertainty. "Should I not turn around?"

"Trust me, I know you'll love this." There it is, that infuriating cocky smirk, tugging the corner of his lip. He stares at me with so much self-assurance I can't help but trust him because my body is now buzzing with anticipation.

Slipping out of my heels, I spread my legs and back into him until I'm between his legs. I stare captivated as he wraps his hand around the base of his cock and pumps a few times as I stand on my tiptoes and my pussy hovers over it.

"Do me a favor?"

"Yeah?" My mind is running rampant, knowing exactly what we're about to do.

"Keep your eyes on the mirror."

And I do. I follow his every movement, hand gripping my hip, fingers digging into my heated skin, his palm around his dick, positioning himself at my entrance, soaked and ready to take him in.

My lips part and I hold my breath as he guides me down until I feel the tip between my folds, and when I sink down and the crown of his head disappears inside of me, we both faintly gasp.

I pulse and clamp down on him the deeper he goes, stretching me in a way that feels unreal.

"Lola," he huskily groans. "Your pussy feels amazing. I know you can take more of me. Can't you?"

I nod, moaning at the erotic sight before me. His dick is halfway inside of me, slick with my salvia, but now with my arousal. I feel lightheaded but in the best way possible and that gives me a boost to let myself quickly sink down into him.

I moan louder, not holding back because it hits a spot it never has before and I feel so full. My eyes almost pop out of their sockets and my jaw physically drops at how full I feel.

"Oh my God," I whimper at our reflection. My legs are spread wide, my pussy on full display for both of us to see, my clit swollen and throbbing faster than it had before. But nothing looks more filthy than the sight of his cock buried deep inside of me.

Heat rises up my neck to my cheek, making it hard to breathe because I'm slightly embarrassed by how much I'm enjoying this. It's perverse and so dirty, but it excites me so much, I can physically feel myself getting wetter.

"Fucking hell, Lola, don't move." He drops his head to my shoulder. His fingers flex and dig at my skin, and his hot breath fans my back. "Stay still for a second because I swear to God I'm going to come."

I should listen to him, but I can't help myself because I'm desperate for relief. So I slowly roll my hips, back and forth despite how I feel his body tense against me.

"Louise." It's a rough warning, but I don't listen. I let my body take over, my mind clouded and lost, chasing the euphoric road. "I swear I love you," TJ says before regaining his control over me and lays his huge palm over my stomach, forcing me back until my back is flushed against his chest. He slides his palm down between my thighs and lazily rolls his finger around my clit.

I want to keep looking, but I can't stop my eyes from rolling back until all I see is black. I become a mess, my moans and whimpers mixing and my words far from unintelligible.

"Faster, baby," he harshly breathes in my ear. "Move your hips faster." He slaps the side of my butt.

I hiss in pain from the sting, but when he does it again, I alternate between rotating and rocking my hips, moaning as he does it again. It hurts, but it feels too good. I don't want him to stop.

It happens too quickly as the orgasm takes over my body. Numbing me from the face down, trapping me in a never-ending high. My pussy spasms uncontrollably against him, and my entire body trembles.

"Open your eyes, Lola." He doesn't stop the assault on my clit, but he stops hitting me and rubs soft, soothing circles on my blistering skin. "And just look at yourself, filled with me. You're doing so damn good, taking my cock like this. Just look at how drenched you are. I bet you taste good."

My head lolls as I try to pry my eyes open but snap open when I catch sight of TJ bringing his two wet fingers to his lips, and he sucks them.

"Yeah, you taste better than I imagined. Taste." He brings them to my mouth. Blowing a shaky breath, I part my lips and let him slip them inside my mouth, faintly tasting myself. "Good, right?"

I nod, still sucking on his fingers as he snakes his other hand around my throat and squeezes lightly.

I don't know how it manages to sneak up on me, but I come again. I don't have time to process it. I'm bucking my hips, grinding them every so often on him until my legs are shaking.

"Oh!" I mewl against his fingers, my body shaking and slick with sweat. "Oh fuck."

I don't know what possesses me, but as I feel a third one teetering over the edge, I begin to bounce on him. The loud slaps of his balls against me only encourage me to move faster and frantically.

My breasts sway with every movement, and my pussy squeezes and grips him hard. TJ's grunting and groaning for me not to stop as he removes his fingers from my mouth and throat and lays one hand on my back and the other on my hip. He pushes me slightly forward and in the mirror, I watch his heated gaze drop to my ass, and he stares at it with stupefaction. And as he licks his lips, it sends my mind into a frenzy.

"That's it, like that. Fucking hell, move your ass like that." He pants, his jaw clenching and ragged breaths leaving him.

The look on his face and all of his self-control withering away has me spiraling out of my mind and I come hard as I feel him release inside of me with a guttural groan.

Every nerve and fuse in my body combusts before my very eyes, and I swear I see nothing but a white, bright light. My legs are shaking violently, I'm panting and breathing like I've run a marathon, my clit and pussy are extremely sensitive, and my heart feels too full.

My entire body gives out on me and I slump onto his slick chest that rapidly rises and falls.

I'm not sure how long we sit like this, him still inside of me, his cum leaking out, but we don't say nothing. All we do is attempt to catch our breaths and cool down, though that's hard to do because every second that passes by, my brain replays this moment.

"Fuck," he hoarsely says and clears his throat. "I've never... that was...you were...fucking hell, Lola, you broke me."

Talk about an ego boost. "That's going to go to my head."

"It should."

TJ's arms wing around my shoulders, his tattooed arm stark against my pale skin. I trace the ink on his arm, particularly on the one of me.

"I love you," he says, kissing the top of my shoulder.

I smile, happily sighing. "I love you."

55

LOLA

"So where are we going?"

TJ reaches over the console, lays his palm on top of my thigh, and squeezes it lightly. "Stop being impatient. We're almost there."

"It's hard not to be when you're being so mysterious."

"I promise it'll be worth it." He squeezes my thigh again.

I heave a sigh. "Okay."

He chuckles, giving me a quick side glance before focusing back on the familiar street. "Are you going to tell me your news?"

"Not until you tell me yours?" I ask with hopefulness in my voice.

"I can wait."

I roll my eyes. "You're frustrating, you know that?"

"You weren't saying that last night when you were riding my face, or when you were screaming into your pillow," he whispers.

A shiver rolls down my spine, heat spreads throughout my body, and my throat becomes dry, making it hard to swallow with the memories of last night flooding my brain.

Once we left the museum last night, we went to the apartment. Cara was still up when we got there, and once she saw us, a knowing smile grew on her lips. It wasn't just the big hickey on the side of my neck that gave us away, but our wrinkled clothes and disheveled hair. I tried to get myself together, but there was only so much I could do.

Because Cara took care of Nix, he ended up falling asleep in her room.

We didn't plan round two. It just sort of happened. One moment, I was drying off after my shower. The next, I was sitting on TJ's face, holding on to my headboard. And sometime in the middle of the night, round three happened. He bent me over on my bed and fucked me until the sun rose.

"Shut up and try the coffee."

The smile on his face turns smug. "Yes, Peaches."

This morning, after our third round, he told me he had a surprise for me but wasn't going to tell me because he needed to take me somewhere first.

All he said was to get ready while he got Nix ready. We stopped by for breakfast and afterward picked up two different coffees. Ever since that first time he got me coffee, it's just become our thing. It wasn't intentional at first, but we just fell into a routine, and now we're determined to try every coffee out there.

He breaks at the red light and takes a chance to take a small, tentative sip from his hot caramel brûlée latte, and me from my iced butterscotch latte. We look at each other, our lips rising at the same time. Neither one of us has to say anything to know we picked well. Unfortunately, it's not always the case and there have been times we've gotten some pretty gross drinks.

We exchange drinks as the light turns green, but before I take a sip of his, I eye him warily.

"What are we doing here?"

He pulls into the parking lot of Gabby and Polly's apartment complex. I scan the area, waiting for the girls to pop out or for the guys to be around, but aside from a group of girls walking out of the building, none of our friends are around.

A sheepish smile creeps on his face as he parks his G-Wagon.

"TJ, what are we doing here?"

"Come on." He takes his seat belt off, climbs out of the SUV, and opens Phoenix's door. He makes sure he's bundled up since the February cold is frigid, and takes him out.

"Daddy, Win." Nix points at the bear sitting next to his car seat.

"Oh, I'm sorry. How could I forget." The tense look on his face withers and brightens despite the cold, gloomy day. TJ grabs the bear and hands it to him.

The way TJ smiles anytime our son calls him da or daddy gets me every time. I just want to capture each moment because the look on his face is always priceless.

Blinking out of the haze, I remind myself that I still don't know what we're doing here.

Getting out, I follow him into the building and up the elevator to the third floor. I must have asked him a few hundred times what we're doing here but to no avail. He doesn't answer.

"Are we going to Gabby's..." I trail off as we walk past her apartment and walk two down until we stop in front of a door with the polished brass numbers *3010*.

He twists the doorknob and gestures for me to walk in before he does, but I don't go in. I stay rooted in my spot.

"What are we doing? Isn't this breaking and entering?" I drum my fingers along the cup, looking from side to side, expecting someone to come out and yell at us for trespassing.

"We can't break and enter if it's our home."

"I'm sorry, what?" I stare at him, dumbstruck, but the weight that was holding me down lifts off me as TJ ushers me inside. "Our home? Did you just say our home?"

He sets Phoenix on his feet and immediately he takes off with his bear, giggling excitedly. "Yeah, our home for at least the next year."

I watch the mop of his curls disappear farther into the apartment while I still stand in place.

TJ takes my hand in his, lacing our fingers together. "Come on, let me give you a tour."

We only make it to the ample but empty living room before I pull my hand from his and stand in front of him. My gaze follows Phoenix as he runs around, his soft footsteps echoing from one room to the other.

I direct my attention back to TJ, trying but failing to wrap my head around his words and where we're at. "Seriously, what are we doing here?"

A broad smile stretches across his face as he raises his hands, wiggling his fingers. "Surprise."

I shake my head. "Please tell me you didn't."

"I did."

Now I regret not telling him sooner, but I got caught in the moment between him telling me that he loved me and then everything else that transpired after that.

I'm too deep in my thoughts, and he takes my silence as a sign to explain.

"I've been thinking a lot about you and Phoenix, and I've decided that I'm going to wait until next year to enter the draft."

Everything comes to a staggering stop. My lips part, but he cuts me off. Wrapping his arms around my waist, he tugs me closer to him.

"TJ, you—"

"I know what you're thinking, but I meant it when I told you I don't want to be anywhere you and Phoenix aren't. I'm sorry that I made you choose between me and school. That was stupid and selfish. I didn't think that through, but I've put a lot of thought into this." He waves a hand over the living room and readjusts it back on my waist. "There are three bedrooms, so Daisy and Cara will have their own, and the apartment is just ten minutes from campus."

If my heart could, it'd combust. God, I'm so in love with this man.

Standing on my tiptoes, I drape my arms around his neck and connect our lips. It's a quick peck, but it's enough to set me ablaze. I also don't want Nix to find us making out.

"I love you, TJ," I say against his lips.

"And I love you, Lola." He kisses my forehead and pulls back a little. "I don't ever want you to have to do anything alone because as long as I can, I'm going to help you and be there for Phoenix. And please don't start overthinking. This is my choice. I want to do this. There's always—"

"You have to go."

He stares at me, taken aback. "No, did you not—"

"I did and I love you too much to let you not follow your dreams. I know how much you want this, how badly you've wanted this since you were a kid."

On the verge of falling asleep, one of the many nights he refused to go to bed until I did, I had him tell me when he knew he wanted to play for the NBA. We talked for hours even after I was done.

I know how much he loves the game, but that conversation added more assurance to how extremely passionate he is about it.

"Yes, it's my dream, but there's always next year. You and Phoenix are my priority. Which means you guys come first and everything else is second or irrelevant."

I cup his cheek, feeling his stubble under the pad of my thumb. "You'd do that for us?"

"I'd do anything for you both. Even if it means putting it off for one more year because as much as I love basketball, I want nothing more than to have the two people who mean the most to me. And I can't play if you guys aren't there. Basketball serves a purpose in my life, but you both *are* my purpose too."

There's a sting at the bridge of my nose, but I wrinkle it and push away the tears that pool at the corner of my eyes.

Thankfully, Nix comes running in, distracting TJ from seeing me become an emotional mess. It wouldn't be the first, but I need to get myself together before I drop my news.

TJ lets go of me and crouches down, setting his cup on the floor as our son runs to his arms. "What do you think, Little Bear? This is going to be our new home."

Nix gasps, his big brown eyes shining brightly. "Home?"

"Home." He smiles, softly tapping his nose and then the bear's because God forbid TJ forget about the other important member of the family.

A tsunami of emotions hits me as I look at them, my family.

My best friends are my family too, but I knew eventually we'd part ways. One day, Cara's going to be a kick-ass lawyer but somewhere in Boston or New York. She's always loved the big cities. And Daisy, she'll be doing something with fitness and nutrition, but traveling. She's always wanted to see the world.

So I knew one day it'd be just Phoenix and me. But now, it's not just us. TJ's in our lives. And he's not just someone who's going to be here from time to time, but someone who's going to be here forever.

"We need to tour the rest of the apartment, so you can—"

"Phoenix and I won't be staying here."

His smile falters and his brows pinch together. "I promise you're going to love this apartment. It's bigger than Gabby's, and Daisy and Cara will have their own bathrooms. The patio is also bigger, and there's storage for all of your art supplies. I promise you're going to—"

"We're not going to stay here because we're going with you." I finally spill my news.

He stands. The corner of his lips twitches, but he doesn't smile, only stares at me with skepticism. "You're what?"

"I've also been thinking a lot about everything that has happened since we saw each other again. But the longer I sat on those thoughts, I realized how little they matter. I don't need to stay here because it wouldn't be fair for Phoenix. He adores you and loves to be with you any chance he can. I can't imagine what it'll be for him if you're gone. And I can't imagine being away from you."

The vulnerability makes me a little anxious. I don't have to be, but being vocal about how much I need him makes me feel just a bit overwhelmed.

"I'm not going anywhere. I'm here," he assures me.

"But you don't need to be here. You need to be wherever it is that you get drafted to, and Phoenix and I will be with you."

"But what about school and your business? I know how important they are to you. I can wait another year."

I smile at his concern. "I've talked to my advisors and I can finish my last year online, and the beauty of my business is that I can pack up and take it wherever I want."

Thanks to TJ and Saint, my business is flourishing. I even created a website, and Saint pretty much bullied me into raising my prices. He did the math and apparently said that I was undercharging. I hesitated at first, worried my clients would think it was too much, but like Saint said, if they don't like the prices, they can find business elsewhere. I shouldn't have doubted him because no one has complained, and I even get tips. I don't ask for them, but I'll never turn them down.

"Daddy, I want down." Phoenix wiggles in TJ's arms.

He puts him down but not before he ruffles his hair and the bear's head. "Be good."

Nix giggles and scurries off into one of the bedrooms, dragging his companion along with him.

I set my cup on the ground next to his and snake my arms around his shoulders. "You shouldn't have to miss out on this opportunity. Don't let this go to your head, but you're extremely talented to stay here."

He flashes me a crooked grin, slipping his arms around my waist. "You think I'm extremely talented?"

"I told you not to let it go to your head." I roll my eyes but can't stop my smile from rising. "But all jokes aside, you need to be out there. Wherever it is, we'll be with you."

His face softens. "Lola, are you sure? Don't feel obligated to do that. I told you, I'm okay with waiting another year."

"I know, but there's really no reason why you should wait. I promise I don't feel obligated. I want to do this."

"I..." TJ pauses, his silence stretching with every passing second. "Are you sure? Because where you go, I go."

"I'm sure."

"Okay." He picks me up and spins us around. A squeal mixed with a giggle slips past my lips, but I can't control it. His excitement is too contagious.

As he puts me down, a thought crosses my mind. "Wait, but how did you get the apartment and what will happen with it now?"

"Perks of being an athlete and Coach pulling some strings. It's been unoccupied because it's getting remodeled but should be ready by July. But I guess since I don't need it anymore, then I'll get my deposit back and the months in advance I paid for."

"Can Cara and Daisy keep it still? I'll pay you back."

"You're not paying me anything, and I'll speak to the office manager. I'll make sure they get to keep it."

"Seriously, let me pay you back."

"I don't want your money, so stop being stubborn. I'm not going to take it," he deadpans.

I shake my head. "I can't take your money."

He grips my chin. Tipping my head back, his lips hover over mine. "Your pussy is mine, so my money, your money. Stop. Being. Stubborn." He enunciates each word before he pecks my lips as Nix shows up again.

I press my lips together to suppress my smile, but it's useless because it continues to stretch across my face. "Okay, fine."

"That's more like it." He smirks, but then he blows a disappointed sigh as he picks up Phoenix. "Sucks we won't get to christen the bedroom anymore."

He would say something like that.

I chuckle, picking up our cups.

"Lola?"

"Yeah?"

"I'm thankful for peach juice."

"Me too." I smile.

56

LOLA

One month and a half later

"We're going to get caught. We need to stop."

I peer above his shoulder, staring at the red light that surrounds the buttons on the number panel on the elevator wall. The red light switches from number to number as we continue to ascend to his floor.

"You keep saying we're going to get caught and we need to stop, yet you're grinding your needy, wet pussy on my hand so..." he trails off, his lips peppering warm, wet kisses down the side of my neck.

I blow a shaky breath, my eyes fluttering closed, and the pulse beneath my jaw is close to imploding from how violently it's beating.

"Shut up."

He grabs my throat and captures my lips with his, nipping my bottom lip before he slips his tongue into my mouth.

I lose myself in him. Gripping his shirt, I pull him closer to me despite how his body is already pressed to mine.

It's not until the elevator comes to a stop and we hear the soft ping, letting us know that we're on our designated floor, that we pull apart.

As the door slides open, I quickly run my fingers through my hair while TJ adjusts himself, making sure his erection isn't noticeable. But at a glance downward, I suppress my laugh because it's anything but invisible.

"Look at what you do to me," he gruffly says.

"Looks like a personal problem." Shrugging, I speed walk down the hall, giggling as he curses under his breath, but in quick strides, he catches up to me.

Spinning me around, he bends down and it takes me a few seconds to realize what he's doing, but as it registers in my head, it's too late. He wraps his arms around my thighs and lifts me up, throwing me over his shoulder.

I fight the urge not to laugh. "Put me down. We're going to get in trouble and you don't need to get in trouble again."

"Be quiet then." He slaps my butt twice before he wraps it around my thighs again.

I try to conceal my giddiness with annoyance, but I only sound breathless and flustered. "You're frustrating, you know that."

"For you, always."

I smile, not bothering to tame the way my lips spread from ear to ear. My hair dangles, swishing from one side to the other with every step he takes down the hall.

I debate on saying something else, but it's pointless because every time I part my lips, I can't help but laugh or clench my thighs.

"I fucking missed you." He sighs.

"I missed you too."

It's been an extremely hectic and busy month and a half for the both of us.

At the beginning of March, we celebrated Phoenix's second birthday at Daisy's parents' house. All of TJ's family members came, and so did all the guys and faculty of the basketball team. Along with Daisy's family and Cara's, it was packed, but Phoenix had the best time.

He loved all the attention he got from everyone and the gifts. Especially the electric car Landon gifted him.

After his birthday, March Madness began and I got extremely busy. With finishing my assignments for school, preparing for finals, working in the museum, and doing live paintings, and TJ with games and practices, we've hardly seen each other.

We didn't let that deter us from still speaking or seeing each other. Whether that's FaceTiming, staying over at each other's places, and staying up until we're ready to go to bed.

Now it's the beginning of April, and this past week we hardly spoke or saw each other. After winning another round, the guys made it to the final four. Coach Warren has a rule for what happens when they make it this far into the tournament, and that's not being on their phones unless it's for emergencies. Everyone is already high on emotions and they don't need the negative energy from social media to affect them.

He's not wrong. While the guys have had a tremendous amount of support, it only takes landing on the wrong side of social media for your mental health to deteriorate.

But yesterday, after they made it past the final four, Coach gave them the yellow light to be on their phones and rest for the big day tomorrow.

And it's yellow not green because despite letting them take it easy, they can't leave the hotel or be messing around. Earlier, Saint and Jayden got in trouble because they were shooting each other with nerf guns, but because of them, everyone got in trouble.

Funnily enough, Coach Warren wasn't mad they were being loud or disruptive but worried they could trip over something and get hurt. So he gave them a choice to be in their rooms or hang out in the lounge.

Everyone is currently there, along with the girls and Phoenix. I was planning to be with them, but as soon as I saw TJ, he asked Cara to watch Nix for two to three hours tops, and pulled me to the elevator.

So now here we are, going to his room.

We could get into so much trouble if Coach Warren finds out, but this is one of those fuck it moments.

We can't bring ourselves to care, and he did say they could be in their room.

"Are you wearing it?"

"Wearing what?" I coyly ask.

"Lola." My name leaves his lips in a rasp, full of desperation. "Don't play with me right now."

I may or may not have sent pictures of myself to TJ in nothing but an emerald green lingerie. And I may or may not have sent him videos of me touching myself in bed or in the shower.

"Maybe I am," I tease, lazily dragging my finger around his back.

I laugh as he picks up his speed until he comes to a stop in front of what I assume is his door and uses the keycard the hotel gave him to unlock it.

He pushes it open, slapping my butt again. "I swear you're going to regret teasing—"

The rest of his words die out and he comes to an abrupt stop at the entrance.

"Was any of this real?"

That voice sounds familiar. Why does it—Daisy?

As if he's reading my mind, TJ puts me down. I stare, too stunned to speak, at Saint and Daisy, who are standing in front of each other.

Their heads whip in our direction. Saint's eyes are vacant and Daisy's are flooded with so many emotions it shocks me momentarily before I snap out of it.

"Forget it. Fuck you."

"Daisy, I—" He grabs her elbow, but she jerks it away.

"Touch me again and I swear to God, I'll break your fucking hand," she angrily spits out before she storms in our directions and steps out of the room.

"What did you do?" I ask, shaking away the stupor, but I

don't wait for his reply. I'm out of the room, following Daisy, and TJ stays behind. "Daisy, wait!"

She gets in the elevator, but before the door closes, I manage to squeeze inside.

She still hasn't pushed a button, only stares at them, but her gaze is distant like she's not here.

"Daisy," I cautiously say.

She snuffs a laugh, blinks, and looks at me with a smile on her face that doesn't reach her eyes. The emotions from earlier are extinguished. "It's nothing."

"That didn't seem like nothing. I'm here for you. You don't have to—"

"Lola." There's a bite in her tone, but she sighs. "There's nothing to talk about, okay? I'm fine. Everything's fine. Okay?"

I want to say something, but I know if I push her, she'll push back.

"I'm here. Cara and I both are. If you want to talk. We're here for you. Always." I want to hug her, but I refrain from doing so, knowing she'd hate that.

"I know." She smiles and this one is genuine.

She pushes the button where the lounge room is and, in silence, we descend.

57

TJ

I CROUCH DOWN IN FRONT OF MY TWO-YEAR-OLD AND hold my hand down, palm facing up. "Can I get a good luck high five?"

He enthusiastically slaps his tiny hand on my palm, the slap hardly audible, but Nix giddily smiles, content with how hard he hit me.

"Thanks, Little Bear, now can I get a good luck hug?"

He giggles, spreading his arms as wide as he can before wrapping them around me.

Wrapping my own around him, I pick him up, eliciting more of those cute giggles that turn into bubbles of laughter.

"I love you, Phoenix." I rest my forehead against his tiny one.

"Luh you, Daddy." He cheekily grins.

I hold on to him for as long as he'll let me, relishing this moment before he and Lola have to leave for the night.

They shouldn't be in my hotel room, but what Coach Warren doesn't know won't hurt him. Plus, I'm not doing anything to hurt myself. I'm just spending time with my family. I barely saw them in the month of March. If I get a chance to spend time with them, better believe I'm going to take advantage of it.

Despite tomorrow being the final against Baylor, it's only

going to get more chaotic after it. Not only will I be declaring for the NBA draft at the end of this month, but I'll be training rigorously, traveling to meet teams, and doing private workouts with them. I'll be busy for almost two months until draft day in June.

So if I want to spend time with my family, fuck it, I'm going to spend time with them.

Nix seems to have had enough of our bonding time because he pulls back and wiggles against me. "I want down."

"Oh no." I dramatically gasp and he gasps too, his big brown eyes going wide. "I can't put you down. I think I'm glued to you."

I pretend like I'm having a hard time pulling away from him and that earns me a few more laughs as he also attempts to pull away.

"See, we're stuck together. I can't let you go now."

With his palms at my chest, he tries to push away, and he almost gives up until Lola encourages him to push harder.

She sits on the edge of my bed, legs crossed with her iPad on her lap. "You got it, baby. You're almost there."

Blowing a loud breath, he pushes one more time until I finally relent and let go. His eyes light up, a triumphant grin on his face as I set him down on the floor.

"Fine, I guess you win this time." I ruffle his hair, smiling as he holds his arms up for Lola to pick him up.

She lifts him up and plops a kiss on his cheek before he settles at one end of my bed, nestling in the duvet, and plays with his stuffed bear and dog. He resumes watching TV as if nothing ever happened.

I sit next to Lola, wrap one arm around her back, bring the other under her legs, and lift her up on my lap so that she sits sideways. As she rests her head on my chest, I hold her tighter, inhaling the sweet scent of vanilla, and bask in the warmth and comfort she brings to me.

Kissing the top of her head, I peer down, staring at the lit up screen. The calendar is pulled up and almost every day is filled with something.

"You think you can fill me in on your busy schedule?" I twirl the brown leather bracelet around her wrist.

"I don't know...I'm a very busy woman. I don't need distractions."

"It's the good kind."

She cocks a brow. "The good kind?"

I lower my voice. "Yes, it'd be very beneficial for both of us. You'd get off, I'd get off. It's a win-win situation."

Her lips curve upward, her voice just as low as mine. "And how exactly would you get me off?"

"Fill me in and find out."

"I guess I can find time." She looks up at me. Those earthy-colored eyes soften when they meet my gaze, and a breathtaking smile spreads across her face.

"I love you." I capture her lips in mine, but I keep it brief since Nix is in here.

"And I love you." She plays with my hair at the nape of my neck, making the last bit of tension resting on my shoulders subside. "I should get going. You need to rest."

Tomorrow is the big day, the NCAA final. It feels surreal and as confident as I am, I'm also nervous. We're the eighth school to ever go to the final back to back. To say the pressure is real is an understatement. I've tried not to put too much thought into it, but occasionally, the nerves slither their way inside of me and fuck with my head.

"Stay." I know I'm probably suffocating her with my hug, but she doesn't complain.

"I wish I could, but Nix had a lot of sugar today. If we stay, he'll be up all night and not let you or Saint sleep." She pauses, her eyes flickering to his empty bed. "Speaking of Saint...did he tell you anything?"

There are many things I expected to happen while being in New Orleans for the final, but Daisy in the hotel room Saint and I are sharing is not one of them. She made it abundantly clear so many times that she wasn't interested, and while they weren't necessarily doing anything, something happened.

"I tried to get him to talk to me, but he didn't say much, and then he had to leave because he was meeting up with his father. Did Daisy say anything to you?"

She sighs. "No. She said everything was fine, but I don't believe her. But I didn't push because she doesn't like when people hover."

"Don't stress. I'm sure they'll tell us, eventually. Just give her some time. If Saint tells me something, I'll let you know, okay?" I kiss the top of her head, hoping to see the pretty smile again.

Her lips tilt up, and she nods. "Okay."

"Now how about you and I sneak into the bathroom, and you give me a blow—"

"Tempting, but no, you need to rest. You have a big day tomorrow."

I chuckle. "I'm kidding. Maybe a hand—"

She softly swats my shoulder, but her smile grows wider.

One minute and fifteen seconds left in the second half. The score, 82-78.

Unfortunately, those 82 points belong to Baylor.

Logically, we still have more than enough time to catch up and take the lead, but time feels as if it's going by too fast. It also doesn't help that we're playing against Landon's step-brother, Ashton, and Saint's rival, Xavier.

Ashton and Xavier have been talking shit, getting in their faces, taunting them with all sorts of bullshit. While Landon has been surprisingly but eerily calm, Saint looks like he's going to lose it. He doesn't look mad, but there's something about the look in his eyes despite the smile on his face that feels like he's close to punching him.

Thankfully, Baylor took their last time-out, and now Saint

seems to have mellowed out, the agitation in his eyes gone. He smiles as if nothing ever happened and didn't spend almost two hours having someone at his back.

The refs blow his whistle, signaling time's up and we need to get back on the court.

"Kingston," Saint calls me, holding his fist out. "We got this."

Even though we only played for a year, I'm going to miss him and our fist bumps. It's become our thing throughout the season. At the beginning or the end of the game, win or lose, we always bump our fists.

I'd gotten to know Saint a few years ago, playing at camps, and anything that revolved around basketball, but we'd never gotten close until last year. Living in the same house, being the godfather to my son, and sharing hotel rooms really brought us together.

It's not a goodbye forever, but unless we both play for the same team in the NBA, we'll never get to play again.

So I'm not going to focus on the nerves that once again slither inside of me, the rambunctious arena that drowns out the sound of my chaotic heartbeat, or the time left. I'm going to enjoy the last few minutes I spend with guys I call my best friends and this moment.

And there's no way in hell I'd let anyone talk shit and think we choked.

I pound my fist to his. "We got this."

It's Baylor's ball. Number eleven dribbles it at the line before he passes it to Xavier. He dribbles it down the court, Saint blocking him, and as he goes to steal it, Xavier throws it in the hoop, but it bounces off the rim and Landon catches the rebound.

He hands it off to Jagger as we jog down the court, Baylor on our asses, jogging lightly backward as they follow our every move.

We set our lay up right as number twenty-two charges at Jagger as expected before he passes it to Jayden and then he passes it to me. Dribbling it down, I throw it to Saint. He smiles with all the confidence in the world, jumps, and releases the ball in the air. It sinks swiftly and effortlessly, granting us two points.

Thirty seconds reset on the shot clock displayed above the backboard, with less than a minute left in the game. Baylor has the ball again. Ashton dribbles it halfway down the court, Jayden guarding him, but another Baylor player blocks him, and Ashton manages to slip away.

He sidesteps Landon, spinning to shoot the ball, but Landon blocks the hell out of the ball, slapping it away from his hand before it can ever leave his grasp. Saint catches it and dribbles it, then passes it to me.

I run it down, a Baylor player hot on my heel, but it's too late because I jump up, dunking the ball. My fingers glide along the rim before I let go and Baylor takes possession of the ball.

A sea of blue and black and green and gold goes fucking wild, both sides on edge and restless because we're tied now. We're just seconds away from the game being over or going into overtime.

I know I'm not the only one who feels the anxious energy from the crowd. Every player on the floor radiates with the same energy, knowing what's at stake. The arena is louder with screams and chants than it was just a minute ago, the floor vibrating with how hard everyone is jumping and stomping their feet, and my heart is close to exploding from the force of its beats.

Number three dribbles the court, passing it to Ashton, who is wide open, but Landon jumps in the nick of time and steals the ball and passes it to me.

Two defenders double-team me, pressuring me to give up the ball, but the dumbasses don't take into consideration that Jagger is free.

I pass it to him, but I hold my breath and I swear everyone else does too. With only two seconds left, determination sets on his face as he jumps from half the court and shoots the ball in the air as the buzzer goes off.

Time slows down, the once booming crowd now quiet,

holding their breaths as we all watch the ball soar in the air. My lungs burn with the need to breathe, but I don't release it.

Not until the ball smoothly sinks in. The swish of the net echoes throughout the arena, but it's muffled by the most satisfying, intense screams I've ever heard. Waves of blue and black drown out the green and gold, their hands in the air, and cameras flashing.

Jagger just made that shot.

Holy fucking shit! Jagger just made a half court shot!

We won!

We all run toward Jagger, ambushing him in a hug, along with the bench and the rest of the members on the team. The camera crew is in our faces, recording and taking pictures of us as we continue to celebrate.

I revel in adrenaline still rushing through me, the amped up crowd that's loudly cheering us on, my teammates who are hugging each other, and the last time I'll be wearing this jersey.

I attempt to keep my giddy smile at bay when we shake hands with Baylor, but I can't tame it down. And when they hand us hats with NCU NATIONAL CHAMPIONS, it splits wider across my face as I place it backward on my head.

Pushing past my teammates and the camera crew, I run toward the erratic crowd until I'm in front of the two people I want to celebrate with the most.

Lola is adjusting Phoenix's earmuffs and once they're situated, she sets him on her hip. He's beaming, excitedly clapping his hands as Lola laughs.

As our eyes lock and I stand in front of them, everyone else disappears. The noise, the pats to my back, the ripple of blue and black become nothing but a blur because having them both here is *all I need*.

"Congra—"

Cutting her off, I pull her into my arms and connect my lips with hers.

"Congratulations! I'm so proud of you!" She manages to say before I give her another kiss.

When I break apart, I take Nix from her and lift him on my shoulders and take her hand in mine, threading our fingers together. As I pull her toward the court, we're rained down with black, white, and blue confetti.

Lola smiles, eyes glowing, staring awestruck at the thin paper showering over us. I don't have to look at Nix to know he's just as happy because his tiny feet kick at my chest and he bounces on my shoulder.

"This is incredible. I can't believe this." Bubbles of laughter evade her as she pulls out her phone and takes pictures of me and Nix. "I'm so freaking proud of you!"

Gabby appears with her camera in hand, standing in front of us. "Let me take a picture. You guys look so adorable!"

I slip my arm around her waist and pull her to my side as Gabby preps her camera. Right before she snaps the picture, Lola tucks a stray, damp curl that managed to slip past my cap underneath it and smiles.

"Okay, we're good now." She gives her a thumbs-up.

Giving Nix a quick glance to make sure he's looking at Gabby, I look down at Lola.

"Smile, golden girl."

And she smiles, breathtaking as ever.

As the pictures are taken, I squeeze her side and she looks up at me.

"I'm thankful for peach juice."

"Me too."

EPILOGUE

LOLA

ONE YEAR LATER

"Are you still thinking about it?" TJ reaches over the console and takes my hand in his, interviewing our fingers.

"Yes, I just can't get over it. It's just...so unexpected."

"It really is. Seeing them together is..." He chuckles, at a loss for words.

All of our friends came to Miami to celebrate our birthday but also came with shocking news.

Since we moved to Toronto after TJ got the first pick in the draft, we've hardly seen them. Especially these past few months as they've been hectic and kind of wild.

Toronto made it to the conference finals but lost the fourth game. Despite that, TJ's gotten a lot of press for how he handled the season after their best starter, Jeremiah, tore his ACL right before the season started.

So many people doubted and were extremely skeptical until they started winning. On top of having a pretty good season, he got NBA rookie of the year last month and has had many brand deals reaching out to him.

With all the press, there are a lot of new fans. I don't mind it. Sometimes it becomes a lot because everyone not only wants to know every tidbit about his life but also mine. It made me a little nervous, but everyone has been nice, for the most part. There are still shitty people online, but I've come to terms that that's never going to change.

I graduated with my degree this month, but I didn't make it to the graduation. My business is still thriving, but I've had to cut back on the number of live paintings I do. Once TJ got popular, people started recognizing me at the events. I can't say this happens all the time, but when it does, I'll be stopped in the middle of painting just so someone can talk about TJ's stats or the teams, meeting him, or taking pictures with me. And I have gotten hit on a few times.

TJ, of course, didn't take that last one well and hired someone, yes, that's right, hired someone to guard me, but only when I'm at an event. I would say it's an exaggeration, but after a drunken encounter with one of the groomsmen, I decided to bring Silas, the bodyguard, with me.

The highlight of my year was when I got hired by my favorite actress of all time, Josephine Flores, to paint for her brother's wedding. It took everything in me not to fangirl, but I was able to maintain my professionalism until I got home.

After I painted for her brother, she recommended me to her other friends and people she knows. And now I occasionally paint for celebrities and hang out with Josephine.

"Daddy, I'm hungry," our three-year-old whines from the back seat.

Three months ago, Phoenix turned three, and it makes me sad because my baby is growing. But I am happy that I get to share all of Nix's milestones with TJ and that we're living together. It's made things a lot easier for our son, but I think it's mainly due to him being able to go with his dad to the arena. He loves to visit and see the guys on the team.

"I'm sorry. I didn't—"

Because everyone arrived today, we decided to have dinner at TJ's parents' house, and tomorrow we're officially celebrating.

But we're not going to their house yet. TJ said we needed to make a quick stop somewhere first.

"I packed some snacks." He glances at my purse. "Graham crackers and apple slices."

I'm not sure how I didn't notice, but sure enough, there are two snack-sized Ziplock bags. One with crackers, and the other with bite-sized apple slices.

I hand him one snack at a time. The last thing I need is for him to choke even though they're the perfect size. It's better to be safe than sorry.

"I thought you said we were making a quick detour?"

"I figured Nix probably wouldn't be able to wait until then. The boy loves his snacks."

"That he does." I smile and hand him an apple slice. "So where are we going?"

"Somewhere."

"Where is somewhere?"

"A place..."

"You're doing that thing again."

"What thing?"

"Where you're being cryptic."

"Am I?"

I grumble, "You're frustrating, you know that?"

"For you, always." He grins, rubbing the pad of his thumb over my knuckles. "You look beautiful."

"Don't try to be sweet. It's not going to work." Unfortunately, a smile betrays me because he always causes these wild butterflies to roam in my stomach when he says sweet things like this.

"Well, I can't be dirty, Peaches. We have a kid in here."

I force myself not to smile again and shake my head. "You say the sweetest things to me, Teddy."

"I do my best." He winks at me.

We spend half of the drive talking about our friends and what we've missed since we've been in Canada, but the other half is me talking. TJ's quiet for the most part, except for a couple mumbled replies.

At one point, his knee starts bouncing. That's his telltale sign when he's anxious. I'm not sure why and I ask him what's wrong, but he says it's nothing. He's being strange, and I want to be able to take away whatever's bothering him.

He dealt with a lot after Jeremiah had to be put out for the rest of the season, and after losing the conference final just a few days ago, it's been tough. He takes a lot of responsibility for it. I wish he didn't, but it's hard for him to let go.

All I'm able to do is physically be here for him and remind him that I'm always here.

I bring my hand to the nape of his hair. Unfortunately, he got a haircut, so I can't tangle my fingers through his curls, but fortunately, he looks ten times hotter than he already did.

"Hey, I love you."

"And I love you." He smiles, bringing my hand to his lips, and kisses my knuckles.

"I'm here."

"And I've never been more thankful."

His bouncing knee stops, but now his fingers drum along the steering wheel.

I want to say something, but before I can, he pulls into a very familiar parking lot. The Miami Davenport Marina, to be exact.

My brows furrow. "What are we doing here?"

"I have to show you something," he simply says before he gets out and grabs Phoenix.

I don't have time to ask any more questions as he walks to the door that says Pier B.

After quickly getting out, I follow him until we're on his dad's yacht. I'm still not sure what we're doing here, and I don't have the chance to ask questions because he asks me to get the bottle of juice from the fridge and to meet him at the bow.

As I make my way there, I overlook the blazing horizon as the sun dips below it but clings to the light blue sky that's slowly transitioning to dark. Streaks of gold burn into the puffy clouds, making the celestial sky look incandescent, like it's caught on fire.

Casting my gaze straight ahead, I stop in my tracks, gripping the neck of the bottle as I look at the large canvas next to TJ and Phoenix.

"Is that—"

"You Decide." A soft, sweet, tender smile curls on his lips.

My heart skips a beat, and my hands become clammy as I close the distance between us. "You bought it." I gape, staring in disbelief at the painting I haven't seen in four years. The one TJ and I saw on our pretend date during senior week.

He takes my hand in his, the other holding Phoenix. "I didn't understand it at first, but then you explained it and it all made sense. Just like when you showed up in my life again, slowly everything started making sense. With all the chaos and peace in my life, *I decide* I want no one else to spend it with than with you. I want the calm and the crazy as long as you're in it."

Letting go of my hand, he sets Nix down and whispers something in his ear before he takes off. I go to grab him, but TJ stops me and kneels before me.

My eyes widen, my heart stops beating, and my lungs burn as I hold my breath.

"Read the label on the bottle."

I blink past the water that blurs my vision and release a shaky breath.

Peaches,
marry me.

The tears I was desperately holding back fall like a waterfall as TJ opens a little black velvet box. A diamond the size of a boulder lies in the middle, glimmering brightly.

He takes my left land, gliding the pad of his thumb over my knuckles as he blows a breath. "We're young, really, really young. We still have a lot in this world to experience, a lot to see, a lot to learn, and so much to do. But, Louise, there's no one, absolutely no one in this world I'd rather go through life with than with you." He takes my hand and lays my palm flat on his chest where his heart lies and thunders erratically. His whiskey-colored eyes darken, filled with an intensity that burns my soul.

"This world is filled with infinite possibilities. Some are in our control and some aren't. Meeting you was out of my control, but loving you was something I had complete and total control of. You're my most favorite and unexpected possibility, and I don't want to stop exploring the endless possibilities life has to offer as long as you're in it."

He pauses, smiling up at me.

"How would you like to have a husband for the rest of your life? What do you say, Louise, marry me?"

"Yes!" I choke on the word, wiping the tears away as he takes the ring and slips it on my finger.

He hops on his feet, sweeps me in his arms, and kisses me.

As he puts me down, Nix runs to us, clapping and laughing. I'm sure he has no idea what's going on, but he's happy none-theless.

"Come here, Little Bear, I'm going to marry your mommy." TJ picks him up and holds us in a long embrace.

Life may not have turned out the way I wanted, but in the end, it turned out to be everything I needed.

The End

THANK YOU FOR READING

If you enjoyed *All I Need*, I'd greatly appreciate it if you left a review on Goodreads and the site you bought it from.

Want more? Follow me on Instagram at e.salvadorauthor to get an update on book 2 in The Knights Series.

ACKNOWLEDGMENTS

I keep typing and deleting because it genuinely feels unreal that I'm actually typing this!!

I should start first with thanking all you wonderful readers who came and stuck around in this journey of mine because without you, I wouldn't be publishing my debut novel! So thank you all for the kind words, the messages, the comments! All your love has been nothing but overwhelmingly but in the best way possible!

To my Love, thank you for encouraging and listening to me talk about this book for the past year and a half! I wouldn't have been able to continue pushing through without your constant support!

B, for all your unconditional support! For believing in me and listening to me when you could be doing better things.

Norhan, "for being the beacon of light in my life, and for always lifting me up on the hardest days. If I wasn't already married, I would've proposed marriage to you already." Thank you for beta reading, thanks for putting up with me when I'm overthinking, and thanks for just being there! So happy you exist, you pterodactyl!

Ana, thank you for not only beta reading but putting up with me when I'm going through it! Thank you for sticking with me in this journey, and listening to my immensely long voice memos. There's no one I love switching languages more than with you. You're the sweetest soul, and I'm so lucky to call you my friend!

Ruby"rock chalk"(I don't wan to hear it), thank you for all

your amazing help! You truly are a gift of a human and wouldn't know what to do with you! I promise that one day I'll stop feeling bad for asking you for so much help.

Madison Montgomery, you forced your squirrel ways into my life so I had to make it even and force my book on you. Despite your lack of love for romance books, thanks for making mine exception! You just know how to make a girl feel special.

Jodie, for allowing me to talk your ear off at work about my book and after a year, still listening me go on about it. Thank you for not judging me and supporting this dream of mine! You're an amazing friend!

Kay, thanks for coming into my life and making it better! You're stuck with me for life, so I apologize in advance because I'm never letting you go!

Savanna, for being the biggest cheerleader! I can't wait to see you do big things!! I adore you!

To my amazing cover designer at Books & Mood, Julie, you are a freaking gem! Thank you ten fold for bringing my cover to life!

Emily, thank you for helping me edit this monstrosity of a book!

Lastly and once again to all my readers! Thank you for making this dream a reality! I'm thankful for all of you!

ABOUT THE AUTHOR

E. is a Mexican-American romance author who loves a good happily ever after and iced coffee with light ice.

When E. is not overthinking or creating multiple Pinterest boards for the hundred book ideas she has, she's writing or reading. And when she's not doing any of those things, she's spending time with her two sons and husband.

Instagram/TikTok: e.salvadorauthor
Goodreads: e. salvador
Pinterest: esalvadorauthor

Printed in Great Britain
by Amazon